SAVING GRACE

SAVING GRACE

BARBARA ROGAN

OPEN ROAD

INTEGRATED MEDIA

NEW YORK

This edition published in 2014 by Open Road Integrated Media, Inc.
345 Hudson Street
New York, NY 10014
www.openroadmedia.com

For Benny

The author is grateful for the generous help of Dr. Larry Riemer, Dr. Zachary Apfel, Dr. Stuart Apfel, Leslie Savan, and Maria Laurino.

The network of support fashioned by Tillie Fisher, David and Eleanor Rogan, Joy Harris, Laurie Bernstein, Ben Kadishson and Jonathan Kadishson allowed the author the time and space to complete this work, for which she is deeply grateful.

Saving Grace is entirely fictional; however, the kind of corruption described herein has its analogue in the real world. For a first-rate, nuts-and-bolts account of political corruption, the author recommends Jack Newfield and Wayne Barrett's *City for Sale,* published by Harper and Row.

THERE WAS A MAN IN THE LAND OF UZ,
WHOSE NAME WAS JOB; AND THAT MAN
WAS PERFECT AND UPRIGHT, AND ONE
THAT FEARED GOD, AND ESCHEWED EVIL.

THE downfall of the Fleishman family began deceptively, without augury, as is common in our times. The same story set twenty-five hundred years ago would have been preceded by the standard omens of disaster and betrayal: comets plunging through the heavens, steaming entrails presaging death, solar and lunar eclipses. The reader would have been forewarned, the participants forearmed. They could have taken precautions, useless though they would have proved.

Nowadays we have no auguries, or none of supernatural note. In our distance from the gods there is inevitably bereftness, but also benefit. When a man of substance sits at ease in the midst of his family, he is not wont to anticipate disaster; and if he could, what would it profit him? Who could support this life, knowing that a single snag could unravel it all, like a stocking with a run; or that a family, solidly if complicatedly meshed, might split asunder at a touch? Better not to know, and bless the flow of time that keeps us in our innocence.

1

GRACIE ANSWERED THE DOOR. A bearded stranger stood on the step. Beat-up leather jacket, jeans, a friendly smile, and sharp, reporter's eyes.

"Hi," he said. "Would Jonathan be in, I wonder?"

"Who are you?"

"Barnaby. I write for the *Probe.*"

Her gray eyes narrowed. "He's not in. If he were, he'd slam the door in your face."

He noticed that she didn't and leaned against the lintel. "You know who I am, then. He's mentioned me."

"Sure. In the same breath with Jack the Ripper."

"Well, he's pissed," he said with an aw-shucks kind of look. "I can understand that."

"Michael Kavin happens to be his best friend."

"That's why I'm here. Look, do you mind if I come in for a second? I don't want to be crude, but I'm about to burst."

Gracie stepped back. After using the bathroom, Barnaby detoured into the living room. He looked about appraisingly. Then he looked at her the same way.

Her face was coming back to him now. Last time he'd seen it, it was attached to a little girl, ten, eleven years old. A picture came to him of a skinny kid standing on a stage, haranguing a roomful of adults. The hoyden had metamorphosed into a beautiful girl, with a feminine version of her father's face; she had Jonathan's high cheekbones, olive skin, black hair, and gray eyes with flecks of green. Barnaby smiled.

"Little Gracie, all grown up. How old are you now?"

"Eighteen," she said.

"You look a lot like your old man, only prettier."

"You've got nerve, showing up here."

"It's the job." He sat in her father's armchair, stretching out his legs. "In private life, I'm a very bashful guy."

"I can tell."

"So, you've read my stuff?"

"Everybody reads your stuff."

He nodded. In the circles they moved in, everyone did read his stuff. "What do you think?"

"I used to think you were pretty good."

"Till it hit too close to home?"

"Till you lost your fucking mind."

"You think I made it up, all that stuff about Kavin?"

"You'd better get your ass out of here before my father comes home."

" Answer the question."

"What's it to you what I think?"

"I'm curious. You don't remember me, but I remember you. You still have opinions, Gracie?"

She looked at him. Her eyes were older than her face, which lent her an air of anachronism, like a sepia portrait in modern dress.

"Good-bye, Barnaby," she said.

He let her walk him out. Halfway down the path he turned to look back. Grace was leaning against the door with her arms folded, a watchful sentry. He heard himself say, for no fathomable reason, "Come see me. Come to the *Probe*. I'll show you around."

"Why?"

"Beard the lion in his den?"

She turned and went into the house.

One week later, Gracie gave her name to a receptionist and sat for some minutes in the dingiest waiting room she'd ever seen. Just as she was about to leave, regretting the impulse that had brought her, Barnaby appeared. "You came. Good for you!" He showed her around the office, introducing her by first name only to people whose names, first and last, were well-known to her. Later they sat in a coffee shop on East Broadway and talked for hours about all sorts of things. Jonathan was not mentioned.

* * *

On a fine spring morning, one Sunday early in May, the Fleishman family sat in the breakfast room, French doors open to admit the sweet herbal breeze that wafted in from Lily's garden. The table was laid for five. Jonathan sat at the head, Lily at the foot; between them sat their son, Paul, ensconced in the financial section of the *Times*, and beside him Clara, Jonathan's mother. The fifth setting was untouched.

Gracie wandered in as they were finishing, holding a book before her face. Without looking up, she took her customary seat beside her father. Lily put aside the *Times* Entertainment section and sat up straight, as if the new arrival were her governess rather than her daughter.

"Say good morning, Gracie," prompted Jonathan.

She glanced briefly round the table. "Good morning."

"Did you sleep well?" Lily asked.

"Okay."

Clara clicked her tongue against her dentures. "The food's cold already. You want I should make you an egg?"

"No, thanks." Gracie turned a page.

"Eyes not even open, and already with the books. You can't live from books, my darling."

"I'm not hungry."

"Why should you be hungry? You don't do nothing."

Jonathan and Lily exchanged a look. Jonathan shrugged slightly. When his mother got going, she could not be stopped, only tuned out. And Gracie was good at that.

Gracie contrived to pour a cup of coffee without lifting her eyes from the page.

Clara said, "It's not right. A young girl should go out, meet people, not sit home alone."

No one answered her, but Paul sighed.

"And you, Mr. Big Shot College Boy, you can't bring home a nice boy for your sister, such a beautiful girl?"

Paul, who privately felt his friends could do better, shrugged behind the paper.

"Mama," said Jonathan, "I don't think Gracie needs a matchmaker just yet." He turned to his daughter and, with the clear intention of changing the subject, asked what she was reading.

"*Lord of the Rings.*"

"Didn't you read that years ago?"

She raised her eyes to his. "I read it every year. I like it. You can tell the good guys from the bad."

Jonathan flushed. This was Grade's specialty, the unprovoked assault disguised as conversation. This time, though, he was determined not to be drawn in. "Then you ought to read westerns," he said. "I recommend Zane Grey."

"Again with the books," Clara complained. "A man she can't bring home. Whoever heard of a eighteen-year-old girl don't go out?"

"For your information," Gracie snapped, "I am going out with someone."

In the silence that followed, Paul lowered his paper and stared at his sister. "You?" She stuck her tongue out at him.

"Who is he, Gracie?" Lily asked.

She pushed back a wedge of long black hair and scowled into her cup. "Just somebody."

"Thanks God," Clara said. "What does he do, this somebody?"

"He's a writer."

"A *writer*? From this he makes a living?"

"Good question, Grandma. I'll check his tax returns."

"What does he write, this writer?"

Gracie shrugged.

Her father gave her a suspicious look. "What's his name?"

"Barnaby," she said reluctantly.

Jonathan turned his hands palm-upward on the table and gazed into them, as if reading his own fortune. "Oh, Gracie."

Lily looked from her husband to her daughter. "Barnaby...not that bastard who wrote about Michael?"

"That's the one," Gracie said.

"How could you?" said Jonathan.

She found she could not quite meet his gaze. "You used to like him. You called him the best goddamn investigative reporter in the city."

"He used to be. Then one morning he woke up and discovered he was God."

"He's not like that."

"Christ Almighty, Gracie. Everything else aside, he must be twice your age."

"Age doesn't matter," she informed him airily.

Jonathan slammed the table. "He's crucifying Michael! Does that matter? He's damn near destroyed him already with his lies!"

"If they're lies, how could they destroy him?"

"Don't talk like a child."

"Jonathan," Lily said, "take it easy."

He glared at her. "Our daughter is dating the Charles Manson of journalism and you want me to take it easy?"

"Really, Dad, chill," Gracie said. "It's not like he's writing about you."

"Not yet," Jonathan said grimly. "Let me tell you something that should have been obvious. If that son of a bitch is chasing you, he's got a reason."

"Naturally *I* couldn't be the reason."

He looked at her and softened. "Use those brains of yours. Ask yourself what does a man of his age and experience want with a teenager?"

Gracie threw down her napkin and strode to the door she'd entered just minutes ago.

"Get back here!" Jonathan bellowed. "Gracie, I forbid you... "
But she was already gone.

"Of course she's getting at us," Lily said serenely. "That's the whole point." She sat at her dressing table, watching Jonathan in the mirror.

"What the hell are we being punished for? For giving her a beautiful home, *two* beautiful homes? The finest education, travel, the best of every goddamn thing?" As he spoke, Jonathan paced up and down. Spacious as their bedroom was, it offered little scope for his rage. "What awful thing did we do to her, that she should treat me with such contempt?"

"God knows," sighed Lily, who also had some idea, but wouldn't think of voicing it. They had tacitly agreed to treat Grade's attitude as normal adolescent rebellion, carried to her usual extremes; Jonathan's question was rhetorical. Catching his eye in the mirror, she said soothingly, "Not contempt."

"She's arrogant and hypercritical. Sometimes I think that girl lives to thwart me."

"She loves you, Jonathan."

"She's got a hell of a way of showing it. Thank God we have one normal child."

"Don't call him normal in that condescending tone!" cried Lily, Paul's constant protector.

"I didn't mean it like that," Jonathan said, but he had. Though he had long since schooled himself against comparisons, the immutable fact remained that Grace was the child of his heart: She shared his nature; she was, even in strife, undeniably his. Whereas Paul, a good boy, polite, grateful for what he was given, ambitious for more, a kid who knew how to use his advantages, seemed to Jonathan a separate entity, a satellite supported by but unattached to his base.

Paul was a good student who had to work for every *A* he got. Gracie was different, cursed or blessed with both passion and a driving intelligence that had manifested itself almost from infancy. She was a difficult baby, a tempestuous toddler, prone to tantrums when ability fell short of desire, a self-taught reader from the age of four, a politician from the day she started school. In kindergarten she negotiated with the teacher for more free play for the class, and got it. In fourth grade she fought a successful campaign to ban Styrofoam in the lunchroom. In class she was outspoken, attentive and negligent by turns, impatient with superficial explanations, a human litmus test for good teachers. Jonathan had delighted in her conversation, her prodigious vocabulary. Gracie, in turn, adored him. She saved all his clippings and speeches and pasted them into a scrap-book. A photograph of Jonathan with Martin Luther King Jr. took pride of place on her desk.

Jonathan loved his son, but in his life he'd had no greater pleasure than watching young Gracie unfold her wings. Remembering those days before his daughter walled herself off from him saddened Jonathan. He could no longer reach her.

Alone in her room, Gracie wrote in her diary, which in brevity if not in matter appeared less like a teenager's journal than a captain's log.

If he's after you, Dad said, he's got a motive. As if I hadn't thought of that. As if I didn't know I've got nothing to attract a man like Barnaby.

Naturally Dad hates him. Like Jonathan, Barnaby has principles. Unlike Jonathan, he lives by his.

* * *

Jonathan walked through the garden, which was beginning to bloom after a cold April. The rush of city traffic, diffuse and muffled, wafted in on the breeze, but within the terra-cotta walls of Lily's bower the air was fragrant with a warm earthy smell. He sat on a cast-iron bench beside a small reflecting pond. The water cast up an image of a successful, well-tended man in early middle age, a face still lean but softened by comfort, black hair streaked with gray, weathered skin, watchful gray eyes that absorbed more than they revealed: a handsome, even distinguished face, but not the one he thought of as his. In this, Jonathan was rather like an actor who has played one role for so long that his character's features have melded inseparably with his own.

He tossed a pebble into the pool, and the image fractured. There was a knot in his gut, compliments of his daughter, tough little Gracie. When she was young and adoring, Jonathan used to brag about that toughness. Now that she had turned it against him, the trait was less endearing.

A stupid misunderstanding had started it all, a molehill she'd made into a mountain. Six years ago, they had quarreled; since that time, Gracie had hardened her heart against him. Her eyes, once full of admiration, regarded him with suspicion. His every word was subject to willful misconstruction. She would not see him as he was.

As a child she used to sit at his feet and beg for stories of the time he and Michael Kavin traversed the country as troubleshooting civil-rights lawyers, Have-Writ-Will-Travel adventurers. Since their quarrel, however, when he told those stories Grade's eyes would glaze over and she would soon find an excuse to leave the room. All her cleverness and ingenuity, once allied to his, she turned to goading him. And Gracie knew how to goad.

The last fight before the Barnaby affair had been the worst of all. In the middle of a festive family dinner celebrating her acceptance to Harvard, Gracie announced her decision not to go to college.

Jonathan's head had clanged like a construction site; he could scarcely hear his own voice for the ringing in his ears. "You don't know what you're throwing away," he told her. "For the rest of your life people will talk differently, listen differently, think differently of you because you went to Harvard."

"There are more important things in life than going to Harvard."

"Not many. And you wouldn't know them if they up and bit you on the nose."

Gracie gave him a look of horror. "How can you say that?"

Jonathan wondered himself, wondered too at the perversity of the fate that caused him to say to his daughter just the sort of that had driven him wild as a kid. Perhaps it wasn't fate, but some perverse quality in Gracie. Jonathan often had imaginary talks with his daughter in which he calmly, rationally explained his life and values. But even in imagination she was unruly: she answered back impertinently, turned his own words against him, goaded him to anger. His actual conversations with the girl rode the crest of the imaginary ones, so that even before she opened her mouth, he was angry and defensive.

And when she did open her mouth, it was worse. With Jonathan's inanities about Harvard echoing in the room, Gracie had stared into his face and begun whistling a tune. He'd taught her to whistle, and she was good. The tune was "Blowing in the Wind." His generation's anthem, not hers.

Now he sat in the garden and tossed stones at his reflection in the pool. He thought about that damn Dylan song and Gracie's gift for fracturing continuity. Jonathan was and had ever been a man of his times. By sabotaging the transitional years, she made a mockery of what he had become.

He closed his eyes and inhaled the sharp, clean scent of fallow earth. I know who I am, he thought. I haven't changed. And if he was a proud man, he had reason to be; for he had faithfully adhered to his principles without sacrificing his family. He had done well and done right, and how many men could say that?

The screen door creaked and he opened his eyes. Gracie was coming into the garden. As soon as she saw Jonathan, she turned and went back inside the house.

That evening, she stood before Barnaby's door, panting slightly from the stairs. Apartment 503 had no name on the bell, but a jaunty green feather was stuck under the apartment number. She put her ear to the door and listened for a long time. There was noise from the street and adjacent apartments, but none from inside. He's not home, Gracie thought. He forgot. The invitation had been vague, tossed off as they parted. "Sunday evening at Maxie's, a bunch of writers and other lowlife. Come along if you like." A favor carelessly bestowed. Convinced he hadn't meant it, feeling like a fool, Gracie knocked once for the hell of it and turned to go.

Suddenly the door opened and he stood in the entrance, a tall, loose-jointed man with a beard and mustache and shaggy brown hair. He had enormous, capable farmer's hands, an easy grin, and warm brown eyes bracketed by laugh lines. Gracie thought of a benevolent Jesse James.

"Hello, Grace," he said, smiling down at her.

"I thought you'd gone already," she blurted.

"Now, why would I do that?" He threw open the door and stepped back. "'Come into my parlor,' said the spider to the fly."

She laughed and followed him in.

Barnaby's apartment was about the size of her parents' bedroom, a large uncluttered studio with bare arched windows that faced onto a blank factory wall across the street. A covered mattress lay atop a sleeping platform on the far end of the room; a small sofa, two chairs, and a desk with a computer furnished the living section. She sat on the sofa. Barnaby disappeared behind a red beaded curtain and returned with two glasses and a bottle of wine.

"Not up to your father's standards, but it ain't Ripple, either. Care for a glass before we go?"

She nodded. He sat beside her and poured. When he handed her the glass, their hands touched. A spark flew between.

"I wasn't sure you'd come," Barnaby said.

"I said I would."

"I thought you'd have second thoughts."

"Why?"

"Have you thought about how inappropriate our friendship is? You're eighteen. I could be your father."

"One father's enough for me, thanks."

"I meant I'm old enough to be."

"Want me to leave?" she asked, knowing he didn't.

The next morning, Barnaby arrived at the *Probe* to find Ronnie Neidelman loitering outside his cubicle. She followed him inside, perching on his desk with a short-skirted show of leg. "Dating jail-bait now, I hear."

"She's not jailbait," he growled.

"Who is she?"

He knew for a fact that if he didn't tell her, she'd find out for herself. "Jonathan Fleishman's daughter."

Ronnie raised her long nose and sniffed the air.

"What? I got work to do."

"I smell trouble."

"Give me a break. She's just a kid. A sweet, confused kid."

"He said, licking his chops."

"Lay off, Ronnie. I prefer mature women, as you know."

She stood up, offended. Ronnie was thirty-six and gaunt, her biological clock a ticking bomb. They'd been lovers, she and Barnaby, off and on for three years. It was a relationship adapted to the peculiar ecology of New York City: committed on her part, wide open on his.

Barnaby had nothing against Ronnie. She was a damn good reporter, easily the best of his protégés, and when she wasn't on the warpath, she was funny as hell. If she were a man they'd have been friends. But as a woman, with her sharp tongue, freckled face, and that lamentable nose, she was no great catch.

You had to look at it logically. The way Barnaby saw it, marriage was the single greatest investment a man made in his lifetime. So why settle for a Ronnie Neidelman when he knew damn well he could do better?

The affair had dragged on too long already. Ronnie was getting ideas above her station. Lately she'd been making noises about wanting a baby. Personally, Barnaby could think of no prospect more revolting than a child of theirs. He pictured it as a fat, bespectacled kid with a magnifying glass in its hand, collecting evidence for an exposé of waste and mismanagement in the nursery.

Now she curled her lip at him. "And I suppose your interest in her is strictly avuncular."

"No," Barnaby said tightly. "Strictly professional."

"I see. Does she know what you're working on?"

"What do you think?"

"Did you get anything?"

"Not yet."

"You're a real sweetheart, aren't you? What happens when the sweet, confused kid lets something slip?"

He scowled. "What do you think, I cover my ears and hum?"

"A prince," she said.

"Darlin', I'm just doing my job," Barnaby said.

2

WITH THE ONSET OF SUMMER THE Fleishmans, like urban birds of paradise, migrated eastward to the Hamptons, where five years earlier Jonathan had converted an embarrassment of riches into a waterfront house and a forty-eight-foot ketch. Part of the deal had been consummated in cash, relieving him of the unwieldy surplus; the rest was a tax deduction.

Although Lily had been deputized to find the house, she knew nothing of its financing, nor did she ask. That was Jonathan's bailiwick. Strange how life and age had brought them from an undifferentiated sharing to a system of airtight departments, he with his, she with hers; stranger still how their original, equal partnership had imperceptibly become a corporation, with Jonathan as CEO— for despite Lily's autonomy, there was no doubt as to who reported to whom.

But it was a good life, she told herself, strolling barefoot across the lawn toward the dock. Indeed, it was generally agreed that in all of New York City there were few women more fortunate than Lily Fleishman. She had health, wealth, two beautiful homes, a brace of clever children, and a successful husband who honored her and was faithful in all the ways that are supposed to matter. She had social position and the respect of her peers, and, in addition to their two houses, she and her husband owned other real estate, as well as stocks and bonds and ample life insurance.

Their house in East Hampton was built on water. A landfill had created the spit over which their house presided, protected on three sides by seawalls. The shallowness of the topsoil did not impede the growth of her garden, but rather lent it an air of hectic gaiety, a kind of here-today, gone-tomorrow exuberance, like the bloom in the cheeks of a tubercular. Lily was a loving but rather wistful gardener, always surprised when she reaped what she had sown.

A breath of wind brought the fragrance of her sea-spray roses, and she turned aside to visit them. These wild shrubs were the pride of her garden, hardy plants that thrived on briny air and exuded, not the insipid sweetness of overbred domestic roses, but a heady, dangerous scent, a siren's call, a glimpse of foreign ports and lost dreams.

But she had no time now to linger in the garden. She was meeting with her friend Margo, an interior designer married to a fashionable architect. Lily drove over and they lunched outdoors, beside the pool. Margo asked, "How's Jonathan?"

"Fine," Lily said. "Overworked as usual."

"Is he coming out this weekend?"

Something peculiar in her voice drew Lily's eyes. "No, he's in Albany, giving a speech."

"And you're not by his side? Tsk, tsk, darling."

"No need. It's not as if he's running for office."

"Thank God. I can just see Jonathan kissing babies. Or you!"

"The benefits of nonelective office."

"So everything's all right?" Margo asked.

Again that odd tone. Lily hugged herself. "Why ever not?" They're not having an affair, she thought. Margo wouldn't do that to me.

"Just checking," Margo said, and went into the kitchen to get dessert.

Afterward, they went shopping.

In the boutiques of Bridgehampton, the shopkeepers greeted them by name, rejoicing at the sight of them. Lily bought a dozen bars of French soap and a packet of scented drawer liners in the dry-goods store. Next door, in the boutique, she found a silk camisole in a lovely shade of peach. Margo bought a T-shirt for their friend Christina, whose birthday was approaching. Christina was divorced and shopping around. The T-shirt read, "How Do I Love Thee? Let Me Count Thy Money."

Then they took a few dresses from a rack of cotton prints and went into adjoining fitting rooms to try them on. Margo said, "Robert was out yesterday."

Margo's brother was something in the New York City Department of Investigations. They weren't close and he rarely came out to the Hamptons. "Oh?"

Margo came into Lily's fitting room, wearing a halter dress. She studied her reflection. "The way they cut these things, if you're five pounds overweight, forget it. I like that, darling! Definitely take it."

Lily looked at herself without enthusiasm. She dressed herself as she decorated her houses, diligently, with taste and style but no particular pleasure. As a girl she had scorned fancy clothes, and she got through the sixties on three pairs of jeans and half a dozen T- shirts. When Jonathan entered city politics, he took to wearing suits and ties, which he called camouflage; without actually saying anything, he conveyed his expectation that Lily would follow his lead. By now she didn't even think about it. Summering each year in a place where clothes make the woman, one adapts.

Lily said, "What did Robert want?"

Margo took out a lipstick and leaned closer to the mirror. "He asked questions about you and Jonathan, especially Jonathan."

"What kind of questions?"

"Money questions. What is their house worth, and how much do they entertain, and does Lily have her own money?"

Lily sank down onto a stool. "Why?"

"He wouldn't say. He *ordered* me not to tell you. I said, 'Darling, do you think you are talking to one of your nasty little paid informants? Lily happens to be my dearest friend.'"

"Why is he doing this?"

"I thought you might know."

"I have no idea."

"Forget about it." Margo shrugged. "Probably just some political nonsense. Or a routine check; they do that, don't they?" She put away her lipstick and turned. Her expression changed. "What is it, darling?"

"Nothing."

"Damn. I should have kept my big mouth shut. It's just he made such a point of my not telling, I thought I'd better."

"I'm glad you did," Lily said. "But I'm sure it's nothing."

* * *

She got home late that night, after dinner with friends and a gallery opening. Clara sat in the living room, crocheting yet another sweater for Gracie that Gracie would never wear.

"Still up, Mother? I thought you'd be asleep by now." She perched on the edge of an armchair, longing for her bed.

"I napped in the afternoon," Clara said, peering at her work. "The house was quiet."

Correctly interpreting this remark, Lily said, "You should have come. Margo was disappointed."

"You don't need an old lady. What did she serve?"

Lily cast her mind back but found it wouldn't go. This frightened her. She had sat over lunch for two hours and could not recall a single dish. Clara peered up at her. "Spinach salad with avocado," she invented hastily, "quiche, lovely fresh raspberries for dessert."

"What's the matter, *tochter?*"

"I'm exhausted," she said. "I'm tired of smiling."

"You worried about Gracie?"

"That's a chronic condition."

"Believe me, Jonathan was worse at her age. A holy terror: long hair, beard, wild talk. Big revolutionary. Went out with *shiksas*, even"—she dropped her voice—"*shvartzas*. He got over it, she'll get over it."

"I hate to see her hurt. And I *hate*," Lily said, with more animation than she'd yet shown, "the thought of that bum touching my little girl."

Clara leaned forward. "You know?"

"I presume. She's obviously crazy about him."

"So maybe it wouldn't hurt her to get hurt for once."

"I hope you're right, because it's in the cards." Lily got up, stretched and yawned delicately.

"Jonathan called."

Lily did not reply.

Clara peered over her glasses. "He wants you should call him back."

"Good night, Mother."

In her room Lily donned the old nightgown she wore when Jonathan was away. The hotel number was written in Clara's scratchy hand beside the telephone. She ought to call, to tell him about Robert. Her hand reached for the phone, then fell back. It was all so insubstantial; talking about it would make it seem more than it was. Better leave it alone. She got into bed and pulled the covers up to her eyes, as she had when she was small and frightened of monsters. She would cry out for her mother, who always came at once, as if she had lain awake waiting. Only then, safe within the magic circle of her mother's arms, would Lily sleep.

Her mother was long gone, though, and of her father, not even memory remained. And one could not call Clara. Lily smiled at the thought of Clara clumping in in her orthopedic shoes, wiping her hands on her apron, saying in her earth-inflected voice, "Monsters? *Vus is dus?* It must be the quiche." If only it were the quiche, something substantial instead of the vague, nameless fear that haunted her.

A sense of vulnerability is as endemic to wealth as hopelessness is to poverty. If Lily's anxiety had more specific causes, they were nothing she felt compelled to examine. But during those late nights when Jonathan was attending some function, or in the early-morning hours when she awoke and could not sleep again, images came to her, she saw her good life as a field full of seeded dandelions, vulnerable to every puff of wind, given to dispersion. In the morning, when the shadows receded and she could see her house and possessions arrayed about her, solid and wind-resistant, Lily's fears dissolved into grateful acceptance.

Lately, though, she had taken to dreaming of death. Jonathan, Gracie, Paul, her parents (resurrected for the occasion), or someone she barely knew; everyone and anyone except herself.

Lily closed her eyes, willed her mind to stillness. She sought the secret place, her haven. In her recurrent dream, Lily traveled alone through Europe, wandering without destination until she reached a familiar place, a city whose name, waking, she could never recall. Through its center ran a wide green canal, where she walked with light steps along a dream-lit bank, moist earth crumbling gently beneath her bare feet. Breathing in the soft, fragrant air, watching the water flow, she felt an air of ease and tranquillity that, waking, she had never known.

Once she told Jonathan about her dream. "The meaning is obvious," he said. "Canal equals birth canal: classic back-to-the-womb stuff, no mystery there, love."

He was wrong. He didn't understand that there are two kinds

of places, the ones you go to and the ones that come to you; and Lily's was of the latter sort. No act of will could summon her dream city, which came when it would and bore with it, like an exile's memory of home, the power to restore and comfort. Nonetheless, her city was real, it existed somewhere. She knew this because each time she dreamed of it, she awoke with a deep, intractable sense of loss.

It's perfectly possible to feel nostalgia for a place one has never been. It's not even unusual. Assimilated Jews long for Jerusalem, Armenians dream of Ararat, Palestinians pine for the hills of Galilee.

Clara, too, lay sleepless. What was the use of sleeping when her bladder was shot? The incessant surge of water against the bulkheads, whose sound pervaded the house, exacerbated the problem. If she dropped off, she would only wake up in an hour, ready to burst. Or, the thing she really dreaded, wake too late.

Long past midnight, Clara heard the front door open. She fumbled for her teeth, put them in, got up heavily, and trudged to the door. "Gracie?"

"What is it, Grandma?"

"Come, sit a minute."

The girl sat huddled in the armchair beside the bed, arms crossed, silent.

"Where was you so late?"

"In the city."

"With that man?"

"Yes."

"You're wasting your time."

Gracie got that look in her eye. "No," she said. "I'm afraid he's wasting his."

"A girl like you can do better."

"You don't even know him."

"I know enough. Where does he live?"

"On the Lower East Side."

"He rents?"

"A studio."

Clara sniffed. "A grown man, hardly makes a living."

"He makes a living. Besides, money isn't everything."

"Of course money isn't everything, but without it you got nothing. Your poor father works himself to the bone so you can throw yourself away on some *nebbish?*" She raised her eyes to the ceiling. "Everything she has; nothing she wants. *You* don't know nothing; *I* know nothing. I grew up with nothing."

Nothing was a presence, not an absence, in Clara's life. *Nothing* looked you in the eye and said: You're worthless; you live in dirt and you'll die in dirt; your name will be erased. *Nothing* was banished from her life but forever lurked outside the door, waiting.

Gracie drew herself up. "You have no right to call him names, just because he's not rich. He's a man of integrity, a political watchdog—God knows the system needs them."

"What watchdog? He's a mutt." The old woman cackled till she choked, and Gracie had to pound her on the back.

"So, *maidele,*" Clara said, wiping her eyes, "you think you're in love."

"I never said that."

"Libeh iz vi puter, s'iz gut mit broit."

"Speak English."

"Love is like butter, it's good with bread."

Gracie stood. "It's no use talking to you."

"Sit, Gracie. At night," Clara said, "I can't sleep, I walk around the house, I hear you crying."

"I won't be spied on!"

"A man makes you miserable, that's not love."

"You're the expert, right? You really know what love is."

"I know. Love is helping, not hurting. Love is you do for him and he does for you. All I want is you should be happy."

"You want me to be happy? Get off my case, I'll be happy."

Then she ran out, and Clara removed her teeth and shuffled in her mules to the bathroom, where she relieved herself. After that she took some seltzer from the small refrigerator Jonathan had installed in her room. Though she'd berated him at the time— "What's the matter, I'm too feeble to walk to the kitchen, I want a little something?"—the icebox had proved useful. Getting old was not so great.

Her hands were shaking. Razor-tongued Gracie had struck again, like that swordsman on the old TV show *Zorro.* She was a foolish, ungrateful child, but Clara was the last one to expect loyalty from a girl. She knew girls; she had had a daughter once, and lost her, lost her husband too. People assumed Clara was a widow, and she let them, but in fact her husband and daughter, Jonathan's sister, were alive and well in Israel.

Though she blamed Jacob for splitting their family, Clara, to her credit, never denied she had been warned. The very first time she met Jacob Fleishman, at a dance in the basement of her aunt's synagogue, he told her: "One day I'm going to live in Palestine. I'm going to join a kibbutz and make the desert bloom."

"That's nice," she'd replied. His hands were so white. He was a furrier. What would a furrier do in the desert, skin rattlesnakes? She knew it was important for a man to have dreams; woman's job was to harness them. He wanted to make things bloom, she'd buy him a geranium. Jacob was a socialist, a union man. Clara didn't know from socialism; she knew from bread on the table and a decent place to live. They both had responsibilities, family to bring over. Clara was certain that a baby or two would lay the ghost of Jacob's dream.

Two years after they married, their first baby was born, a girl they named Fanny after Jacob's grandmother Faigele. The next year they bought a two-family house in East New York, Brooklyn.

They sent money to their families in Poland, begging them to get out while they could, for an ominous cloud was settling over Europe. Jacob's sister wrote to say that they were coming, but that was the last they heard from her or any of them. No one came. When Jacob and Clara wrote home, their letters came back marked "Addressee unknown."

Every day Jacob rode the train home from his workshop on the Lower East Side, sank into his armchair, opened the radio, and listened darkly to the news, ignoring his wife and child. When the Nazis invaded Poland in 1939, he began reading the Bible. Clara thought at first that he was getting religion, but his reading seemed only to incense him, and he never set foot in synagogue, not even on Yom Kippur. Not even the birth of his son, Jonathan, could dispel the fog of his depression. Without telling Clara, Jacob tried to enlist in the United States Army, but was rejected for a triviality— flat feet.

On the day the Warsaw ghetto fell, he came home early from work. Clara was in the basement, hanging laundry.

"What's the matter?" she asked through a mouthful of clothespins.

"We're going to Palestine," he said.

Her shoulders tensed, but she took a pin from her mouth and clamped a diaper onto the line. *"Vus is dus?"*

"We're going to Palestine."

She turned to look at him. Something settled and certain in his face made her cry out so that the clothespins spilled out of her mouth and down her front. "We can't," she cried. "We have the house, the children."

"Sell the house," he replied inexorably, "keep the children"; and a wholly unaccustomed grin split his face.

Clara rented the house (she wouldn't sell it, no fool she) and they sailed away to Palestine. Jonathan was a toddler, Fanny eight years old. Now Jacob was the one who sang all day, while Clara paced the decks, frowning and muttering to herself.

Jacob had a *landsman* on a kibbutz in the Negev, and it was there they went after landing in Jaffa. Jacob and Fanny fell instantly in love with the primitive settlement and surrounding wilderness; but Clara hated the kibbutz, that bare, ugly outpost sandwiched between the Dead Sea and the towering, sere cliffs of the Judean wilderness. When they took her children away to the children's houses, she wept inconsolably. The scorpions, snakes, and desert beetles the size of rats terrified her. Their little room with its concrete floor was an oven, and ventilation could only be had at the cost of privacy.

Clara mourned her house in Brooklyn, her beautiful furniture bought all new, never secondhand, her carpets, her electric stove. Here the bathrooms and kitchen were communal. Even in the shtetl, Clara's mother had had her own kitchen; and though their outhouse had been primitive, at least it was theirs alone. In Poland, even the poorest of the poor had some link to the civilized past—a pair of Sabbath candlesticks, a hand-stitched linen tablecloth, something of value. Here there was nothing; like primitives, the people subsisted on visions she could not perceive.

"You call this a home?" she cried to her husband. "This is a prison camp."

"No, Clara, no." Jacob patted her awkwardly. "Here is our home, come look." Outside, the stark, massive hills of the Negev cradled them, the sky of a blueness so pure and sharp the heart soared to see it. In the air was the arid smell of undisturbed time, of a land unmodified by man, a majestic continuum.

"It's ours," he told his wife, holding her with one arm and with the other tracing a broad sweep of the land. "It was given us to take and make into our very own. 'For the Lord thy God bringeth thee into a good land, a land of brooks of water, of fountains and depths that spring out of valleys and hills; a land of wheat, and barley, and vines, and fig trees, and pomegranates; a land of oil, olive, and honey."

But Clara said scornfully, "Him who eats *trafe* and never goes to shul, not even on Yom Kippur, he talks about God? This one who don't even believe?"

"Just because I don't believe in God," he said with dignity, "don't mean He don't have to keep his promise."

In his eyes she saw a reflection of the land of brooks and fountains, ripening fields of wheat and barley, green vineyards and fragrant orchards. But when she looked around her, all she saw was barren wilderness, savage, useless, intimidating beauty.

"Fool," she scolded. "You don't live from scenery. You can't eat hope." She pointed back into their dark shack. "This *nothing* is all there is."

But it was as if they spoke different languages, and neither could understand the other's. To Jacob, a large house or a small room, fancy furniture or plain, was no matter. To him it was the dream that mattered; to her, the bed. He took his wife's hand and said passionately: "Here is a great canvas, and we hold the brush. Clara, we can build a whole new society, a light to the nations."

"Let them light their own light," she said. "I want a decent home."

"Here we can live free in our own country, we can shape this land to our dreams. Clara, this is where we belong."

"What was so bad with Brooklyn?" she cried. "We had a home, carpets on the floor, drapes on the windows, all from our own work: what was so bad?"

"It wasn't our land," Jacob said patiently.

"I don't want a land," she cried. "I want a life."

They gazed at each other in perplexity. "Ach, what's the use?" Clara sighed. "For stubbornness there's no cure."

She was assigned to work in the toddlers' house, where Jonathan lived. By day Clara tended to the six babies domiciled there, and at night she traded off with the other mothers, spending one night out of seven on a cot in the children's room.

She made no effort to get along with the other women or to learn the language. Several months after the Fleishmans arrived, a group of veterans accused Clara in a general kibbutz meeting of favoring her own child over others.

"Of course I love my own children more," she replied scornfully. "I'm not their mother?"

A pall of collective disapproval settled over the room. The kibbutz secretary said sternly, "Our children are loved, not only by their parents, but by every member of the community. We love our children without smothering them in bourgeois family bonds. We treat them as people, not possessions. And we never, ever favor one over another."

"Ha!" crowed Clara. "You think I don't see how Rivka gives her boy the biggest bowl of soup, and Miriam skims the cream off the milk to fatten her little Rochele? And you think I blame them? I don't blame them! They're mothers, like me. If a mother don't look out for her children, who will?"

Jacob and Clara were asked to wait outside. The discussion lasted only a few minutes: the kibbutz had held longer, more impassioned debates on buying milk goats from the Bedouin. The secretary came out alone. "Maybe you should try a moshav," he told Jacob.

Jacob put his arm around his wife and they walked back to their room. As the door closed behind them, Clara said calmly, "I'm going home."

"Home," said Jacob, "what home? We *are* home."

"Home to Brooklyn, and I'm taking the children with me. You can come or no, it's up to you."

"We don't need this kibbutz. To hell with them. There's others. Or we'll go to a moshav. Would you like that, Clara?"

"I'm going home," she said.

"We'll move to a city—Jerusalem or Tel Aviv. You'll like that." In her face he saw that inexorable intent that she had seen in his the day the Warsaw ghetto fell. "I can't go back," he said.

"So." Clara turned up her hands, saddened but not surprised. Jacob wanted something she couldn't understand, much less give him. That he wanted it more than he wanted her and the children seemed to her a terrible betrayal, but she did not argue. Even if she could force Jacob to come home, what good would it do? What use would a bitter, resentful man be to her? *"Zai gesunt,"* she said, in sorrow and anger—Go *in health*, as if it were he who was leaving.

Not for a moment did she anticipate Fanny's reaction. The

child had grown away from her mother, going so far as to change her name—she answered now only to the name of Tamar, Hebrew for the date palm. Tamar flatly refused to leave Israel. "If you try to take me back to Brooklyn," she said, "I'll run away."

"Is this my daughter?" Clara cried, striking her breast. "I gave you life, nursed you, fed you, and now you spit on me?"

"I can't leave. This is my true home."

This mystical nonsense was precisely what Clara could neither understand nor abide. "Your home is with your parents. With your mama," she amended, casting a defiant look at Jacob, who stood listening silently with his arms folded.

Tamar looked from one to the other. "You want to stay too, don't you, Papa? Mama, you can't leave us."

Clara groaned. "This is all your fault," she told Jacob, "you with your Palestine *mishugas!*"

He replied: "Remember Ruth's words to Naomi. 'Whither thou goest, I will go, and where thou lodgest, I will lodge; thy people shall be my people, thy God my God.'"

"She could talk. What did she leave behind, a tent in the desert? I left *mein* own house. You want I should follow you? From Brooklyn to Queens I'll follow you. From Queens to Long Island I'll follow you."

"God gave us *this* land, not Brooklyn or Queens, not even Long Island."

"Don't talk to me about God, you atheist! And who asked him anyway? Some gift He gives! A desert full of scorpions, snakes, and Arabs, and by you fools it's Paradise. He can keep his gifts, the big spender! Oy," she cried, "what am I doing so bad? All I want is to make a life for myself and *mein kinder;* and for this I'm a criminal?"

But Jacob did not relent, nor did Tamar. One month later, light one child and a husband but laden with a bitterness that would last a lifetime, Clara boarded ship with Jonathan in tow.

Who was right and who was wrong? Clara knew: the proof was in the children. Clara's boy had grown into a fine, wealthy, successful family man. Jacob's girl had a good profession, but nothing to show for it. Tamar's husband had been cut down by an Arab's bullet, her only child was adopted. So who was right?

3

"HEY, HEY, LBJ, how many gooks did you kill today?" the two men chanted, then slapped hands and laughed.

The locker room, which stank pleasantly of sweat and Lysol, was deserted except for the club attendant, and if he found anything incongruous in this juvenile greeting between two impeccably dressed middle-aged men, he was far too well-trained to show it. They themselves saw nothing strange in it, for though on the outside they might look fiftyish and comfortable, inside they were still twenty-three year old radicals.

"I really appreciate you coming," Michael Kavin said, clasping Jonathan's shoulder.

"What the hell? We've been golfing together for twenty years— suddenly you've got to kiss my ass?"

"That was before I came down with leprosy," Michael said.

They finished dressing and left the locker room for the clubhouse, where a dozen men and women were waiting their turn to tee off.

"Good to see you, Mike," the club manager said as he handed over their scorecards. "How're you doing, Mr. Fleishman? You guys want caddies?"

"Not today," Michael said.

"Go right ahead, then."

As they walked past the people waiting on benches, straight out to the first hole, Michael cast a proprietary glance around him. He owned a piece of the club, a gesture of appreciation by the club's directorate for his help in settling a zoning dispute with the municipality. Though his interest was too small to matter much financially, it was good investment property and it did wonders for their waiting time. Gone and unlamented were the days of rising at six to tee off at ten.

Jonathan teed off first and hit a long straight shot down the fairway. Michael's shot went wide. When they converged at the hole, Michael laughed and said, "Darling, we can't go on meeting this way."

Jonathan looked at him. "Why not?"

"I wasn't kidding about the leprosy. Did you see Callaghan duck into the john as I walked by?"

"Fuck him. He was happy enough to see you coming a month ago—"

"That was then," Michael said morosely. He was a large man, a head taller than Jonathan and half again his weight. As a young man he'd been built like a moose; it was often said, unkindly, that Jonathan was the brain and Michael the brawn of their partnership. But over the years his muscle had turned to fat. He was fair in complexion, and as they climbed the hill, his face turned florid.

"You want to watch your health," Jonathan said. "Don't let the pricks get to you. It'll blow over."

"You really believe that?"

"Sure I do."

"Tell it to the marines," Michael said, puffing as they reached the top. It struck Jonathan that Michael's father, who had died of a heart attack while they were in law school, couldn't have been much older than they were today.

They'd been best friends since their undergraduate days at Columbia, but in those days there were three of them: Michael, Jonathan, and a black kid from Eastborough named Lucas Rayburn. People called them the Three Musketeers.

They shared a drafty prewar apartment on the Upper West Side, supplemented by a migrant population of girlfriends. Though Michael's father was a minor clubhouse pol in his home borough of Queens, none of the three came to Columbia with any particular interest in public affairs. Jonathan planned to become a doctor, like his sister in Israel. Michael was going to join his father's accounting firm, and Lucas, who got into Columbia on a basketball scholarship, hoped for a career with the pros. But they were thoroughly sidetracked by the civil-rights movement. Within a year of matriculation, all three had switched their majors to political science; by the time they were juniors, they'd decided on law as a precursor to political careers. The three went through Columbia Law School together. Immediately after passing the bar, Jonathan and Michael joined SNCC (still in its infancy, still welcoming whites) and traveled down south to join the black-voter-register drive; but Lucas, who had a younger sister starting college that fall, stayed behind to take a job as an assistant district attorney in Eastborough.

For five years Jonathan and Michael worked in tandem as roaming Have-case-will-travel lawyers, ranging from voter registration in the South to the struggle of migrant workers in the southwest, antiwar and black nationalist movements. Along the way they accrued wives and children, but precious little money with which to support them. In 1973 Jonathan and Michael returned to New York with the certainty of having done their bit and the intention of settling down at last.

Michael joined a Brooklyn law firm with close ties to the local Democratic Party. Jonathan opened a practice in Eastborough, where Lucas Rayburn, now chief assistant to the D.A., introduced him to powerful mainstream city and state Democrats.

Jonathan's politics underwent a subtle shift. Not in principle, but in practice. The clients Lucas sent him were people who did business with the city, and the problems they presented— zoning variances, building permits, tax abatements—were more prone to resolution over dinner in a fine restaurant with a few influential people than in court. Jonathan learned the art of keeping his personal and professional lives separate. He guarded his opinions, observed the boundary of consensus, cultivated political friendships, learned golf over Lily's objections ("the first downward step on the road to Republicanism," she called it), and kept a strict account of favors disbursed and received. He and Lily bought their first house, a modest Colonial just slightly beyond their means in the middle-class township of Martindale.

When the Democratic borough leader of Eastborough and two of his aides were forced to resign after indictment on corruption charges, the party cast about for a new broom. Jonathan, the outsider with a national reputation as a reformer, was tapped for the job. He was meant to be a stopgap, to hold the spot until the dust settled enough for one of their own to take over. Young, attractive, and very clean, Fleishman was the perfect dark horse.

Barnaby once wrote of him that he'd built his career of being a dark horse; by the time people figured out what Jonathan wanted, he generally had it.

They'd made their intentions clear enough ahead of time, and Jonathan had seemed amenable. Before the ink was dry on his appointment, however, he had grasped the reins of power, and within two weeks he'd won over some of his predecessor's people, fired the rest, and replaced them with his own. The party leaders sat on their hands. They knew what was going on; they saw how Jonathan had finessed them. If you can't stop it, they figured, lie back and enjoy it. By the time party elections came around, his power was consolidated.

Slowly but steadily, in a motion parallel to but always a little behind Jonathan's, Michael Kavin too was rising in the ranks. With a little help from his friends, he was appointed associate counsel to the Board of Estimates. Later he became chairman of his home-district planning commission, with power over neighborhood zoning.

Thirty years of friendship. Outside of his family, no one meant more to Jonathan than Michael and Lucas; and this was due less, perhaps, to his affection for them (which nevertheless was very real) than to his need for an occasional glimpse of that self found only in the smoky mirror of long acquaintance. Michael in particular was a witness to the continuity of Jonathan's life, an antidote to Gracie's critical eyes, a reminder of where he had started and how far he had come. Because Michael knew him to his core, in his company Jonathan felt more himself than at any other time. With Michael by his side, he felt both younger and lighter, disencumbered of the weighty knowledge of *how things work.*

Now his friend stood leaning on his club, huffing and puffing and sweating profusely.

"Are you okay?" Jonathan said. "Want to chuck the game and grab a beer?"

"We need to talk, and this is the only place I feel safe. Even here..." Michael looked around warily. "They've got these long-range directional mikes."

"Christ, you're paranoid."

"The hell I am. You haven't got a fucking clue. I haven't taken a shit in the past two years that hasn't been recorded."

Jonathan had a vision, a mental snapshot of three stooges

standing amidst the urinals in a dingy john, fumbling an envelope from hand to hand. He sighted along a club. "What are they looking at, specifically?"

"Everything. Think about the last two years. That's how long they've been on my tail."

"And by 'they' we mean specifically... ?"

Michael stared at him. "Come on."

Jonathan smashed his club onto the ground. "I heard it. I just didn't believe it. You're not even in his goddamn jurisdiction. What, is he going out of his way to fuck a friend?"

The other said quietly, "It's not me they're after."

A long look passed between the two men. Michael said in a conciliatory voice, "It's not actually Lucas. It's that bitch who runs the anticorruption unit, Jane Buscaglio."

"She wouldn't take a piss without his blessing. I still can't believe it. We go back so fucking far. He wouldn't be U.S. attorney now, if it wasn't for me. Now he turns on us?"

"It's the climate. He's got to cover his ass. Especially in view of our history."

Jonathan picked his club up off the ground and lined up his shot. "Did they offer you a deal?"

"Sure. My ass for yours."

"Bastard," he exploded softly.

"Aren't you going to ask what I said?"

"Hell, no." He tapped the ball. It disappeared into the hole.

Michael bent down, took it out, and tossed it to Jonathan. "I told her to stick it."

"Did I ask?" he replied, offended. "I know you."

They walked on, heads bent together. "You don't know what it's like, Jonathan. They're into everything. I can't tell you. They're like roaches, like cancer." Michael laughed shakily. "It's affecting my marriage. I keep thinking that Buscaglio broad's in bed with us. What a fucking turn-off."

"How is Martha taking it?"

He grimaced. "You want the party line or the truth?"

"I'm sorry, man," Jonathan said, and he meant it, despite the nasty little voice inside that said, *You married a bitch. Lily would never let me down like that.*

"Don't be sorry. Be careful."

* * *

Lily closed her book and looked up, shading her eyes. "How was your game?"

"Lousy," Jonathan said, sinking into a deck chair.

"How's Michael?"

"Shaking in his goddamn boots. Paranoid as hell." He'd decided, driving home, to say nothing about Michael's warning. Why open that whole can of worms when most likely nothing would come out of it? He looked around. Paul was swimming laps in the pool. "Where's Gracie?"

Lily pursed her lips. "City."

"She spends more time there than she does out here. Is she still seeing that shmuck?"

"I presume so."

"You presume so? Are you her mother or her goddamn maid? You presume so?"

"Jonathan, don't you dare take it out on me."

"I'm sorry." Jonathan leaned back and surveyed his domain. His wife lay near him on a chaise lounge, her eyes hidden behind dark glasses, her body firm and tan in a white suit of exquisite simplicity. An elegant, sophisticated woman, nothing like the shy, pretty girl he had married. Her transformation was a mystery to Jonathan, who could not see his own, but it was also a source of great pride. He had done for his wife and children what his own father had so dismally failed to do for his. Watching his children grow up with everything was a deep solace to the boy inside who had grown up wanting, never having.

Paul waved from the pool. Across the lawn, the ketch's mast bobbed up and down above the level of the dock. Bees droned, and water slapped rhythmically against the bulkheads. Lily's roses filled the air with a briny sweetness.

"It's a good life," Jonathan said.

There was something in his voice. Lily propped herself up on her elbow and removed her dark glasses, but could not read his face.

Gracie leaned against a boulder by the lake in Central Park, reading a small leather-bound edition of *Pride and Prejudice*. She wanted Barnaby to find her lost in her book, careless of the time, but she was finding it hard to concentrate.

He was late again. Every time it happened, Gracie told herself she ought to be mad, she ought to leave. But then she would look up and see him flying toward her, with his jacket bellowing out like a sail and that wonderful crooked grin, and she was full of gratitude and wonder that he had come at all.

She applied herself to her book. "It was plain to them all that Colonel Fitzwilliam came because he had pleasure in their society.... But why Mr. Darcy came so often to the parsonage, it was more difficult to understand." Difficult to Elizabeth, maybe; to Gracie it was obvious that Darcy, however unwillingly, was in love with her. His visits were not to satisfy a lover's craving, but to seek out any flaws or vulgarity that he might use to extricate himself. To no avail, for like a man struggling in quicksand, Darcy sank deeper and deeper into the mire, until he succumbed through sheer exhaustion. "In vain have I struggled. It will not do. My feelings will not be repressed. You must permit me to tell you how ardently I admire and love you."

The page blurred. Darcy's face dissolved into Barnaby's. She saw him sick with desire for her, struggling against feelings he could not contain. His honest, creased face bent close to hers; he murmured, "In vain have I struggled...."

A shadow fell over her book. Gracie looked up, blushing as if her thoughts were visible. The man looming over her was not Barnaby at all, but a seedy-looking stranger in filthy jeans and a torn sweatshirt. He leered. She gave him her fiercest look and he backed away.

Gracie stood and looked about. All around, people were strolling in pairs, playing Frisbee, sunbathing; there was no sign of Barnaby. A small boy pulled a sailboat on a string along the edge of the lake, beaded with sunlight and rippled by the breeze. Grace reached back to lift the hair off her neck, and a deep voice, cloying as caramel, said quietly: "Hey there, darlin'."

She looked over her shoulder. The seedy man had returned.

"Go away," she said, with a shooing motion.

He slid forward, hand brushing his crotch. "I've got something for you, baby doll."

She wasn't afraid. He was bigger than she was, but there were people all around and besides, she knew how to fight. Big brothers were good for that if nothing else. She faced the man head on, fists clenched. "I told you: get lost."

"Don't you want to see what I got? I guaranfuckingtee you're gonna like it." He reached for her—she drew back.

Then a voice behind her yelled, "Hey!" Gracie turned. Barnaby was scrambling up the rocks, moving faster than she'd ever seen him move. He blew straight by her, threw both arms around the stranger, and hurled him onto the boulders.

The seedy man found his feet and scuttled away. Barnaby turned to Gracie. "Are you okay?"

"Sure."

"What did he say to you?"

"Nothing worth repeating."

"I'm sorry, Gracie."

"For what? Rescuing me?"

"For picking such a stupid place to meet. Come on." He took her arm and they started walking, just walking, heading nowhere in particular.

"Nice to know you've got my back, anyway," she said after a while.

"Anytime. Not that you needed rescuing." He smiled, thinking of the first time he'd laid eyes on her. Must have been eight, nine years ago, at a town meeting in Martindale at the height of the busing furor: Jonathan Friedman at the podium trying to make the pro-integration case, and the audience drowning him in catcalls. Suddenly a little girl marched up onto to the stage, faced the audience, and pointed a scrawny finger at the lead heckler. "Sit down!" she said, in a voice so commanding and so incongruous that the man obeyed out of sheer surprise.

The girl scanned the crowd. "You folks can disagree all you want, after you've heard him out. Maybe if you really listen, you won't want to disagree."

Then she went back to her seat. It wasn't exactly a *To Kill A Mockingbird* moment. Hearts didn't melt, minds didn't change. But Jonathan finished his speech without another interruption.

"What are you smiling at?" Gracie asked.

"I was just remembering the first time I saw you." He told her the story.

She laughed. "I had a big mouth."

"You loved your old man . Nothing wrong with that."

The laughter left her face. She shrugged.

"I saw you at lots of events," Barnaby probed. " You were his biggest fan. I was his second biggest. I guess we have that in common."

"I was a kid," she muttered. "What was your excuse?"

With an almost audible click, Barnaby shifted into professional gear. She had something for him, he could smell it. But he didn't stop walking or do anything to spook her, just continued the conversation. "What changed?"

"I grew up." She looked away from him, and her eye fell on the Central Park carousel. "Oh, look! Let's go on it!"

Barnaby bought two tickets. Gracie chose a black stallion with a fiery mane, and he took the horse beside hers. The music started, and the carousel jolted into motion. Gracie laughed and gathered up the reins.

He gazed at her. She wore an apple-green halter dress that left her brown shoulders bare. He kept flashing on the scene among the boulders: Gracie in full concentration mode, that wretch grabbing at her. He saw her through the other man's eyes, and it was a shamefully arousing image: a juicy-sweet young thing, alone and unprotected.

Gracie flashed a smile. Her dress streamed out behind her, the soft fabric clinging to her breasts. His horse rose in counterpoint to hers. As they passed in midair, Barnaby reached out and laid his hand on her leg.

The carousel spun, the horses rose and fell. Their motion carried his hand up and down her thigh. He felt the warmth of her flesh beneath the thin cotton. Their eyes met and held. She did not remove his hand. When the ride ended, Barnaby could barely walk.

They sat on a bench. Maybe he could have his cake and eat it, too, he thought. He was only human, for Chrissake. And Gracie was of age. She leaned against him, and his arm settled itself around her shoulders. A small girl on skates shuttled back and forth in front of them, careening from a wastebasket to her father's arms.

"Where are we going?" Gracie asked.

"Good question."

"Let's go to your place."

It'll come out, he thought, *and I'll be fucked. This is nuts. Why am I even thinking about it?* His eye fell on a Good Humor cart. "Care for an ice cream?"

"Instead? Seriously?"

"Gracie, have mercy on an old man."

"Do you have a girlfriend?"

"No."

"A boyfriend?"

"No! Jesus."

"Why then?"

"You know why. I'm no Humbert Humbert."

"And I'm no Lolita. That's bullshit." Gracie studied his face. "There's something else."

"What else could there be?" Stupid question. He could see her considering it.

"My father?"

Barnaby gave her his wounded puppy look. "Have I ever asked you about him?"

"You wouldn't," she said thoughtfully. "You'd wait."

She was too damn smart. Barnaby had no choice. He pulled her to him and kissed her. She kissed him back, hard. When they finally broke apart, Barnaby noticed the father of the young skater leading her away, casting a disapproving look back over his shoulder. He shrugged it off. A man's got to do what a man's got to do.

4

IT WAS A HOT SUNDAY, late in June. The Long Island Sound was full of brightly colored speedboats and water-skiers. Sailing the *Water Lily* was the only thing Jonathan and Gracie still did together, but they did it well, with an efficiency born of long practice. As long as they kept working, the morning passed in harmony. Then they put into a quiet cove for lunch, and over sandwiches and a thermos of coffee, Jonathan launched into his speech.

"A man like Barnaby," he said, "lives through his work. He has to; he's got nothing else. It's his mission from God, his obsession. He couldn't shut it off if he tried."

"You've got it all wrong," Gracie said.

"Set me right, then."

"He likes me. I like him. Our relationship has nothing to do with you or his job."

"Is that what he tells you?"

She flushed. "I know when people are lying to me."

"Sweetheart, you haven't got a clue." The worst part of this whole thing, he wanted to say, is knowing you're going to get hurt and being helpless to prevent it. But what was the use? She would only get that look on her face, the look he'd known since she started walking. *Hands off,* it said. *I've got this.*

"Why are you so suspicious?" Gracie said. "Barnaby's always been one of your greatest fans."

"That was before he sank his teeth into Michael. Now he's tasted blood. It's made him hungry. I hear him clawing at the door; I hear him scrabbling on the roof."

"I hear a touch of paranoia. He's not the big bad wolf, Dad."

"That's precisely who he is."

Gracie made a face and turned away. Kneeling on the seat, she reached down, cupped a handful of water and splashed it on her face and neck. The sun streamed down on water so clear she could see crabs scuttling along the cove's sandy floor. The small pebbled beach was dotted with sunbathers. Distorted by rising waves of heat, the scene resembled a painting by Matisse. Distant voices mingled with the cries of sea gulls. Grace closed her eyes and imagined Barnaby was with her. Would he like sailing, or would he despise her for having such a decadent toy?

Jonathan said, "I cannot understand how you live with what that man has done to Michael and his family."

She opened her eyes. "I'm sorry for them. But if Michael did what they say—"

"Michael's no more guilty than I am!"

Gracie leaned forward, arms around her knees. "Then why doesn't he defend himself? If he's innocent, why doesn't he speak out, why doesn't he sue the Probe?"

"Because the media distorts everything. Anything he said would be twisted and turned against him."

"If someone called me corrupt and I wasn't, nothing in the world could keep me quiet."

"It's not that easy, Gracie. Michael has a good lawyer, and he's taking his advice. Mud sticks. In the real world you have to do what works, not what feels good."

"Seems simple enough to me. Either he did the stuff they say, took bribes and all that, or he didn't."

Jonathan collected the sandwich wrappers and stuck them in the cooler Lily had packed. The silence between them stretched out. Finally he said, "That's not simple, it's simplistic. You've got to look at the whole man. I'm not talking just about the glory days with the Freedom Fighters; I'm talking about his whole career. The man's paid his dues and then some. He could have hung up his spurs years ago and no one would have said a word. But no, he goes on struggling, fighting the good fight: minority hiring, integration, women's rights, day care, public schools, decent health care—the same old horses we've been flogging for decades. One step forward, two steps back, but he never gives up. For longer than you've been alive, he's been fighting."

Gracie started to reply, but he spoke over her. "How do you

judge a man like that? On legal technicalities, the difference between a bribe and a contribution? Even politicians have a right to look after their own. Show me where it's written that a man can't look after his own family. Or do you think that to fight for the poor and homeless, you've got to *be* poor and homeless? That's lazy, childish thinking. If you were down and out, who would you want on your side? Some poor *shlub* who can't even buy himself a cup of coffee, or a man of power?"

"It matters, doesn't it," Gracie broke in, raising her face to his, "how you get the power?"

Damned knowing eyes she had, he thought, and was suddenly seized with anger. "You have no right to judge me!"

"I thought we were talking about Michael."

She knew exactly who they were talking about. Jonathan took a deep breath. His heart was pounding. One of these days she was going to give him a heart attack. It never ceased to amaze him how the person he loved most in the world was the one who made him the angriest.

"When you grow up," he said, in a measured tone, "you will learn that it takes power to achieve your goals. Not good intentions—power. If you want to change the rules, first learn to play the game."

"Monopoly?" she asked. "Risk?"

Roger Hasselforth blew smoke at the ceiling. He squinted at the fluorescent fixture, removed his glasses, and wiped them with a crumpled linen handkerchief. "Rumor has it," he said to the overhead fan, "you've been sleeping with the Fleishman girl."

"*Rumor has it?* Who told you that, Ronnie Neidelman?"

"No," Roger said, which meant yes.

Barnaby glared at him. "And you believed her? Do you think I'm stupid?"

"You're a lot of things, Barnaby, but stupid you're not. I still need to ask."

"I've met the kid a few times. I'm sure as hell not balling her." Barnaby paced the editor's office, weaving among stacks of old *Probes*. "This place is a fire hazard, apart from smelling like a stinking ashtray. Why don't you clean it up once in a while?"

"We're talking about your disgusting habits, not mine. Is the girl a source?"

"Not yet, but she's got something for me, the little tease."

"Does she know what you're working on?"

"What do you think?"

"What happens when she finds out?"

Barnaby shrugged.

Roger stared up at him, and not for the first time realized that he loathed Barnaby's way of looming over people. "Sit down, damn you. What do you need her for, anyway?"

Scowling, the reporter sat. "Do you want Fleishman or not?"

"Don't be an ass. There's no 'either-or' here. Of course I want him. She can't be your only way in."

"I can't run an investigation and play nursemaid at the same time. I told you I'm not balling the girl, so drop it."

"All right, all right. How's the story coming?"

"I've just about nailed it. The scam is neat and tidy, and right where you'd least expect it: in the minority set-aside program."

"His baby."

"That's right, it's his baby and he controls it. Contracts awarded through the program are exempt from normal bidding procedures. They're supposed to be vetted by a special affirmative-action board headed by the borough president; in reality, the B.P. just turns it over to Fleishman. He's turned a program to help minority businesses into a stocked pond that he and his buddies fished dry."

Roger shook his head sadly. "Hard to believe."

"How do you think I felt? I fucking hero-worshiped the guy. When I was a kid, I wanted to grow up to be Jonathan Fleishman."

"You supported that set-aside program. You called it the most progressive in the country."

"It is. That's the brilliance of it. All the companies he extorts are legitimately minority-owned. Fleishman's brought equal opportunity to graft."

"And this ties into Michael Kavin how?"

"They're partners," Barnaby said. "Those guys had their fingers in more pies than they had fingers, and every one of those pies does business with the city."

Roger tipped his chair back, balancing perilously. "Can you prove it?"

"I'm gettin' there."

"When? We're not the only paper sniffing around, you know."

"Then you'd better quit wasting my time, hadn't you?" Barnaby said, pleasantly enough. But his face darkened as he left his editor's office and barreled through the rabbit warren to Ronnie Neidelman's desk.

"Bitch!" he said, in a carrying voice.

Heads craned over partitions all around them. Ronnie looked smug and nervous, not a pretty combination. "What's up, Barnaby?"

"You told Roger I'm balling that girl."

"Aren't you?"

"Hell, no!" he said righteously.

She studied his face. "But you'd like to be."

"Why, because she's young and beautiful?" He laughed derisively. "That's no crime."

"It is by me."

"That's your problem. Better learn to check your hormones at the office door."

"Asshole!" she yelled as he stalked off. Barnaby didn't look back.

In size, Barnaby's cubicle was halfway between Roger's private office and the three square feet of semi-partitioned desk space allotted to the Probe's plebeian reporters. The weekly journal had outgrown its facilities years ago, but its steady increase in circulation was no match for the spiraling cost of space in the city. With moving unthinkable, each new addition to the staff reduced the per-capita allowance of space. Thus status at the *Probe* was defined in square feet and the possession of such luxuries as a door. The last inhabitant of Barnaby's cubicle had died of AIDS. Barnaby launched his campaign for the eight-by-ten glass-enclosed cubicle the day he found out about his predecessor's illness; he was as relentless in pursuit of the space as his corporate counterparts were of corner offices and executive-washroom keys.

The door also had the functional benefit of reducing the racket to a muffled roar. Barnaby slammed it shut and reached for his phone book. He had told Hasselforth some, not all, of the story. It wasn't that he didn't trust his editor, it was just his nature always to keep something in reserve.

He dialed the number of the Department of General Services and asked for Arthur Speigel. Speigel was a mid-level functionary in the DGS, one who, like many others in the municipal bureaucracy, owed his job to Fleishman's recommendation.

This made him the journalistic equivalent of a hostile witness. Barnaby, of course, had no power of subpoena. His power was discretionary, vested solely in his troublemaking capacity. Speigel didn't like taking his calls, but he didn't dare refuse them. Now he came on with a wary "Hello?"

"Hey, Artie, how's it going?"

"What is it, Barnaby? I'm busy."

"Then I won't waste your time. Have you got those figures I asked for?"

There was a pause. "I've got 'em. But I'm telling you up front, they're misleading."

Barnaby uncapped his pen. "So, what is Rencorp paying the city?"

"You can't look just at the rent. There are a lot of other factors—"

"What are we, playing patticake here? Just give me the goddamn rent and I'll go bother someone else."

"A couple thousand a month," Speigel said unhappily.

Barnaby laughed deep in his throat. "Two thousand? You're kidding."

"The building's in a lousy neighborhood. Before Rencorp took it over, it was occupied by some printer that hadn't paid rent in months. The place was a wreck. They spent a fortune fixing it up."

"And the building is how big?"

There was a rustling of paper. "About forty-five thousand square feet. You got to understand that this building is located right in the heart of south Eastborough. Rencorp's employees weren't exactly thrilled about the move."

"So Rencorp's doing the city a favor," Barnaby said.

"You could say that. Their move opened up a lot of jobs for the borough; and as a gesture of support for the community, they opened up a day-care facility, which your paper is always bitching we don't have enough of."

"That's very touching, Arthur, considering their savings in rent. Do you know what that kind of space is worth on the open market?"

"You guys are always looking at the down side."

"And Fleishman approved this sweetheart deal?"

"What are you talking? These things go through a dozen city

agencies till they end up here. It's got nothing to do with party politics."

Barnaby cackled rudely. "Please, dude. You know and I know that nothing goes down in Eastborough without our friend's approval."

"If you know so much, what are you asking me for?"

"Arthur, Arthur," Barnaby sighed. "Why all the indignation? Now you've got me thinking something's not kosher."

"What's not kosher? You know Jonathan. He sees a chance to snag hundreds of jobs and a day-care center for his borough, he's not exactly gonna spit on it."

"He's a prince," Barnaby agreed. "Did you know that Rencorp got a massive tax abatement when they moved to Eastborough? For the next ten years they'll be virtually exempt from state and municipal tax."

"So what?" Speigel said. "Jonathan's supposed to bring business into the borough. All you're telling me is that he's good at his job."

"He good at something. But I'm sure you're right, Artie. Jonathan's personal ties to Rencorp have nothing to do with the company's good fortune."

There was a long pause. When Speigel spoke, his voice was hollow. "I don't know what you're talking about."

"You don't know he's the company legal adviser?"

"That's no business of mine."

Barnaby didn't speak.

"You're barking up a bad tree. If ever there was a right guy, Fleishman is it."

"Did he ask for your help on the Rencorp lease?"

"I don't remember. What if he did? That's his job. If he pulled a few strings, he did it for Eastborough. Hell, you ought to give him a medal."

Barnaby said, "Quite a guy, Jonathan." He thanked Speigel and hung up, rubbing his hands together. The morning's unpleasantness was wholly subsumed by glee. He was onto Fleishman now. He knew the man's spoor, recognized his signature, that overlay of altruism. Rencorp was the paradigm, the case that would blow the lid off Fleishman's scam.

The company fitted the profile precisely: it was a legitimate, minority-owned company that met all the criteria of Eastborough's set-aside program and had done spectacularly well since moving onto Fleishman's turf. In 1984 Rencorp was a small electrical contracting firm with billings of about $300,000, located in the Bronx. In 1985 the company moved to Eastborough and was awarded, through the set-aside program, a federally funded subcontract for city rehab projects. Between 1985 and 1986 their billings shot up to 1.7 million.

In 1987, two years after moving to Eastborough, Rencorp expanded into electrical supply. Despite competitive bids from two veteran minority-owned supply houses, it received another set-aside contract to supply lighting and cables to Eastborough's subway stations. The company seemed extraordinarily lucky. They had only to wish for a job and it was theirs. Their requests for variances met with sweet understanding; and when they outgrew their parking lot, the city conveniently put in a municipal lot next door. Blessed with either a potent guardian angel or an earthly facilitator, Rencorp was currently grossing over seven million.

Barnaby had pored over all the company's public filings and literature, but found Jonathan Fleishman's name in only one: a 1984 press release in which he was named as the company's legal adviser. By the time Rencorp got its first city contract, Fleishman's name was nowhere to be found. On the list of shareholders, Barnaby found something interesting: one Solomon Lebenthal, whose name had cropped up during his investigation of Michael Kavin. He was a partner of Kavin's in a print shop that did work for Eastborough. Barnaby made a note to follow up on Lebenthal.

It was long past dark by the time he walked home through a light drizzle. On the stoop of his building, a man lay sleeping in a foul- smelling cardboard nest, a blanket wrapped around him. Barnaby stepped over him and climbed four flights to his studio, unlocked three bolts, and went inside, locking the door behind him. He showered, then sat naked on his bed and rolled a joint. The red message light on his answering machine was flashing, and he played back an incoherent message from Ronnie Neidelman. Drunk again, he thought disapprovingly. He smoked a couple of joints in quick succession. He was horny, but it wasn't Neidelman he wanted. When he closed his eyes, visions of Gracie danced through his head.

He didn't like it. Barnaby wasn't the kind of man to chase schoolgirls. But he had a yen for Gracie, a wicked desire, light-years from the tepid attractions of recent years. Seeing her accosted by that low-life scum had aroused in him something very far from paternalism. Touching her on the carousel made it worse, and then she had to twist the knife. She knew what she was doing, too. Women always knew.

But his hands were tied. There was honor involved, as well as reputation. Barnaby guarded both as jealously as other men guard their daughters—more carefully than Fleishman guarded his—because what else did he have?

Men his age, no smarter or more industrious than he, were racking up condos, country homes, cars, and boats. Barnaby rode the subways and lived in a rented fifth-floor walkup in a roach-infested building sandwiched between a parking lot and a sausage factory. The studio was decent enough inside, but he was long past the age of pretending there was anything romantic about his cesspool environment or of taking an inverted pride in his poverty.

Once, years ago, his mother had flown in for a visit. As she walked down the street from the subway stop, her face began quivering with disgust, and as soon as they got inside, she threw up her hands. "This is how you live?" she cried. "Such a smart boy, by now you should have a home, a family, money in the bank. What have you got? Nothing!"

His mother's name was Selma Reiser Goldfarb. Barnaby had been born Howard Nathan Goldfarb, but took the single name of Barnaby when he moved to New York. Once a year, Howard Nathan Goldfarb rose from the dead and flew to Chicago to celebrate Passover with his parents and sister. But for the rest of the year he was gloriously self-named and self-made, free of chattel.

Usually his poverty didn't bother him. On principle he despised consumerism; by nature he was not particularly acquisitive. Other forces fueled his fire. The city was infested with corrupt politicians who siphoned off the wealth of the city while people slept in the gutter and children grew up abused, illiterate, and hopeless. Barnaby despised those vermin politicians. He considered himself privileged to be numbered among their exterminators.

No one got rich in his line of work, not if he was honest; but there were other forms of capital, and reckoning by those, Barnaby was a man of substance. The governor took his calls; congressmen courted him. In fifteen years on the job Barnaby had broken more major stories off the city beat than any other reporter in town. He had the respect of his peers and a name that struck fear in the breasts of the powerful and corrupt.

Little enough, but too much to jeopardize for a fling with the poor little rich girl.

5

"WE'VE KNOWN EACH OTHER twenty-five years," Martha Kavin said, "and during that time I don't believe we've ever met without our husbands. When you think about it, it's amazing how little we've had to say to each other."

"Still, you came," Lily said, beckoning the waiter.

"The timing was curious. I wondered what you're after."

"I'm not *after* anything. I just thought you could use some moral support."

"How touching," Martha said.

They were within months of the same age, but Martha looked ten years older. Her eyes were sunk in a mottled pool of failed concealer and smudged mascara, her skin was pasty, and her graying blond hair cried out for attention. Martha was a senior editor at Simon and Schuster, where she had tarried long enough that the bright young things shooting past her into management were half a generation younger. Too late to change houses; at this point, she'd be lucky to hang on to her job. One of the most dispiriting aspects of Michael's fall from grace was its effect on her own career. It was a bitter discovery to find that as his stock plummeted, so did hers.

The Japanese waiter came and took their orders. When he was gone, Lily leaned toward Martha. "This must be hell for you. I wanted you to know that if there's anything I can do—"

Martha cut her off. "You've done enough, thank you, you and your husband."

"What do you mean?"

"You know exactly what I mean. If you didn't, you wouldn't be here."

"I believe in Michael's innocence. I came to tell you that, not to listen to you badmouth Jonathan."

"Not just Jonathan; you're as complicit as he is. What do you think pays for your fancy estate in Highview, the house in East Hampton, that monstrous boat? You don't even work. Where do you think all that money comes from, Jonathan's salary?"

Lily gave her icy look. "I didn't know you kept such careful track of our expenditures."

"Ducking the question: Why am I not surprised?"

"Not that it's any of your business, but Jonathan happens to have made some excellent investments."

"Oh, really. In what?" When Lily didn't answer, Martha laughed and said, "You're such an ostrich."

The waiter served their lunch and slipped away. Lily stared down at the dainty little rows of rolled sushi, whose fishy odor was suddenly overwhelming, and found she'd lost her appetite. Martha attacked her squid grimly, as if she weren't hungry either, but expected this meal to be her last.

Lily's head hurt. The headache had started on the jitney from East Hampton but suddenly it was much worse. The restaurant swam in and out of focus. Martha's vermilion mouth jabbered soundlessly, and the sushi wriggled on Lily's plate. She pressed her hands to her temples and shut her eyes.

Gradually, like the downside of a labor contraction, the pain ebbed. Martha's voice resurfaced. "What's wrong?"

"Headache," Lily said.

"You've gone white."

"Let's get out of here."

Martha signaled for the check, but Lily was recovered enough to grab it when it came. She paid, and they went outside into the heat. Though they had no wish to go on together, their paths led the same way, toward Columbus Circle. After a while Martha said, "Win or lose, this fight has cost us everything. Not just money. We're talking divorce, when this nightmare is over. We're talking kids who want to change their names and move to Arkansas. We're talking my career down the tubes. And you know what kills me? We didn't need it. Maybe in the beginning, but later, between his salary and mine? It's not worth it, I told him; but Jonathan wouldn't leave him alone."

"I wish you would stop saying that. Jonathan loves Michael."

"Sure, in his own twisted way. That's why he had to drag Michael down with him. If they were both doing it, it had to be okay."

They'd reached the southern edge of Central Park. Lily stopped and glared at Martha, who suddenly remembered a younger, more formidable Lily. Where had she gone, and when had Tapioca Woman taken her place?

"That's enough," Lily said, sounding more like her old self. "I'm sorry if Michael's done things he shouldn't have, but he's responsible for his choices, not Jonathan."

"We'll see," Martha said. "I'll tell you this: the buck won't stop with my husband."

"I don't believe you. Michael would never drag Jonathan into his mess."

Martha let out a bitter laugh. "Michael will do what he has to do." The women glared at each other, all semblance of liking gone. "You know what your problem is?"

"No, but I'll bet you do."

"I finally figured you out. Behind that Mrs. Ramsay act you do so well, you're nothing but a common coward. You take what Jonathan gives, but you don't have the guts to ask where it comes from. You just drift along on the current."

Lily flushed. "That's absurd."

"Is it? Listen." Martha moved closer. Her breath smelled of squid. "I'm strong. Somehow I will survive this nightmare, and when it's over, I will rebuild my life. But you, Lily: what's going to happen to you?"

Lily had heard enough. She turned and fled into Central Park, where she wandered aimlessly, too upset to go home. After some time she found herself in the Sheep Meadow, where she and Jonathan used to attend the free concerts when they first came back to New York. They would arrive early in the morning to stake out a good spot, settle in, and get acquainted with their neighbors. Gallon jugs of wine circulated, and a sweet cloud of marijuana smoke lay over the meadow. She sat on the grass, legs outstretched, leaning back on her elbows. When she closed her eyes, she could see the bare-chested boys with flowing hair, the girls in Indian prints holding half-naked babies with peace signs stenciled onto their diapers. It seemed like yesterday. Where had the time gone? People stared at her, an elegant middle-aged lady in silk and high heels lolling in the grass, but for once she didn't care.

* * *

The door marked "Jonathan Fleishman, Eastborough Democratic Leader" was usually left ajar, for the incumbent ran an open shop; but this morning's unexpected caller had carefully closed it behind him.

"It wasn't so much what he said," Arthur Speigel said, "as how he said it, if you know what I mean."

"Let's start with what he asked."

"He asked what the city was getting for the Rencorp lease."

"Did you tell him?"

"What else could I do?" Speigel said. He was a pink-faced twitch of a man, with thick glasses and an air of perpetual worry. "It's city property. I had no grounds not to tell him. Anyway, he could have got it through Freedom of Information."

"You told him." Jonathan sighed. "Let me explain something, Arthur. The Freedom of Information Act does not say that every time a reporter asks a question we have to fall all over ourselves to answer it. The law lays out procedures to be followed—detailed, time- consuming procedures. Reporters still have to work for a living; we don't have to do their jobs for them. Do you hear what I'm saying?"

"Sorry, Jonathan. I just thought it was better not to seem obstructive. I didn't want to make a big deal of it. It's not like there's anything wrong, right?"

Jonathan leaned back in his chair and gazed at the ceiling. The chair was a custom-made orthopedic rocker, an expensive item, but the party had picked up the tag. Jonathan's bad back was a badge of honor, like Jack Kennedy's, and a part of his legend; it stemmed from a savage beating in an Alabama lockup some twenty-five years ago.

Except for the creaking of his chair, the room was very quiet.

"Did you mention the day-care center?" Jonathan asked.

"The day-care center, the jobs. I told him the deal was made with the city, not the party. I reminded him Rencorp is a minority business, I said it's the opening wedge in a whole revitalization project for south Eastborough."

"And?"

Spiegel lowered his eyes. "He kept coming back to the rent. He asked about you, too."

"What about me?"

"He asked if you had some kind of side deal with Rencorp."

There was a moment of silence. Jonathan leaned forward, folding his hands on his desk. "And you said...?"

"I said not that I know of."

"Are you shitting me?"

"I'm sorry. He came at me out of left field."

"That was the best you could do?"

Speigel pulled a large red handkerchief from his pocket and mopped his forehead. "So maybe I didn't handle it so great. He took me by surprise is all. I guess I should have seen it coming."

"How so?" Jonathan asked with ominous softness.

Speigel took off his glasses and wiped his eyes. "Ever since the *Probe* tore into Mike Kavin, people have been waiting for the other shoe to drop."

"And I'm the other shoe?"

"I didn't mean it like that. Hey, don't kill the messenger, my friend. I'm here, aren't I?"

There was, nonetheless, a look in his eyes Jonathan had not seen before, a speculative glint. He walked Speigel out, an arm around his shoulders.

"Do me a favor, Art. Next time Barnaby calls, if there is a next time, duck the call. And if somehow he does get ahold of you, be less accommodating. Stonewall. You don't know, you don't have time, you're not authorized, you need it in triplicate—know what I mean?"

Afterward, Jonathan poured himself a shot of bourbon from a bottle he kept in a cupboard. Spiegel's after-shave had left a sweet, brackish odor in the room. The man was no rocket scientist, but he was useful and he had a good political nose: the kind of guy you could throw cold into a meeting of strangers and in ten minutes later he could tell you with absolute accuracy that A, ostensibly allied with B, was secretly playing footsy with C.

Respect bordering on the obsequious was his usual manner with Jonathan. Today there had been an undertone of doubt, the sound of a man hedging his bets.

His secretary buzzed him. "It's your bank, Jonathan. The woman's called twice; she says it's urgent."

"Thanks, Maggie. Put her through."

"Mr. Fleishman, this is Maria, Mr. Gonzalez's secretary from the bank? You remember you helped me out with my son a few years ago?"

He remembered doing some small thing—making a phone

call when her boy was busted, getting the kid rehab instead of jail. "Of course," he said heartily. "How's the boy doing?"

"Fine, thank you. Mr. Fleishman, something terrible is happening here. Mr. Gonzalez couldn't call you 'cause they're sitting right in his office, but he gave me a sign and I came out to the lobby."

"What's the problem, Maria?"

"These people came with a subpoena, Mr. Fleishman. They're auditing your account."

"Who is? The IRS?"

"No, sir," she whispered. "I heard them say the U.S. attorney's office."

Jonathan felt a dull impact, like drilling on an anesthetized tooth. "They had a subpoena?"

"Yes, sir, because Mr. Gonzalez didn't have no choice, he had to let them look. Only he gave me a wink to go call you. You better come right down here, sir."

The bank was only two blocks from his office. He was there in five minutes. Maria was hovering by the entrance. As they strode through the front room toward the manager's office, the tellers looked at him, then looked away. Maria opened the office door and stood aside to let him enter. When Jonathan squeezed her arm in thanks, she turned away, wiping her eyes.

Luis Gonzalez glanced up, and a look that was half-relief, half-embarrassment flooded his face. He spread his hands. "Nothing I could do, Jonathan."

Three people were seated at a table strewn with computer printouts and ledgers. Two clerkish men glanced up incuriously, then went back to the papers before them. The third—a woman, red-haired, hard- faced, striking—took the time to scowl at Gonzalez. Then, without a word, she stood and thrust a subpoena at Jonathan.

He skimmed it and tossed it aside contemptuously. "What grounds did you give for this fishing expedition?" he demanded.

"I can't answer that."

"Don't be a smart-ass—Bugalio, is it?" He knew damn well who she was—the bitch who was after Michael's blood.

"Buscaglio, and we both know I don't have to cite grounds to you, sir." The "sir" was late and ironic.

"Lucas knows about this?"

"Of course."

He needn't have asked. Buscaglio might be flavor of the month in the U.S. attorney's office, but she had nowhere near the authority or the clout to take him on herself.

They're like roaches, Michael had said, but he was wrong: they were maggots. Jonathan felt a spreading sickness in his gut. It was happening to him. He'd seen it done to so many others, he knew just how the process worked. It was inexorable. Once they started, they never let go till they found something to justify their efforts; and if they couldn't make a case, they'd manufacture one.

He stood in the doorway, paralyzed by the realization that after all these years of fighting for the system's victims, he had finally joined them. It was all wrong; it was never supposed to happen. This pawing through his bank records was pure harassment. What else could they expect to accomplish by it—or did Lucas reckon him stupid as well as corrupt?

But he had to remain calm. People were watching. He told himself that he was an honorable man, and honorable men cannot be humiliated. Nevertheless, he couldn't stop himself saying bitterly, "Lucas didn't have the balls to confront me himself. Tell him I thought he had more guts."

"You should leave now, Mr. Fleishman," Buscaglio said with an insolent look.

Luis Gonzalez jumped up and came around his desk to stand beside Jonathan. His face was red. "Mr. Fleishman is an honored customer of this bank and he has every right to be here."

Jonathan clasped his shoulder. "It's all right, my friend. Let them look. They're just wasting time and money."

"My time," Gonzalez said, "my tax money. I'm sorry, Jonathan, this just burns me up." He turned to Buscaglio. "I grew up in Eastborough, and all my life this borough has been run by crooked politicians who got fat off the people. Nobody ever did a goddamn thing to them. Finally we get someone decent, someone who cares about our problems, and that's who you go after. Lady, you want to do some good, why don't you go after the drug money that flows like water through this borough? Why don't you go after the dealers who sell crack to our children?" Why don't you one-tenth of what this man has done?"

Jonathan could have kissed him.

Jane Buscaglio shrugged and picked up a ledger.

* * *

Clara sat at the kitchen table in the light, bright house that was built on water and wrote in a crabbed, uneven hand:

> Dear Tamar,
> How are you? And Micha? He should get out of the army. Seven years, enough already. He should go to college, get a real profession.
> And you, my daughter, I'm very proud they made you chief of surgery. Maybe now you'll think about what I said, about coming to America. Here such a respected doctor could live like a queen, with a beautiful house and fine things, good as your brother. What you got there on the kibbutz? A couple rooms, a few sticks furniture, not even your own telephone or car they give you. I ask you, this is fair?"

Of course it wasn't fair. What was the good of being a doctor if you had to give away all you earned? Helping others was very nice, but first you got to help yourself. Okay, so the kibbutz put her through medical school, very nice, but was that a reason they should live off her the rest of her life?

It was a terrible thing to work and work and never see the good of it, terrible and unnatural. Clara knew. In Poland, her poor mama and papa had struggled from dawn to late at night just to survive; from year to year they never saved a penny. Here in America, if a person worked hard, he made money; and if he was smart and saved, he could have anything. A person was lazy, didn't want to work, he stayed poor—that was his choice. That was the American way, and it was fair. Jonathan worked hard and he grew rich. Tamar, in Israel, worked just as hard, had even greater responsibility, and what did she own? Nothing. Not even her little house was hers; everything belonged to the kibbutz. Very nice, she had respect; but respect you can't sell, you can't eat.

Clara sighed. No point getting aggravated. Tamar wouldn't listen, never had. She was as stubborn as her father.

> "Everyone here is fine, thanks God. Gracie sees a young man, nice Jewish boy, runs a newspaper in the city. I don't know if it's serious. Jonathan don't like him, and what's not

smart is he shows it. I told him, Lily too: you
say black, she's bound to say white. Gracie's
just like you and your papa, contrary to the
bone. Don't know what's good for her. Lives
in an empty room like a bedouin. Now she says
she won't go to college, even though Harvard
and all those ivory schools want her. Says
they're 'elitist.' Just like your papa, him with
his socialist mishugas. But that's how it goes
in families. One side gets the sense, the other
gets the stubbornness. Same with Jonathan's
children—Paul with his feet on the ground,
and Gracie with her head in the clouds."

So the boyfriend wasn't such a fine young man. So he didn't
run the newspaper. Where did it say she had to tell her daughter
everything?

"Lily's got some tsuris, but she don't talk
to me, really talk, I mean. Maybe she's mad
at Jonathan, but I don't know what's to be
mad at. He works too hard, but he's a good
family man, a mensch. Maybe it's the change
of life, but then why don't she tell me, I'm not
a woman? It's not like she has her own mother
to talk to."

Clara sat back and shook the cramp from her hand. Lily had
called her "Mother" since the day she married Jonathan, but only
from her mouth, not from her heart. Not because they didn't love
each other— they did—but because of a barrier erected by Lily,
which Clara's best efforts had failed to breach. Perhaps it was
loyalty to her own mother, who had died so tragically, poor soul,
or perhaps a simple disinclination toward intimacy: Clara had
noticed that although Lily had many friends, she had no intimates.

"So, tochter. Give a kiss to Micha, and to the
old man a good kick in the pants.
                                        Mama"

* * *

On her way through the park, Lily was mugged from within. The pain had not gone after all, but merely lain in wait, biding its time. She was walking slowly down the path, a little distracted, wondering what had come over her and whether the grass stains in her beige silk would ever come out, when suddenly she had the sensation of something alive and alien trapped inside her skull, fighting desperately to escape. Her sight narrowed; she staggered to a bench and slumped onto it. After a while she became aware of a voice somewhere close behind her. The voice was a woman's, singing in a German accent. *Hush, little baby, don't say a vord, Mama's gonna buy you a mockingbird. And if that mockingbird don't sing, Mama's gonna buy you a diamond ring.*

There was a gathering stillness in the air, a warm anticipation, like the pause before a thunderstorm. Lily knew that voice, though it had been twenty-five years since she'd heard it. Who could forget her mother's lullaby?

And if that diamond ring turns brass, Mama's gonna buy you a looking glass.

But that was impossible. Lily had buried her mother. Someone else must be singing that song. Someone with an accent like her mother's. Someone with the same voice.

And if that looking glass gets broke, Mama's gonna buy you a billy goat.

Greta never sang or spoke or read in German, nor could she abide to hear it spoken. She gave up her native language after the war. Lily was brought up on English nursery songs sung in a German accent.

Her eyes began to clear. The pain shrank to a single point, then vanished. In its wake came a sense of tremendous well-being.

And yet the singing continued. It was a mystery she had only turn her head to solve; yet Lily was oddly reluctant to do it. At last she made herself look around.

She saw no one. Lily stood, turned in a full circle. People were walking past, but there was nobody standing close by and singing.

And if that bully goat von't pull, Mama's gonna buy you a cart und bull.

6

TAMAR KIMCHI INSERTED HER HAND in the hole and sifted the sandy earth. Decades of surgery had given her fingers eyes: as they palpated the hidden object, she saw the smooth curve beneath the encrusted surface. "Yes," she murmured, "yes. Let's expose it."

"Drink first." Micha held the canteen to his mother's lips, then to his own. They set to work using trowels. *Go gently,* Tamar coached. *Where there is one piece there are more. See through your instrument.* But none of it she said aloud, for there was no need.

She and Micha had been on many such expeditions together, starting from the time he was five and had to trot on matchstick legs to keep up with the adults. Tireless and incapable of boredom, he would haul bucket after bucket of excavated dirt away from the dig, then sit for hours in a patch of shade, patiently sifting for small artifacts. The archaeologists treated him like a mascot, patiently submitting to interminable questioning: what is this and how was it made and who made it and what did they use it for—and always, interestingly: How do you know? The child took nothing on trust, not even Tamar, whose adoption of him had been incremental, a slow annexation of the little orphan boy taken in by the kibbutz. When he was eight, Tamar taught him to map finds on a site grid, and a few years later to excavate and photograph artifacts in situ. Micha had good hands, an eye for the land, and a boundless curiosity that Tamar thought would stand him in good stead as an archaeologist; but Micha chose instead to follow his adoptive father's footsteps and make the army his career.

He had done well—his fond mother thought he would have done well in any field—but lately she had sensed his dissatisfaction. The army was not what it had been in her day, when it had faced the massed might of five Arab nations and prevailed, like David over Goliath. Nowadays *they* were Goliath. Their soldiers fought schoolboys and women in a hopeless struggle; if they won, they lost. But Micha had not yet spoken, and it was not her way to force a confidence.

"Try now," Micha said, when they had dug all around the hidden object. Tamar gently wriggled it back and forth, gauging the ease of motion before slowly lifting it out of the hole and laying it on a ground cloth. Despite its encrustation, they could see at once that it was an intact earthen pitcher. While Micha dusted off the superficial dirt with a brush, Tamar used a dental pick to chip sediment from the space between the curved handle and the body of the pitcher. When it was clean they put it back in the hole and Micha photographed it.

"Assyrian?" he asked when he was done.

Tamar picked up the pitcher and closed her eyes, sighing a little in perplexity. "It's at least that old, but it's not the right shape. Look." She handed it to him.

"Maccabean?"

"Possibly." She marked the pitcher's location on a grid of the test ditch, then numbered and logged the artifact.

Micha squinted at the sun, though he wore a watch. "Getting close to dinner."

His mother laughed. "Ah, well, I know better than to stand between you and a meal." She packed the little pitcher carefully in a cloth bag and stowed it in her backpack. They shouldered their equipment and set off on foot.

They were inside Nachal Arugot, a wadi whose spring-fed waters cut a swath of green bounty from deep within the Judean wilderness downward to the Dead Sea, where it ran parallel to Ein Gedi, the Spring of the Wild Goat: ancient even in biblical times, the oasis in which David hid from the wrath of King Saul.

Tamar was a surgeon by vocation, an archaeologist by avocation. Convinced that there had been significant early habitation beside the spring's source, deep in the heart of the Judean desert, she had tried for years to persuade the archaeologists of Ben-Gurion

University to mount a serious expedition. Her conviction was based not on hard evidence, for all she had amounted to little more than a few potsherds that might have come from anywhere, but rather on her instinct for the past harbors of desert dwellers.

Some people reach enlightenment through visions, some through music, some through meditation; but the lowly instruments of Tamar's enlightenment had always been her feet, which were to her like the deep roots of the acacia that suck the sap of the earth. The stones underfoot were known to Tamar, and the hidden pools, and the generations of ibex that browsed among the prickly acacia trees. Like the worm that burrows into flesh and makes its way to the heart, so did the ancient memories of the earth wend upward to lodge in the marrow of her bones. Though little was known about the prehistoric Judean desert dwellers, Tamar saw traces of their passage in the worn bone of the ancient path that rose from and descended to the wadi floor, and heard the desiccated echo of their voices in the desert wind that preserves all it touches: for even as the desert's light is a transparent meld of brilliant color, so is its silence a vast, mute repository of ancient sounds.

But her instinctive certainty did not convince the professionals, nor could she blame them, scientist that she also was. Funds were scarce, not to be allocated on speculation alone. When Tamar offered to carry out a preliminary probe of her own, the archaeologists agreed. It was no skin off their backs if she failed, their glory if she succeeded.

The initial soil analysis had been promising but inconclusive. Tamar waited for Micha to come home on leave to begin digging a test pit. Two days ago he had returned for a week's furlough. Tamar was able to arrange a few days off from the hospital in Arad, where she was chief of surgery. She and Micha drove to the entrance to Nachal Arugot, then hiked four miles to the site she had chosen. On the second day of digging, they had found the pitcher.

Veteran desert rats, they did not waste breath by talking as they walked. When they reached the jeep, Micha said, "This ought to convince them to start a real dig."

"No, it's not nearly enough. We've got to get down deep enough to see the stratification; then maybe we'll have something."

Micha took the wheel for the short drive to Kibbutz Ein Gedi.

On the way, Tamar said, "I got a letter from your grandmother today."

"What does she say?"

"You should quit the army and get a serious job. I should quit the kibbutz and the hospital and come get rich in America."

He laughed. "Anything besides the usual?"

She was slow to answer, and he glanced at her. "Something's wrong," she shouted over the rattling of the jeep.

"With her?"

"No. With your cousin, Gracie."

Micha glanced warily at his mother, whose wide-brimmed straw hat sheltered a face as brown as parchment, with sensible blue eyes and a weathered look. "What about her?"

"She's seeing someone Jonathan disapproves of."

He downshifted for the long, twisting climb up to the kibbutz. "So? What is she, nineteen, twenty?"

"Eighteen."

"Still in school?"

"Just graduated."

"What's it got to do with you, Dr. Mom?" Micha said in a warning voice. His mother had a tendency to pick up strays that he, as number-one stray, found threatening. On several occasions she'd brought home children who for one reason or another had been abandoned in her hospital. The kibbutzniks in charge of the children's houses complained behind her back, but no one dared say a word to Tamar's face.

"She's an interesting child. Intense."

"Uh-oh," he groaned. He pulled into the parking lot beside the dining room and they got out of the jeep.

"She's refused to go to college. Jonathan's angry, and something's wrong with Lily. I don't know. I think this might be the time."

"The time for what?" He raised a hand. "Stop. Go back to question one. What's it got to do with you?"

"I liked the girl," Tamar said. "She was unhappy, but it was a robust kind of unhappiness. I looked at her in that Stepford family and I thought, There, but for the grace of God, go I."

"And you've been biding your time all these years, waiting to get your hands on her."

She grinned and ducked her head, like a kid caught red-handed. As they passed the dining-hall entrance, Yaacov barreled out of the kitchen to intercept them. "Find anything?" he asked his daughter.

"We did all right. I'll show you later." Looking at the dish towel he wore around his throat like an ascot, Tamar asked, "Did they stick you in the kitchen again?"

"Goddamn Yossi," Yaacov snorted. "Whoever thought I'd come to this?"

She made sympathetic noises. Eighteen months ago, riding through a field of alfalfa that the kibbutz cultivated to keep the ibex out of their real crops, her father had fallen from the tractor. For over two hours he lay in agony on the damp ground. By the time someone noticed the idling tractor and came to investigate, the wet cold had seeped into his bones. His broken hip healed well, but he developed rheumatism and a strain of pneumonia that proved highly resistant to antibiotics. He spent three months in Tamar's hospital, but as soon as he was back on his feet, he began fighting with Yossi, the kibbutz secretary. Yaacov insisted on being reassigned to his old job in the fields; Yossi, on orders from Tamar, adamantly refused.

Tamar linked her arm in his. "I had a letter from Clara."

He grunted. "What's she got to say for herself?"

"She sends regards."

"I bet."

"I'm thinking of asking Grace to come."

Yaacov's face lit with pleasure, then turned dour. "Clara won't stand for it."

"If Gracie wants to come, she'll come."

"Stubborn, is she?" said the old man, who had never met his granddaughter.

Tamar smiled. "She comes by it honestly."

"In my opinion, she won't come. Your mother's poisoned her mind against us."

"Can't hurt to ask."

Micha made a face at her behind Yaacov's back. "Remember last time."

"Gracie and Paul couldn't be more different," Tamar replied firmly.

"Then I like her already," Micha said. His cousin Paul's one and only visit, at the age of 18, had been disastrous. Tamar had arranged for him to live and work with the volunteers, young people from all over the world; but Paul refused to work, pointing out that he was on vacation and adding that where he came from, dinner guests were not expected to wash the dishes.

Tamar curbed her tongue and arranged for his transfer, at her expense, to the kibbutz guest house. On his first night there, Paul put his dusty shoes outside his door for cleaning. Next morning, when he found them untouched, he carried his complaint all the way to the kibbutz secretary, who laughed in his face and to that day took pleasure in retelling the story.

A few nights after that incident, someone crept into Paul's room, stole his shoes, and left a pair of stinking galoshes from the coop, caked with chicken shit and mud. Paul was not amused. The following morning, without a word to anyone, he took the bus to Tel Aviv, where he stayed in the Hilton until he could get a flight back to New York.

Micha didn't care; the kid was nothing to him. But Yaacov, who felt in Paul's desertion a painful echo of his wife's, was deeply hurt. Tamar said it was a shame, but not entirely the boy's fault; it was a matter of upbringing.

"Gracie is different," she said later, as they lolled, pleasantly tired, in deck chairs on her lawn. Half an hour to go before dinner, the sun was setting over sandstone mountains that glowed pink and gold. This was the breathing hour, when the air was sweet and cool and the parched earth sighed with relief.

"Mother seems obsessed with this child," Micha said lightly to his grandfather. "The daughter she never had, perhaps."

"I've reconciled myself to having a son," she said, with a complacent look at him. "But I do feel it's a shame there's been so little contact with the other family."

"Thank your mother for that," Yaacov said automatically.

"It's not a matter of fault; it's just a shame." Her muscles ached from the digging. Micha moved behind her, and began massaging her shoulders. Tamar closed her eyes and Gracie's face appeared before her.

The girl had been fourteen when they met. It was one year after Tamar's husband died. She didn't choose to go to New York; the hospital sent her to deliver a paper at an international oncology conference in New York.

She had disembarked at Kennedy Airport, rumpled and jet-worn from the twelve-hour flight, to find the whole family waiting at the gate. Even before Tamar recognized them, they caught her eye with their elegance. Lily and Clara in furs, Jonathan in a suit.

Clara spotted her first and ran forward, crying her name. The others followed. Lily offered a cheek, soft as rose petals, and Jonathan gave her a quick hug. The son followed his father's example. Tamar looked around for the daughter, and spotted her standing some feet away dressed in blue jeans and a baggy sweatshirt, remote and watchful. A slender child, with a thin, dark face much like her father's, raven hair that hung straight to her shoulders, and bangs that came down to her eyes, giving her a hooded look. Summoned by her father, Grace came forward and shook Tamar's hand but did not kiss her.

They drove to Jonathan's house in Highview, a three-story brick mansion on the outermost edge of the borough over which he presided as Democratic leader. It was beautifully decorated but oppressively large; though she felt provincial doing it, Tamar could not help counting the rooms and estimating the number of kibbutz families that could be accommodated in comfort. On the ground floor, spacious reception rooms flowed one into another, and original art was displayed without pretension. A sunlit music room led through French doors into a greenhouse, which opened into three acres of varied and delightful gardens, designed by Lily and maintained by a small army of gardeners. Yet all this splendor served only to sadden Tamar, for it seemed to her that its creator had lacked a worthier object for her talents and energy; she noticed too that although it was all her handiwork, Lily did not seem to own this house, but rather wandered through it like a guest.

They dined *en famille* the first evening, at a table laid with white linen, silver, and crystal, groaning with food and French wines. The meal was excellent but the conversation languished. The gap was too wide. Tamar found it hard to look Jonathan in the face, ashamed for him that he should need so much.

She stayed with them for a week. Her days were taken up by the conference, where she delivered her paper and listened to many others, and her evenings by the family, who seemed determined that like it or not, she would enjoy New York. They went to the theater and concerts, which she did enjoy, and to dinner parties, which she did not. When Jonathan introduced her to his friends, he invariably used her title: "My sister, Dr. Tamar Kimchi." She saw this as a sign of embarrassment, a means of compensating for her plainness, her unfashionable clothes and short, choppy hairstyle, so convenient in the operating room but so difficult elsewhere.

Tamar enjoyed Clara, felt an unexpected affinity for her, and spent several amusing hours trying to imagine what had ever brought two such disparate people as Yaacov and Clara together. Clara was as voluble as Yaacov was quiet, as practical as he was dreamy. The one thing they had in common, Tamar finally concluded, was the very thing that had torn them apart. Both were convinced that they'd found that elusive grail, the good life.

Toward her brother Tamar felt no affinity, perverse or otherwise. He was too smooth, too rich, too secretive—the kind of man, she guessed, who kept secrets even from himself.

Despite the affluence of her brother's home, Tamar sensed in it an uneasiness embodied in the little girl, who stood out from her glamorous family, a little waif amidst the riches. Gracie rarely spoke, but followed her aunt with watchful, guarded eyes. In this family of charmers, she seemed indifferent to being liked, self-possessed beyond her years.

Gracie's room, which Tamar, to her surprise, was invited to see, made a statement at striking and deliberate odds with Lily's. Mother and daughter clearly shared a taste for simplicity; but while Lily's was realized through exquisite, costly materials, Gracie's took form in raw brick and plywood. Her bedroom was sparsely furnished with a mattress on the floor, a desk, a simple pine dresser, and rows of homemade bookshelves, unvarnished planks balanced on bricks and anchored by the weight of hundreds of books. A dozen locked diaries were the only personal belongings displayed in a room too arid to support even a stuffed animal or rag doll.

The doctor in Tamar diagnosed a kind of material anorexia; Gracie's appetite seemed fine, but she could not stomach *things*.

Several days after her arrival, Jonathan invited Tamar into his study. It was the first time since childhood that they'd been alone together. They studied each other in silence, intimate strangers wondering at their resemblance to one another, which was much greater than their resemblance to either parent. Both had olive complexions, small neat features, black hair, and wiry builds; only Tamar's eyes were robin's-egg blue, Jonathan's greenish gray.

"You have a fine family," Tamar said. Talking to Jonathan, she was conscious of the oddness of her English, fluent but stripped of regional accent, spoken with a lilting Hebrew inflection.

"I'm sorry I never had the chance to meet yours," Jonathan said.

He astonished her. He could have come to her wedding. He *should* have come to Zach's funeral. They'd invited him to Micha's bar mitzvah; he sent the boy a ridiculously large check but stayed away. She knew that he had often traveled through Europe, had even visited Egypt; but he never came to Israel. Fair enough, he owed her nothing; but their father was another matter. Jonathan's cold indifference was an unending source of pain in Yaacov's life.

"Never mind my family," Tamar said in her forthright way. "Why have you never visited our father?"

He considered before he spoke—he was the kind of man, she thought, who always would. "I invited him to come here."

"He wants to. He'd love to see his grandchildren. But he doesn't believe he'd be welcome."

"I asked him. I offered to pay his way."

Tamar waved this aside. "But you've never come to him."

"I'm not the one who deserted him," Jonathan said. "He left us."

"Clara left us and took you with her," Tamar said. "I remember. You were too young."

"That's not the way I heard it. But why should we fight their battles now? It's ancient history. We're all grown-up."

Tamar agreed; but, having dismissed the only subject that bound them, they fell into an awkward silence. She walked around the room, which was far less stylish than the rest of the house and had about it an air of sanctuary. Massive bookshelves lined the walls, filled with law books, volumes on public policy, money management, real estate, and political biographies. In a dim corner of the room, behind a worn leather armchair, were older-looking paperbacks, carefully preserved but exuding the faint, forlorn odor of books long unread. The wall behind the large captain's desk was papered in deep-crimson-and-black print and covered with framed photographs of Jonathan with various important-looking people. Tamar recognized three: the governor of New York, the mayor, and a former president. Lily, who photographed like an angel, appeared by his side in many of the photos.

On top of the desk was a portrait of the family. Tamar picked it up and studied it. Jonathan was standing between Paul and Lily, an arm around each of their shoulders. All three beamed at the camera. A little to the side stood Gracie, aged twelve or thirteen. She stared unsmiling at the camera, her body canted away from the others.

"What is it with Gracie, if you don't mind my asking?"

Jonathan bristled. "What do you mean?"

"She doesn't talk. I've yet to hear her speak one word to you, civil or otherwise."

"A bad case of adolescence. My daughter is convinced she knows better than anyone. She is the supreme judge of human conduct, especially mine, of which she strongly disapproves."

"What does she disapprove of?"

"We had a falling out a while ago, when we built this house. She didn't want to move. But I had the chance to acquire this place at an exceptionally good. In fact," he couldn't resist adding, "in two years it's already doubled in value."

"Why should moving house upset her so much?"

Jonathan hesitated. She thought he was going to blow her off, but he surprised her by answering. "Our last house was in a town called Martindale. A short time after I sold it, the city announced a plan to integrate Martindale through clusters of low-income housing. My charming daughter had the gall to accuse me of selling out ahead of time, for fear housing values would plummet."

"Did they?"

"For a while. They've recovered."

"But if you sold before the plan was announced, you couldn't have known."

"Oh, I knew," Jonathan said offhandedly, "of course I knew; I was on the Commission. But that had nothing whatsoever to do with our decision. No one who knows me would ever accuse me of white flight, except my daughter."

Tamar said nothing, but looked troubled.

Jonathan put his hands on the desk and leaned forward. "You have to understand how hurtful that was. I despise racism. It's been the great battlefield of my life. I happen to believe that racism and xenophobia are root of most social evils."

"I despise cancer," Tamar said quietly. "I fight it every day. But I know I'm not immune to it."

"The housing plan was never a factor, was it, Lily?" he said as his wife entered the room, bearing flowers.

"We never mentioned it," Lily said. "Why would we?"

Jonathan, finding this answer less supportive than expected, raised his eyes to his wife's face.

Tamar turned away. On a shelf, unostentatiously displayed, was a photo she had not noticed before. In it was a much younger version of Jonathan, shaggy-haired and bright-eyed, standing beside a man she recognized at once as Martin Luther King Jr. It wasn't a posed photo, but a snapshot of the two men deep in conversation on a city corner. King's right arm was slung round Jonathan's shoulders; in the background was a blur of running men.

Lily slipped out of the room as quietly as she had entered it. Jonathan came over to Tamar, took the photo from her hand and studied it.

"This was Gracie's," he said. "For years it was her most prized possession. She kept it on her dresser. She took it to Show and Tell. Then we had that ridiculous fight about the Martindale house, and two days later Lily rescued this picture from the trash."

Jonathan's story had crystallized everything Tamar sensed about her brother's household. Despite its opulence, there'd been a deep dissonance in that family, a sadness at the core. It would be good for Gracie to come here, she thought. She'd known the desert to cure many a festering wound.

The sun dipped over the mountains, and at once the air turned chill. "Dinner time," Micha said firmly. Tamar got up out of her chair and ran her hands through her graying hair. Her father took one of her arms and her son the other, and together they walked along the path to the dining hall.

7

JONATHAN, YOU HAVE TO DISTANCE yourself from Michael. He's going to drag you down with him."

"What is that, woman's intuition?"

"Martha said so."

Jonathan looked at his wife, who was cutting rose stems over the sink. He threw his briefcase onto the seat of a chair and hung his wet raincoat over its back. "Martha Kavin? When did you see her?"

"I went into town yesterday. We had lunch."

"Since when are you two lunch buddies?"

"I invited her. To show we weren't going to drop them just because they have trouble."

"That was nice of you."

She turned to look at him. "She told me to go to hell. Michael is going to turn on you."

"Not in this lifetime."

"Martha hates us. She blames all their troubles on us. She says you seduced Michael into whatever it is he's supposed to have done. She implied that you're corrupt and I've closed my eyes to it. She called me an ostrich."

"Bitch. I never liked that woman."

"Jonathan, is Michael going to be indicted?"

"Probably."

"Can he hurt you?"

"He wouldn't even if he could," Jonathan said firmly, because if he couldn't rely on that, he might as well pack it all in. Lucas Rayburn had turned on him. Barnaby was targeting him. Rumors were flying; even Spiegel was hedging his bets. Soon the leaks would begin. "Fleishman Under Investigation..." "Eastborough Democratic Leader Suspected..." And once it began, the ending was preordained.

"What is it?" Lily said. "What's wrong?"

"Nothing."

"I'm not blind."

Jonathan hesitated. He couldn't tell her everything. Lily was that part of his life unsullied by politics. If he lost that, what would remain? It was, moreover, his duty to protect her. "It's that bastard Gracie's been seeing," he said at last. "He's been talking to people, asking questions."

"What kind of questions?"

"The offensive kind," he snapped.

Lily took the roses from the sink and began arranging them in a crystal vase. A thorn scratched her finger, and a drop of blood fell onto the counter. "Have you told Gracie?" she asked.

"No, and I don't want you to."

"Why not?"

"Wouldn't help."

"Why do you say that?"

"She wouldn't stop seeing him." It hurt him to say it.

"Of course she would," Lily said, but she wasn't sure either, and it showed in her voice.

"I guess I don't want to find out."

Lily carried the vase into the living room and set it on a side table. Jonathan followed, throwing himself into an armchair. She stood at the picture window overlooking the bay, and in the rain-streaked glass saw her husband sitting in a pool of light, leaning forward, hands on knees, watching her. In the reflection his face was blurred, mutable; for a moment she saw the face of her young lover of that first summer, when they lived together in the back of the van they called Rosinante, traveling through the south.

Nothing was forbidden then, nothing hidden. "What are you thinking?" one would ask, purposely picking the most incongruous time, and the rule was that the other had to tell everything, no matter how silly, irrelevant, or revealing, and not just the primary thought but all the tangled strands of miscellaneous notions, stray impressions, sensations, and feelings that made up the moment.

How unthinkable such a game was now. How dangerous.

Outside, the rain-bearing wind blew across the bay, lashing the sentinel cypresses, pressing against the window, groping for a crack, a crevice, any way in. Beyond the long, manicured lawn, the moored ketch rode the waves; rain-whipped, the tide was high tonight. The ketch's mast rose and fell high above the dock, and its bumpers thudded against the piles, sounding like a distant drum.

Sudden darkness engulfed the boat. Even as Lily watched, a great tidal wave rose from the bay. Smashing over the bulkheads, it inundated the lawn, washed away her shallow garden, and loomed over the house. She covered her face and awaited the crash of shattering glass. But nothing happened; and when she peeked through her fingers, the wave was gone.

Her husband's reflection wavered and aged. Framed by lamplight, he peered in on her as if the glass were between them.

"Lily," he whispered, "I need to know: are you with me?"

"Where else would I be?" she said.

"You look so far away."

"I'm frightened." She leaned her forehead against the cool glass and waited for him to come up behind her and say: No need, my love.

"I'm going to confront Lucas," Jonathan said from his armchair.

Many questions occurred to her, but the one she asked was, "Is that wise?"

Three days later, they faced off in the living room of the Highview house.

Lily said, "I don't think this is a good idea."

"So you've said."

"You used to take my advice."

"You used to give advice worth taking," Jonathan said.

"I used to have the information."

"You used to want it."

They were saying forbidden things, picking at the fabric of the marriage. Outside, a car door slammed. "Be careful," Lily whispered.

The bell rang. Lily opened the door, said, "Hello, Lucas," and held up her face to be kissed. Rayburn bussed her cheek, glancing past her at Jonathan.

He came forward, not smiling. "Glad you could make it. I wasn't sure you would."

"Neither was I," Lucas said. They shook hands briefly—Lucas's hand dwarfed Jonathan's—and Lily led them into the living room.

"Lovely room," Lucas said.

She stared at him. "You say that as if you've never seen it before."

"He's seeing it now through different eyes," Jonathan said

Lily settled herself on a sofa. They had quarreled earlier about her sitting in. Jonathan said it would look as if he were hiding behind her skirts, but Lily for once was adamant. "This affects me as much as you and Lucas better know it."

"Coffee?" Jonathan asked Lucas. "Or a drink?"

"Nothing, thanks."

"Afraid it might be contaminated?"

"Poisoned," Lucas said, and they all pretended to laugh.

Jonathan sat beside his wife, Lucas opposite in an armchair, stretching out his long legs. "So, buddy," Jonathan said, "you want to tell me what's going on?"

"If that's why you asked me here, this is going to be a short visit."

"You can't say it to my face? You sent that woman with a subpoena to paw through my goddamn bank records—what did you think you'd find?"

Lily, who had not known about the subpoena, felt that she was falling, drifting slowly downward into the bottom of a deep, still well, a listening place. She did not look at her husband, nor he at her.

Lucas studied his hands. "You know I can't discuss my office's activities with you."

"Then why are you here?"

"I thought maybe you had something to say to me."

Jonathan snorted. "I know Buscaglio offered Michael a deal to implicate me. You're coming after me, and you don't have the basic decency to say to my face what you're doing behind my back."

"You talk about decency," Lucas Rayburn said, with a flash of bitterness.

"You could have come to me. Anything you wanted to know, you could have asked. I've got nothing to hide. But this dirty business, this going behind my back, suborning friends and colleagues, that's despicable, man. That's beneath you, or so I thought."

"I've got a job to do. Friendship doesn't come into it."

Lily found her voice at last. "It did before you had the job, when you needed Jonathan's support to get it. For God's sake, Lucas, you know what Jonathan has done for this city, what he did before we came here!"

"I do," Lucas said in his deep, slow voice. "He's done pretty well for himself, too."

"How dare you!" Lily cried. You know us! I thought we were all on the same side."

Lucas clasped his hands so tightly his dark knuckles gleamed. "I know what you were," he said softly. "I haven't forgotten a thing. That's what makes it so sad."

"So you will not listen to reason," Jonathan said sadly. "You persist in trying to make something out of nothing."

"No one can do that."

"Except God," Lily said, "and that's who you're playing."

When he was gone, they stood for a while in the large living room without speaking. Finally Jonathan said, "You stuck up for me. Thank you."

"What did you expect?"

"No less."

"Why is Lucas doing this?"

"Because I'm Michael's friend. Guilt by association." They looked at each other. He expected her to drop her eyes and turn away or melt into him, but she just stood there.

"Jonathan," she said, "what have you done?"

"Nothing I'm ashamed of. This is about Lucas's ambition, nothing more or less."

"He seemed so...sad."

"Crocodile tears. He'd sell his soul to be mayor, but there's heavy competition. You want maximum publicity, who do you go after? Not the bad guys—that's too easy. No, you go after the biggest good guy you can find and pull *him* down. All the better if it's a friend. Let everyone see how impartial you are."

"How could you not tell me they subpoenaed our bank records? Don't you think it concerns me too?"

"No. It's nothing to do with you, and I won't let them drag you into it."

She stared at him. His brow was beaded with sweat. "Are you frightened?"

"Not frightened; concerned. Despite your parting exchange with Lucas, it's very easy to make something out of nothing—it's called fabricating a case, and it happens every day."

Lily's headache was back. She sank into a chair. A woman was singing. "*Rock-a-bye baby in the treetop, ven the vind blows, the cradle vill rock...*"

The voice faded away. Lily shivered. "Did you hear that?"

"Hear what?" said Jonathan.

"What I can't make out," Barnaby murmured, "is how you got from there to here." They were in his apartment because Gracie, testing her strength, had insisted that she would meet him there or nowhere. Barnaby would have fortified himself with a visit to Ronnie Neidelman, but they were still on the outs. Gracie sat on the edge of his bed, legs tucked beneath her. He clung to his armchair as if to a slippery rock in a tempest.

"What do you mean?" Gracie said.

"I remember you as your old man's shadow, Jonathan's little coat-bearer. What changed? What happened to the two of you?"

"What's it to you?"

"I'm interested. I want to know what makes you tick."

"You make me tick." She aimed for sexy but couldn't quite pull it off straight-faced.

"Was it a gradual disillusionment, or did something happen?"

"We had a falling-out."

"What about?"

Gracie didn't answer.

He went and sat beside her on the bed. She wore a sleeveless denim shift with a zipper down the front. The thought of opening that zipper had been with him since he first opened the door. No doubt that's why she wore it, seductive little baggage. Her father had seduced, then fucked him over. Barnaby was damned if he'd fall for the daughter's line of goods. Yet somehow, a moment later, he found himself kissing her.

When he released her, Grace was a dusky red. Her blush was delicious, like the skin of an apple; he longed to sink his teeth into her cheek. In her admiring eyes, he saw himself as wise and courageous, a man of the world, a person of substance. He pulled her to him. She was light and sweet in his arms, and her hair smelled like fresh-cut grass. When he cupped her breast, it nuzzled his palm like a puppy. *This is fucked up*, he told himself.

This is really stupid. But it was already too late. He tugged down the zipper, and her dress fell open. Barnaby pushed her onto her back and lay on top of her. He thought he would have stopped if she'd objected, but it was just as well he wasn't tested.

Afterward, he petted her and kissed her and told her she was beautiful. She stretched languidly, shameless in her nakedness, and her long black hair fell over her breasts just as he'd imagined it would. He stroked the smooth curve of her thigh and said, "You're a wicked girl, Gracie, seducing a poor weak man like myself."

"You feel taken advantage of?" she asked. He smiled at that, and something in his smile made her uneasy. "What?"

"I was just thinking: If your old man could see us now…"

"He said you have evil intentions. He just doesn't know how evil."

Barnaby laughed, his mouth warm against her ear, his hands caressing her back in long, slow strokes. "What happened between you?" he murmured.

She stiffened in his arms. "Why do you keep asking?"

"Because I want all of you, Gracie, not just this part, sweet as it is." He leaned back and gazed into her eyes. "Because I'm in love with you, you doofus."

A vision came to Gracie. She saw herself living in this apartment, Barnaby's lover. Sometimes their friends would come to visit, and they would spend long evenings sitting around, talking and laughing. But when Barnaby was busy working on a story, she would protect him from intrusions and they would stay home alone, he at his desk and she curled up on the sofa. They would talk about his work. She was a stern critic with an eye for the weak points, and sometimes he would get angry; but in the end he would listen to her. He would grow to depend on her.

Barnaby was waiting. She couldn't distrust him anymore, not after what he'd just said.

"Do you remember when the city announced it was building low-income housing in Martindale as part of a plan to integrate the town?" she asked.

"Sure."

"There was a huge town meeting. My father spoke."

"I was there. I remember that speech." He remembered the article he'd written, too. There were references to Martin Luther King Jr. and Bobby Kennedy.

"It was good, wasn't it? He told them, 'Don't panic, don't sell, don't do the blockbusters' dirty work for them. Integration doesn't destroy neighborhoods, white flight does.' And they trusted him, because he wasn't just a politician, he was their neighbor. I was so proud I started bawling. You were right, I was his coat- bearer, literally that night. I looked in his pocket for a handkerchief."

"And found?" Barnaby asked, with a hint of impatience.

"Papers. Documents. When I saw what they were about, I went into the ladies' room and read them thoroughly, twice. I couldn't believe it."

"Believe what?" More than a hint now.

"He'd sold our house," Gracie said, the wonder of it still in her voice. "Right out from under us. Our house in Martindale. Those were the papers."

His hand faltered, then resumed its steady, soothing stroke. "You must have confronted him."

"Sure, that night."

"How did he explain it?"

She answered flatly. "We needed a bigger house. An opportunity came up and he had to sell our house quick to take advantage of it. The timing was pure coincidence."

"But you didn't you believe it?"

"Would you? They kept it a huge secret. If I hadn't found those papers, they wouldn't have told me till the moving vans arrived."

Barnaby frowned. "But you didn't move right away. I'd have noticed; everyone would have. People would have raised a huge stink."

"We moved a year later," she said. "We stayed in the Martindale house as tenants. That was part of the deal. And I wasn't allowed to tell anyone or talk about it outside the family."

He sat up and reached for his jeans. "He panicked."

"My father doesn't panic."

"Did he ever admit it to you, that he sold out because of the housing project?"

Of course not, she thought. He never admitted it even to himself. But there was an edge to Barnaby's voice she hadn't heard before, and suddenly she felt Jonathan's presence in the room, heard him inside her head. *Always working.... You can be damn sure he's got a motive.* She glanced up at Barnaby and caught an avid gleam in his eye.

Gracie pulled the sheet up over her breasts. "Never," she said.

8

"A reporter is supposed to be objective. If he's not, he owes it to his readers to say so up front.
"In the interests of fairness, then: I'm not objective about this particular story. On the contrary, I confess to being deeply embarrassed by it, both personally and professionally."

BARNABY stared balefully at the words on the screen. Soft, soppy lead, New Journalism crap. Though his politics were liberal, Barnaby's professional ethic was conservative; he considered reporters who wrote in the first person to be as inept as photographers who shot their own shadows. Accordingly, he'd written the Fleishman story without any reference to himself.

Roger Hasselforth had read the draft and called him in. The editor's office had one of the few outside windows in the *Probe* warren, but it was thrown away on him. No one could see out of it. The small area that wasn't blocked by piles of old newspapers was covered with years of uncut city grease and grime.

"You've been in this guy's corner since he came up." Roger said from within a cloud of smoke. "Wouldn't hear a word against him. Didn't I say to you a year ago: 'Fleishman's living awfully high on the hog, what's the story there?' And what was your answer? 'The guy's a lawyer, what do you expect?' Look at this shit." Roger disinterred a clipping from the clutter on his desk. Barnaby recognized his own column. "The best choice by far to unseat the mayor, if he could be persuaded to run, is Jonathan Fleishman, Eastborough's gutsy reformer.'"

Barnaby winced. "Don't rub it in."

"That was just four months ago. Suddenly Dr. Jekyll is Mr. Hyde? You owe readers an explanation. What happened? Did Fleishman change, or were you duped all along?"

Barnaby slammed the desk with an open palm, raising a cloud of ash and dust. "You want me to cock up a first-rate piece of investigative journalism with some totally irrelevant personal confession? The piece is damn good as it stands; in fact, it's so strong I wouldn't be surprised..."

"What? A Pulitzer? A call from the *Times?*"

"So what, it's a crime to want recognition for good work? It's not like I get paid decently."

Roger ignored the bait. "You helped put Fleishman where he is, and now you're the guy who's knocking him down. That makes you part of the story."

"Damn straight I put him where he is. I'm the one who broke the story on Fleishman's predecessor, who also got caught with his hand in the cookie jar."

"Before my time," said the editor, who'd been with the *Probe* for only eight years, less than half the time Barnaby had put in.

"Yeah, well, guess who my informant was."

Roger fell back in his chair. "Fleishman? You're kidding."

"Nope."

"How come you never told me before?"

"No reason to. Ulan knew." Ulan had been the *Probe's* editor at the time.

"So Fleishman blew the whistle on this guy, then took his place?"

"Yup."

"Didn't that bother you?"

"At the time, no. I figured why can't the good guys play hardball, too?"

"Still, it casts a light on Fleishman." Roger rubbed his stubble. "Can we use it?"

"I promised him anonymity."

"Way back then."

"Why? Is there a statute of limitations?"

"Fine. But this just supports what I'm saying. You need to work on this piece, put yourself in it."

They argued a while longer and finally compromised. Roger would run the story as written, and Barnaby would write a mea culpa sidebar.

* * *

The rest of the morning Barnaby spent trying to track down the elusive Solomon Lebenthal, Michael Kavin's business partner who was also a major shareholder in Rencorp. His home number was unlisted. The printing company he owned jointly with Kavin claimed ignorance of his whereabouts. By their tone, Barnaby could tell he wasn't the only one looking for Lebenthal. On a hunch he phoned Jane Buscaglio in the U.S. attorney's office. She took his call at once.

Barnaby told her they'd be breaking a big Fleishman story in the *Probe*'s next issue. Buscaglio asked in a pro forma sort of way if he could wait a week; he replied, "No way;" she thanked him for letting her know, and then there was a pause. Neither said good-bye. Barnaby could hear the aimless scratching of her pen as she doodled. "So," she said at last, "what have you got on Fleishman?"

"You know, Jane, I'd love to go into that, but I really need to track down Solly Lebenthal."

A moment passed. "Who?"

"Once again, with conviction."

"Off the record?" she said.

"Okay."

I don't care what you write about Fleishman. But I'd appreciate it if you'd leave Lebenthal out of your story."

Barnaby had nothing on Lebenthal anyway, but he wasn't about to tell her that. "What's in it for me?"

Buscaglio said she would call him back, and she did, fifteen minutes later: just enough time for her to have checked with Lucas Rayburn. "What do you want?" she asked.

"An overview, for starters."

"I'll give you an exclusive when I'm free to discuss it."

Barnaby snorted. "I'm not writing your memoir, Jane."

"You'll leave Lebenthal out?"

"For now. Has he been subpoenaed by the grand jury?"

"Not served," she replied carefully.

"But one was issued?" If he was right, she wouldn't answer: that was how they handled delicate exchanges.

She said nothing.

""Is he talking with you?" Barnaby asked, jotting notes.

"Not directly."

"Through an intermediary? A lawyer?"

Silence again: confirmation.

"So you're looking to cut a deal. What's he got? Something on Fleishman?"

"*Something?*" she said ironically.

Something big, then. Barnaby's heart fluttered. This could be the missing link in the narrative he'd been constructing, the one piece of the puzzle he hadn't been able to find. "Was he Fleishman's bagman?"

Another long, pronounced silence. Then Buscaglio said, "I've gotta go. Remember your promise."

Barnaby finished his notes on the conversation while it was fresh in his mind. Only then did he turn to his computer to write the sidebar Roger had demanded. First the lead: "A reporter is supposed to be objective..." Then the rest:

> "*Probe* readers know that this reporter has long touted Jonathan Fleishman as the best politician this city has to offer. I backed him for mayor and saw no reason why he should stop there. He was a sharp, effective reformer with a genius for using the system against itself. His credentials were impeccable. Fleishman was a freedom rider from the early days of the civil rights movement. He spent his first decade as a lawyer to the oppressed; there's hardly a civil-rights battle he didn't fight in. As Democratic leader in Eastborough, he worked aggressively to eradicate longstanding housing and school segregation. He brought thousands of jobs to his borough and created a minority set- aside program that set the standard in affirmative-action programs. His office door was always open to constituents. Jonathan Fleishman was the ultimate buck-stops-here politician.
>
> "What I did not know, because I refused to see, was that he was also the worst kind of hypocrite: a white-collar crook in blue jeans and a cloth cap, who hid his corruption beneath a veneer of high principle and social responsibility. For years the warning signs were masked by his

golden tongue, which never failed him even
as the corruption deepened. Indeed, his voice
seemed to gain in resonance, issuing from the
hollow shell of a once-ethical man.

"The signs were masked but they were there.
I know, because other people read them. I didn't,
despite having every opportunity. I've followed
Fleishman's career since my high-school days.
The man was right up there with Rudd, Seale,
Dellinger, Hayden, and Hoffman as the heroes
of my youth. When our paths crossed in New
York, I grabbed at the chance to meet him.

"We never became close personal friends. I
didn't visit him at home, sail with him, or eat
at his table. I did, however, fuck his daughter."

Barnaby didn't intend to write that last sentence. It seemed to
type itself. He deleted it quickly and went on.

"We were, however, political allies, and I think
that for both of us that counted more. I watched
with admiration as Fleishman backed his way
into the municipal Democratic machine, a
radical Trojan Horse decked out in moderate
trappings. At my urging this paper endorsed
him for Eastborough Democratic leader.
After he won, I reported on his activities with
satisfaction and a regrettable sense of hubris:
Barnaby the Kingmaker."

Barnaby the Kingmaker: was that going too far? It was hard to
judge. Once you let yourself get started, this kind of writing was
hard to control. Barnaby was aiming for the sort of confession
that would induce colleagues to slap him on the back and say,
"Lighten up, man, you're not omniscient," not the sort that would
make them think: "Hey, the guy really *is* a jerk."

He deleted the phrase and went on.

"In retrospect it's obvious, as these things
usually are. I should have realized that no one
could have devoted the time Fleishman did to

his political job and still manage to make a private fortune, unless his public and private affairs overlapped. But even after my eyes were finally opened by the Kavin affair, the evidence of his corruption was hard to discover.

"To some extent this is because Fleishman's been careful to cover his tracks. But the greatest impediment to my investigation has been the fact that his constituents don't care. 'The guy works hard for us,' they say; 'he's entitled to look after his family, too.' You hear it from Democrats and Republicans alike: 'Jonathan Fleishman is the best thing that ever happened to Eastborough.'

"It's a sad commentary on the state of politics in our city that, corruption notwithstanding, they may be right. Fleishman's achievements were real, not imaginary. My disappointment and, yes, my anger at Fleishman are directly proportionate to the esteem in which I'd held him.

"This, then, is my confession. Because I liked Jonathan Fleishman, because I respected him and took pride in his success, because I expected great things of him—because, in short, I invested too much in the man—I allowed myself to be blindsided.

"Ultimately, there is no justification. It was my responsibility to look harder, to look deeper, to take those hard-won lessons on political hypocrisy and apply them to our friends as well as to our enemies. If Fleishman is about to take a big fall, I feel partially responsible for helping to erect the pedestal. That's not a reporter's job. A reporter's job is to see things as they are, not as we would wish they were. *Mea culpa.*"

Maudlin self-pity, that last bit, Barnaby thought when he read it over, but he let it stand. It was all bullshit anyway. He'd confessed to every sin in the book except the one thing he felt slightly guilty about, and that was balling the Fleishman girl. Amazing Grace; Lord, what a sweet thing. Barnaby used to despise older men who dated young girls; now he saw the matter in a whole new light. Girls were different from women, body and soul. One saw so little innocence in his line of work. Gracie reminded Barnaby of something he'd lost so long ago he didn't even remember what it was. Under any other circumstances he'd have gone on seeing her, and to hell with what people thought. Even now his main regret was that their affair had been so short.

Anyway, it was over and done with; no point worrying about it now. Opportunity had knocked and he'd opened the door. He was human. Barnaby had been in the news business too long to imagine that reporters were made of different stuff from the people they reported on.

Still, it nagged at him, eroding the pleasure he deserved to feel at exposing Fleishman. He kept imagining Gracie opening the *Probe,* reading his article, including the story she'd given him, and discovering she'd been used. He thought of calling to forewarn her, but he couldn't envision the conversation going anywhere useful. What he really wanted to explain was that he had a higher responsibility, a calling, it was fair to say, beside which any claim she had on him was insignificant. It wasn't as if he'd raped her, after all. She'd initiated the encounter. Besides, he'd done nothing to her that her old man hadn't done to the city.

Her story about the Martindale house was not essential to his article. But it was true, he'd checked it out; and it effectively established Fleishman's hypocrisy. When he made the decision to use it, Barnaby had considered the possibility that Grace might retaliate by exposing their relationship. Unlikely, he'd decided; no woman likes to admit she's been used. She'd cover it up for her own sake. And if worst came to worst, it would be her word against his, and his carried weight.

If only he could be sure. It was hard to predict what Gracie might do. Barnaby hadn't forgotten the time they played chess in Union Square Park. He was a good player, but he made the mistake of underestimating Grace. She won in twelve moves and they never played again.

* * *

Lily slept fitfully.

Her mother's voice came to her day and night. It wasn't that Lily imagined her mother alive. She knew full well that Greta was dead; but the knowledge made no difference.

Once she got over the initial shock, this haunting was not surprising, but rather seemed long delayed. Greta had died by her own hand, of her own free will. If she changed her mind, if she found she had something left to say, could not one act of will be reversed by another?

The suicide had been carefully planned. In Greta's apartment they found books on pharmacology, the relevant sections underlined in red. Before taking the pills, she posted a letter to the local police precinct, so that they and not her daughter would find her. Pinned to her dress they found a note addressed to Lily.

"I am so tired," it said, in Greta's ornate Germanic script. "My strength is used up. I waited until you were settled. Now I can't wait anymore. Forgive me, darling Lily. I love you. All that was mine, I leave to you."

The words were no comfort and the legacy was tainted. Everything Greta had had was both more and less than Lily wanted. Solace came only now, two decades later, from the sound of her mother's voice.

Lily told no one about Greta's return. The matter was personal, and besides, she knew what others would advise, what she herself would have advised another.

She didn't want to see a doctor. Nothing was wrong with her. If her mother's voice was a symptom, it was of no disease Lily cared to have diagnosed. To her it seemed a blessing. Those nursery songs carried with them their original aura of warmth, security, enveloping love. Who would exorcise such a welcome visitation?

On the morning of the day Barnaby's story would appear, Lily woke from an uneasy sleep to a sense of Greta's presence. With her eyes shut, she could almost feel the warmth of Greta's soft flannel nightgown and smell her scent, a blend of Ivory Snow and violet sachets.

She imagined herself a child again, walking down a street with her mother. Greta had a small compact that she carried in her hand whenever she went out. There was no powder in the compact; Greta didn't wear makeup, not even lipstick. She used it for the mirror, which she consulted surreptitiously, angling it this way and that. Lily had never asked why, just as she never asked the meaning of Greta's blue tattoo.

The memory faded, and with it the sense of Greta's presence. Lily opened her eyes and turned toward Jonathan, but he wasn't there. She remembered that it was midweek and he was staying in the Highview house, close to his office. She got out of bed, washed, and dressed. The house was silent; Clara, for once, was sleeping late. Lily put up a pot of coffee and discovered they were out of milk. She took her purse and walked outside. A light mist rose off the bay, and the air was salty. She stopped to clip a vine that had tangled itself around a rosebush; then she drove to the deli on Main Street.

It was early, no customers in the store. Old Henry Blue behind the counter blushed inexplicably when Lily came in. She took a half-gallon of milk from the refrigerator and placed it on the counter. Henry glanced involuntarily toward a stack of papers on the floor. Lily looked down. Nestled between *Newsday* and *the New York Times* was a stack of the *Probe*. Above the logo, a banner headline screamed up at her: "THE LONG FALL OF JONATHAN FLEISHMAN."

She picked up a copy and skimmed the piece. Henry busied himself with his back to her, stacking packs of cigarettes. Lily couldn't take it in. Phrases jumped out at her. Secret probe, indictments, racketeering, extortion, bribes—this wasn't her Jonathan they were writing about, this was some other man. Influence peddling, Rencorp, Martindale...Lily stopped then, and read the section about Martindale slowly. Tears came to her eyes, and she leaned her forehead against a glass display case.

"Are you all right, Mrs. Fleishman?" Henry kept his eyes on the counter.

She nodded at the stack of *Probes*. "How many do you have?"

"About forty, ma'am."

"Would you put them in my car, Henry?" She laid a hundred-dollar bill on the counter.

"What's the point?" he said gently. "You can't buy them all."

She tried to lift the stack herself. Henry Blue sighed and came around to help.

Clara sorted through the morning mail. She recognized her daughter's doctorish scrawl and started to open the envelope before noticing it was addressed to Grace. There was a second letter from Israel, this one to her. She hadn't seen the writing in many years, but she knew immediately whose hand it was.

She didn't open it at once. She returned to her room and placed the envelope on her dresser. She washed her face, combed her hair, took off her nightgown, and put on a brassiere and girdle and over them a dress, not a *shmatta* for the house but a real dress. She made her bed. Then, at last, Clara sank into her armchair and opened the letter.

"Dear Wife," he had written, which incensed her at once. True, they had never divorced. But what kind of marriage was it when the husband and wife never met, never talked, never even wrote to each other?

And why suddenly now? she wondered, crumpling the letter in her hand. It couldn't be good news. It came to her that in his old age, Jacob was getting lonely. Maybe he wanted to remarry. She imagined him asking for a divorce, and a rusty twinge of jealousy ran through her old bones. The feeling made no sense; how could you lose what you didn't have? She smoothed out the letter and read on:

"Tamar wants Gracie should come visit us here. We all want to know her. Tamar wrote to the child but I'm writing to you. Don't you stop her, Clara. It wouldn't be right. She got family here, a grandfather, an aunt, a cousin she never met. She's got a right to know us if she wants. Tamar says Gracie will make up her own mind, but she don't know you like I know you. Once you set your mind, that's it. If you decide to stop her, she don't come. So please. What's right is right."

Clara snorted. The nerve of the man. First he stole her daughter. Now he wanted her granddaughter. Clara hadn't minded Paul visiting Israel. She knew her grandson, and she knew the kibbutz. He was in no danger. Gracie was a different story. With that girl you never knew what would be, except trouble.

Besides, was it right she didn't know her grandson? How many times did she ask Tamar to send Micha for a visit, and all she got were pictures. But such pictures. What a handsome boy, and smart, she knew from his letters.

"Over my dead body you'll get Gracie," she scolded, shaking Jacob's letter as if it were his throat. "She'll go to Mecca before she goes to Israel."

A car drove fast up the driveway, scattering gravel. A door slammed. Lily's staccato heels clicked up the path, across the deck, and into the kitchen. Clara went to meet her, waving Jacob's letter. "Lily, I want to talk to you."

Her daughter-in-law did not look at her. Her arms were full of newspapers and her face was smudged with print. Clara had never seen her so pale.

"Lily, *mammale*, what's the matter?"

Lily dropped the stack on the table, took a large black trash bag from a drawer, and started stuffing the newspapers inside.

"What you doing? Lily, talk to me. At least look. What am I, a ghost?" Still Lily did not respond. Clara snatched a paper from the table and held it close to her eyes. Her lips moved. "Oy Gott."

Paul strolled into the kitchen, dressed for tennis, carrying his racket. A handsome boy, tall, blond, clean-cut, and if he was overly conscious of his good looks, it was natural enough at his age. He walked past his mother and grandmother to the refrigerator and took out a carton of juice. He turned and his eyes fell on the *Probe's* banner headline. He read it aloud and looked at his mother, who shook her head helplessly. Paul uncrumpled the paper and read the story standing, still holding the Tropicana.

The phone rang. Paul put down the carton and answered it. "He's not home," he said.

"No comment," he said.

As soon as he hung up, the phone rang again: same questions, same response. The third time, Paul grabbed the receiver and yelled, "No comment, goddammit!" Then he gasped. "Oh, God. I'm sorry, Jessica. We've been getting these crank calls. I was just leaving....I see.... I understand.... Yeah, another time. 'Bye."

He smashed his racket to the ground. His handsome face was bright red. "Goddammit! Do you know who that was? Jessica Dumont, daughter of *the* Jason Dumont. I've only been trying for a whole year, finally I'm asked to the estate for tennis, and now this fucker Barnaby... What the hell has Dad done?"

Lily slapped him. Her diamond ring scratched his cheek and a few drops of blood surfaced. Paul touched his face, then looked at his fingers. Lily turned and walked through the French doors into the garden. He ran down the hall to Gracie's room and threw open the door.

She lay on her mattress, fully dressed in jeans and a T-shirt, but sound asleep. "God damn you, Gracie!"

She woke with a start. Her eyes went from her brother's face to the newspaper in his hand. Then they closed.

"I hope you're pleased with yourself," he cried. "I hope you're fucking proud of what you've done to me and everyone else in this family." He threw the *Probe* at her and slammed the door. Gracie batted the paper away in disgust, as if it were a roach. Moments later came the roar of Paul's Camaro.

She went to the window and peeked out. Lily was kneeling in the dirt with her back to the house, furiously yanking weeds. As if she felt her daughter's eyes, she turned and looked up. Their gazes locked. Lily's reproach passed through glass as through water. Gracie covered her face and turned away.

Barnaby woke from the sleep of the just to the sound of a phone that had been ringing for a while. He grabbed it. "Yeah?"

"I'll get you for this."

He sat up. "Gracie?"

"When you didn't call, I knew something was up. I hoped it wasn't this. But I knew it was."

"Hey, listen, I'm sorry you had to—"

"Fuck you."

"Baby, I understand you're hurt. If it's any consolation, I'm hurting, too. But someday when you've got a little distance on this thing, you'll understand that I just did what I had to do."

"And now I'm going to do what I have to do." Gracie hung up.

9

THE FIRST PART WAS BAD ENOUGH. Jonathan read it again, sitting in a parked car on a small lane near his house in Highview. He couldn't go home; the house was surrounded by reporters. His office was under siege too. What he longed to do was to drive out to East Hampton and lay his head in Lily's lap, but his daughter would also be there, and he wasn't ready to deal with her. Thus was Jonathan Fleishman, a self-made man of substance, reduced by the stroke of a charlatan's pen to sheltering in a car like a poor homeless person.

In the first half of the article, Barnaby accused him of conspiracy, extortion, racketeering, and influence peddling. He named six minority-owned companies that did business with the city and also employed Jonathan as a consultant or legal adviser. Barnaby harped particularly on Rencorp, calling Jonathan the company's "corporate fairy godmother" and implying that he profited from their good fortune.

Barnaby's witches' brew of innuendos lacked the essential ingredient of proof. There was no law against Jonathan's being retained by companies that did business with the city, and no evidence that he had perverted the political process to help them. But Jonathan didn't delude himself. Proof sometimes matters in a court of law, never in the court of public opinion. No one reads that carefully. Impressions, not facts, count; implications alone can kill.

A smear job in the *Probe* didn't carry the weight of one in the *Times*. People were onto the *Probe's* tactics of insinuation and damning by association. Nevertheless, the piece was strong

enough and contained enough grains of truth to force Lucas
Rayburn to react. Which way would he jump? If their longtime
friendship came into play, it would probably be as a negative
factor, compelling Lucas to bend over backward to deny him the
benefit of the doubt. If indictment was hanging in the balance,
Barnaby's piece could tip the scale.

In his heart, though, Jonathan could not believe it. After all,
he was innocent. He had always played hard, but he played by
the rules. They couldn't change the rules on him in the middle
of the game.

Lucas was a reasonable man. If he were here now, if they
could talk freely, Jonathan could explain this to him. "Lucas,"
he would say, "I did what everybody does. We all have the same
problem. How do you live on a politician's pay when you've got to
deal with people whose income makes your salary look like milk
money? You don't take Donald Trump to lunch at McDonald's,
not if you want to score points for your constituency. Everyone
has to have something on the side; you know that, Lucas."

A face Jonathan knew as well as his own materialized in the
passenger's seat. Lucas said, "There are limits, my friend. There's
a code."

Jonathan pounded the steering wheel. "Precisely! And I have
adhered strictly to that code, the real one, not the written one,
the one that tells you what's okay and what's beyond the pale.
The same code you follow, and every other honest politician."

Lucas leaned back in his seat, his head just grazing the roof
of the car, and laughed that deep, slow, mellifluous laugh that
Jonathan had always loved. "Oh, man," he said, wiping his eyes,
"you always had a mouth on you. Only, since when did you start
buying your own crap?"

Then, before Jonathan could reply, he vanished, and Jonathan
was alone.

He turned back to the paper. The first part of the article was
politically devastating. The second aimed straight at his heart.
It was a paradigm of hypocrisy: the story of the sale of the
Martindale house, attributed to an anonymous source, but told
as only Gracie would tell it.

Jonathan read it and wept.

It was as if his own hand had risen up against him, his own
mouth defiled him.

If it were in his power, he would have cast her from his heart and home; he would have paid her back as she deserved. But hard as he tried, Jonathan could not imagine doing that. Gracie was a part of him. Not even her treachery could sever the bond. Against his will, he suffered her pain as well as his own, for he was certain that Gracie, too, had been betrayed.

"Great story, man." Lou Bone, the *Probe's* custodian, lifted his hand for a high five. Barnaby slapped it.

All through the newsroom he heard, "Nice work, Barnaby," "Good going, man." Roger came out of his office with a cigarette dangling from his lower lip, pumped Barnaby's hand, and pulled him inside.

"The *Time's* metro editor called," Roger said, shutting the door.

"Yeah? Does he want to offer me a job?"

Roger glowered. "They want to interview you for their story on Fleishman."

"What the hell for?"

"You're part of it. It's like I told you: Fleishman's staunchest supporters blows the whistle on him, that's news."

Barnaby threw his head back and boomed a laugh. He was in an excellent mood. "This is nothing. Wait till Kavin rats him out."

"You think he will?"

"Do bears shit in the woods? I've already got the headline: 'Kavin Caves In.' What do you think—too hokey?"

There was a disturbance in the newsroom, shouts, sounds of a struggle. Roger cracked the office door and peeked out. Three men, including the burly custodian, were hanging on to the arms of a furious intruder.

"Let him go!" Roger said. "Come in, Jonathan."

Jonathan Fleishman strode toward them, eyes fixed on Barnaby, with a look that sent the reporter scuttling backward. Roger stood in the doorway, barring the way. "We're not going to do anything foolish, are we?"

"You're scum, Barnaby," Jonathan said. "You're a sleazy, no-good, schoolgirl-seducing bastard."

Roger slammed the door so hard that dust flew from the lintel. "What are you talking about, Fleishman? Nobody here seduced any schoolgirls."

"You hear him denying it? Ask *him* what he did to my daughter."

"Nothing," Barnaby said. "I never touched her."

"That's not what Gracie says."

Barnaby hesitated. "Bullshit," he said, a moment too late.

Roger gave him a hard look, and Jonathan's face darkened. "You screwed my little girl. You used her – you led her into a betrayal that will hurt her for the rest of her life."

Barnaby came around the desk and sat on the edge, crossing his arms. "You're avoiding the real issues. We've got serious stuff on the table; why don't you answer the charges?"

"Why don't you?" Jonathan turned to Roger. "Do you condone his seducing a teenager to get at her father?"

The editor, still staring at Barnaby, lit a cigarette. "He wouldn't do that."

"Fire his ass," Jonathan said. "You want to protect your paper, fire the bastard."

"Your concern for the *Probe* is touching."

"This is bullshit," Barnaby said. "I've got a story to write." He stood and came around the desk. Jonathan stepped back as if to let him pass—and then he swung. There was a distinct crack as his fist connected solidly with Barnaby's nose. The reporter flew backward into a stack of old newspapers. Blood streamed from his nose into his beard.

Jonathan turned and walked out, pushing through the crowd outside Hasselforth's office. No one tried to stop him.

After they stanched the flow of blood from Barnaby's nose, Roger picked up the phone.

"Who are you calling?" said Barnaby.

"The cops."

"Hang up."

"The man assaulted you. I'm a witness."

"So what? I just trashed his life."

"He fucking broke your nose! That's a crime. Not to mention you can sue his ass."

Barnaby shrugged, pressing a wad of paper towels to his nose. "I'm not making a federal case over a pop to the nose. We've got him on bigger stuff."

Roger hung up the phone. "So you did fuck her."

"I didn't seduce her, okay? If anything, she seduced me. And forget that schoolgirl shit. She's of age."

"Barely. What is she, seventeen?"

"Eighteen."

"Fleishman's right: you *are* a prick."

Barnaby scowled. "You got the story, didn't you?"

"How much of it came from her?"

"Only the bit about the house in Martindale. It checked out."

"Did she know what you were working on?"

"Give me a break."

"You fucking lied to me, Barnaby, and you've put me in a hell of a position."

"So what? Am I fired? Let me know, Roger, because if you don't want me, there's a lot of papers that do." He stormed out.

Ronnie Neidelman was waiting just outside. "Oh, poor baby, did the big bad man hurt you?" He tried to pass her. She blocked the passage. "So unfair. Just because you screwed his precious *teenaged* daughter."

"Move!"

"Did you really think you could have your cake and fuck it, too?"

"What if I did?" he shot back, provoked beyond endurance. "It beat fucking your bony ass."

She slapped him hard.

"Not again," he wailed, as blood spurted from his nose. Laughter rolled through the newsroom. Barnaby scanned the room, but the sound seemed to come from whichever way he wasn't looking.

10

AT LAST LILY HAD SOME SOLID WORRIES to anchor her anxiety. Things that yesterday were as clear as glass had abruptly turned opaque; she could not foresee where they would be a year from now, or what would become of her family. And yet the matter that most occupied her mind was the shocking state of her garden.

As if a veil had been lifted from her eyes, she saw that her beds were sadly overgrown, her valiant rosebushes choked by weeds. It was a great mystery. Her life (which she now saw in retrospective, as if it were over) had been so leisurely, so free of constraint; why, then, was her garden in such disarray?

"Off with your head," Lily said, kneeling in the dirt, bareheaded. "Take that, weed. Who asked you here? Who planted you? You don't belong—out, weed!" Each intruder uprooted gave her a pinprick of satisfaction.

Beside her on the grass, the cordless phone shrilled. She answered cautiously, but it was only Jonathan's secretary again.

"I just spoke to him," Maggie O'Rourke said in the brogue forty years of exile had not eradicated. "I don't know where he is, he wouldn't tell me. All I know is he's on his way to you. And he told me to have the service pick up calls to the house. You can ring them anytime for messages. Have you been getting calls?"

"Lots. Mostly reporters. And a few good friends calling to cancel engagements."

The older woman clucked her tongue. "Here I got wall-to-wall reporters. They keep badgering me. I don't know what to tell them."

"Tell them nothing."

"I'd like to tell them what I think of them, harassing a fine, honest man like Mr. Fleishman. It's enough to make a body sick. Oh, Mrs. Fleishman," she cried, "he should be here. Tell him he should be here."

Poor old thing, Lily thought, he's got you good. They say no man's a hero to his secretary, but Jonathan's always adored him. Maggie's motherly brand of hero worship was harmless; the last girl had been a different matter. But it would not do, Lily told herself, to think about that now.

She told Maggie that Jonathan surely knew what he was doing, and promised he would call when he got in. She said, "It will be all right, you'll see," an assurance Maggie seemed to accept, though Lily herself didn't believe a word of it. To her, the matter looked quite hopeless.

It wasn't so much what had happened as how it had happened, falling upon them suddenly, with an air of inevitability. It wasn't Barnaby's story, but the way he had crept into their lives through the back door of Gracie's anger, the way he snaked into the heart of the family, dividing them, setting one against the other. His wily treachery meshed with Lily's secret dreams and premonitions: she saw with certainty and something close to resignation that their lives were undone, like a singular composition burning in a fireplace, a garden uprooted by a cyclone. And the strangest thing of all was her sense that it was happening *again*. Why again, when until now their lives had been graced by such good fortune?

And yet she was not surprised. Something in her knew that joy is stalked inexorably by sorrow, that good is ephemeral, but evil endures. This knowledge was transmitted through both her mother, who never slept, and her father, for whose message death was the medium. Potent messengers indeed, for had they not known this destruction in their own lives, and had it not come upon them similarly, without warning? Survivors of the Holocaust, they were called, but in reality they were its final victims, dead of seeing too much, too clearly. Innocence may be hazardous, but knowledge is deadly. This principle Lily had applied to her marriage, treading the narrow path between awareness and ignorance.

Now she was paying the price, learning a lesson she ought always to have known. Lily had been a blind woman wandering through a mine field as if it were a garden; now her eyes were open, but she saw no way out.

Sunlight glinted off the glistening bay and the white stucco walls of the house, baking the top of her head. Like her mother's visitations, Lily's agonizing headaches had grown more frequent. Sleepless nights she spent wandering through the dreaming house, touching her possessions, doing crosswords, resting on the chaise, counting shooting stars. Sometimes she dozed, only to waken with a start, as if someone had called her name.

Now, close beside her, a voice began to sing:

"Humpty Dumpty sat on a wall,
Humpty Dumpty had a great fall.
All the king's horses and all the king's men
Couldn't put Humpty together again."

That was all. The voice, the presence, were gone as abruptly as they had come. She had no control, no power of subpoena. But lately she had realized that the songs seemed to comment on what was happening to her. Like Humpty Dumpty, her family had fallen and shattered. Not all the king's horses or all the king's men would put them back together again.

The commentary was not edifying. It was not charitable. It was even faintly mocking. But it was relevant: communication, not just memory.

I walk down the street, dressed in black, wearing a hat that hides my face. It's early, just before dawn. The construction site is deserted. A homeless man sleeps in a cardboard box in front of his building. Silently I climb the stairs to the fifth floor. The green feather is on his door, where the name is meant to be. I knock. For a long time no answer comes, but I keep on banging.

Finally his voice says, "Get the hell out of here."

I don't speak. I knock again.

The bed creaks as he gets up. Bare feet patter across a wooden floor. The door opens. He stands before me, shirtless, in a pair of jeans.

"Jesus," he says.

I step forward. He gives way.

"I've missed you, Gracie," he says. "You don't know how many times I wanted to call."

The studio's a mess. He clears a space on the sofa for me, sits opposite. Empty bottles, overflowing ashtrays, an open carton of congealed Chinese food on the computer.

"Forgive me," he says. "I find I'm in love with you."

I open my purse and take out the gun. His pupils dilate.
"Gracie?" he says.
I aim it at his heart and release the safety catch.
"Grace, please." He holds out his hands. "Don't!"
I pull the trigger.
I watch him die.

Gracie laid down her pen and reread the passage, sighing with pleasure. Then she frowned. It was only fiction. Fiction was easy. Writers put words in people's mouths, manipulated events, started and ended things wherever they chose. In real life, the story would continue. The cops would come and arrest her. She'd be taken out of the house in handcuffs, photographers and film crews jostling for shots. She wouldn't care. She would hold her head up high. But her family would suffer. She, who had already done so much harm, had no right to inflict more.

In any case, fictional revenge was no response to actual injury. Gracie knew Barnaby for the worst kind of evildoer, the kind that masquerades as good, and that knowledge carried with it the responsibility to act. There was a hollow, aching core where her self-esteem used to reside, and only vengeance would fill that vacuum.

She imagined Barnaby laughing after she left his apartment, mocking her later to his friends. Humiliating as the images were, they served as a barrier to others, more painful still. When her thoughts touched on her father, Gracie's face would scrunch up, her knees would roll up to her stomach and her chin down to her chest, as if she would disappear into herself.

It was not his anger she feared, but rather the unbearable burden of guilt: the knowledge that she, unnatural child that she was, had destroyed her own father. For years she'd told herself she hated him. Only now that she'd forfeited his regard forever did Grace realize she'd never stopped loving him. The wrong her father did, he did not do to her; the betrayal was hers, not his.

The crunch of gravel announced the approach of a car. Moments later she heard her father's voice, calling out for Lily, who did not reply. A moment later Grace heard him in the study, shouting into the phone.

She crept into the hallway and stood outside the room, listening.

"I don't care how many times," her father said. "How the hell did he get onto you, anyway?...It *is* simple. You don't take his calls and you don't return them. He's just a goddamn reporter... Really. Tell me one thing, Solly. What are you worth today and what were you worth six years ago?... Hell, no, and neither would Michael...Why don't you take a little vacation, get out of town for a while?... So what? It's hotter here... Okay, buddy. Talk to you later."

He hung up. Gracie heard a deep sigh, then silence. Before her courage could fail, she opened the door and stepped inside. Jonathan, seated at his desk, lifted his head from his hands. His gaze touched on her, then glanced off. She understood that he could not bear the sight of her.

"I'm sorry," she said. "I know it's too late, but I'm sorry."

"Go away, Gracie. I'm busy."

She'd expected anger, not the cold disgust she heard in his voice. "I know how you must feel," she said.

"You don't. I hope you never do. You hurt me, daughter, more than I thought I could be hurt."

"I never meant to. I never meant any of it. I thought he really...I was stupid. It's all my fault."

She was crying. Gracie never cried. Jonathan looked at her for a moment, then lowered his gaze to the papers on his desk. "Don't flatter yourself. Barnaby was out to get me. You were just a bonus."

"He betrayed my trust."

"As you betrayed mine," he said, "but I had more call on your loyalty."

"I didn't know."

"How can you say that? I warned you myself."

"I don't expect you to forgive me. I don't forgive myself." She stood, head bowed like a convict awaiting sentencing. Sunlight spilled through the tall paned windows onto the bleached- wood floor and ash furniture, illuminating everything in its path except Grace. She had stopped crying. Her face was haggard and pale. Jonathan was torn between two impulses: to comfort her and to beat her.

" You're a fool, you know that? Not because Barnaby conned you. I could write that off to inexperience. But what you said, the way you made me look like a complete hypocrite."

Now it was she who looked away. Her silence contained echoes of old arguments, and they enraged him. Jonathan struck his chest. "I *know* who I am. Who are you to judge me? Where were you when I marched in Birmingham? Where were you when I was beaten in Selma, jailed in Montgomery? Where were you when Martin Luther King Jr. called me brother? You didn't exist; you weren't even a thought."

"You've changed," she said, as if that were obvious.

"I've changed, yes. I'll tell you how: I now have the power to do more good than ever before. And that power is well-placed and it was hard-won, and you have no right to judge me—you least of anyone. No one has ever called me a hypocrite."

"Who would dare?"

He stared. "Have you come to ask forgiveness or to twist the knife?"

"I don't know. I don't know what I'm doing or saying. I only know I'm sorry I hurt you."

Jonathan stood abruptly and walked to the window, hugging his arms to his chest. Outside, at the bottom of the drive, a black-and-white patrol car wove among the reporters' vehicles, like a sheepdog herding its flock.

"Go away," he said, weary to the bone. "I have nothing more to say to you. Where is your mother?"

"In the garden."

"Naturally," Jonathan said in a much-put-upon voice. "Perfect day for gardening."

Clara had been baking earlier, and the kitchen was warm and fragrant with challah. She caught Jonathan on his way out to the garden, emerging from her room with the *Probe*.

"Didn't I tell you?" she demanded, wagging a stubby, ink-stained finger under his nose.

Jonathan let out a groan. "Yes, you told me. Whatever it is, you told me."

"Be a lawyer, I said. Be a businessman. But stay out of politics. Politics and Jews don't mix, I said."

"You also said that in America a man can be anything he wants to be."

"Can be, not should be," she replied tartly. "Who needs it?"

"Not now, Mama."

"But no, you wouldn't listen. Too much like your father; you had to save the world. So what happens? You stick your neck out, the goyim cut it off. All my life I've seen it happen."

He indicated the paper. "That particular goy's a Jew."

"No! With a name like Barnaby?"

"Howard Goldfarb, originally," said Jonathan, who'd gone to some trouble to find out. " He changed it."

" So Gracie was going with a Jew after all." Suddenly her face crumbled. She covered her eyes with her hands and rocked on her heels.

Jonathan touched her arm. "Mama?"

Pushing his hand away angrily, she glimpsed her own blackened fingers. Her eyes, enlarged by thick glasses, turned liquid. "Such filth he writes, it sticks to the fingers. Jonathan, you got to make him take it back."

"What's said can't be unsaid. The harm is done. I have to find Lily now, Mama."

Clara grasped his arm with a grip that could crush a scrub brush. "So maybe I'm a stupid old woman, but I don't understand what you did so wrong. You helped so many people. So you made a good living—suddenly in America it's a crime to make money?"

"No. But you see, Mama, Barnaby thinks you can't do good and do well at the same time, because he hasn't managed it."

She huffed. "Jealous."

"Sure he's jealous. You should see where he works. He lives in a dump, works in an ant farm—he's a loser."

Predictably, her face crinkled with disgust. The uncompromising materialism of Clara's philosophy gave it the advantage of easy calibration: prosperity was the scale. Jonathan had grown up to the sound of her litany: "In America, you work hard, you do well." The corollary, less frequently stated though always implied, was that anyone who didn't do well in America was either lazy or stupid. Now he suffered a moment's unease, a sense that he was not only playing to his mother's value system but also buying into it.

The moment passed. Detaching his mother's fist gently but firmly from his shirt sleeve, he went out the French doors into the garden.

Lily's garden was deafening with color: brilliant yellows and flamboyant reds, hot pinks, lavenders and purples set off by the royal blue of the bay. "Lily!" he called, but there was no reply.

Jonathan checked the garage and found her car in its usual place. For a moment he wondered if she could have gone out to talk to the reporters waiting like vultures outside his gates; but that was the last thing she would do. He walked back into the garden. "Lily, where are you?"

Suddenly he noticed a trowel and a pair of garden shears lying with an air of abandonment beside a cluster of rosebushes. He walked over slowly, a hollow ache in the pit of his stomach.

Lily lay in the grass behind the shrubs. Her eyes were closed, her hands black with dirt. There were streaks of mud on her cheek and twigs in her hair. A bee hovered over her lips. She was as beautiful as Snow White.

Jonathan fell to his knees beside her, calling her name. Her eyelashes trembled, like those of a child pretending to be asleep. But she did not stir.

11

HOW MANY TIMES, HOW MANY thousands of times have I told you not to work outside without a hat? You never listen."

"Sorry," Lily mumbled.

"Leave her alone, Jonathan! What's the matter with you? Go, wet this rag again." As soon as he was gone, Clara leaned toward her daughter-in-law. "Tell me, *tochter.* What is it?"

"I'm fine. Really."

"Sure you're fine. Lying out in the dirt God knows how long, that's fine."

"Jonathan's right. Too much sun."

"Maybe it's change of life?" Clara whispered. "I don't suppose it could be... ?"

Lily laughed. "Oh, God, Mother, no."

Jonathan came back in. Clara put her strong arm under Lily's shoulders. "Here, drink a little, I made some nice tea." She looked at her son, who had tossed the washcloth to her and was now pacing the room, and her voice sharpened. "Did you call the doctor?"

"No!" Lily sat up on the sofa. "No need, it was just too much sun."

Jonathan gave her a brisk nod. She'd scared the life out of him. He'd carried her senseless into the house, shouting for his mother. But moments later, after Lily woke from her faint, he had succumbed to a searing irritation with his wife. What a thing to do, what a stupid stunt to pull, at the very moment that he needed her most! What was she trying to prove, working out in that sun with no hat, fainting and scaring them all to death? He had returned home after the worst day of his life, and this was what greeted him: his daughter a traitor, his son AWOL, his mother hurling I-told-you-so's, and now this. It was too bad, it was really too bad. He deserved better from his family.

"I have to make some calls," Jonathan said. "When you're feeling better, Lily, come see me in the study."

The two women watched him out the door. They looked at each other.

"He's not himself," Clara said.

"Who is he, then?"

Jonathan sat at his captain's desk of gleaming teak and brass, head in hands, revisiting his phone conversation with Solly Lebenthal. There was a time, long ago, when he had assumed that every phone he regularly used was tapped. Years of success, acceptance, and prosperity had eroded his caution; he'd been slow to see that if Lucas had gone so far as to subpoena his bank records, he might well have gone further still. He'd spoken foolishly to Solly. The wretched man had caught him off-guard, with his wild talk about going in together, cutting a deal with the U.S. attorney's office. What deal, for Christ's sake? What did they have to confess to? Was it a crime for a man to support his family?

Barnaby's outrageous portrayal of Jonathan seemed possessed to have reached into his life and skewed it. Even Solly Lebenthal, who of all people should have known better, acted as if the reporter's accusations were true, as if his lies and distortions weren't perfectly obvious. A man can have overlapping spheres of public duty and private interest without being corrupt. It was only natural that most of his clients did business with the city, Jonathan's expertise being the very reason they came to him. How can you have a crime with no victim? If his private interests meshed with his public interests, did that not serve to make him more zealous in pursuit of the public good?

He was choosy about his clients. He didn't work with deadbeats. I he sponsored a company for a set-aside job and that company screwed up the job, they were never going to work for the city again, no matter how many retainers, consultancies, or campaign contributions they offered him. They had to do the job:

that was an essential part of the deal, and Jonathan made sure they knew it.

That these companies had prospered was a tribute to his skill in picking winners, minority companies with the stuff to make it big. All they needed was a leg up; all they lacked was access to the white power grid. Jonathan supplied those needs—for a price, admittedly, but man cannot live by pro bono work alone.

So he told himself, and yet Jonathan was uncomfortably aware in a rarely consulted corner of his mind that others might characterize his activities differently. To forestall misunderstandings, he needed urgently to sit down with the presidents of all six companies Barnaby had named in his piece, to find out what they'd told Barnaby and whom else they'd been talking to.

That morning he'd asked Maggie to arrange the meetings, but his normally indefatigable secretary had failed to reach even one of the six. Jonathan picked up his desk phone and dialed the direct line of Rencorp's president.

His secretary answered.

"Hilary, it's Jonathan Fleishman. Put him on, would you, dear?"

"Sorry, sir, he's not in."

"Where is he?"

"Out of town, sir."

"Where? I need to reach him."

"I'm sorry, sir, I don't have that information."

Sirring him to death. One after another, he dialed the other five companies. Each time he got the runaround. By the time he hung up on the last know-nothing secretary, Jonathan was livid.

There was a knock on the door. "Come in," he barked, expecting his wife. But it was Paul who entered, shutting the door behind him.

"Finally," growled Jonathan. "Where the hell have you been?"

"Driving around." Paul sprawled into a chair, stretching out his. "Did you know there's a bunch of reporters and a sheriff's car outside the gate?"

"Of course I know. I sent for the cops to keep the reporters off the grounds. You didn't speak with them?"

"Hell, no! Someone in this family knows how to keep his mouth shut. This is a fine mess Gracie's gotten us into."

"It's not all her fault. That bastard had his sights on me all along. Gracie was just the icing on the cake for him."

"Look, Dad, the stuff I said this morning...I've thought it through, and I want you to know I've got your back."

"What did you say this morning?"

"Mom didn't tell you?"

"Your mother's not feeling well."

Paul looked relieved. "I was just venting. This thing couldn't have happened at a worse time. I had a date to play tennis with Jessica Dumont, who happens to be the only child of Jason Dumont of Dumont Industries? Two minutes after I read that thing, she called to cancel. She made some excuse, but I knew her father made her do it."

With an effort, Jonathan brought his attention to bear on his son. "So her old man's an ass. If you like the girl and she likes you, you'll find some other place to meet."

"She's not the kind of girl. Besides, it's the father I really wanted to meet. Fucking bastard Barnaby. I blame Gracie, too."

"Who else?" said Jonathan, seeing which way the wind blew.

Paul reddened. "So she *did* talk to you. Don't blame me for being upset. I mean, we're your family, for Chrissake. You're supposed to protect us from this crap."

Jonathan said nothing, only looked, and Paul turned redder still.

"Anyway," he went on, "as I'm driving around, I start realizing I'm not the only one hurt by this thing."

"And this came as a revelation?" Jonathan said. "Trumpet blasts, voices from on high?"

Paul was and had ever been impervious to sarcasm. "That's right. So I turned around and drove back to tell you: for what it's worth, and to the extent I can do anything, I'm here for you, Dad."

"Thank you, Paul, for what it's worth and to that extent."

"I figure we're in it together. I never asked where the money came from, did I? I just took what you gave; so that makes me like an accessory."

"Like a what?"

"Isn't that the right word?"

"Depends on what you mean. An accessory is someone who aids and abets a crime."

"Well, maybe I didn't do that exactly."

"But I did?"

"I didn't say that."

"Didn't you?" Jonathan looked around vaguely. "Someone did."

"Come on, Dad. Even I know a man is innocent until proven guilty."

Jonathan pounded his desk. "Goddammit, I *am* innocent!"

"That's the spirit, Dad."

As Paul left, Lily came in and took his seat.

"Did you hear what your son said to me?" Jonathan demanded, holding the edge of his desk.

"I heard. You intimidate him."

"He scares the hell out of me."

"Have you seen Gracie yet?"

"Briefly," he said coldly.

"I hope you weren't too hard on her."

"I should have thought your first concern would be for me. Gracie is not the injured party."

"She's injured, too. And you're a lot tougher than she is."

"What does that mean? I'm tough, so I don't need my family's support? I deserve better than this."

"Yes, you're right," she said. "It was damned inconsiderate of me to faint in the garden."

"Don't start with me, Lily."

"I'm as furious with Gracie as you are. She had no right to expose our private family business to that stranger; it was foolish and dangerous, but it wasn't malicious. She didn't know what that creature was up to. She cared about him, and he used her."

"Of course she knew. I warned her."

"But she didn't believe you. She was in love with him. Darling, we're so used to treating Gracie like an adult, we forget that emotionally she's still a child. She trusted him because she loved him."

"She's not that stupid."

"What did she tell you?"

"What difference does it make? Of course she claims she didn't know what he was doing. What else would she say?"

Lily's rigid posture relaxed a little. "You know Gracie never lies. She's much too arrogant."

"She knew, she didn't know, what the hell's the difference? She betrayed me. Do you realize how that Martindale story made me look?"

"Made *us* look. I was a party to that decision."

"So you were. And did we ever discuss or even mention the effect of integration on our home's value?"

"Of course not," she said.

He nodded approvingly.

"We didn't need to say it." Lily felt as if someone else were speaking through her mouth, not quite a stranger, but someone she had known a very long time ago. The feeling was alarming and exhilarating, like riding a roller coaster. But Jonathan looked as if she'd stabbed him in the heart.

Lily rarely entered Gracie's room. This was partly because Gracie never invited her, and partly because the room's barrenness felt like a reproach, a declaration that they had nothing to give Gracie that Gracie wanted. In Martindale her bedroom had been charming and feminine, furnished by Lily in white French Provincial. But after her quarrel with Jonathan, the girl discarded the furniture together with all remnants and reminders of childhood, including photographs. All she kept were her books, locked diaries, and a minimum of clothing; and thereafter she maintained this Spartan order by never acquiring a new possession without discarding an old. Lily had never forgotten something that Jonathan's sister Tamar had said, during her only visit. "Gracie lives like a refugee in her own home."

She knocked on the door, waited a moment, and walked in. Gracie looked up angrily, slipping a letter under her pillow.

"Tell me that's not from Barnaby," Lily said.

"No! It's from Tamar."

There was no chair, so Lily lowered herself gracefully to the mattress on the floor. "Your aunt? What does she want?"

"She invited me to visit the kibbutz."

What *chutzpah*, thought Lily, to write directly to Gracie instead of to us. Though she hardly knew her sister-in-law, it seemed to her typically high-handed, just the way Tamar would go about things. Lily suspected Tamar of intending to steal her daughter away, though she had no evidence, only the fear that it might be possible. She knew her own deficiencies as a mother. Lily loved her daughter dearly and understood her even better than Jonathan, who was too close to see Grace clearly. But love isn't everything; it isn't even enough. Lily had always felt that Gracie needed more from her, needed something Lily did not possess and could not even name.

Lily knew she could defeat Tamar in a moment, merely by urging her contrary daughter to accept the invitation. But did she want to? Leaving home might not heal the wound of Gracie's disastrous love affair, but it would take her out of the public sphere. It would separate her from Jonathan, too, which would not be a bad thing.

"I don't think that's a good idea," she said.

"It's a very good idea," Gracie said predictably. "I'd go if I could. But I can't desert Dad now, not when this whole thing's my fault."

"Just part of it. A relatively small part."

"He warned me. I wouldn't listen."

Lily knelt on the mattress, facing Gracie and pressed a hand to her cheek. "Listen to me, Gracie. Barnaby was out to smear your father with your help or without it. He knows that. If he didn't tell you that, it's only because he's angry at you for saying what you did. As he has every right to be."

Gracie removed her mother's hands. "I'm sorry I was stupid enough to tell that story to Barnaby. But I didn't make it up. It really happened."

Lily wasn't going there. "No matter what you think happened, you never should have told it to a reporter. Really, Gracie, where was your head?"

"If you've come to scold me, you're wasting your time. There's nothing you can say I haven't already said to myself. I'm a traitor. Daddy hates me now, and I deserve it."

So dramatic, thought Lily, so proud. So like Jonathan. "He doesn't hate you," she said. "He's angry and hurt; but he could never hate you."

"Leave me alone." Gracie flung herself down and buried her face in the pillows. Lily stroked her long black hair, soft as the fine black down she was born with. Lily closed her eyes. Her thoughts turned to the day her daughter was born.

When her labor had started, two weeks early, Lily settled herself for a long wait. But Gracie was in a hurry. Jonathan drove her to the hospital, weaving through rush-hour traffic. By the time they arrived, the contractions were continuous. As she lay on the examining table, Lily felt the first unmistakable urge to push. "It's coming!" she gasped.

A bleary-eyed young resident dressed in jeans and a plaid shirt glanced between her stirruped legs and shouted for a stretcher. "Don't push," he told her. "Don't push," as if Lily had anything to say about it. The baby was pushing, and it was stronger than both of them.

Time passed, an agonizing blur. Lily found herself in a delivery room, lying flat on her back on a table. Jonathan was behind her, holding her shoulders. The young resident, still in street clothes, joked about express deliveries as he held up his hands to be gloved. Another contraction swept over Lily. She felt the baby pushing, pushing at the door.

The doctor's hand slipped inside her. She felt him pressing it back. "Let it out," she screamed. "Let it out!"

But the doctor stood very still, staring downward, his face a mirror that suddenly turned dark. "Huh," he said.

"Almost there," Jonathan whispered encouragingly, his mouth to her ear. "One arm's already out."

"Idiot!" she snarled, for she knew the baby hadn't crowned yet, and who but a man could think that delivering a baby fist-first was good! Then another contraction bore her away. "Pant, don't push!" the doctor commanded, but he was just a voice: all the urgency in the world was concentrated on the life within her, struggling to emerge. On the next contraction, Lily felt herself tear open and heard a lusty wail coming from both within and without her body.

"It's a girl," the doctor said, and he held up the baby, still connected to the umbilical cord. She was brick red, wriggling and bawling. Her little face was scrunched up with indignation, and her skull was an odd shape, flattened on top. Lily looked up at Jonathan. He was gazing at the baby as if he'd never seen anything so beautiful.

After the cord was cut, the nurses cleaned the baby, swaddled her, and carried her over to Lily. But Lily was mid-contraction, expelling the afterbirth. Jonathan took the baby instead, and smiled down at her face. "Grace," he said. "Amazing Grace."

Then Lily held out her arms, and Jonathan passed the baby to her. "Hello, Gracie," she said, and suddenly the baby stopped crying. Her eyes met Lily's with a look of recognition that said as plainly as words: "It's you!"

And she'd never changed, Lily thought. Gracie went through life as she entered it, fist-first and with that odd, discerning look. Lately, though, judgments had accrued to the look, like bits of barnacle adhering to a rock.

Gracie's breath was slow and deep, as if she had fallen asleep. Lily was not deceived. "Can we talk about Barnaby?"

"No!" was the muffled reply, so immediate and inevitable it made her smile.

"Then don't talk, just listen. I'm speaking not as your mother, but as an older woman. Barnaby deceived you. He's spent his whole career manipulating people, and he has no scruples at all. You didn't have a chance, Gracie."

"I should have known," said the muffled voice. "I just closed my eyes."

Lily sighed. "Don't we all?"

"But I don't want to be like that," Gracie said. *Don't want to be like you,* she meant, and Lily knew it.

In a small artery close to the heart of old Greenwich Village stands a run-down, dingy old tavern called Maxie's. Never renovated, never sold, the bar is run by the same man who opened it in 1942, Max Horowitz, then a twenty-three-year-old greenhorn from Galicia. Within months of arriving in New York he knew what he wanted to do, but it took two years of backbreaking eighteen-hours-a-day labor as a stevedore to accomplish it. Even after he had the money, it took six months to find the premises: a sprawling workshop in an alley near MacDougal. The owner had died and the widow was selling cheap. Max put in plumbing, installed a bar, and purchased a mismatched assortment of tables and chairs off the back of a truck. The tavern was almost ready; all it lacked was a name.

All the best bars of the day bore their proprietors' names: Clancy's, Reilly's, O'Malley's. The Irish names had a ring that "Horowitz's" lacked. Max couldn't imagine the guys he had worked with on the docks calling out to their mates, "Meet you for a beer in Horowitz's." Of course, it wasn't just the name. Who ever heard of a Jewish barkeep? A good *yeshiva bucher* could grow up to be a storekeeper, sure; a scribbler, maybe; but a barman?

Max Horowitz was what he was, a Jew. Couldn't hide it and wouldn't if he could. He named the joint Maxie's.

The walls were a dingy olive and hadn't been painted in ten years. Horowitz had a thing about hiring workers and kept saying he would do it himself, but everyone knew he was past it. The drinks were your basic drinks. He could manage a Scotch and soda, but Horowitz wasn't big on cocktails. Ask Max for a White Russian and he'd send you to Siberia; but his shots were generous and cheap, and though he couldn't be bothered to serve food, the peanuts were the best in town. Reporters from the *Probe* and the *Village Voice* began frequenting the tavern soon after it opened, and never found a reason to stop. Its air of embedded neglect sheltered it from the waves of gentrification that periodically inundated the Village; and if he liked you, Horowitz was a soft touch for credit.

So it was natural and fitting that Barnaby should repair there after finishing his day's work. His reception was gratifying, especially by his Voice colleagues; indeed, Barnaby would have been quite overwhelmed by all the drinks and the accolades had it not been for his consciousness that they were well-deserved and overdue. Fleishman's psychotic interlude had blighted what should have been the best day of his career. But no outsiders knew about that, and chances were they never would—because no matter how obnoxious they were to your face, *Probe* staffers didn't wash the paper's dirty laundry in public.

At least, he found himself rather fervently hoping they didn't. Somehow the business with Gracie had grown from a niggling discomfort into a full-blown hassle. Barnaby couldn't understand his colleagues' attitude. It hurt him that they credited Fleishman's accusation. Why should they? Fleishman had every reason to accuse him falsely, and this seduction story was a perfect red herring. The fact that it was true didn't excuse their believing it—for after all, Barnaby was not the kind of man to do what he had done, and his colleagues above all should have known that.

And even if Gracie confirmed it, what did it matter in the greater scheme of things? There's no law against sleeping with an eighteen-year- old woman, no matter how old you are. And there sure as hell wasn't anything original about sleeping with a source, which sometimes seemed more the industry rule than the exception.

Half an hour after Barnaby arrived at Maxie's, Brian Rossiter walked in and was greeted with much genuflection and uncovering of heads by the assembly. Never before had anyone from the *Times*, let alone one of its most powerful editors, been seen at Maxie's, which was strictly a low-rent press tradition.

A portly Irishman of about sixty, Rossiter had recently suffered a heart attack and was rumored to be headed for early retirement. A fierce game of musical chairs was raging at the *Times*; the situation was fluid. Rossiter walked into the saloon, looked about purposefully, and headed straight for Barnaby, who stood in the center of a group at the bar.

A path parted before him like the Red Sea for Moses. "Fine story, Barnaby," Rossiter said, shaking hands. "You sure as hell left us in the dust. Was that stuff true, or did you make it up?"

"Pure fiction, of course. What else is left when the *Times* monopolizes all the news that's fit to print?"

Rossiter smiled without even trying to look like he meant it. "Got a minute?"

"Sure," said Barnaby, who was wishing he'd gone a bit lighter on the free drinks. They took a corner table, and Max himself came over to take their orders—beer for Barnaby, bourbon for Rossiter.

"We'll be playing catch-up for a while on this one, damn you," Rossiter said.

"Glad to hear it," Barnaby said.

"Of course, once the Kavin story broke, we started looking hard at Fleishman."

"Not hard enough, considering you've got ten times my resources."

"Not hard enough," the editor conceded, "assuming your story checks out."

"It checks out."

"Sorry to hear it. I liked Fleishman. Respected him."

"Me, too," Barnaby said. "I'd have said he broke my heart, if I had one."

"Just a shame so few people will read the piece. What's your circulation at the *Probe,* around a hundred, hundred twenty thou?"

"Thereabouts."

"Makes me wonder what a guy like you could do with some juice behind him."

Barnaby's heart fluttered like a girl whose boyfriend has just taken a knee. "Funny you should say that, because just this morning I was saying to myself, 'Barnaby, a man with your talents is wasted on the *Probe.*' My very words."

The editor smiled. Barnaby smiled back. Over Rossiter's shoulder he saw the street door open. Ronnie Neidelman walked in.

Barnaby shifted his chair to put his back to her, forgetting that Ronnie knew his back better than his front, having seen rather more of it. She headed straight for his table

"Hey, sweetie," she said, bussing his cheek. "Thought I'd find you here. How's the nose?"

He could smell booze on her breath. "Not now, Ronnie."

"Aren't you going to introduce me, lover?"

"She calls everyone that," Barnaby said to Rossiter *sotto voce.* "Brian Rossiter, Ronnie Neidelman. Ronnie's one of our best and brightest, when she's sober."

Uninvited, Ronnie pulled up a chair from a neighboring table and squeezed between the two men. "I thought I recognized you," she said to Rossiter. What's the Times' Metro editor doing slumming in Maxie's?"

"Hardly slumming," Rossiter replied; then, to Barnaby, "Maybe we should continue this another time."

"Ronnie was just leaving."

"Am I embarrassing you, Barnaby?" she cooed.

"No, you're embarrassing yourself. Go home and sober up."

Ronnie turned to face Rossiter. "Continue what? What are you boys up to?"

"I was just congratulating Barnaby on his Fleishman piece."

"Speaking of Fleishman's piece—"

Barnaby cut in hastily. "That's enough!"

She ignored him. "You weren't by any chance offering him a job, were you, Mr. Rossiter? Because if you were, there's something you should know."

Barnaby got to his feet and yanked Ronnie up with him. The clear-eyed malice of her smile told him that she wasn't nearly as drunk as she pretended; instead she was laughing in his face, taunting him, daring him. He'd never hit a woman in his life, but now it was all he could do to refrain. He put his mouth to her ear. "Leave now, or I swear to God I'll have you fired in the morning."

"Relax, Barnaby," she said loudly. "I'm on your side. I was just going to tell Mr. Rossiter that whatever he hears, it wasn't your fault. That sort of problem usually starts very young. I wouldn't be surprised if you yourself were abused as a child."

"Excuse me?" Rossiter said.

Ronnie gave him an earnest look. "I can assure you that normally, Barnaby would never let his little problem interfere with his work. Besides, for all we know, the Fleishman kid seduced *him*."

Rossiter's eyes widened. He put down his drink and stood up. "Got to run. So nice to have met you. Kudos again, Barnaby."

They watched him leave, Barnaby and Ronnie and the rest of the bar. Then Barnaby took a step toward Ronnie, and she took two steps back.

"Calm down," she said, not a bit drunk now. "This is a public place."

"Isn't that why you picked it?" He gestured abruptly at the table. "Sit."

Warily she took a seat. Barnaby joined her. He looked down at his hands. Kind hands, Gracie had called them, silly little bitch. He'd like to wrap those kind hands around Ronnie's scrawny neck, but he kept his hands and voice down. "What the fuck did you do that for?"

"Same reason people climb Mt. Everest," Ronnie said. "Because it's there."

"What's there?"

"Your monumental ego. Your arrogant male superiority complex."

"My balls!" he hooted, playing to an attentive gallery. "Look who's caught the feminist bug!" And he looked with disdain at the lanky, indignant woman with her brown hair, sallow skin, and long nose, nostrils reddened at the tip. Barnaby had both the impression that he could see past her skin to the web of fine vessels that irrigated her brain, and the discomfiting sensation that she, too, could see through him. Their long affair had just ended, yet already it was a distant memory. He couldn't even remember what had attracted him.

He lowered his voice. "Why are you and Roger so convinced I did that thing?"

"You didn't deny it."

"I do deny it—of course I deny it."

"Too late. Besides," she said, "I know you."

He laughed scornfully, flicking his hands toward his lapels. "You know me? What do you know?"

"I know that if you hadn't screwed his daughter, you would have charged Fleishman with assault."

"Then you know nothing. A guy throws a punch after you bring down his whole life, so what? That's penny-ante bullshit."

"Yes, it is. But you're a penny-ante player."

"You don't know me. Do you realize what you've done? And for what? Jealousy? Did you really think that because I balled you now and then, you had some kind of claim on me?"

"Don't flatter yourself."

"Then why?"

She leaned back and regarded him with half-closed eyes. She took a pack of Camels from her purse and, for the first time since he'd known her, lit a cigarette.

"Since when do you smoke?"

Ronnie shrugged. "You know how it is. You give up one bad habit, you take up another. I don't like what you did to that kid. It turned my stomach, the way you chewed her up and spit her out. It was like watching one of those repulsive drivers'-ed movies in high school. You're my worst nightmare about what this profession can lead to. Which is funny, because I used to really admire you."

"How many times do I have to say it? I never touched the little bitch!"

"And the pathetic thing is, you didn't even need what you got from her. It was just piggishness. So I won't allow you to profit from it."

"*Won't allow?* Who the fuck are you, the morality police?"

"Just another bitch," Ronnie said.

12

MONDAY MORNING, JONATHAN sat in his Eastborough office with his door open as usual, but even though he could hear people all over the building, no one came in or even passed by. His corridor, usually the hub of activity, seemed cut off from the rest.

He was sorry but not surprised. His colleagues took their lead from the bigwigs in City Hall, who had adopted a wait-and-see policy. The mayor, questioned by reporters, said on television: "If the *Probe's* allegations against Fleishman turn out to be true, that would be very serious indeed. Personally, though, I put a lot more stock in Fleishman than I do in that reporter fellow, Barnaby."

Beneath the surface message was a perceptible distancing; suddenly he was just plain Fleishman to the mayor, when two weeks ago it was "my dear friend Jonathan." Even so, qualified support was better than none, especially considering how many times the mayor had been stung. But when Jonathan called to thank him, the mayor wouldn't take his call.

Since none of the six company presidents had returned Jonathan's calls, he concluded that they were talking to Rayburn's people; they had joined in the conspiracy against him. He remembered Michael Kavin as he had seen him last, standing on a hill, peering around him and jabbering about long-range directional mikes. Paranoid, Jonathan had called him to Lily; but now he knew how Michael had felt. Lately it seemed as if all certainties had been repealed, as if he had strayed across an invisible boundary into a world where anything at all could happen and the foundations of his life were no more than two-dimensional *trompes l'oeil*.

The only calls all morning came from reporters, and those were screened out by Maggie. Just as Jonathan was leaving for lunch, the phone on his desk rang at last. The caller was Robert Mazur, a political aide to the governor and Jonathan's liaison to Albany. Close political allies for years, they'd also done some serious sailing together.

"How're you doing, buddy?" Mazur's tone was a shade too hearty.

"Not bad, all things considered. I've still got my health."

"I know you must be busy, so let me get to the point. First of all, I want you to know that no one here gives Barnaby's smear piece any credence. We know you. Your integrity is not an issue for us."

"Thank you, Bobby." Jonathan was moved. Gratitude and loyalty had been thin on the ground. "I won't forget this."

"That said, the perception is bad. There's a feeling it might hurt the party."

"Are you fucking kidding me?"

"Have you given any thought to stepping aside for the duration?"

"The duration of what?"

"The investigation."

"No, Bob, I haven't. Why, do you know something I don't?"

"No, how would I know? All I know is what I read."

Jonathan got up and kicked his door shut. "What are you saying? You're asking me to commit political suicide. I'll be damned if I'll cut my throat for you, the governor, or anyone."

"Don't even think like that, Jonathan. This is just a temporary thing. I'm not saying quit. I'm talking leave of absence, on salary, of course."

"You're talking suicide. Dammit, man, I thought you were my friend."

"I *am* your friend." But he sounded uneasy, and Jonathan was certain other people were listening in. He cut the conversation short, practically hanging up on Mazur. To hell with him. To hell with them all.

His heart was pounding and his palms felt clammy. It wasn't so much the pain of betrayal, to which he had lately grown inured, as it was pure funk—fear, not of the outcome of this ordeal, for of that he would admit no doubt, but of the cost to his family. Jonathan was too much his mother's son to live beyond his means, but the life-style he had chosen to provide for his family, and which he deemed necessary for a man in his position, kept him stretched to the limit. Ever since Barnaby's first articles on Michael Kavin had appeared, several major sources of income had dried up. His private practice was suffering; no one wanted a lawyer with problems of his own. Now Mazur had popped up with the suggestion Jonathan take a hike—"step aside on salary," he'd called it, but he knew and Jonathan knew that was bull. You don't walk away from power and expect it to be there when you get back.

He wasn't hurting for cash yet, but it wasn't so far down the road that he couldn't see it coming. He could eliminate the frills— the cruise to Bimini was out of the question now—but Jonathan's real trouble was with basic living expenses. It was damned expensive to keep up two houses, and Paul's tuition was astronomical; thank God, he thought, Gracie had turned down Harvard. Then he was appalled at the thought. It was all so humiliating.

Maggie buzzed. "Michael Kavin on line two."

"About time." Of all the phone calls he had not received since Black Thursday, Michael's had hurt the most. Jonathan lifted the receiver. "Where the hell have you been, *paisano?*"

"Up shit creek," Michael said comfortably, "lookin' for a paddle, just like you. How're you holding up?"

"I've had better weeks. Mostly I'm pissed as hell. That shit Barnaby..."

"Tell me about it."

"You were right, man. They are like cockroaches. You can't see 'em but you know they're there, the buggers."

"Don't I know. Tell me something: have you heard from Solly?"

Jonathan winced. The caution of his salad days, when Hoover's FBI really was on his tail, had returned in full measure. Perhaps fear is like bicycle riding, something that once learned cannot be forgotten; but if so, Michael should have known better than to mention Solly's name on the phone. "Where are you calling from?" Jonathan said.

"A booth. I make most of my calls from public phones these days. I walk around jingling like Santa Claus from all the change in my pockets."

"Yeah, well, I'm in my office."

"I can't get him at home or in the office. I even called his bookmaker; *he* hasn't heard from him either. Do you know where he is?"

"I don't know what the hell you're talking about."

There was a silence; Michael had caught on at last. "Never mind," he said appeasingly. "Who the fuck cares? Are we still on for Sunday?"

"As far as I'm concerned, we are."

"I read Barnaby's piece. Fucking douche bag."

"You know what? I slugged the son of a bitch." Jonathan didn't care who heard that.

" Barnaby? You're kidding. When, where?"

"In his office. Broke his nose, I hope."

"God bless. How'd it feel?"

"Like a really good appetizer.

Michael laughed. Then his voice turned sober. "How's Lily coping?"

"You know her. She's a trouper." In fact, since Barnaby's story appeared, he and Lily had hardly spoken except to quarrel. But he'd never tell Michael that. He wouldn't put Lily on a par with Martha.

Some of their worst fights were over Michael. That morning at breakfast, Lily had predicted that Michael would break their standing golf date. "And if he doesn't," she'd added, "you should."

He'd glowered at her. She was wearing an old robe of his and no makeup. There were deep shadows underneath her eyes, and her hair was uncombed. He'd never realized how much work went into making Lily look like Lily until she ceased to make the effort. "We're talking about Michael here, my old buddy, remember?"

"Lucas was your buddy too."

"Lucas has lost his marbles."

"Michael is not going to have any choice in the matter."

"There's always a choice."

"You know how they work; they use the small fish to catch the big. Don't you think they'd trade Michael for you?"

"They might. He wouldn't."

"First there were three," she said in a singsong voice, "then there were two, now there is one."

"You're talking nonsense."

"Then how come you understand me?"

"Understand you? I'll lay odds you don't even understand yourself."

She blushed. They were both aware that lately Lily had not been herself. Sometimes she was so distracted that he had to call her name three times before she answered. When she spoke, her words surprised her as much as they did him. It seemed as if this business had jolted something loose inside, jarring to the surface thoughts that would normally have been repressed.

Until the past week, Jonathan, if asked and perhaps even if not, would have pronounced his marriage the most successful of his acquaintance. Granted, since that regrettable incident of two years back, they did not, perhaps, talk quite as much as they used to; and for many years there had been areas of his life about which Lily, by tacit agreement, knew little. But that was only natural in a long marriage; there was nothing wrong with moderate reticence and a decent respect for each other's privacy. One couldn't, after all, live forever in one's spouse's pocket.

But ever since Barnaby's attack on him, Lily had started breaking the rules, as if the story were a natural barrier behind which she could stand and snipe at him. Such un-Lily-like behavior. Just last night, dining alone in Highview, Lily had suddenly and with no discernible change of tone or expression asked, "Was Melanie your only affair, or were there others?"

Jonathan choked. She came over to pound on his back. "What are you talking about?" he sputtered. "We haven't got enough problems, you've got to excavate for more? This is extremely ancient history you're talking."

"Two years is not ancient history. Two years is unfinished business."

"But why now, for Chrissake? We need to conserve our energy, not waste it settling old scores. Why now?" he repeated angrily.

Lily's face was strained. "I don't know. It just seems necessary."

"No. Uh-uh. When it *was* necessary, you wouldn't talk about it. Now, in this context, it's like picking up a baseball bat and swinging at my head."

Back then he could have explained it simply, made her see how insignificant the affair was: a one-night stand that Lily through the sheerest bad luck had discovered. He hadn't planned it when he took his secretary with him to Washington for a three-day conference. They had dinner together, a few drinks; she flirted with him, he flirted back. Melanie was an attractive woman, thirty, divorced... she knew he was happily married. Jonathan never asked her to come to his room that night, dressed in nothing but high heels and a trench coat; but she did, and what was he supposed to do about it, throw her out? It would have been like throwing out good food, a cardinal sin in any household of Clara's. Nothing at all would have come of it if he hadn't made the lethal mistake of letting her stay the night. When the phone rang at seven in the morning, they were sound asleep. Melanie picked it up and said sleepily, "Hello?"

There was a long silence, during which Melanie realized what she'd done and elbowed Jonathan awake. He saw the phone in her hand and grabbed it. "Hello?"

He heard his wife breathing. Lily hung up without a word.

When Jonathan returned home to Highview the next day, he found her in the den, alone, sitting in the old oak rocker with an open book on her lap. He entered carrying a dozen long-stemmed yellow roses. Lily lifted her head and gazed just past his left ear. Said nothing, didn't smile, only looked blankly in his general direction. The clock on the mantel ticked loudly.

"How are the kids?" Jonathan asked.

"Fine."

"Good." He held out the flowers. "These are for you."

She shifted her gaze to his face but said nothing.

"Where should I put them?"

"In the trash," she said, and went back to her book. Jonathan stood awhile longer, feeling like a fool. Then he went upstairs.

That was all. She never brought it up, and cut him off when he tried to. Even when he told her, several days later, that Melanie had left his employ, she said nothing.

From then on, Lily talked as if nothing had happened but acted as if everything had. Jonathan could not bridge the gap. Several times he alluded to his trip to Washington, but these oblique references deflected off the glass of her Mona Lisa smile.

Her anger spoke through silence. The long, voiceless dialogues that were once the mainstay of their intimacy were now saturated with suspicion and anxiety. When they sat silently together, he watched her thoughts butterfly across her face and tremble at her lips. To restrain them, she pressed her lips together with such force that sharp little lines appeared in the corners of her mouth. This unwonted severity gave her face a whole new look, not one he particularly admired.

Given half a chance, he would have made her see that a loveless affair was no betrayal. Men of a certain age have affairs: it's a fact of life, required, almost, as a rite of passage, a tunnel through which one must pass in order to come out the other side.

It was not, after all, as if he made a habit of it. Compared to Michael Kavin, who cheated on Martha every chance he got, Jonathan was a monk; though in fairness, it had to be allowed that he had come out far ahead of Michael in the marriage sweepstakes. Martha Kavin was an untamed shrew who'd grown worse with age.

If Jonathan were allowed a harem of five hundred women, Martha wouldn't have made the waiting list; whereas Lily was more beautiful and desirable now than on the day he married her.

Lily gave him no credit for temptations resisted. It wasn't, after all, lack of opportunity that had kept him faithful. It was love. If a man was resolutely faithful, despite many temptations and opportunities, was it fair that he be condemned for a single indiscretion? Condemned, moreover, without a hearing?

And, having condemned him years ago, was she now entitled to throw the thing in his face?

These past few weeks had been hard on Lily too; he realized that. The tension of not knowing how the cards would fall, the feeling of having lost control, surely afflicted her as well as him. She did not say so, but he saw it for himself in the way she wandered through the walled garden of the Highview estate like a prisoner taking exercise. Several times he'd come upon her standing with unnatural stillness, as if listening to something he could not hear.

Her intention, he knew, was to be a loyal, warm, supportive wife in their time of trouble. She had come to Highview expressly to appear at his side, and in public she was pure grace under pressure. The problem lay in the private realm. When they were alone together, another side of Lily emerged, one not even remotely familiar to Jonathan.

Jonathan was not blind to her suffering, but he perceived it through a cloud of resentment. His pity for her did not dispel his hurt and surprise at the fact that at the time when he needed her most, his wife had turned against him.

They lay side by side in the master bedroom of the Highview house, a room larger than the apartment in which Jonathan had grown up. Lily wore makeup and a pink silk negligee. She'd had her hair done.

He hadn't expected to see her that evening. Clara kept calling from East Hampton, where she had stayed with the children. Gracie wouldn't talk, wouldn't eat, wouldn't even come out of her room. Clara made some delicious chicken soup and Gracie wouldn't touch it. "I'm an old woman," she said. "I can't take the aggravation. She's your daughter; you come home and deal with her."

Since Jonathan couldn't leave, they'd decided that Lily would return to East Hampton alone. Never mind that Lily was the last person in whom Gracie would confide; better to blame their separation on Gracie's problems than to admit that these days, it was easier for them to be apart than to be together.

But when he drove up the circular drive to the house that evening, Lily opened the door to him. Gracie could wait another day, she said. That evening she was her old self, and as they lay in bed waiting for the eleven-o'clock news, Jonathan felt a stirring of desire. He ignored it. Potency had never been a problem; lately, however, so many things that had never been problems turned out to be problems, that he dared not open up another front.

The top story on the news was a cop killed while making a drug bust. Then a blown-up photo of Jonathan flashed onto the screen behind the announcer. "U.S. Attorney Lucas Rayburn isn't talking, but NBC has learned from prosecution sources that the grand jury investigating charges of corruption in Eastborough has handed down a sealed indictment against Jonathan Fleishman, the borough's powerful Democratic leader. Mr. Rayburn refused to comment on this report; however, well-informed political sources note that the U.S. attorney, a longtime friend of Jonathan Fleishman's, has recused himself from involvement in the case.

"In a related development, the city's Department of Investigation today confirmed that they are investigating Mr. Fleishman in connection with recent published reports of widespread corruption in Eastborough's set-aside program. NBC's attempts to reach Mr. Fleishman were unsuccessful. He did not return repeated phone calls."

The station switched to a commercial. A man sat at a desk piled high with bills, his head in his hands. His wife stood behind him, massaging his shoulders. "I think," she murmured tenderly, "it's time to call a lawyer."

Lily switched off the television with the remote control. They sat without speaking, staring at the blank screen.

Lily said, "Jonathan, we have to talk."

"Not now."

"Please, darling. Look at me."

The face he turned toward her was taut with anger. "What?"

"Everyone in the world will have seen that."

"That's what concerns you? That your friends will see, and you'll be embarrassed?"

"Jonathan, please. We're on the same side."

"Are we?" A spasm passed over his face and he pressed his hands to his temples. "I'm sorry, Lily. It's just that sometimes I wonder."

"We have to do something."

"Do what? What can I do? They're assassinating me. They're killing me slowly."

"Fight back. Hire a lawyer. Sue the *Probe*. Do *something*. We can't just lie here waiting for the steamroller to crush us."

He shook his head. "It's all talk. Nothing's happened. Nothing will."

"Wake up and smell the coffee, darling. It's happening now."

There was a long silence. Jonathan rubbed his eyes. "What do you want me to do?"

"Hire the best goddamn lawyer you know. We should have done it sooner, the minute Lucas subpoenaed our accounts."

The "we" was generous. He knew she was right. Somehow, though, hiring a lawyer meant accepting the reality of this nightmare, admitting the possibility that he could actually be indicted, finally giving up the hope, which Jonathan still harbored, that one morning he would wake to find the whole mess evaporated, everything back to the way it used to be.

"It's terrible not knowing what's going on. Just waiting to find out, like everybody else."

His wife's voice was so sad, so terribly resigned, it frightened him out of his self-absorption. He reached out to her. Lily came into his arms, buried her head in his shoulder.

"It will be all right," he said, stroking her hair.

"No, Jonathan."

"We just have to stick together, that's all. I promise you, sweetheart, it will be all right."

He held her tight. Lily didn't say anything. Her mother's song was running through her head: "All the king's horses and all the king's men/ Couldn't put Humpty together again."

13

"COME IN," JONATHAN SAID. "This is my wife, Lily. Lily, Christopher Leeds."

"A pleasure, Mrs. Fleishman."

"May we offer you some supper, Mr. Leeds?"

"No, thank you. I've just come from a dinner."

"Very good of you to come to us, and on such short notice," said Jonathan, who was in fact wondering what this house call would cost him. What did a lawyer like Christopher Leeds charge? Even with professional courtesy, he was bound to be expensive.

"I'm honored that you thought of me," Leeds said.

Lily led the way into the living room. "Lovely," said the visitor, looking about with appreciation. Leeds was a man of indeterminate middle age, with a round, smooth face, thick steel-rimmed glasses that magnified his eyes, and a circle of tonsured hair surrounding a bald pate. He looked more like a doctor than a lawyer, and more like a priest than a doctor. Indeed one could easily imagine him in brown robes, a cloistered monk with a boyish enthusiasm for Aquinas or St. Anselm.

Jonathan had numerous lawyer friends, including several renowned litigators, but when he finally brought himself to hire an attorney, he went to none of them. Years ago he had seen Christopher Leeds in action, and since then, with the respect of a journeyman craftsman for an artist, he'd taken every opportunity to watch him. He'd always known that if he ever found himself in serious difficulties, this was the man he'd go to.

Prosecutors feared him, judges walked gingerly in his presence. Leeds was known to have turned down dozens of proffered judgeships for the sheer joy of exercising his art. His forte was cross-examination. Unlike many of his colleagues, who ranted at and bullied opposing witnesses, Christopher Leeds never got angry. Instead, he got sad. The more the witness lied, the more sorrowful he became. To the jury he appeared a kindly old Gepetto, watching dolefully as the nose on Pinocchio's face grew longer with each lie. They felt for him and, by extension, for his client. The oddity was that when you read the transcripts, you saw that Leeds's questions acted quite separately from his gentle demeanor: innocent in isolation until, like Hitchcock's birds, they flocked together to fly at witnesses and peck their testimony to shreds.

The men sat on facing sofas in front of the fireplace. Lily placed herself in an oversize armchair in a corner of the room, out of their line of vision.

Seeing Leeds in his living room, Jonathan was suddenly acutely embarrassed. He felt as if he had exaggerated his peril, called in a top neurosurgeon to treat a minor headache. Lily's presence was paralyzing. He'd asked her to stay out of this meeting, but she'd refused; the echoes of that quarrel were still in the room.

Jonathan spread his hands. "I've admired your work for years, but I never thought the day would come... I'm not sure even now... "

Leeds's understanding smile sent shafts of comfort through Jonathan's soul. "It takes time to shift gears," he said. "This kind of thing is like an unexpected bereavement or a sudden accident. It takes a while till you even realize you've been hurt."

"Oh, I know I've been hurt, all right. There's a gaping hole in my belly, and money is pouring out."

Christopher Leeds laughed. He had a surprising laugh, giggly and a bit high, like a kid who knows he's going to get punished for laughing in class but can't help it.

"I know I'm being investigated," Jonathan said. "But as far as I know I haven't been indicted."

Leeds's tonsured head nodded gravely. "You will be."

"How do you know?"

"I know a few people. After you called, I took the liberty of contacting them."

Dusk had fallen and the room had grown dim, but neither Jonathan nor Lily moved to switch on the lights. Jonathan cleared his throat. "What will I be charged with?"

"Conspiracy. Extortion. Bribery. Racketeering. Influence peddling." Leeds's face grew longer with each word. Jonathan had a fleeting vision of a Seder he had attended as a small boy. At the head of the table sat an old man who dipped his finger into a goblet of wine and shook one red drop after another onto his plate. "Blood," he'd intoned. "Boils. Locusts. Darkness. Death of the firstborn."

Jonathan walked to the bar and stood for some time with his back to the others. He poured some Chivas into a glass and raised the bottle inquiringly to Leeds and Lily. Both of them shook their heads. He carried his drink back to the sofa. "I'm innocent of those charges. That's where it starts and that's where it has to end. I have done nothing to be ashamed of."

Christopher Leeds nodded politely.

"I've gone against the tide all my life," Jonathan said. "There are people who hate my guts politically. But no one has ever questioned my integrity."

Leeds bridged his hands and rested his chin on top. "Of course, I don't know what the U.S. attorney's office thinks it has in the way of evidence," he said. "But these kinds of charges generally fall into a kind of twilight zone. This is what I meant by the need for adjustment. You spoke of integrity. Integrity is a moral value that is outside the purview of the court. For the coming months, you, I, and the prosecution will be concerned solely with appearances and evidence."

"Both can be deceptive."

"They can be deadly. Everything depends on the construction placed upon them."

"If Jonathan really is the grand jury's target," Lily cut in, "why hasn't he been called to testify?"

Both men looked at her in surprise. Lily touched a plate on the wall and the recessed lights came on. She came forward and took a seat beside her husband.

"It's not a good sign that he hasn't," the lawyer said. "It may mean they're saving him for last because they want as much ammunition in hand as possible before questioning him. But it doesn't matter."

"Why not?" she asked.

Leeds opened his soft, plump hands, unadorned but for a plain gold wedding band. "Because he won't testify."

"Why shouldn't I?" Jonathan demanded. "You're talking as

if indictment is a *fait accompli*. Testifying before the grand jury might be my last hope of preventing it."

"Unfortunately, it doesn't work that way. Grand juries almost always return whatever indictments the prosecutors ask for. Even if we got use immunity, and I doubt they would agree to that, your testimony would only serve to give away valuable information about our defense to the prosecution. At this point, the less said to anyone, the better."

Lily gave him a measuring look. "Mr. Leeds, did your friends tell you anything about Michael Kavin?"

"We didn't discuss Michael."

"Can you find out if he's cooperating with the U.S. attorney?"

"That would be difficult."

"I think you'd better try. My husband has a date to play golf with him this Sunday."

"My wife," rasped Jonathan, "has contracted an acute case of paranoia."

Leeds's eyes, magnified by his glasses, were deep, lucid pools. "In this sort of situation, Jonathan, there's no such thing as paranoia. The fact that Mr. Kavin has not yet been indicted is cause enough for speculation."

"Put it out of your head. There's no way Michael would ever turn on me." But even as he spoke, Jonathan remembered Michael's uncharacteristic obtuseness on the phone, mentioning Solly's name, then harping on his disappearance.

"A wild animal in a trap will gnaw off its own leg to free itself. Mr. Kavin is trapped. One cannot be sure what a person will do under such pressure. But this is mere speculation. I shall try to find out."

Lily said, "We also have to deal with the press. It's impossible to stay silent any longer about the Probe's accusations."

"When the time is right—"

She interrupted him. "The time *is* right. Every day that goes by without a refutation makes us look worse."

Christopher Leeds and Jonathan exchanged a look, which was not lost on Lily. "I'm afraid the publicity will get even worse before it gets better," Leeds said gently. "But eventually it will get better, if we lead with our brains and not our hearts."

"Don't patronize me, Mr. Leeds."

"I wouldn't dream of it, Mrs. Fleishman."

"Despite what my husband just told you, it's obvious to me that you're building your defense on the premise that he's guilty."

"No, ma'am. But I do believe that in this imperfect world, the innocent are in no less need of protection than the guilty."

"Assuming," Lily heard her new, irrepressible voice say, "the innocent can afford it."

Ten more minutes, Barnaby told himself, and I'm out of here. What a goddamn waste of time, shlepping all the way up to Eastborough on the strength of a single cryptic phone call. And then the bastard doesn't even show.

Unless Tortelli was already there, sizing him up. Barnaby looked around the bar. Some effort had been made to tart it up Polynesian style; the drinks came with little pink-and-purple parasols stuck in them and the waitresses, all well past their sell-by date, wore grass skirts. He saw a few solitary men sitting at the bar, but none that matched his image of the owner of the gravelly voice that called itself Tortelli.

Chances were the guy was phony. When you shook a tree as big as Fleishman, all sorts of nuts fell out. But the art of investigative journalism begins with triage, and Barnaby had always prided himself on his ability to weed out real informants from grudge-holders and attention-seekers. Tortelli had sounded on the level.

He had phoned Barnaby at the *Probe*. Gave his name, said he was a printer in Eastborough. "I read your story about Rencorp and Fleishman. It was good as far as it went. But you only got half the story."

"Yeah?" Barnaby said. "So what's the other half?"

"That ain't for the phone," Tortelli said. "You want to know, come talk to me."

"Hey, buddy, you want me to schlep all the way up to Eastborough, you got to give me something more to go on."

"You don't know the whole story behind how Rencorp got their sweetheart lease. I do. That's all I'm gonna say."

Rationally Barnaby should have let it go. What could a printer in Eastborough know about Rencorp or Fleishman? His time would be better spent following up more solid leads, like tracking down the elusive Solly Lebenthal. But there was something in Tortelli's voice...

"Where and when?" Barnaby asked.

It took sixty minutes by subway. He'd have taken a cab, but if nothing came of this, Hasselforth wouldn't reimburse him, the cheap bastard. Another ten minutes to find the bar. And then he sat for thirty more, cooling his heels.

At eight-thirty he signaled the waitress, paid his tab and headed for the door. Just as he got there, it opened, and a burly man with blue fingers entered. "You Barnaby?" the man asked.

"Me Barnaby. You Tortelli?"

The man grinned, and a gold tooth gleamed. Tortelli was older than Barnaby had expected, somewhere in his sixties, tall, dark-complexioned, and still handsome, though gone a bit jowly. You could see he'd been a lady-killer in his day and probably still kept the secretaries hopping. He wore a tweed sports jacket and a white shirt, but no tie. "Sorry I'm late. Got held up in the office. Lemme buy you a drink."

"What's the story, Mr. Tortelli?" Barnaby said when they were seated in a corner booth.

"The story is, I'm the guy got kicked out to make room for Rencorp," Tortelli said.

Suddenly Barnaby recalled Arthur Speigel saying that Rencorp had taken over the premises of a printer. "Didn't I hear you went bankrupt or something?"

Tortelli glowered. "No way. I was a couple months behind on rent, but that's not why they evicted me."

Barnaby had a feeling a tape recorder would spook the printer. He took out his notebook instead. "I'm listening."

"It was the first time in eight years we'd missed a payment and it was no big deal. I worked the whole thing out with GSA. They agreed to let me pay off the debt in installments, no problem—in fact, they was decent about it. I made the first two payments on time, and then outta the blue I get an eviction notice."

"Why?"

"Because Fleishman wanted that building for his buddies at Rencorp, and what Fleishman wants, Fleishman gets."

"Is that your opinion or can you prove it?"

"I can't prove it, but it figures."

Barnaby laid down his pen with a sigh. Man with a grudge. Garbage run. "Why?"

"Because they warned me something bad would happen. 'Fleishman giveth and Fleishman taketh away,' they said."

"Who said?"

Tortelli didn't answer, and Barnaby didn't push him. A

waitress hobbled over and set two beers on the table. Under her grass skirt she wore support hose and orthopedic shoes. After she clomped away, Barnaby asked Tortelli why he'd been late paying his rent.

"I lost my biggest account."

"Who was the customer?"

Tortelli pulled at his beer and didn't answer.

Barnaby glanced at his watch. "Look, man, you called me."

"Maybe I'm having second thoughts."

"Not after dragging me way the hell up here, you don't. Why'd you call me, Tortelli?"

Tortelli took out a cigar and lit it. He studied his hands, gnarled and blue-ridged like a map of his life. "I was mad," he said. "Mad don't come close. When I read your story about Rencorp paying that pissant rent and getting all them minority tax breaks, I was like, I don't care what happens to me as long as I get those bastards. Lemme tell you something. I was paying more than twice the rent Rencorp pays, and every guy in my shop I hired local. They was all blacks or Puerto Ricans, except one Jewish guy does the books, but it's not a 'minority business' cause I ain't a minority. Never mind that; I never asked for nothing. But these bastards went after my business, and it's not just me they screwed. What about the guys I had to lay off and their families— who's looking after them?"

"Sounds like a sad story, Mr. Tortelli, but I don't see how it ties in with Fleishman."

" I'm gonna tell you how it ties in. I've had plenty of time to think about it, and what I figure, it all comes down to good old American greed. You asked who the customer was who dumped me? It was the Eastborough Democratic party."

Barnaby suddenly felt very smooth, as if he were skating alone in the center of a frozen pond. "Why did they fire you? Did they have a problem with your work?"

"Fuck no! We never had a single complaint."

"So what was the problem?"

"They wanted kickbacks," Tortelli said simply. "I wouldn't pay." He sighed a long, shaky sigh, and Barnaby knew then he had him: the dike was down, and suddenly the printer was talking so fast that Barnaby had to switch to shorthand to keep up.

It all started with a visit two and a half years ago from

Michael Kavin, Tortelli said. Kavin told him that the Brooklyn Democratic party was shopping around for a printer.

"He tells me his friend Jonathan Fleishman recommended me," Tortelli said, puffing on his cigar. "He tells me Fleishman says I'm not only a good printer but also a solid, public-minded citizen.

"Now, I'm as public-minded as the next guy, which ain't much, so already I'm thinking: What's with this guy? Plus what, they don't have printers in Brooklyn? But he's talking a lot of work, big bucks, so I'm not about to contradict the man. Sure, I tell him, I'm real public-minded. So he goes on bullshitting about how important it is to him and his buddy Jonathan that businessmen who take from the city give something back, through charity or political contributions; but all the time he's talking I see him doodling something on a piece of paper, the same thing over and over: a dollar sign followed by an eight and three zeros."

I'm being set up, Barnaby thought. This is too good to be true. But he didn't believe it. Tortelli was real.

"I'm staring at this paper," Tortelli said, "not really taking it in, 'cause this is like outta the blue; and then Kavin takes it, crumples it up, sticks it in the ashtray, and lights it with a match. And then uses a second match when it don't burn completely. Then he looks up at me and finally he shuts up; in fact he don't say a word till the silence gets so thick you could choke on it. It's clear he's waiting for me to say something, so I says, 'I understand,' and he says, 'Good,' and he leaves. And the next day they send Lebenthal to me."

Barnaby looked up, slack-jawed as a rube at a county fair. "Solly Lebenthal?"

"Yeah, that was his name. Measly little guy, wears fancy three-piece suits, but every time I see him he's got egg stains on his lapels. Anyway, he shows up the next day and says Mr. Kavin sent him to collect my donation to some Jewish cultural foundation. Now, I don't know this guy from Adam, you understand, so I says to him 'What donation?' and he says 'Eight thousand bucks.' 'What the hell,' I says to him, playing dumb, see, 'I mean, no offense, but I'm not even Jewish.' So he says, 'Mr. Fleishman and Mr. Kavin will be very disappointed,' and I says, 'Mr. Fleishman knows I give good value for money and always have.'

"See," Tortelli said, "I was up all night thinking it over, and I didn't believe that Fleishman was really involved. I know

Fleishman, see. He's a decent guy. I figured these two bozos were using his name to shake me down, and I wasn't about to go for it.

"So next thing you know, Kavin's back, only this time he won't sit in my office. He takes me out to a diner and we sit in a corner booth and he starts talking, and again he's making with the doodling. So I says, 'Mr. Kavin, you dragged me all the way out here, now talk straight to my face. What do you guys want from my life?'

" This city's been damn good to you,' he goes. 'We think it's only fair you put something back in the pot.'

"'Whose pot?' I says. 'Does Mr. Fleishman know what you're doing?'

"Kavin laughs in my face. 'So that's your problem,' he says. 'Don't you know that me and Jonathan are like this?' And he holds up two fingers, like that.

"Well, the truth is, I did know they were close friends, but I never once heard that Fleishman was on the take, and I didn't believe it. I'd been doing his printing for years, and he never asked me for nothing. So I told Kavin I want to hear it from the horse's mouth.

"The very next day, Fleishman calls me. And he says he's sorry about the misunderstanding with Mr. Lebenthal, and that actually it's not just a Jewish cultural foundation but a whole bunch of different charities they support, and he hopes I'll reconsider making a contribution."

Tortelli stopped. By now Barnaby was having hot flashes. "Then what?" he demanded.

Tortelli snubbed out his cigar. "I wouldn't have done it for the new business. If it was just Kavin, I'd have told him to shove his job up his ass. But I couldn't afford to lose Eastborough."

"So you paid."

"Once," Tortelli said softly. "Only once. And I wouldn't give it to that slime-bucket Lebenthal. He tried to pressure me, but I told him, 'Hey, if Fleishman and Kavin want the money so bad, let them take it from my hand.' "Mr. Fleishman and Mr. Kavin are busy men," he says, so I say, 'If they're too busy to pick up eight grand, then they don't need it and I won't pay.' So he set it up."

Barnaby gazed at the burly printer with a feeling as close to love as he ever came. "Sets what up?"

"The sitdown. Me, Fleishman, Kavin."

"You paid them?"

"Didn't I just say that?"

"Personally, I mean. You put the money in their hands?"

"Sure."

"How'd you pay?"

"What do you think, MasterCard? Eighty C-notes in a fat manila envelope."

"Where?"

"Right here. We went into the john and I handed Fleishman the envelope. Made them open it and count it in front of me. Kavin did the counting. All the time, I'm watching Fleishman's face. He looks like he's eating shit, but what the hell—it's my fucking money."

"You handed Kavin and Fleishman eight thousand in cash."

"What are you, deaf or something?"

Barnaby rubbed his face. "What happened afterward?"

"I got the work that Kavin promised me. But after I refused to pay anymore, that went away, and then I lost Eastborough, and next thing you know, I'm out on the street."

"Did you know that Kavin and Lebenthal are partners in a printing business? They bought into a small shop in Brooklyn just about two years ago. Doing quite well, I hear."

Tortelli's face went purple. "The fuck you say."

"Why'd you stop paying?"

"It offended me." Tortelli hit his head, still shaken by the news on Kavin. "See, I never heard a bad word about Fleishman, and if a guy's dirty, you generally get to hear about it. I figured they were singling me out, see, and I resented it."

"Why would they single you out, Mr. Tortelli?"

"I'm Italian, right? No secret about that, with a name like Vito Tortelli. A lotta people, they hear an Italian name and right away they think Mafia, they think crook. I'm no crook, godammit. I'm the son of immigrants and I built my business up from nothing, the old-fashioned way, with plenty of elbow grease. I started out running a press and now at sixty-two I'm back to doing it, but I'm not ashamed of that. I never paid a bribe in my life. So okay—it offended me, them figuring all they had to do was ask and I'd roll over."

"Have you told anyone else?"

Tortelli gave him a look and tapped his temple. "What for? Whaddaya think, they're gonna admit it? 'Oh, yeah, Tortelli, we took eight grand off him once but then he quit paying, so we fucked his ass'? Fuck no! Of course they'll deny it, and who's gonna believe me? Who's gonna take my word over Jonathan Fleishman's?"

14

AFTER JONATHAN FINISHED, no one spoke. The dining room was so quiet they could hear the swaying of the cypresses, the restless lapping of waves against the bulwark at the foot of the lawn. Clara sighed deeply into her soup, and matzo balls skittered round the bowl like rudderless boats in a high wind.

At last Gracie said, "What are they indicting you for?"

Jonathan could not bring himself to repeat the charges Christopher Leeds had predicted, though they still echoed in his mind. "You read that article."

"But that's the *Probe.*" Barnaby's name was no longer spoken in the house; it was "the *Probe*" or "that bastard." "They distort everything, they publish lies. You told me."

"They're in it together; the *Probe*'s hand in glove with the U.S. attorney's office."

"But that's impossible. They need evidence to indict."

"Maybe they have evidence," Paul said.

"You traitor!" Gracie cried.

"Look who's talking! If you hadn't shot off your mouth to that bastard, none of this would have happened."

She lowered her head. Her brother was only saying what she herself believed.

"This has nothing to do with Gracie," Jonathan said. "Lay off, Paul."

"Lay off? That's typical! That's exactly the problem with this family. It's poor Gracie this and poor Gracie that, as if she wasn't the one to blame. You're all so concerned about Gracie, you never think of what this will to me."

"What will it do to you, Paul?"

His eyes watered. "It'll ruin me at Columbia. I was doing so good there—I was making the right sort of friends. Now it's all down the drain. I was supposed to head the pledge drive for my fraternity next year. Forget that. They'll probably kick me out altogether."

"Heavens," Jonathan said.

Paul threw his napkin onto the table. "You think it's trivial. All my problems are trivial to you. No one in this family gives a damn about me." He ran out of the room.

Jonathan watched him go, then looked at Lily. She gave him a slit-eyed glare and followed Paul.

Only his mother and Gracie remained. Gracie leaned toward him, dry-eyed and focused, more like her child-self than she'd been in many years. "You have to tell me more. We have to plan our counterattack."

"I don't know any more." It was not the first lie Jonathan had ever told his daughter, but the first he was conscious of.

"The charges have to be answered publicly. We can't skulk around like Michael did—we've got to tackle them head-on."

"No one," he said slowly and precisely, "is to speak to the press. Not one word."

Clara snorted.

"That goes for you too, Mother."

"What am I, a dog you should muzzle me? I got plenty what to say."

"I can't stop you, Mother. Go ahead and talk, if you want to destroy me."

"Dad's right," Gracie said. "He should be the spokesman, not us."

"I'm not making any statement."

"You have to!"

"I've been advised against it."

"By who?"

"By my lawyer," Jonathan said testily, "and considering what his advice costs, I'm damn well going to take it."

"It's bad advice. But if you won't speak out for yourself, at least make the others do it. All those companies the *Probe* said paid you—they need to come out and say you never took a dime."

"They're not going to say a thing. No one sticks his neck out in a case like this."

"You're only asking them to tell the truth."

He hesitated. Their eyes met and a spark of intelligence flew between. Then Jonathan turned away. "It's out of my hands."

Her eyes blinked rapidly. Twice her mouth opened and shut without utterance. At last she asked, "*Did* they pay you?"

"I'm a lawyer. I represent clients. It's the custom in this country to get paid for work. It so happens that my legal work provides the bulk of this family's income, which you would know if you'd ever taken an interest. I do not take bribes; I do not take kickbacks; and why the hell I should have to defend myself to you," he shouted, "I will never understand!"

Jonathan's voice echoed in the silent room. A Dylan Thomas verse came back to him, a favorite from his college days: *Do not go gentle into that good night/ Rage, rage against the dying of the light.*

Gracie tottered out on legs gone stiff as stilts.

Hearing her brittle step in the hall, the firm, final closure of her bedroom door, Jonathan thought: I've lost both my children. He tugged at the lapels of his jacket in a vestigial gesture of mourning.

The next morning, Wednesday, Jonathan rose before six, dressed quickly and quietly, and left for the city. Lily woke to the sound of the closing door. She had taken two sleeping pills the night before and consequently her sleep had been unbroken, though troubled with elusive nightmares. For some time she lay back on the pillows, watching dappled sunlight play along the wall opposite the bay window. When she closed her eyes, the fresh salt breeze reminded her of the air in her canal city. It had been a long time between dreams, and there was no telling when she'd be allowed back.

Once she'd read of an isolated tribe that believed man's highest task was learning to control his dreams. They practiced their belief by taking responsibility for their own dreams and teaching their children to do the same. If a boy dreamed of hitting another boy, for example, he would have to go to that boy the next day and atone for his dream aggression.

The idea had stayed with her, though Lily could no longer remember where she had read it or even whether it was fiction or nonfiction (a distinction that in her own life had lately grown less than distinct). Many times she tried to make herself dream of her canal city, and several times she actually succeeded in setting out on a dream voyage; but somehow she always got sidetracked. Like her mother's voice, the dream was a gift that could not be summoned, only received.

After some time, Lily got out of bed and went into the master suite's bathroom. It was while she was lying in her bath, warm and fragrant with attar of roses, that the headache attacked.

It snuck up from behind and pounced without warning: one moment she was soaping her legs (thank God, Clara would say later, she wasn't shaving them), the next she was sputtering with her face underwater and what felt like a python clamped around her skull.

Fighting panic, she turned onto her hands and knees and raised her head like a deadweight from the water. She slumped over the edge of the tub, and water streamed off her hair and shoulders onto the tiled floor. Black spots swarmed like flies before her eyes.

After a while she dragged herself out of the tub and lay on the cool tiles; eventually she made her way back into bed, where she sank exhausted against the pillows. The pain was something like the contractions of labor, though in a wholly different part of the body. While they continued, they seemed endless, out of time; yet there were respites in between the stretches of pain. Also like a contraction, this pain was modulated in the shape of a wave. It started with a slow constriction, tightened in agony, then slowly relaxed: throbbing on a grand scale.

She thought of getting up, but as one thinks of traveling to China: someday, perhaps. Time passed and she heard the family stirring, but no one disturbed her, until at last there came a knock on her door and Clara followed, carrying a cup of steaming tea.

"Lily, it's past ten o'clock already. Your friend Margo called twice... " Then, noticing Lily's face: "What's the matter?"

"Just a headache." Lily tried to sit up, a mistake, since she failed. Clara set the cup on the nightstand and felt Lily's forehead.

"No fever," she muttered. Then she saw the bathroom, whose door was ajar: bathwater still in the tub, soaking-wet towels all over the floor. "Oy Gott. What happened, Lily?"

"Nothing."

"That's some nothing. What is it, you fainted, you fell? I'm calling the doctor."

"No, don't. I don't need a doctor for a headache. I know what it is—it's all the stress."

"Last time sun, this time stress. If you won't call the doctor, I'm calling Jonathan."

"You'll do neither," Lily said, in a voice she had never before used toward her mother-in-law.

Behind their thick glasses, Clara's eyes watered. She walked to the door. "I'll let you rest."

When she was gone, Lily covered her eyes and wept silently. How could she speak like that to Clara, who had been like a mother to her and who was trying to help? The crazy thing was that Lily half wanted to see a doctor. Since the first time in the park, she'd had four more of these headaches. They frightened her. If pain is a warning signal, these were air-raid sirens.

But what if the attacks were connected to the return of her mother's voice? After all, they had started at about the same time. What if curing the headaches meant silencing that precious, soothing voice? Lily had lost her mother once; how could she bear to lose her again?

There was another reason. The intense pain told her that if her headaches had an organic cause, it was nothing minor.

She didn't want to know. More than being sick, she feared knowing she was sick. This shameful realization came to her clearly in the pale, pure light of exhaustion. Martha Kavin had been right: she was a coward.

She was lurking in the supermarket parking lot when Gracie emerged, carrying two bags. The woman was in her thirties, with a long nose, freckled cheeks, and a lanky body dressed in jeans and a checkered shirt. Apart from Gracie, she was the only woman in sight not wearing makeup.

"Grace," the woman said, hurrying over, "can I talk to you?"

"No."

"It's not about your father. It's about Barnaby, what he did to you."

Gracie kept going. "Everyone knows what he did to us."

"Not 'us.' *You.*"

She glanced at the woman, who now seemed vaguely familiar. "Who are you?"

"Ronnie Neidelman."

"You work for the *Probe.*"

"Yes, but—"

"Fuck off." Scowling, Gracie opened the trunk of her mother's car and shoved the bags in so hard she heard something crack.

"Give me five minutes. You don't have to say a word; just listen. It's to your benefit."

After what had happened, Gracie didn't trust herself in the vicinity of any reporter, and she feared what her father would do if he heard of this. But her curiosity was greater than her fear, and she told herself that if she did not speak, it could do no harm to listen.

They sat in the parked car, and Ronnie Neidelman lit a cigarette from the dashboard lighter, took a few puffs, then snubbed it out with a grimace of disgust. "Reporting's a rough business. We spend our lives cajoling people into telling us stuff they don't want to tell us. But despite what you probably think, there are boundaries. If it's true Barnaby seduced you, he stepped way over the line. I wanted you to know that line exists, and there are consequences."

Was he bragging about it? Gracie wondered. She could see him in a bar, surrounded by laughing, leering colleagues. *I didn't just fuck the father, I fucked his daughter, too!*

"Is that his story?" she asked Neidelman.

"No." The reporter looked startled. "No, he denies it, of course. I believe his exact words were, 'I never touched the little bitch.'"

"And you're telling me this because…?"

"Because it offends me. And because you should know that if he broke the rules, he can be called to account. You're not powerless."

"I never thought I was," Gracie said.

Neidelman stared and shook her head. "Some kid."

"I gave up teddy bears a while ago. Is he your boyfriend?"

Now the woman looked flustered. "How do—That's got nothing to do with why I'm here."

"No?"

"I'd like to know, though, if you can tell me. Did you and Barnaby…did he seduce you?"

"Who told you that? You said he denies it."

"Your father."

"What are you talking about?"

"Well, not me *personally*," Neidelman said. "Everyone in the newsroom heard him. Didn't he tell you? The day the story broke, your father burst into the office, called Barnaby out in front of the entire newsroom, and broke his nose."

Gracie smiled.

15

THE DAY AFTER HIS SECOND PIECE on Jonathan Fleishman appeared, Barnaby got a call from Jane Buscaglio asking for a meeting in their usual place, a downtown greasy spoon whose only merit was that it was frequented by no one they knew.

"Good story," she told him after a cursory handshake. "Where's Tortelli?"

"Who?" Barnaby said innocently.

"Your printer friend. You left his name out of the story, but it wasn't hard to find."

He gave up the pretense. "Actually, I asked if he'd been to see you. He seemed reluctant."

"We need to talk to him."

"So who's stopping you? You don't need my permission."

"Can't find him."

Barnaby clucked sympathetically.

"Don't fuck with me, Barnaby. I know you know where he is. I need this guy."

"Why, is your case so weak?"

"We've got a strong case. But if your story's true, Tortelli's a smoking gun."

"Even if I knew where he was, journalistic ethics would—"

"Yeah, tell me about ethics!"

"Jesus, what's the matter with you, Jane? On the rag this morning? You've been acting weird ever since I walked in."

Buscaglio stared at him over the top of her glasses. "Fine, you want to talk about ethics: what's the story on the Fleishman girl?"

Barnaby felt himself blush. "What about her?"

"Did you fuck her?"

"You, too, Jane, really? You've known me long enough. You think I'd do that?"

"I don't hear you denying it."

"I shouldn't have to. Just for the sake of argument, though, even if it were true, what difference would it make? It doesn't make Fleishman any more or less guilty."

"No, but it would put a whole new spin on our relationship. I'd have to think about information flowing both ways."

Barnaby paled. This was an accusation of a different color, and they both knew it. She's jealous, he realized suddenly. She's pissed he never hit on to her. It made perfect sense. Buscaglio was pushing forty, a notoriously sensitive age for single women. On the six-o'clock news, she looked dashing, almost glamorous, but up close, he could see the crow's-feet around her eyes, the gray strands in that flaming red hair. There was ambition in the set of her mouth, and she had a runner's body, lean and mean; no tits to speak of. Not Barnaby's type, but he could have taken one for the team.

Too late now, anyway, with Buscaglio looking at him like he was a roach in her bran flakes. "You disappoint me, Jane. I thought we had some respect for each other as professionals."

"We did have. But never mind the girl. We've got bigger fish to fry. I want Tortelli."

"I want Lebenthal."

She shook her head.

"I just need him for confirmation," Barnaby wheedled. "I've got it figured out. Kavin hits on Fleishman's targets, and Fleishman reciprocates. No one shits in their own stable. Lebenthal's their joint bagman, because neither Michael nor Jonathan like getting their hands dirty." He raised an eyebrow and waited.

Buscaglio said nothing.

Barnaby went on. "I keep remembering what the printer said about the look on Fleishman's face while Kavin was counting money in the john. That didn't jibe with the Fleishman holier-than-God image. So much neater and cleaner to accept little pink deposit slips from Solly Lebenthal. How'm I doing, Jane?"

"No comment."

"Is Lebenthal talking to you?"

"No comment."

"What about Kavin? Why hasn't he been indicted yet?"

"No comment on Kavin either. I didn't come to trade."

Barnaby stuck a toothpick in the corner of his mouth and chewed on it. "Too bad. 'Cause I want Lebenthal just as badly as you want the printer."

"You are skating on thin fucking ice, Barnaby. By withholding this witness—"

"I don't control him!"

"You know where he is."

"If I did, I'd never break confidentiality to tell you."

"Would you," asked the prosecutor, "in return for an interview with Lebenthal?"

He hesitated.

Buscaglio laughed unkindly. "Okay, Barnaby. Now that we know what you are, let's talk price."

Michael Kavin came running into the locker room twenty minutes late. His face was red and he was panting. Jonathan flicked a towel at him.

"You son of a bitch, I thought you'd stood me up."

"Sorry Jonathan. I knew that's what you'd think. Goddamn car conked out on me—bastard needs a new transmission and I've been putting it off."

On the way out, the manager offered them a caddy; they declined in unison. The club was crowded, and it wasn't until the sixth hole that they found themselves thoroughly, reliably alone.

Michael peered over his shoulder, a recent habit Jonathan found irritating. He grasped Jonathan's elbow and stage-whispered, "I've talked to Solly."

"Where is he?"

"He wouldn't say. He called last night. Jonathan, I think he's thrown in with them."

Fleishman's face looked like wood. His eyes were unreadable behind dark glasses. "I'm glad he's okay," he said. "I was worried about him, disappearing like that."

"He's not the one we've gotta worry about. Didn't you hear what I said?"

"I heard. You don't have to spit in my ear. What did Solly say?"

"He said Buscaglio's been all over him. He said they're looking to do a package deal."

"Why'd he call you?"

"He said it was to warn me, but I think he was sounding me out, like would I go in with him. Only my feeling is he's already in."

"I see." Jonathan lined up his shot, sighting along his club.

It wasn't distrust of Michael that made him mask his shock (he would no sooner distrust Michael than he would himself), but rather an instinct for self-preservation forged in the streets and schoolyards of Brooklyn, where he'd learned a fundamental lesson: if you cry when you're hit, you've already lost. Nevertheless, Lily's relentless campaign had had an effect. Though her hints and accusations infuriated him, Jonathan knew that she wasn't often wrong in such matters. To his own disgust, he found himself weighing Michael's every word, answering with care.

"Don't you realize what this means?" Michael demanded.

"It means shit. Fuck Solly. Let's play." Jonathan swung his club and the ball flew down the fairway, coming to rest less than two yards from the hole.

"Jesus," breathed Michael. "Someone still likes you."

Jonathan laughed—this was more like the old days. But when he clasped Michael around the shoulders, his friend stiffened and pulled away.

"Look, Jonathan, we need to consider our options."

Jonathan took off his sunglasses and looked straight at him. "My friend, the only option I'm considering on this fine day is whether to use my five-iron or my putter."

"What's with the attitude, buddy? I've been waiting a long time to get you alone."

"Me too, Kemosabe. Only why'd you jump when I touched you?"

"You startled me. Christ, now who's paranoid?"

Jonathan sank his ball with one putt. It was typical of the man that the more upset he was, the steadier his hands became. Michael had sounded hurt but not hurt enough. His shirt was soaked, and every few minutes he mopped sweat from his brow. Of course, thought Jonathan, clinging to hope, Michael never could take the sun.

They finished the course in near-silence.

In the locker room Jonathan peeled off his shirt and headed for the showers. Michael hung back.

"Jeez, look at the time," he said. "I gotta run. I was supposed to meet Martha half an hour ago."

"Since when do we finish before twelve?"

"Yeah, well, we've got this meeting... Hey, take care of yourself, pal." He waved and walked toward the door. Without seeming to hurry, Jonathan arrived before him. He leaned against it.

"You know, Michael, Lily really did not want me here today, and my lawyer had a fucking cow. I told them to go to hell. I said, 'Michael would cut off his right hand before he'd turn on me.' I'd hate to think," he said, smiling, "that I was wrong."

Kavin's face looked like a red balloon on the point of bursting. He swallowed hard, said nothing.

"Take a shower, Michael."

"I can't, really, Jonathan. I'm running late as it is."

"For what, a meeting with the feds?"

Michael closed his eyes. "I wish you hadn't said that, man. I really wish you hadn't said that."

"If I'm wrong, I'll apologize. Take a shower."

"What are you saying? You think I'm wired, is that it?"

"No, *paisano*. It's just that I had this strange feeling even before we walked in here that you weren't going to shower."

"You're saying I'm wired, you prick."

"I'm saying you stink, Michael. If your best friend can't tell you, who can?"

"Get out of my way." When Michael tried to shoulder him aside, Jonathan grabbed his shirt with both hands and ripped downward. The shirt tore apart and dropped down to his hips. Both men stared at the small transmitter taped to Michael's chest.

Like a drowning man, Jonathan saw his life flash before him: a montage of scenes from Columbia, law school, county jails in the deep south, fights, picket lines, demonstrations, more fights, rallies... Michael was in every frame, always at his side, more faithful than a wife. Michael was no outsider; Michael lived inside him. This betrayal came from within.

"Oh, God." He sighed with a bitterness deeper than tears, beyond anger.

"Fuck you, man." Tears mingled with sweat on Michael's face. "What do you know? What the fuck do you know?"

"I know I wouldn't have done it to you."

"Yeah, you're so self-righteous—wait till you stand in my shoes."

There was a sharp knock on the locker-room door. The knob

rattled but did not turn; Jonathan had locked the door. "What's going on?" a man's voice yelled.

"Get stuffed," Michael shouted back. He ripped the transmitter off his chest, ground it underfoot, and grasped Jonathan's shoulders. "Lebenthal's talking and now Barnaby's dug up Tortelli. They've got us by the balls, *paisano*, we are fucking screwed. You tell me—what was I supposed to do?"

"You're supposed to be a man."

Michael flinched. "That's what I'm doing. I'm sorry, Jonathan, but we're not kids anymore. My first responsibility is to my family."

"I could buy that, if you weren't doing it at my family's expense."

"They promised me you wouldn't be hurt. All they wanted was enough to turn you. You've got to come in, Jonathan, before it's too late. The buck don't stop with us, and they know it. Buscaglio's seeing stars on her dressing-room door."

"What did they give you?" Jonathan croaked. "What did they buy you with, Michael?"

"That's not the way it went down."

"Don't bullshit me, man. You sign a pact with the devil, you damn well better learn to call a spade a spade." He tottered over to a bench and sat hunched over, rocking back and forth like an old man saying Kaddish. This rocking motion, which seemed to well up from the deep desolation within him, evoked a visceral memory of Lily in a rocking chair, staring with frozen eyes at a bunch of yellow roses.

"I thought I knew you," Jonathan murmured, so softly he might have been talking to himself. "I thought if there was one person on earth I knew, it was you."

Outside the locker room the commotion was growing louder. Men were yelling back and forth, and someone was working on the lock with a screwdriver. Michael opened his bag, slipped on a clean shirt, and stood for a moment with his hand on the knob, looking back. But, finding nothing to say, he unlocked the door and went out.

16

"HE COMES INTO THE ROOM," *Grandma says,* "*you walk out. He sits at the table, you get up. He talks, you don't listen. This is how you treat your own father, who loves you and cares for you all your life?*"

"*It's better that way, Grandma,*" *I tell her.*

"*Better than what?*" *she cries, throwing up her hands.* "*He's your father, but he's my son, and I won't sit quiet and watch you hurt him.*"

She can't understand that it would hurt him much more if I spoke. He understands; he knows this is my way of protecting him. Because I know he's guilty. He told me so himself. Not with words, but with his eyes. When I said, "*Make the others come forward, make them tell the truth,*" *his thought was,* "*God forbid.*" *I saw this. He knows I saw it.*

I don't want to lie to him and I don't want him to lie to me. Any more lies would kill us for sure.

But I feel sorry for Clara. These days she wanders around the house mumbling to herself like an old lady. She's dying to go down the drive and tear into those reporters, but she won't go against my father's orders. As far as she's concerned, it's all an anti-Semitic plot. I tried to explain to her about conspiracy and influence peddling, but she refuses to understand. "*So he helped his friends,*" *she said,* "*so what's the big deal? The Italians don't help the Italians? The Irish don't help the Irish?*"

"*But they're claiming he did it for money,*" *I said.*

"*So what, you want he should work for free? You want we*

should live like your friend Mr. Barnaby No-name, with the cock-a-roaches and the rats and the drunkards and dope peddlers?"

Then she tells me, "Honor thy father," like Moses proclaiming the law. As if I didn't want to, as if I wouldn't give anything to believe in him again.

Last night I overheard him telling Mom what Michael Kavin did. I think he was crying. I sniveled some myself. The man's my fucking godfather. But then, Lucas is Paul's. You can't trust anybody.

Which doesn't mean people shouldn't be called to account. I've been thinking a lot about Barnaby, a pig in sheep's clothing if ever there was one. I know it, Needlewoman knows it, but you can tell by the way all those newscasters and reporters genuflect when they mention his name that he's got them snowed. My brain says sit back and shut up, because God knows I've done enough harm already. But my heart says, "Kill. Kill."

It's not just vengeance, though I admit that's a factor. The point is, I know Barnaby. I know what he is. And thanks to Needlewoman, I know I can hurt him. So it follows that if I don't, if I sit back and do nothing, I am responsible for every dirty, rotten thing he goes on to do.

Tomorrow I'll drive into the city.

"'The time has come,' the Walrus said, 'to talk of many things.'"

"'Of shoes, and ships, and sealing wax, of cabbages and kings; and why the sea is boiling hot, and whether pigs have wings,'" concluded Lily.

Christopher Leeds beamed at her.

"Great," Jonathan groused. "I'm dying and my lawyer recites Lewis Carroll." He wasn't complaining, just showing that he too knew his English lit. Since Michael's betrayal, Jonathan's embarrassment about using Leeds had burnt off like a rocket stage, propelling them all forward.

They sat, the three of them, on the deck overlooking the bay, sipping iced tea flavored with mint from Lily's garden. Christopher Leeds in his Hampton mode was a portly Tom Wolfe-ish figure, formally attired in a white linen suit, pink shirt, panama hat, and white ducks. He and his wife were spending the month of August with Leeds's sister, who, it emerged, lived year-round in Sag Harbor. This surprised Jonathan, who could hardly conceive of Leeds's having had parents, much less siblings, but it was certainly convenient: for Jonathan had taken to spending more and more time at the summer house, not to seek comfort in the bosom of his family, but to spare himself the mortification of ostracism.

Jonathan had dreaded telling Leeds about Michael's treachery. The least he expected was an "I-told-you-so;" but in his worst fantasies, the ones that showed up at three in the morning, the lawyer threw up his hands and resigned the case. In reality, Leeds's response was unfeigned sympathy and pain. His face grew luminous with grief; he pressed Jonathan's hand in consolation and said, as if of a death in the family, "I'm so sorry." At that moment, Jonathan felt his liking for the man turn to love.

Now, however, Christopher Leeds had resumed his lawyerly persona. Pudgy hands laced over his knee, he said, "Ms. Buscaglio telephoned me."

Jonathan said, "What did she want?"

"You must understand that this was an opening move on their part, a preliminary tender, if you will. We could certainly do better, if you choose to pursue this option. She offered to drop some counts if you agree to plead guilty to extortion, influence peddling, and racketeering, provide full information and cooperation to investigators, and testify about all your 'illegal activities and coconspirators.'"

"Drop some counts—that's all?"

"That's all she offered."

Jonathan laughed. "In other words, they want me to betray my friends, destroy my reputation, ruin my career, and disgrace my family: and all that is not even worth immunity."

"Correct. From what I could gather, immunity's not on the table."

"What did you say?"

"That I would pass on the message." Leeds's face gave no hint of opinion or expectation.

"Tell Buscaglio and Lucas to go fuck themselves."

"Would you mind if I put that into my own words?"

"Suit yourself."

Lily was sitting with her hands pressed tighdy between her knees. "Jonathan," she said, "have you thought it through?"

He turned to her, his face a dusky rose. "There's nothing to think about. I'd rather rot in jail for life than plead guilty to something I didn't do."

"Of course you realize that fighting these charges will be cosdy," Leeds said neutrally.

"You're saying that guilty or innocent, I'm fucked either way. Thank you; that point had occurred to me."

"I should also point out that pursuing this discussion with the U.S. attorney's office, even to an unsuccessful conclusion, would almost certainly yield useful information about their case, which otherwise will be withheld until discovery."

"It's copping out, Christopher. It's admitting that their charges have some legitimacy. Besides," Jonathan said irritably, "I'm not going to do to anyone what Michael did to me. That's not what I'm about."

"You don't have to decide immediately."

"The decision is made. We fight." Jonathan looked at Lily. She reached over and clasped his hand.

"All right, then," Christopher Leeds said, breaking out his boyish smile. "We fight. Jonathan, there is much to do. Might I suggest that we leave this delightful but distracting setting and immure ourselves in your study?"

Lily understood this, correctly, as a dismissal. To Jonathan's relief, his lately unpredictable wife rose, smiled pleasantly, and said, "I'll let you get down to it, then. Shout when you're ready for sustenance."

"The first thing you have to understand," Jonathan said when she had gone, "is that there are two sets of rules: the written ones and the real ones. It is perfectly possible to commit some minor technical violations of the former while adhering strictly to the latter. I am a man of principle, and the first principle of politics is to get results. Wealth in itself means nothing to me; but in our society, wealth *is* power. That's reality, and in order to function effectively, I must live within that reality."

Christopher Leeds sighed. Given a choice, he would have skipped the philosophizing and gone right to the nitty-gritty; but there never was a choice. God created the world with a word, and thereafter man imitated him. Jonathan would have been mortified to know that he was following the pattern of all Leeds's clients, albeit more eloquently than most: fashioning a context in which every misdeed had its sufficient justification and from every act of seeming venality there emerged, like a butterfly from its chrysalis, an act of altruism.

"They accuse me of influence peddling," Jonathan said. "What does that mean? Patronage is the oil in the political machine; nothing works without it. The real moral issue isn't if you use it, it's how."

Leeds said, "They will claim, presumably, that you used these political appointees to benefit your law clients, and thereby yourself."

"They can say what they like. I'll stand on my record of appointments. I've appointed more blacks and Hispanics than any other politician in this city. And I don't sponsor incompetents. Loyalty counts, okay, but if a man can't do the job, I won't protect him. Anyone who knows me—"

"But the jury doesn't know you. And as someone who's been at this for a while, I must warn you that just because the law mandates a presumption of innocence, that doesn't mean the jury will afford it. I don't care what they say in *voir dire;* some of those jurors are going to come into court with the attitude that if you weren't guilty, you wouldn't have been charged."

"All I'm saying is I have a record to stand on. My law clients are practically all minority-owned businesses. I'm proud of what I've done for them."

"Which is what, precisely? And how did they pay you? Do you own stock in any of the companies?" Leeds took a file from his briefcase and opened it on Jonathan's desk. Inside were neatly clipped copies of Barnaby's two articles, sections of which had been highlighted in yellow. Jonathan's nose twitched disdainfully, as if Leeds had just spread fresh manure over his desk.

"I'm told that Barnaby is very close to Buscaglio," Leeds said. "We have to assume that whatever he's got, she has as well. Let's begin with Rencorp."

"I don't want to talk about Rencorp."

"I'm your advocate," Leeds said gently. "I'm your doctor, your rabbi, your father confessor. You tell me everything."

Jonathan ran his fingers through his hair. "I made that company. They were nothing, they had nothing until Bo Johnson came to me. I made them; and now that fucker won't even take my calls."

"Do you own stock in Rencorp?"

"No."

Christopher Leeds cocked his head, a bespectacled popinjay looking for a worm. "Your wife? Your children?"

"No one in the family."

Leeds waited.

Very unhappily Jonathan said, "Michael held stock."

"On your behalf?"

"His own as well."

"I see," Leeds said without expression. "Well, we must assume the prosecution has that information."

"Michael wouldn't... " he began, but the worn-out mantra died in his mouth, flooding it with poison. He wrapped his arms around himself. "I know they'll twist it. I know they'll make it look dirty. But the honest-to-God truth is that investing in that company was a pure act of faith. Five years ago they were nothing: a room, two typewriters, and a three-legged desk. Today they employ two hundred people. They did it on their own. I enabled them, but they did it. I'm supposed to apologize for that? I'm proud of it!"

"But you had a fiscal interest in the company. By helping Rencorp, you helped yourself."

Jonathan's temper flared; but he told himself that Leeds wasn't judging him, only playing devil's advocate. "That's incidental—it takes nothing away from the benefits to the community. On the contrary: if I profit from the public good, doesn't that make me even more zealous in its pursuit?"

Astonishingly, Christopher Leeds giggled.

"Don't look at the letter of the law," Jonathan pleaded. "Look at the spirit. Weight the good I've done for others against the harm and tell me: which is greater?"

Leeds reached across the desk and pressed Jonathan's hand. "In my eyes, there is no question. But the court doesn't work that way. It's either guilty or not guilty of the charges. 'More sinned against than sinning' isn't one of the options."

Jonathan looked down at the hand touching his, and suddenly his dream of the night before, which had teased at the edge of his consciousness all day, came back to him. He was golfing with Michael on an unfamiliar course. Jonathan hit his ball into a sand trap. When he went in after it, the trap turned out to be a bog. He sank down to his waist and still felt nothing underfoot. The more he struggled, the faster he sank. He screamed for help. Michael stood watching with a furrowed brow. "Michael, hold out a club!" Jonathan cried, buried now to the chest.

His friend drew back, clutching the bag to his chest.. "Not these clubs!"

The quicksand lapped at Jonathan's chin. "For God's sake, man!"

"Sorry, *paisano*," Michael said. "We're not kids anymore." He turned and walked away.

After leaving the men to their work, Lily found herself restless and sick of the house, once her refuge, now her prison. She called her hairdresser, who agreed to receive her at once, and left the house. At the gate she ran the gauntlet of reporters, who howled her name.

"I knew it," Randall said the moment he laid eyes on her. "*You* didn't say so, but I knew you would need color. Well," he sighed, slipping on rubber gloves, "there goes lunch."

"Sorry, Randy," Lily said. "Things have been a little hectic."

"Oh, I know, my dear, I read the papers. It must be terrible for you. But, Lily, you really cannot go on this way."

"What can we do? It's out of our hands."

He stared at her in the mirror. "I was talking about your hair, dear."

"Oh."

"Let's not lose our sense of proportion," Randy said, mixing chemicals in a bowl. "Scandals come and go; hair is forever. Everyone has troubles. I had a woman in here last week—hold this, please—in one month she lost her father and her mother. They come home from the mother's funeral, and out of the blue her husband tells her he's leaving her for another woman, some young gal from his office. On top of this, the bum has the nerve to try for custody of the children. Last Monday she comes in, she tells me, 'Randy, just a quick fix. I don't have time for anything else, I'm going to court today.' 'Not like that, you're not,' I tell her; I stand her in front of the mirror. 'Look at yourself, my dear,' I say. 'You're a mess. The judge will take one look at that face and say to himself, "This woman is not coping."'"

As he spoke, Randy deftly sorted out strands of hair, painted them with a small basting brush, and wrapped the hairs in foil. "To make a long story short, I did not let her out of that door until we had her looking beautiful—hair, nails, makeup, the whole works. P.S., she went to court and the judge awarded her custody."

"Poor woman," Lily said, wondering who she could be.

Sometimes, though, she suspected that Randy's stories were apocryphal; he seemed to have a customer for every occasion.

"The point is, appearances count. They count more than guilt or innocence, more than right or wrong. I'd much rather read about you in the society columns, Lily dear, but if I must see your name on the front page, I want it to read, 'the beautiful and elegant Lily Fleishman.'"

"'Hair by Randall Gray,' " she added with a smile.

"Absolutely. Perhaps a discreet little tag... "

They burst out laughing and once she started, Lily couldn't stop. She laughed until tears streamed down her face. She felt so safe in Randy's chair, so well-protected.

They went a long way back, she and Randy, so far back that it was he who had presided over the sacrifice of her beautiful long hair to Jonathan's burgeoning political career. When Randy had left the Martindale establishment where he worked to open his own salon, Lily went with him. Even after they moved to Highview, she came faithfully, bringing her new, fashionable friends with her. Randy's reputation grew, along with his prices. He expanded the store, added manicure and makeup departments, and eventually opened a second salon in East Hampton, where he catered two days a week between Memorial Day and Labor Day to his migrant birds of fashion.

He was a lifelong bachelor with campy mannerisms. People who didn't know him well assumed he was gay; in fact, Randall Gray was a closet heterosexual. He was discreet, but his lovers weren't always; Lily knew two Hampton women who had been his mistresses, and suspected a third. Though Randy had never made any advance toward Lily, more than once she had caught him gazing at her with more than hairdresserly regard; but when she noticed, he would sigh theatrically and say, "Lord, what an artist I am." She called him her Pygmalion; and in her honor, he named his salons Pygmalion East and West.

He had never visited Lily's home, nor she his. They had never shared a meal, seen a movie, or taken a walk together; yet they were friends, and Lily confided more in him than in anyone else.

Leaning back in the chair, Lily closed her eyes and surrendered to his competent ministrations. The familiar buzz of the salon soothed her spirit: laughter and the high-pitched clatter of gossip, the endless dialogue of the hair washer and the manicurist, the swish of the broom wielded by a sweet-faced young girl who

served coffee in between rounds. Suddenly she heard a familiar
bray of laughter, and she opened her eyes to find Margo bearing
down on her.

"Lily, you naughty girl, where have you been?"

"Hello, Margo."

"Don't 'hello Margo' me! Why haven't you returned my calls?"

"Do you mind!" It was hard to say what bothered Randy
more—Margo's intrusion on his work or her harassment of his
favorite.

"Oh, don't fuss, Randy. Darling, I've been worried sick about
you."

"I'm sorry, Margo. It was good of you to call. I just didn't want
to impose my troubles on my friends."

"Who else can you impose them on? Jonathan's got his own,
poor man. Lily, I am so furious at those goddamn reporters I
could spit. Such filthy lies!"

"It's very strange," Lily said. "I can't tell you how strange. It's
as if someone pulled the rugs out from under your feet and you
look down and see there's no floor."

Randy shuddered. "That reminds me, did you see the revival
of *Metamorphosis?* Baryshnikov was absolutely brilliant.
Imagine waking up one morning and finding you've turned into
a cockroach."

"Oh, please," Margo said, "you should see how I wake up in
the morning." She looked at Lily. "Why weren't you at Christina's
last weekend? Everyone was there. She told me you'd accepted."

"That was before." No need to say before what.

"But, Lily, darling, what's the point of sitting home feeling
sorry for yourselves when you've got tons of friends dying to
show their support?"

"Tons of friends? You're the only one who called."

Margo said nothing for a moment. The little sweeper came
over, bearing coffee: sweet and light for Margo, black for Lily.
"They don't want to intrude," Margo said. "They feel awkward.
It's not like a bereavement, when everyone knows the form. One
can't send a card: 'So sorry to hear of your indictment.'"

"It hasn't come to that," Randy said sharply. He tilted Lily's
head downward to work on the back. "Margo, get washed."

"In a minute. Lily, I'm having a little get-together Saturday
evening, nothing elaborate, just a few old friends. Why don't you
and Jonathan come?"

"Thanks, Margo, but I don't think Jonathan's in a very sociable mood."

"Then come yourself. Come early, so we can talk. I won't take no for an answer, Lily. Just because your husband's unaccommodating is no reason for you to be in purdah."

Lily laughed. Margo's aggressive warmth had melted her icy cocoon; just for a moment, she was tempted to accept. Randy was giving her significant nods and winks in the mirror.... She was startled by her own reflection, failing for a moment to recognize the silver-snaked Medusa head as her own.

"Isn't it funny," she said, "how, to become beautiful, we must first make ourselves hideous?"

"Shut up, Lily, or I'll slap a mud pack on your face," Randy said.

Lily wished her time in Randy's chair would never end, that she would never have to go home. Margo put her face close to Lily's and said earnestly, "You remember when Jerry had that trouble with the IRS two years ago and we had to sell the Palm Springs condo? He got so depressed, he damn near dragged me down with him. Finally I got it through my head that Jerry is Jerry and I am me, and that no matter how much you feel for your husband, you've got to be your own person."

"It sounds good." Lily sighed. "If only saying made it so."

"Saying doesn't make it so; *you* have to make it so. Will you come?"

"It's kind of you to ask, but I'd just spoil everyone's evening."

Margo drew herself up. "Really, Lily, who do you think we are? Maybe your political friends are pulling up stakes—to hell with them if they are—but we are made of sterner stuff. We judge our friends by the really important things, like how they dress and the quality of their parties."

Lily dissolved in laughter. Now she knew how Alice had felt in Wonderland. Everything she'd thought was solid—her marriage, her family, Jonathan's political standing—turned out to be built on sand; while all she had taken for froth was turning out bedrock. "I'd like to come," she said. "I'll ask Jonathan."

Driving home, she rehearsed her arguments. "It would do us good to get out," she told the rearview mirror. "Hiding at home is like admitting guilt. Appearances count." She was in such a good mood that as she drove up to the pack encamped by their gate, she did a Reagan: cupped her ear and shrugged regretfully.

Outside the garage stood a black-and-white New York City police car.

Lily's first thought, oddly, was that something had happened to Grace.

She ran into the house through the kitchen, then followed the sound of men's voices to the front hall. Lily stopped dead. The door was open. Standing in the portico, facing her, were two uniformed New York City cops. Her husband stood with his back to her; in front of him, a barrier between him and the police, was Christopher Leeds. As she watched, one of the policemen handed an envelope to the lawyer.

Jonathan looked around, pale beneath his tan. His eyes passed over her without registering her presence.

Suddenly Greta was in the room, standing just behind Lily, singing softly but distinctly in her ear:

Three blind mice, three blind mice,
See how they run, see how they run.
They all ran after the farmer's wife,
She cut off their tails with a carving knife;
Did you ever see such a sight in your life
As three blind mice?

17

THEY STOOD ON THE COURTHOUSE STEPS in a glare of blinding light. Jonathan and Lily, arm in arm, faced the cameras; his face was somber, hers wore a nervous hostess's smile. At Christopher Leeds's insistence, they did not speak, but were dressed to make speech superfluous. Jonathan's conservative dark suit, ivory shirt, and striped tie asked the question: Is this a man who would sully his hands? Lily's white linen dress was immaculate, yet something about the crimson scarf around her throat and her air of exquisite dignity evoked the image of Jacqueline Kennedy emerging from *Air Force One*, stained with her husband's blood.

Several steps above and behind them stood their children. Paul, dressed in a suit more conservative than his father's, clutched a briefcase in one hand; with the other he grasped his sister's arm, a gesture that looked like solicitude but was actually restraint.

While Christopher Leeds spoke to the press, Gracie glared out at their tormentors. Like a lighthouse beacon, her anger swept in wide arcs, illuminating those it touched with its dark light. She sought one face in particular, and though the blinding klieg lights and flashbulbs made it hard to distinguish features, she knew him the moment she spotted him. Paul, following her eyes, gave her arm a warning squeeze; but Grace was going nowhere.

Uncharacteristically, Barnaby hung back on the fringes of the crowd. His place was up front, shouting questions and demanding answers, but he didn't trust Gracie. She had spotted him and was staring so fixedly that his colleagues were beginning to notice.

Clara was not there. Up until that morning, she'd insisted on coming. They had all moved back into the Highview house to be closer to the courthouse. From six-thirty that morning Clara had kept coming into Jonathan and Lily's room, asking, "Is this dress all right?", "Which hat?", and "Should I wear gloves?", until Jonathan finally snapped, "Mother, wear what you want, just give us some peace." Clara cried. Jonathan, whose women were all decidedly unweepy, had never seen so many tears in his life as during these past few weeks. "Excuse me," his mother said. "I've never been to an arraignment before."

Later he went to her room, and apologized. Then he said, "Mama, there's one thing you can do for me."

"Anything, *bubbele*."

"Don't come to court. Stay home."

"Jonathan, you're my son. I have to be there."

Despite everything, Jonathan had to smile. It was like going back thirty years to when he used to get in trouble at school. He took her hand. "Mama, this is the worst day of my life. Don't add to my pain by making me witness yours."

She pressed his hand to her lips, smearing it with bright red lipstick. "You want I should stay home, I'll stay home. Whatever's best for you." When they left for court in a chauffeured Lincoln sent by Christopher Leeds, Clara saw them off, a stolid figure planted in the garden like an ungainly shrub in orthopedic shoes. No Orpheus, Jonathan kept his eyes on the road.

The others gazed out windows. "Your purpose is to support your father, your husband," Christopher Leeds had told them the day before. "Stand close to him; touch him whenever possible. Look straight into the cameras. Don't scowl," he told Gracie; "Don't pout," he told Paul. He passed approval on their court clothes. Gracie had to change twice before he was satisfied, from jeans to a denim skirt to her one hated "good" dress. "You're a nice family," Leeds instructed them. "A close family. I want the cameras to see that closeness."

They listened with astonishment but did as he bade them, and of course he was right, for of the millions of potential jurors who watched the news that night, many were moved by the spectacle of innocent suffering. In court, Lily, flanked by her two children, sat directly behind Jonathan. Paul and Gracie held her hands when Jonathan rose to speak the only words he would utter in public that day: "Not guilty." After the proceedings were concluded, the three of them crowded round Jonathan and kissed him, even Gracie, who had not said an unnecessary word to him in weeks. Then Christopher Leeds led them out onto the steps, where they posed for the photographers like good little children who are seen but not heard.

The cameras loved them: such a handsome family, strong and graceful under pressure, like a sound ship in a storm. Except for Gracie's scowl, they might have been posing for a picture at a wedding or bar mitzvah. Though they couldn't hear Christopher Leeds's remarks above the baying of the reporters, it didn't matter: they had their orders.

They played their parts well. But when the charade was over, when the car door closed behind them and they were alone with no lights, no cameras, no hostile eyes, no witnesses save Leeds's professionally discreet driver, the center did not hold. They fell apart, each into a silence separate from the others'.

At home, they parted. Lily went out to the garden, Clara to the kitchen, and Paul to his room, where he pored over out-of-state college catalogs. Gracie made a phone call, changed her clothes, and slipped out of the house. Jonathan closed himself in his study and began a task Christopher had assigned him, compiling a list of every business and political transaction he had ever had with Michael Kavin and Solly Lebenthal. But his pen shook so violently he had to lay it down.

During the arraignment, he had felt himself removed from the action, observing foggily from a distance as people went through motions and spoke words devoid of content. Suddenly, scenes from the courtroom replayed before his eyes, obliterating what lay about him; and as he relived those moments, the full force of the pain he'd blocked out at the time broke through.

He saw Buscaglio in her tight, camel-colored skirt and high heels, pacing from the witness stand to the jury box, pausing now and then to turn and point a red-tipped finger at him. "This is the man!" she declared dramatically, wagging a talon at his face as if accusing him of... what? Murder, rape, mayhem? All eyes followed that accusing finger, fastening on Jonathan in harsh judgment. Pens scratched and the eyes of the artists shuttled from his face to their pads and back again. Was there enough innocence in the world to withstand such scrutiny, or was any man lost who received such a look, questioning all that he was?

Unprincipled, she called him. She called him worse things, invectives far more stringent than the relatively mild "unprincipled," but none of them hurt as much. Jonathan prided himself on being a man of strict principle.

The interpretations of his principles had evolved over the years, as was only natural; but to the principles themselves he had steadfastly adhered, and at no small cost to himself. He was proud of the job he'd done, the balance he'd struck between public duty and private obligation. Of course, from time to time he'd been forced to compromise; that was the nature of politics. The important thing was that he had nothing to be ashamed of. Circumstances change, needs change. At twenty-five, Jonathan had needed nothing that could not be carried in a rucksack; now he needed rather more.

Did that justify Buscaglio's calling him, as she did, "a greedy, luxurious man"? And looking at him with a contempt that reminded Jonathan of the looks on the faces of the whites who had lined the streets of Birmingham screaming, "Niggers! Coons! Commie kike bastards!" as the civil-rights demonstrators marched by.

That look cut through Jonathan's fog like a bullhorn. The odd lethargy that had come over him the moment he entered the courtroom fell away, and he started to rise; but Christopher Leeds's fingers tightened on his arm. He murmured, "Don't let her get to you."

Jonathan sat back and glowered at Buscaglio, who taunted him. "Venal," she dared call him; but to accuse Jonathan Fleishman of venality was to rob the word of meaning. Buscaglio knew, they all knew, that what he earned in the public sector was a fraction of what he could have made in the private. Even in his present position, he could have grown rich ten times over if he'd made that his priority. Instead he'd turned down countless opportunities on ethical grounds. Jonathan knew, however, that this defense, the true one, was useless. Like his wife, the law gave no credit for temptations resisted.

He leaned back in his chair and rubbed his eyes. Buscaglio's ferret face, her red mouth and nails, faded from view. When he opened his eyes, he was back in his study. His glance fell upon the framed family photograph that stood on his desk. A beautiful portrait, marred by Gracie's patented I-know-what-I-know look. Jonathan looked her in the eye. "I know who I am," he said, and immediately felt stupid for talking to a picture; but who else was there to talk to? Michael was gone.

She answered back, perverse, unreasonable child: *You know who you* were.

He said: Do I have to give up everything? Does choosing public service mean taking a vow of poverty? I never said I was bucking for sainthood. All I wanted was to lead a decent life, do some good, and provide for my family. And haven't I done it?

You went too far.

Yeah, well, let me tell you something, sweetheart. In the real world, money counts. It buys education. It buys opportunity; and if it doesn't buy good health, it sure as hell buys good health care.

Money isn't everything.

Try living without it. And why *should* I deny my talent for making money? I never sought it; it came to me. I happen to possess the ability to see clearly into the heart of a business, to gauge its soundness: financial dowsing, you might call it. I don't need books, I don't need accountants. I'm like one of those witch doctors who operate on the heart without opening the patient's chest. And why not? In this world some men are born with money, others with good looks. I have a small gift; is it fair, is it reasonable to ask me to renounce it? Do we ask judges to put out their eyes, that justice may be blind? Do we demand that doctors catch their patients' diseases?

It's not the same.

It's exactly the same. Go away, Gracie. Leave me alone.

When word got out that Roger Hasselforth was buying, Maxie's was mobbed. Not only *Probe* staffers but also reporters from the *Voice* and the tabloids gathered to celebrate Barnaby's coup by drinking Roger's booze.

At the epicenter of the milling crowd stood Barnaby, pleasantly drunk, his arms around two nubile young (but not too young) copy-girls as he argued amicably with Jack Flora. Barnaby had no time to cultivate deep friendships, but he had plenty of the collegial variety, spiced by rivalry. Jack Flora, formerly of the *Probe* but now an editor at the *Post,* was his oldest and closest friend of that species. Flora, sucking on his pipe, was saying, "A week's a lifetime, man. You try filing daily and see how much investigation you get done."

"Excuses, excuses," Barnaby said.

"Besides, far be it from me to denigrate your work, my friend, but it's not like you carried the tablets down from Mount Sinai.

For a long time everyone but you knew Fleishman was corrupt; the man left fucking dinosaur tracks."

"So how come no one ever followed them?"

"Fleishman was mentioned in dozens of *Post* stories just this past year."

"Mentioned." Barnaby sneered. "Why didn't you really go after him? Oh, excuse me; you were busy tracking down nasty restaurant inspectors who take fifty-dollar bribes."

Flora's reply was cut off by the rhythmic tapping of a spoon against a glass. Standing beside the bar (tended for the occasion by Max Horowitz himself), the *Probe's* editor-in-chief raised his glass. "Ladies and gentlemen, I propose a toast to my respected colleague Barnaby, whose relentless quest to rid this city of its parasites has resulted in today's arraignment of Jonathan Fleishman."

"Hear, hear," cried Ronnie Neidelman, plastered in a corner.

"Many of you know that Barnaby and I have had occasional little set-tos." Roger paused for effect. "All right, occasional knockdown, drag-out brawls. This is due to no shortcoming on my part, but rather to the stubborn, intransigent, obsessive personality of my reporter."

Laughter and catcalls rippled through the room. Barnaby bowed. Roger continued:

"Paradoxically, ladies, gentlemen, and members of the press, the very qualities that make Barnaby such a despicable human being also make him a superb reporter. This is a sobering thought, and I hope that those of you who are driving home will bear it in mind as you start your cars. Barnaby is the pit bull of reporters, a journalistic piranha, if you'll excuse the mixed metaphor." Barnaby raised his hands in modest protest, but Roger went on. "He is the last man I'd want on my trail if I had something to hide. Champion of the weak, defender of the oppressed, nemesis of the corrupt—"

"Hang on, Roger, wasn't that supposed to be *bane* of the corrupt?"

"I think 'nemesis' is better. You see what I have to put up with, people? The man cannot take editing." The room reverberated with lubricated laughter. "Let us raise our glasses," Roger concluded, "and drink to the health of Brother Barnaby."

They drank. Several people shouted, "Speech! Speech!" but

they were outnumbered by others who yelled, "Forget the speech, bring on the booze!"

Barnaby raised his arms, and silence fell. "Friends, Romans, countrymen, lend me your ears. We have gathered here, not to bury Fleishman, but to praise Barnaby. Before the revelries begin, however, let us take a moment to reflect. To quote the great American philosopher Pogo, 'We have met the enemy, and he is us.' If there is one lesson to be learned from this miserable Fleishman affair, it is that we can take no one and nothing for granted. We must scrutinize our friends with the same critical eye we turn on our enemies, ever alert for the telltale signs of hypocrisy."

"How about scrutinizing yourself?" Ronnie heckled from her seat in the corner.

He raised his voice to drown her out. "Let us drink to the memory of a man once respected and loved by us all, a man, once, of valor and principle, King Arthur in the court of progressive politics. His prospects were bright and nearly unlimited. When a man falls from such a height into the pit of corruption, it is a tragedy in which we all share."

"You would know about corruption, wouldn't you, Barnaby?" This new voice, clear and young, came from the back of the crowd. Heads turned. As the speaker walked forward, a path formed, and a low buzz spread through the room as those who recognized the Fleishman daughter enlightened those who hadn't. She wore a simple white dress and sandals. With her bare legs, flawless olive skin, and black hair, she looked like a teenage Pocahontas. Gracie stopped an arm's length away from Barnaby.

"Wh-what are you doing here?" he stammered. "Max, this kid's underage."

"That's not what you said two weeks ago," she said in a clear, carrying voice. "I was old enough then."

The only sound in the tavern was the swish of Max's broom as he swept around the edges of the crowd. Barnaby reset his dial to paternal solicitude. "Gracie, please, I realize you're upset about your father's problems, but you've got no business here."

"But our affair had nothing to do with my father. Isn't that what you said when you made love to me, when you tricked me into talking about him?"

A collective gasp rose from the audience. Roger Hasselforth slumped onto a bar stool and covered his eyes.

"It's not true," Barnaby said, looking from face to face. "It's obvious she's lying. She's crying rape to try and discredit me. Come on, people; the same thing could happen to you tomorrow."

"I'm not crying rape," Gracie said calmly. "I admit I consented. Of course, it wasn't exactly informed consent, was it? You did tell me you loved me. You did swear you weren't investigating my father. I admit I was stupid to believe you, but I thought there were rules."

Rage puffed out his cheeks and filled his belly with wind. "This is absurd. This is madness. No one's buying this. You're making a fool of yourself."

"I *was* a fool. I thought journalists had some sort of ethical code. I didn't realize you could lie to people, seduce them into telling you things. My father warned me, but I knew better. 'Barnaby's an honorable man,' I said. And then, after you got what you wanted, you dumped me. Not a call, not a note, not even a card for my eighteenth birthday."

"You were eighteen when I—" He broke off abruptly.

"When you screwed me? You know that because you checked, didn't you?"

Ronnie Neidelman hooted. "She got you good!"

Barnaby was turning purple. He sought a sympathetic face in the crowd, but settled for a familiar one. "She's making this up," he appealed to Jack Flora. "Who're you gonna believe, me or her?"

"How's that cute little tattoo on your ass, Barnaby?" Gracie asked. "The anchor that sways as you walk?"

"Do you have a cute little tattoo on your ass?" Flora asked, filling his pipe.

"You expect me to drop trou to refute her? Fuck that!"

But a chorus of female voices had already arisen from the crowd of spectators: "He does, he does!"

"So it's common knowledge," Barnaby said, pivoting on a dime. "Anyone could have told her, and I know who I'd bet on. This is all you, Neidelman. This has spiteful bitch written all over it. What is it you want, Gracie?"

"An apology would be nice," Gracie said. "But I'll settle for the truth."

"The truth? I'll tell you the truth. Whatever you claim I did to you is nothing compared to what your father did to this city. And I'll tell you something else: I sleep real good at night, because ridding this city of a cancer like your old man matters a hell of a lot more than hurting the pride of some poor little rich girl."

"My father is not guilty. But even if he'd done everything you've accused him of doing, he'd still be ten times the man you are." Gracie grabbed a stein of beer from the table beside her and threw it at Barnaby's face, the stein as well as the beer. It hit his already swollen nose, which immediately began streaming blood. He doubled over, hands to his face, blood and beer dripping from his fingers.

Gracie drank in the sight for a moment; then she turned and headed for the exit, moving, for once, as her mother and countless dance instructors had despaired of teaching her: shoulders squared, head erect, eyes forward. Inside, all was tumult, but something deeper than these emotions, a long-dormant sense of self, perhaps, of authority, stirred and woke within her. Like a pin through shattered bone, it held her upright as she walked out of Maxie's.

The bartender wrapped some ice in a dish towel and tossed it to Barnaby, who pressed it gingerly to his nose. No one moved to help him. He looked around the room and saw judgment on every face. "What the fuck? You know that was total bullshit."

Nobody answered. Max went back to sweeping the floor, his face sour, ignoring Barnaby even as he swept between his feet.

"Thanks for the vote of fucking confidence!" Barnaby said disgustedly. "Fine bunch of colleagues you are. I tell you, I never screwed the girl. Tell them, Roger."

The editor turned away and signaled for the check.

"Fuck you, you jealous bastard. Jack, you believe me, don't you?"

Jack Flora took his time, tamping down his pipe and relighting it. "I hope it was the fuck of a lifetime, buddy," he said at last, "because she's sure as hell screwed you."

Barnaby smacked his own forehead. "I can't believe this holier-than-thou bullshit attitude! How many times have you cozied up to sources to develop information? We all do it."

"We don't all sleep with sources," Jack said. "We don't all fuck little girls."

18

GRACIE LET HERSELF IN QUIETLY, tiptoeing past the living room, but her father must have heard the car pull up. "Gracie!" he thundered through the closed oak door. She drew a deep breath before entering. Her father sat in a leather club chair beside the fireplace, a closed book and a half-full tumbler of amber liquid beside him. Despite the hour, he was fully dressed. As she approached, he looked her over anxiously, head to toe. "Where the hell have you been?"

"The city," she said.

"Why did you sneak off like that? Your mother was worried sick."

"I was afraid you'd stop me."

"Stop you? Am I a tidal wave, am I an act of God? Stop *you?*"

"Is that Gracie?" Lily said, entering the room. She wore a nightgown and robe but looked naked to Gracie, who rarely saw her mother without makeup.

"It's me."

"Gracie, where have you been?"

"At Maxie's."

"Who's Maxie?" they said in unison.

"What, not who. It's a bar in the Village."

"A bar?" said Lily. "On this night, of all others?"

Her father said, "Come on, Gracie, spit it out. We're not playing Twenty Questions."

She sighed. "It's where Barnaby hangs out. He was there with a bunch of his friends, celebrating."

Lily sank onto a sofa, dreading in the deepest part of her

being what Gracie would say next, not because she knew what it was, but because she had no idea. It could be anything. There were no limits left in the world, which teemed with a multitude of malevolent possibilities, as if the air had suddenly grown both visible and poisonous. "Careful, Gracie," she murmured helplessly; for when had Gracie ever been careful? Lily always laughed when young mothers moaned "Boys!" in boastful complaint. When her children were babies, Paul was the cautious one, slow to walk, frightened of dogs, cats, even ants, wary of the unknown, always clinging to his mother's skirts. It was Gracie who ran about with her knees raw and her little body covered with bumps and bruises, Gracie whose overall pockets had to be cautiously turned out, Gracie who got into fistfights and broke her arm playing Superman.

"What have you done?" demanded Jonathan.

"I told the truth. I said he seduced me to get at you."

Lily pressed her cheeks with the palms of her hands. "In front of a roomful of reporters? How could you, Gracie?"

"I figured it would hurt him more than it did me," Gracie said. "I was right."

"What did Barnaby say?" her father asked.

"He said it wasn't true, but I proved it."

"How?" He held up a hand before she could answer. "Never mind, I don't want to know. What else?"

"I threw a drink at him."

Despite himself, Jonathan smiled.

"A beer stein, actually," Gracie went on, encouraged. "Got him in the nose. It bled like crazy, but I think it was already broken."

The smile faded. "Jesus, Gracie, that's assault! You could be arrested for that."

"*You* weren't."

"What does she mean?" Lily said. "Jonathan, could she really be arrested?"

"Don't worry," Gracie said. "The last thing Barnaby wants is for this to go further."

"How about all the other reporters in the bar? The prosecutors are bound to hear about it. They could charge you as leverage against me." Her father got up and began pacing the room. Two circuits, then he came to a halt in front of Gracie. "There's only one thing to do. You'll have to go away for a while."

She gasped. "Go where?"

"I don't know yet. Israel, maybe, to your aunt."

"No! Put it out of your head. I'm not leaving."

"You have to, for both our sakes."

"I can't. You don't understand. It would be like I took a swing at Barnaby and then ran away."

"I do understand. But I can't take the risk they'll come after you."

"I thought you'd be mad. I thought you'd yell at me. I never thought you'd throw me away."

"I'm not throwing you away! It's just for a little while, Gracie, till I know you're safe."

"I'm not a rat," she cried. "I'm not deserting you."

He looked at her dark, intense face and saw as if in a mirror his own anger, pride, love. He thought: Gracie is my golem child. The best thing I ever made, and she's going to destroy me. He pictured her bearing down on Barnaby in her avenging Fury mode, and almost found it in his heart to pity the poor bastard. Jonathan knew the look she'd have worn; he'd seen it before, on a summer night nine years ago, before they left Martindale. On his way home from work, Jonathan had come upon a fistfight on his own street corner, two youngsters duking it out in the middle of a knot of cheering kids. He got out of his car and pushed through to the center. The combatants were unevenly matched, but the smaller one was giving as good as he got. It wasn't until he yanked them apart and the little one's Yankee cap fell off that Jonathan recognized his daughter.

"What's this?" he said, tightening his grip on the other kid's arm.

The boy sniveled and wiped his nose with the back of his hand, leaving a red, mucusy streak across his cheek. "She hit me first."

Gracie gave the kid a look that would have been funny on her little face if it hadn't been so genuinely menacing. "He called Mrs. Brand a nigger," she told her father. "When I told him he's a moron, he called me a nigger-lover."

"Well, you are," the boy taunted, braver at arm's length. "You love your teacher, and she's a nigger."

Jonathan let Gracie go but kept hold of the boy. "What's your name?"

"Kyle."

"Kyle what?"

"Kyle Hatwater."

"Your parents know the kind of language you use, Kyle Hatwater?"

"Where d'ya think I learnt it?" the boy snarled. With a sudden twist he wriggled free and escaped down the block.

Jonathan took Gracie home. She had the start of a black eye and a shallow but bloody cut on her forehead. Her knuckles were bruised, too. They must have been at it for a while before he got there. He sat her down at the kitchen table and tended to her wounds, icing the eye and cleaning the cut. Gracie didn't make a sound, though it must have hurt.

"Where'd you learn to fight like a boy?" he asked her.

She frowned. "I wasn't fighting like a boy; I was fighting like someone who meant to win."

"Fine; now that you've corrected the question, answer it."

"The hard way."

It took him a moment to understand. "This has happened before? You've been in fights?"

"A few," she said modestly.

"Why, Gracie?"

"Because they're idiots and bullies, like that jerk Kyle. And I stand up for what I believe in, just like you."

"It's good to stand up for your beliefs," Jonathan said, "but fistfights don't prove anything except who's stronger."

"That's *something.*"

"You have to reason with people."

"They can't all be reasoned with. You said so yourself."

"At least pick your fights. That kid had six inches and twenty pounds on you."

"I was winning when you stopped it."

"That's not the point, Gracie."

"What other point is there? Anyway, I knew he was chicken. He's bigger and stronger than me, but he can't take a punch."

"And you can?"

"I don't like it, but I can. You have to, if you want to win. I'm not a quitter."

Jonathan was silenced, for it was from this very knowledge that he'd worked so hard to protect her. How strange: Martindale was a world away from Brooklyn, yet somehow his daughter had ended up learning the same hard lessons Jonathan had learned as a boy.

Just as well that she had, he thought now. At least she still knew how to take a hit, whereas Barnaby, like that schoolboy bully, could dish it out but couldn't take it.

As he gazed into that dear, infuriating face that was both itself and the reflection of his own secret, integral self, Jonathan felt the last vestige of bitterness remaining in his heart melt away. He put his hands on Gracie's shoulders. "No one would ever call you a quitter. I admire your courage, I admire your heart—but it makes no difference."

"Dad, you can't send me away. Don't you know I'm on your side?"

"I do know."

"If you let me stay, I swear I'll keep my big mouth shut."

"You don't know how long I've waited to hear you say that. And yet now that you have, I find it's the last thing on earth I want."

"I mean it. You need me here." Gracie hugged him, pressed her head against his chest. "Please don't send me away."

His arms flew apart in surprise, then closed around her. As he pressed his daughter to his heart for the first time in years, Jonathan felt his suffering merge with hers, so that the pain of each was heightened, but also, mysteriously, solaced. He kissed the crown of her head and at that moment awoke to the full magnitude of his loss: it came to him that if he sent her away now, it would be forever. Gracie would never forgive him for humiliating her twice in the same manner, fhis was not a new wound, but the rupture of an old one that never healed right. When Gracie discovered that he had sold their Martindale house, Jonathan had tried to make her see the matter rationally; but his daughter, so quick to grasp the dynamics of politics, proved quite uneducable on the subject of economics in general and real estate in particular. "Selling out," she'd chanted, "selling out, selling out, selling out," until he could not bear the sound of the words.

She fought him until she understood that her passionate opposition was no equal to the sheer weight of parental authority Jonathan wielded in the wake of persuasion. Then she quit and plunged into a period of mourning: tore her clothes, locked herself in her room, quit eating. When she emerged from hibernation, Gracie was a changed child, her wild-eyed spunk replaced by watchful reserve, not only in the house but also out of it.

It broke his heart. Jonathan tried to blame their rift on her intransigence and willful misapprehension, but he knew that in her place he would have felt as she did, betrayed and abused. Now, once again, he was plucking her prematurely from the fray, this time even sending her away.

"It's not punishment." He cupped her face, gazed into eyes that blinked furiously, fighting back tears. "I love you, Gracie. I'm trying to protect you."

She backed away from him. "The worst things you do, you say you do for us."

"Maybe so," he said. "But this isn't one of them."

All through the night, Jonathan and Lily lay side by side, thinking and worrying separately about Gracie. Lily was afflicted by an unshakable sense of vicarious déjà vu, reliving an experience that belonged, not to her, but to her mother, and perhaps her mother's mother.... An innocent might attribute Jonathan's persecution to rivalry, jealousy, or changing political mores; but Lily's history proscribed innocence. Anti-Semitism was a many-headed hydra. *They* wouldn't stop with Jonathan. *They* would come for her and the children next.

At last her mother's purpose was revealed. Greta had returned to warn her, remind her that what happened before was bound to happen again, because the world hated Jews, always had, and always would. Save the children, her mother's ghost commanded. When Lily shut her eyes, a memory came, vivid as a dream. She was lying in her girlhood bed, listening as her mother read from a book of Bible stories the story of baby Moses. The volume was illustrated, and one picture, Lily's favorite, showed the pharaoh's daughter and a handmaiden kneeling beside the river, reaching toward a drifting cradle woven of bulrushes, while the infant's mother watched from a hiding place. Pharaoh's daughter plucked baby Moses from the river, Greta said, and raised him as her own son. As she read, she wept, and her sighs were like the rumbling of the el trains that passed outside Lily's window.

Lily watched and wondered why, but did not ask. Surely the story of Moses was a tale of triumph, in which a simple Jewess tricked the mighty pharaoh into fostering a child who would become his nemesis and the savior of the Jewish people. Only now, forty years later, as Lily prepared to set her own child adrift, did she understand what Greta had always known: that salvation comes only through sacrifice of the heart's deepest bonds.

She sighed again and again. Jonathan heard her but said

nothing, only reached out and stroked her back. When she turned toward him, he kissed her, first tentatively, then more urgently. Silently they made love. When talking was too dangerous, sex became the last channel of communication and solace.

But even as he kissed his wife, a small nagging voice inside Jonathan was calculating what it would cost to defend Gracie if Barnaby pressed charges. He wasn't afraid they would lose the case—she had been too cruelly and blatantly abused by Barnaby. But innocence, he well knew, availed nothing without money; and good counsel and expert witnesses were punitively expensive. And there were other costs, greater costs. How could Gracie endure the press scrutiny that was sure to come? While she was just his daughter, they'd left her alone and focused on him. Now that she'd made herself part of the story, they would have no such mercy.

The phone calls started before seven A. M. and stopped when Jonathan took the phone off the hook. He listened to the messages: all reporters, all asking for Grace.

At 9:00, the family gathered around the breakfast table. Clara had made pancakes, but only Paul could eat. He wore tennis whites; his racket was on the sideboard.

"After breakfast," Jonathan said to his daughter, "you're to go and pack. We've already spoken to your aunt. Your flight leaves today."

She put down her cup and stared at him, but didn't answer.

"What?" said Clara. "What did you say?"

He raised his voice. "Gracie's going to Israel."

"Since when?" Paul demanded. "Not that I mind."

"Since your father and I decided," Lily said, "that she's better off away from here."

"And I'm not?"

"Why? Do you want to go to Israel, too?"

"No, but a bunch of my friends are putting together a trip to the Bahamas."

No one bothered to answer him.

"She's your daughter," Clara appealed to Lily, "and you know I'm not one to interfere, but this is not a child you send to Israel. Learn from my mistake. I lost my daughter to Israel."

Jonathan shared her fear. Love was a binding force, but not

a strong one. Gracie was no homing pigeon. Set free, she might very well fly away, never to return. And yet the thing had to be done. To save her, he had to let her go.

"In Israel," Lily said, "she'll be safe."

Gracie spoke at last. "Would anyone care to hear my opinion?"

No one did. They went on talking over her head, discussing her, until she scraped her chair back loudly and rose to her feet. Then they stopped talking and looked at her.

"Israel's out of the question," she said. "I'm not going, and you can't make me."

19

JUST UNDER TWENTY-FOUR HOURS later, Gracie Fleishman walked down the steps of an El A1 plane into a torrid blaze of sun that fused her senses. The great heat, undulating off the ground and ricocheting off the metal surfaces of the planes, made people standing nearby seem to shimmer; others, at a distance, appeared and disintegrated like phantoms. The heat invaded her body and pressed down on the top of her skull, filled her nostrils with a mix of burning dust and jet fuel, parched the roof of her mouth, and coated her tongue in acrid dust.

Gracie looked up into a cloudless sky of palest blue that was higher than any sky she'd ever seen before. In the space between earth and sky, a hawk soared, riding the air currents like spiraling escalators to heaven. All around her the runways bustled with activity; military jeeps darted about the runways, and soldiers, male and female, toted rifles and submachine guns as if they were loaves of Italian bread.

She lifted her loose mane of hair and lowered her head, but the sere wind lapped at her nape with a tongue like a branding iron.

Her fellow passengers hurried toward the glass doors of the terminal, fifty feet away. She began, slowly, to follow.

A man approached from within the heat mist, his eyes fixed on her face. When his features jelled, Gracie found herself looking at one of the best-looking men she had ever seen. He had a head of black curls, almond skin, high cheekbones, and a strong cleft chin; he was lean and sinuous, and though he wore an army uniform, his bearing was more feline than martial.

She recognized him at once, though Clara's treasured snapshots didn't do him justice. He came up to her and stopped, looking her up and down critically.

"Tamar couldn't make it. Welcome to Israel." No smile. Tone polite, handshake cold.

"Thanks," she answered in the same manner.

"I'm Micha."

"I know."

He reached for her bag. "I'll take that."

"I can manage."

He shrugged and let her.

Inside the terminal, passengers from Gracie's plane and another that had arrived minutes before waited in long lines at passport control, but Micha led her to a small office on one side of the entrance hall. The young officer sitting behind the desk jumped up, shook Micha's hand. They spoke in Hebrew; then the officer extended his palm toward Gracie. "Passport, please."

She handed it over. The officer flicked it open. He looked from the passport photo to her face and lingered there. "Very nice," he said. "So, this guy's your cousin, eh? Very bad. Big trouble, Micha."

"I'm used to trouble," she said in a Lauren Bacall drawl. The officer laughed all out of proportion, but Micha, whose strong, silent act was beginning to irritate Grace, gave her a noncommittal stare. He had removed his sunglasses; his eyes were a startling indigo blue.

The officer stamped her passport and returned it. "See you again, I hope," he said to Grace, and he waved them through a door that led directly into the baggage-retrieval area.

"Now we wait," Micha said.

"Wait for what?"

"Your bags."

"I don't have any."

"No bags?"

"Just this." She indicated her carry-on.

"You travel light."

"I don't plan on staying long."

Sliding doors led outside. Something about the height of the sky made Gracie want to duck. Several men rushed her, shouting, "Taxi! Taxi!", subsiding into silence when they noticed Micha.

He led her to a white Peugeot parked in a no-parking zone at the terminal's curb.

"Good connections, huh?" Gracie said.

He glanced at her out of the corner of his eye but did not reply. He hadn't, she thought, much to say for himself at all. No questions about the flight, no inquiries about the family. Clearly her cousin was no more thrilled to have her there than she was to be there.

"Look," she said as they sped down a cypress-lined avenue toward the airport gates, "you might as well know this wasn't my idea."

"I'm devastated."

"Just because I happen to be a Jew doesn't mean I'm a Zionist. I think what you people are doing to the Palestinians is disgusting."

His mouth twitched. "Very perceptive, considering you've been here all of ten minutes."

So he had a tongue after all, a sly, sarcastic tongue. "I watch the news. I read. I'm not totally ignorant."

"Oh, well, then."

Smug, self-satisfied, and conceited, Grace diagnosed, unsurprised. Her cousin was too handsome for his own good. "What are you, anyway?" she said.

"You mean my sign?" he mocked her.

"I mean your rank."

"I'm a captain."

Gracie didn't know whether or not to believe him. "Then why didn't that guy in the customs office salute you?"

He raised an eyebrow. "We both know who I am."

"Aren't you kind of young to be a captain?" she asked severely.

"Israelis age faster than Americans. I know American men my age and older who still call themselves kids."

"Whereas you are a man."

"I am a man," he agreed.

"It must be great to be so sure of yourself."

"It's an easy thing to be sure of," he said with a laugh. Gracie turned away, annoyed at herself for arguing with him, and stared out the window. They were driving through a small dusty village in which all the street signs, shop signs, billboards, even the graffiti, were in Hebrew. This astonished Gracie, who knew that Hebrew was the national language but had imagined somehow that this was just for show, that in the privacy of their own country, Israelis secretly spoke English with a Yiddish accent. Some of the street signs had oddly spelled English translations beneath the Hebrew lettering.

They came to a major intersection, where an arrow to the left indicated Tel Aviv, an arrow to the right, Jerusalem. Micha turned right.

"We're going to Jerusalem?"

"Through it, on the way to Ein Gedi."

Grace rested her head on the cool glass, staring out at the countryside. Her eyes felt gritty and her head ached. She'd sat up for most of the twelve-hour flight, and when she finally fell asleep, had been awakened, it seemed minutes later, by an otherworldly chanting: a group of black-frocked men with wide-brimmed hats praying in the back of the plane.

Outside, the sky was ashen and the land lay flat on its side, like a parched yellow dog waiting for the rains. They passed scattered orchards and irrigated fields, verdant outbreaks on the arid face of the earth that nevertheless had not the same hectic greenness as the trees in Lily's garden, but tended rather toward olive or yellow tones, as if their roots had sucked up the essential color of the earth.

Gradually the land about them grew hilly. They entered into a wide valley dominated by what looked like an ancient fortress surrounded by vineyards and groves of olive trees. "The monastery of Latroun," Micha announced in a dutiful manner. "The bloodiest battle of the War of Independence was fought here."

Beyond the valley the road rose steeply, threading through pale stony hills covered with pines that seemed to grow out of bare rock. Micha cut the air conditioner and opened the windows, and the scent of mountain pine wafted into the car. On the right shoulder they passed a red-rusted ruin of an armored vehicle, then another on the left. Relics, Micha said tersely, of the War of Independence, left to rust as memorials to the men and women who died breaking the siege of Jerusalem. Grace, who had never heard of the siege of Jerusalem but didn't care to ask, glanced upward at the sheer cliffs surrounding the road. If the enemy had ambushed convoys from up there, it was a miracle that anyone had gotten through.

The road took a sudden turn, and suddenly Gracie saw before her a city of shimmering gold, crowning the hills like a celestial oasis. She gasped. Micha glanced over. A slow, sweet smile transformed his face. "Jerusalem," he said.

The illusion of golden light did not dispel as they entered the city, but rather intensified. All the buildings were built of the same pale stone that made up the surrounding hillsides; under the intense midmorning sun, they glowed with a lustrous sheen. The air was hot and dry and mountain-sweet, the light possessed of a clarity that made Grace feel as if she'd lived all her life underwater and never known it till now.

Micha drove to Zion Square, the heart of the city, throbbing with an astonishing and one would think unstable variety of people. Hasidim in black and striped caftans rubbed elbows with Bermuda shorts-clad tourists, bare-legged young Sabras, soldiers, Arab men in keffiyahs and dusty gray suits, peasant women in Bedouin dress, portly matrons arm in arm, schoolchildren in cotton shorts and blouses, gesticulating merchants in shirt sleeves, made up a kind of human crazy quilt.

Micha pulled up in front of a clothing store on Jaffa Street whose jumbled wares spilled out onto the pavement. Without a word, he left the car idling and dashed inside, emerging minutes later with a plastic bag and a wide-brimmed straw hat. "Try this," he ordered Grace, passing the hat through her window.

"I don't need a hat."

"Put it on."

Glaring, she put it on her head. It fitted snugly. Micha nodded approval and got back into the car.

"How much was this thing?" Gracie said.

"Don't worry about it."

"Thanks, but I don't need you to buy me stuff. Especially stuff I didn't need to begin with."

"If you're going to be any use at all," he said in a tone of grave doubt, "you have to acclimate yourself. This isn't New York. One hour, two at most, in the sun without a hat, you've got sunstroke." He tossed her the plastic bag. Gracie opened it and found a metal canteen encased in green burlap, with an adjustable shoulder strap. "Rule number two," Micha said. "Never go out without a full canteen. I bet you didn't even bring one."

"There was hardly time to pack, they hustled me out so fast."

"Why? What did you do?"

"None of your business."

They had left the commercial center of Jerusalem and were

now approaching the Old City, whose massive fortress walls seemed to stretch out in all directions. There were turrets atop the perimeter wall, and apparently an inner rampart, because people were peering over the top. Minarets, church steeples, and terraced rooftops rose within the walled city, and a silver dome sparkled in the sun. From the outside the Old City looked vast; Grace was ashamed of the miniaturized, Disneyesque conception that had been her expectation. She'd had it all wrong. Though overwhelmingly strange, Jerusalem was real, solid, rooted not only in place but also in time. One could tell just by looking that the walls of the Old City extended below the ground as well as above it, as if the portion above the ground were merely a reflection of the portion below. Old lessons from Sunday school, long forgotten, came back to her: during three thousand years of continuous occupation, usually as the locus of armed struggle, the city had been borne aloft on the tide of history—razed and rebuilt, conquered and reconquered countless times, but never abandoned.

They turned left at Jaffa Gate and drove parallel to the wall until they reached the Damascus Gate, where Gracie shouted, "Stop the car!" so urgently that Micha veered sideward and slammed on the brakes.

"What is it?"

"I want to go in there, inside the walls."

"No way." He reached toward the ignition, but Gracie caught his wrist in a grip that awakened his respect.

"It's important," she said.

"Tamar will take you. If you walk there with me, you are a target."

"I'm not afraid."

"Because you're ignorant."

"You wait here, then. I won't be long." Before he could stop her, she was out of the car.

"Wait!" he shouted. But she ran without looking back. Cursing, Micha grabbed his rifle from the back seat, locked the car and chased after her. Halfway down the sloping path to the gate, he caught up and grabbed her arm. "I heard you were smart, but you're acting stupid."

Gracie felt a rare sense of embarrassment. "It's just so different from what I expected. We don't have to stay long—just a minute, to see inside."

Micha sighed. "Okay," he said. "But you must stay beside me all the time, do what I say, and go only where I go. Agreed?"

"Agreed."

They continued down the slope; Micha kept one hand distrustfully on Gracie's arm, the other on his rifle. The broad plaza in front of the Damascus Gate swarmed with Arabs, Bedouins, tourists, donkeys bearing enormous loads. When they reached the city wall, Gracie obeyed an impulse, mysterious yet compelling: she laid her open palm against the stone. Something that felt like electricity but wasn't passed through the wall into her hand.

She wasn't imagining. She hadn't that sort of imagination, and in any case, her expectations were very different. She'd thought of Israel, dismissively, as a Jewish-American colony, a distillation of the Borscht Belt and the Eden Roc. The Jerusalem of her imaginings was a sum of abstractions—a political problem, a nexus of competing religious visions, the otherworldly focus of a Passover prayer: "Next year in Jerusalem." But when she touched the wall, abstraction became, not flesh, but stone.

She and Micha passed through the Damascus Gate. As if the quality of the light had affected all her senses, Grace seemed to see, hear, and smell with hyper-clarity. One impression did not displace another, but rather piled on, until little room remained for any sense of self. The smell of the souk was utterly strange yet strangely familiar: a piquant blend of roasting meat, tobacco, incense, spice, and dung. Its music was the singsong of vendors and the sibilant, polylingual babble of shopkeepers enticing customers: "Please, miss, come look. *Venez ici, mademoiselle. Ich sprechen sie Deutsch.*"

No one called to Gracie. With Micha, she walked in a pocket of silence and sullen glares.

"This used to be the busiest market in Jerusalem," he said, "but Jews don't shop here anymore."

"Why not?"

"Too many incidents. Stonings. Knifings."

She was quiet for a moment. Then she said, "If you were a Palestinian, what would you be doing?"

He resumed his tour-guide voice: "This is the Via Dolorosa, the Way of Tears. Jesus walked through here, carrying the cross on the way to his crucifixion."

The stone-paved streets, too narrow for cars, were worn to a smooth gloss. Gracie, never prone to mysticism, had to fight off a persistent, illusory sensation that seemed to rise through her feet, a spectral thrumming, a deep vibration like the unseen passage of countless sandaled feet. A distant male chanting reached her ears, and this too seemed illusion, until they turned a corner and came upon a procession of dark-bearded men in black wool cassocks, who held aloft a silver crucifix and chanted as they walked.

"I will take you to one place," Micha said, "and then we must go. I have to return to my base today."

"Where are you based?"

"The West Bank."

Gracie forced herself to hold her tongue, but couldn't control her eyes. Micha dropped her arm.

They turned off the Via Dolorosa and entered a narrow alley lined with small stone houses and shops. Behind the latticed iron gates of the houses, and atop their terraced roofs, Gracie caught glimpses of grape vines, lemon trees, and flaming bougainvillea. Small children, playing in the street, ran into their houses as Micha walked by.

Wherever she looked, her eye touched on nothing that could not have existed in the same form one thousand years ago. Her family, their problems, seemed infinitely remote in time and space. She was lost in both dimensions, her only anchor the stranger beside her.

Their path led through twists and turns. Once they passed a spice shop that illuminated the street with the scent of unlimited possibilities. Beyond, the alley curved sharply and opened up into an unexpected white square. They sat on a stone bench. Gracie looked about, enchanted by its architectural harmony, the pale stone houses that looked more like natural outcroppings than constructs. There was not a soul in sight, nor a voice heard, only the unfamiliar calls of the birds perched in rooftop gardens and a faint strain of Arabic music that wafted over the fragrant square.

"What is this place?" Grace whispered.

"Just a place," Micha said, smiling faintly. "If it has a name, I don't know it."

"It's so peaceful, so lovely. How will I ever find my way back here?"

"Jerusalem is full of beautiful spots. You don't need to come into the Old City. Sometime I'll take you to Ethiopia Street."

"What's there?"

"A convent of African nuns who've been here so long even their church has forgotten them. Every day, at dawn and sunrise, they have services; they sing, and their voices are like manna from heaven."

Suddenly Micha froze. He raised his hand to silence her. Someone was running toward them, down one of the alleys that opened into the square. The clatter of footsteps echoed off the stone houses: impossible to say where it came from. Micha jumped up. Rifle in hand, he spun around. The sound stopped; there was a momentary silence followed by a low whine, a sharp crack. A rock the size of a baseball flew past Gracie's ear.

She wheeled around. In the entrance to the spice alley, a skinny boy of thirteen or fourteen shifted a rock from his left hand to his right and drew it back.

Micha shouted and ran toward him. The boy let the rock fly, not at Micha but at Gracie. She ducked and felt a searing pain race along the top of her head. Then she was on the ground, and blood was dripping onto the stone pavement. Grace touched her scalp and her hand came away bloody.

The boy ran. Micha started to follow, looked back at Gracie, hesitated, and returned. He knelt beside her. "Where are you hurt?"

She touched the crown of her head.

A woman came out of one of the houses bordering the square and slowly approached them. She asked a question in Arabic. Micha answered in her language. She pointed to a doorway and they spoke for some moments.

"Can you walk?" he asked Gracie.

"Of course," she said haughtily. She raised a hand, and he hauled her to her feet. The little square spun around her, and she would have fallen but for his strong left arm. His right, she noticed, remained on the stock of his rifle, and behind the dark glasses his eyes darted about the square.

Across the threshold the light was wonderfully dim, and the temperature dropped twenty degrees. The stone walls of the house must have been two feet thick, more effective than air conditioning. The Arab woman led them into her kitchen and seated Grace beside a primitive sink. Beneath her shapeless dress she was thin to the point of gauntness and her face was deeply lined, but Gracie perceived that she was younger than she'd thought, no more than thirty.

Her cousin disappeared. They heard him moving quickly through the rest of the house, opening and closing doors. Gracie lowered her eyes in shame, but the woman seemed to accept the intrusion as a matter of course. She soaked a clean white towel in cold water and began sponging blood off Gracie's face and head. Micha came back into the kitchen. Gracie said at once, "Why did you search her home?"

He didn't reply, but came close and examined the gash on her scalp. His face was stern. "Superficial," he said. "But close enough. A centimeter lower and I'd have been in big trouble with Tamar."

"I asked you a question."

"Do you want to go to hospital?"

"Of course not."

"Then I'll just clean that up a bit and we'll go on to Ein Gedi. Tamar can deal with it there."

It hurt but she didn't make a sound as he washed the cut and poured something over it. When he finished, the woman gave her glass of water. Gracie remembered Clara's last words at the airport. "Don't drink the water. And don't take anything from the Arabs." Though faintly brackish, the water was very cold and refreshing. She drank it all.

"You'll feel a slight burning and then no pain. Try not to move. Good girl. Micha, how could you be so stupid? Taking her with you into the Old City—you might as well have painted a bull's-eye on her back."

"Sorry, *Ema*." Micha stood awkwardly in a corner, a large man growing smaller by the moment.

"What next? A stroll through Hebron, a picnic in Gaza?" Tamar snorted, unappeased. Meanwhile her deft hands probed and parted, snipped and cleaned with the autonomous competence of long practice. "He must have got you with a flat edge," she informed Grace. "It's a deep scrape and it's still oozing a little, but there's no puncture and I doubt the impact was enough for a concussion. If we can just keep it from getting infected..." She pulled down the overhead lamp and peered closely. "What did you put on this?"

Micha answered in Hebrew.

His mother grunted. "He's a fair medic, I'll say that for him. But stupid, very stupid."

Grace opened her eyes and squinted upward into her aunt's bright little monkey face, framed by a cap of dark hair. "It wasn't his fault," she said. "I made him go."

Tamar hooted. "Did you put a gun to his head?"

"Not quite."

"Then it was his fault. Wasn't it, Micha?"

He sighed. "Yes, Tamar. It was my fault."

Later, after dark, Micha and Tamar walked to his car; actually it was the army's car, but he had the use of it. He was quiet, brooding.

"Must you go back tonight?" she asked.

"Yes." He used to love going back to the army after leave, used to feel like a sea lion slipping back into the sea. But lately the water had tasted bitter; the sea was polluted. He would fight for his country anywhere, but he hated playing cop.

"So," said his mother, "what did you think of the girl?"

"Not quite as bad as I expected."

"God knows what you expected."

"The female equivalent of Paul."

"Not much like the brother, is she?"

"Not much. I'll say this for her: she didn't whine when she got hurt."

"Didn't snivel when I patched her, either." Tamar looked so satisfied at this that Micha felt a pang of apprehension, almost jealousy. Unlike him, this girl was her own flesh and blood.

"She didn't want to come, you know," he said.

Tamar stopped short. "No, I didn't know."

"Her parents forced her."

"Oh, no. I can't have that. I won't keep her here against her will."

She looked like a kid whose new puppy had just been snatched away. Micha relented. "You'll bring her around. Could be she doesn't have much to go back to."

They'd reached his car, but in unspoken agreement they walked past it to the edge of the parking lot. The kibbutz was set atop a steep hill; at its feet, the Dead Sea glistened darkly. Micha and Tamar gazed downward. Bats darted soundlessly overhead.

"I'm thinking of leaving the army," Micha said.

"I thought you might be."

What would it take, he wondered, to surprise her? He laughed suddenly and kissed the top of her head. "Good luck with your stray cat."

20

LILY WAS CUTTING SALT-SPRAY ROSES for the house when something stung her on the back of the head. She yelped and spun around, but nothing was there. Suddenly there was buzzing all around her, a swarm of invisible bees. She covered her face with her hands and ran toward the house, but the insects flew with her, attacking, stinging. She knew she was going to die. She screamed—and woke, safe in her bed, in East Hampton.

Sunlight streamed through the window. She was alone in a bed soaked with sweat. The buzzing was gone, yet the pain remained. Something's wrong, Lily thought. Something's very wrong. The telephone rang. She grabbed it.

"Hello?"

There was a hollow sound on the line, a slight echo to the caller's voice. "Lily, it's Tamar."

"Tamar. What's wrong?" She struggled to sit up. "Is it Gracie?"

"Gracie's fine. Micha picked her up at the airport this morning. When I left for the hospital, she was sleeping off the trip and Yaacov was pacing the floor like an expectant father."

But Lily had heard something in her voice. "What is it, Tamar?"

"Clara's concerned about you," Tamar said in her blunt fashion.

"About me?"

"I had a letter. She says you've been having severe headaches, that you fainted, and something—I can't quite read this part—about crawling out of a tub?"

"Oh, Lord. I told her, the headaches are just a reaction to what's been going on in our lives. Perfectly natural, under the circumstances. But she gets so fussed."

"She also said that sometimes when she talks to you, you don't seem to hear her. She says it's as if you were sleepwalking while awake."

Lily didn't answer.

"Were you aware of that?" Tamar asked gently. Her voice was calm, interested, not overly concerned.

Lily was weary. The dream was still with her, the pain unabated. Keeping it a secret took a greater effort than she could summon. That she had never felt close to or even comfortable with Jonathan's sister emerged now as an advantage: when she spoke, it was to the doctor in Tamar.

"The headaches are terrible. Frightening. They make me think I'm going to die."

Tamar was silent; then: "What else?"

"My mother visits me."

"Do you see her?"

"No. I hear her. Sometimes I smell her scent. Do you think I'm crazy?"

"No. How long has this been going on?"

"Since the beginning of summer."

"Have you seen your doctor?"

"I didn't care to. I like hearing her voice."

"Have the occurrences increased in frequency?"

"At first there were intervals of a week or more. Lately it's every day, sometimes several times."

"Are they associated, the headaches and your mother's voice? Do they occur together?"

"Sometimes. Not always."

"What does your mother say to you?"

"She doesn't talk. She sings. Nursery songs."

"Songs you remember?"

"Yes, but it's not remembering, it's hearing."

"I understand," Tamar said, and to Lily's relief, she sounded as if she really did, as if hearing one's dead mother sing were nothing out of the ordinary. Lily felt a deep sense of relief, as if she'd been speaking in tongues and had stumbled at last on someone who knew the language. Once started, she held back nothing, but described her symptoms in detail, with a sense of wanton luxuriance. It had been a very long time since she'd held anyone's attention the way she now held Tamar's. Lately, all conversations had centered on Jonathan, with a smattering of Gracie; the rest of the family had faded into the background.

Suddenly Jonathan walked in. Lily fell silent and clutched the phone to her chest with a guilty start. For one dizzying moment, Jonathan imagined she was talking to a lover. "Who is it?" he mouthed.

She brought the phone up to her mouth. "I must go. Thanks so much for calling. Please give Gracie our love."

"Is that Tamar?" Jonathan reached out. "Let me talk to her."

"Don't hang up!" Tamar shouted in her ear.

"'Bye now," Lily warbled, waving Jonathan off.

"Lily, listen." Tamar spoke urgently. "The constellation of symptoms you describe could be caused by a number of things, some of them relatively trivial, some quite serious. Stress alone is definitely not the answer. Do you hear me?"

"Yes."

"You must see someone without delay."

Lily's voice was resolutely social. "We'll talk again soon. Take care, now."

"Is Jonathan there? Put him on."

"I'd rather not. He's got enough on his plate."

"This comes first."

"What the hell is going on?" Jonathan said. He snatched the phone from her hand. "Tamar, it's Jonathan. What's the matter?"

For the next ten minutes he said very little. He paced the room, cradling the phone, time and again casting a baleful look at Lily, who felt as if he were seeing her for the first time in months. He took a pen and pad from his pocket and wrote down a number and a name. After he hung up, he sank into a slipper chair beside the bed and gazed out the window at Paul swimming laps in the pool. Beyond him, the *Water Lily* bobbed on gentle waves. Finally he looked at Lily.

"Why didn't you tell me?"

"I didn't want to worry you. I thought it would go away by itself."

"Bullshit."

"You'd have made me see a doctor."

"Damn right I would have."

She frowned. "I didn't want to. She's *my* mother. You think I wanted some doctor telling me, 'Take two pills and your mother will go away'?"

"You're a mother and a wife. If you didn't care enough about yourself to seek the proper care, at least you had an obligation to me—"

"Pompous, pompous," Lily mocked. "You have no right to talk."

"Didn't it occur to you that something might be wrong?"

"Why shouldn't my mother visit me, goddammit? Yours *lives* with us."

"*My* mother's still alive."

"Alive, dead, what does it matter?"

"Now you're scaring me," he said.

His head was in his hands, a hangdog pose that begged for pity. Poor Jonathan, Lily thought reflexively, but stopped herself. No. It was "Poor Lily" now. For once, the fuss wasn't about Jonathan or Gracie. It was about her. "Would you take my mother from me, too?" she asked.

"Take her from you? Lily, she took herself out of the picture twenty years ago. That's a one-way door. No one comes back."

True, thought Lily, and yet her mother *had* come back.

"And why *too*?" Jonathan continued, with rising indignation. "What have I ever taken from you? All I've ever done is give, give, give, to you and the children."

She rolled her eyes.

"What's that supposed to mean?" he demanded.

"It means we have a son who's spoiled rotten with excess and a daughter who can take nothing from our hands."

He lifted his face to hers and she saw him naked, all his pain exposed. "That's cruel, Lily."

"Life's cruel."

He ran his hands through his hair. "I'm beginning to feel I don't know you."

"It's a beginning."

"I don't know why you're so angry with me. I don't know why you didn't trust me enough to tell me what was happening. We used to tell each other everything."

Lily raised an eyebrow. "Twenty years ago. Besides, I tried to tell you."

"When?"

"A week ago. I came to your study. I told you my head hurt."

He didn't remember. "What did I say?"

"You said, 'Take an aspirin. Take two.'"

"You didn't say enough. I'm not a goddamn mind reader. And there's a hell of a difference between having a headache and—"

"You found me unconscious in the garden. That didn't worry you?"

"You said it was too much sun."

"It probably was."

"Not according to Tamar."

"I don't care how good a doctor she is, she can't diagnose from seven thousand miles away."

"She didn't diagnose anything. All she said was it's got to be checked out, which any idiot—" Jonathan choked to a stop as bitterness flooded his mouth and throat. "What if you're wrong? What if it *is* something serious? How am I supposed to live with that? Damn you, Lily," he cried, torn between a compulsion to fall at her feet and another, just as strong, to beat her with a stick. "How could you do this to me?"

"Tell me," she said, "if you'd found Gracie lying in the dirt, would you have let it go at 'too much sun'?"

They both knew the answer to that. The real question was why she'd asked it. Was she implying that he cared more for his daughter than he did for his wife? Jonathan was beginning to see himself as the hero of a Greek tragedy, a mortal persecuted by a malevolent god. He dared not ask "What next?" for fear his house would come tumbling down about his ears.

"How does everything end up being my fault?" he asked. "You hide your symptoms, then blame me for not discovering them. At work I run a clean shop, I play by the rules, I tolerate no cheating, no shoddiness, no discrimination; and suddenly in mid-game they change the rules and claim I cheated. In my life I never cheated."

"You cheated on me," Lily observed.

Her words tugged on his soaring indignation like an anchor, bringing him up short. Jonathan saw Michael, standing in the locker room with his shirt in tatters and a black bug clinging to his chest like a leech. He saw himself facing Lily with an armful of yellow roses.

"I'm sorry," he said. "I've always been sorry. I never did a dumber thing."

"You know," Lily said, "Martha Kavin was right. I *am* an ostrich."

He sat on the bed beside her and took her hand, which quivered in his like a wounded bird. "You're not yourself. Neither am I. I hardly know who I am anymore. Jonah, maybe, in the belly of the whale. It feels as if my life has risen up and swallowed me. I can't get out. And I keep wondering: Why don't they know me? What have I done that's so terrible? Am I really such a monster?"

"We're neither of us monsters," Lily said, but she didn't sound sure. The phone rang. Jonathan picked it up. "Yes?"

It was Christopher Leed. "Jonathan," he said, "we've got a problem."

21

"CAN THEY DO THAT?" JONATHAN ASKED.

"The short answer is, it's been done and upheld all the way up the line."

"They have no right. There's such a thing as presumption of innocence."

"That statement presumes rather more innocence than I would expect in a fellow attorney," Christopher Leeds said with a smile. "The rationale is that they're not confiscating your assets, they're protecting them."

"I just can't believe it of Lucas."

"I've been expecting it ever since we refused to enter into negotiations. It's the logical next step: they're turning up the heat."

"Is it possible Buscaglio did it on her own? After all, he removed himself from the case."

"No," Leeds said. "As U.S. attorney, he had to sign off on the motion."

Jonathan sighed deeply. Through owlish spectacles Christopher Leeds regarded his client worriedly. Jonathan seemed unusually slow on the uptake today, more than a little distracted. Leeds hoped nothing was wrong at home. So often, in these cases, something was; and not necessarily because the family lacked loyalty. Crises like Jonathan's invariably widened preexisting familial fault lines, precipitating events: a breakup that might have been coming five years down the line accelerates; fledglings leap from the nest on untried wings.

After a while Jonathan asked, "Can you stop them?" and

Leeds replied, "I'm sure as hell going to try," which, though uttered in the mildest of tones, was the first profanity Jonathan had ever heard from his monkish lips. "I said I expected it; I didn't say I condone it. In my book, it's dirty pool."

There was a knock on the door and Leeds's secretary, Rachel Brown, walked in. She was a young black woman, quite beautiful, with whom Jonathan had chatted earlier while waiting for Leeds. She was working her way through law school, which she attended five nights a week. She had told him that she came from Eastborough and named one of the poorer projects.

"Tough place to grow up," Jonathan had said sympathetically.

"It got better," she said, "after you came up."

He gave her a look of startled gratitude.

The young woman nodded. "My mother still lives there. I know what the people think. We know who our friends are, and it don't... it doesn't always go by color."

Entering the office now, Rachel flashed him a smile. She stepped behind Leeds's desk, bent, and spoke softly.

Leeds excused himself and followed her out of the office. Left alone, Jonathan occupied himself by surveying the books on Leeds's shelves, which, surprisingly, contained relatively few legal tomes but a preponderance of fiction. Good fiction, too, and eclectic—the collection of a serious and unapologetically idiosyncratic reader. Lesser- known works of classic writers rubbed elbows with contemporary masters. Gaddis, Coover, Percy, Carver, Gordimer; genre fiction, too, but top-of-the-line: Philip K. Dick and Stanislaw Lem, Peter Dickenson, Sayers, and an enviable stash of Damon Runyons. Some were books Jonathan himself owned, and meeting them here was like discovering that he and Christopher Leeds had close friends in common. Others he'd meant to read but hadn't gotten around to. If I go to jail, he thought to himself, I'll have time to read; maybe Christopher will lend me some books.

The sickly laugh he tacked onto the end didn't obscure the fact that somehow, the unthinkable had become thinkable.

If I go to jail.

It was possible. Lily was right: anything *could* happen. When twelve strangers had the power to send him to prison, his fate was no longer in his hands.

Had it ever been?

Jonathan had lived his life like a high-flier suspended over a safety net, only to discover at the age of forty-eight that there was no net and never had been. Nothing to catch you if you fell, no bottom to the hole, no up, no down, no cause, no effect. Things happened; that was all. People acted as if the world were a rational place, as if the laws of physics were paradigms of an underlying moral order, but really it was just whistling in the dark. Jonathan longed for a rational explanation of his travails, but so long as he'd held fast to his innocence, nothing that had happened in the past two months made sense. His iliad of unearned woes had torn great rents in the camouflage, through which gaped the void: a chaotic world in which anything at all was possible.

When Leeds returned, Jonathan complimented him on his taste in fiction.

The lawyer beamed fondly at his books. "Yes indeed. My professional literature." He smoothed the perimeter of hair that surrounded his baldness like an empty corral. Jonathan waited, head cocked, for an explanation or punch line. Reluctantly, because he was a private man who liked to observe boundaries, Leeds explained: "Trial lawyers, you know, are basically storytellers. Each case has certain givens, evidence, witnesses— the particulars vary, of course—around which the prosecution and defense weave their tales, competing for the jury's belief. The better story wins; it's as simple as that."

"Where's the justice in that?"

"There is none. Litigation is not about justice, nor is it, strictly speaking, about truth. It's about good, plausible storytelling. Alternate visions of reality. Fiction."

"I never took you for a cynic."

"That's not cynical. I've always believed that fiction, good fiction that is, is a reasonable vehicle for truth. But of course there are limitations. One can't just fantasize wildly. 'Aliens made me do it' is not going to wash with the jury, unless one's trying for insanity."

"I noticed you have science fiction on your shelves."

"For fun," Leeds whispered behind his hand.

Jonathan smiled. "What story will you make of me?"

"I'm not sure yet. But I'm beginning to feel that in this instance, our best defense is offense."

"Specifically?"

"Shift the focus from the accused to the accusers. A hoary

old tactic, but sometimes it works, especially in political trials where the jury is predisposed to the possibility of prosecutorial vindictiveness."

Vindictiveness, Jonathan thought, was precisely the word. Though Michael's betrayal had been a crushing disappointment, it could at least be said to have occurred under the gun. But no one held a gun to Lucas' head. Lucas could have nipped this in the bud. Instead, incomprehensibly, he had let it escalate until the damage was irreversible.

Leeds stood up. He clasped his hands behind his back and proclaimed: "Ladies and gentlemen of the jury, we will demonstrate that in the execution of both his public and his private affairs, my client, Jonathan Fleishman, never strayed outside the norms of the municipal marketplace; that he therefore had no reason to believe he was engaged in any illegality; and that, in fact, no illegality occurred. We will also show, beyond a shadow of a doubt, that the charges against my client were politically conceived and maliciously prosecuted."

Jonathan applauded. "Bravo. Bravo." The phrase "municipal marketplace" at once pleased and worried him. It conjured an image of a gigantic, bustling department store whose registers rang incessantly with a brisk trade in sinecures, contracts, leases, subsidies, seats on commissions, and appointments to boards. A not altogether inaccurate image, he thought, but risky.

Leeds sat. "Most of their case, what I've gathered of it, is weak. Your ties to those companies are not easy to document, and not, in and of themselves, illegal. They need to prove you exerted undue influence, and that is difficult to do; the facts lend themselves to many interpretations. The worm in our apple, Jonathan, is Vito Tortelli."

All the air went out of Jonathan. He slumped in his seat.

"If he tells the same story under oath that he told that *Probe* reporter..." Leeds paused tactfully.

Jonathan gnawed the inside of his cheek. He didn't want to talk about Vito Tortelli, but Leeds had to ask. Finally he said, "I have no reason to suppose Tortelli will change his story."

Christopher Leeds lowered his eyes, centered a pad on his desk. "The difficulty, you see, is that if the jury believes that you accepted a cash-stuffed envelope from Tortelli in a men's room, not only does that taint their image of you, it also implies consciousness of guilt."

"Tortelli blames me for losing his place. He's got a chip this big on his shoulder. I've seen you work. You'll tear him to shreds."

"But Kavin was there too, he says, and we know they've got Kavin... and then there's Solly Lebenthal."

"So what are you advising me, Christopher—I should go fall on my sword?"

"God forbid!"

Leeds looked so shocked that Jonathan felt compelled to reassure him: "Just a manner of speech, my friend."

"We'll know more next week, when they present their motion to freeze your assets. I told you, Jonathan. I intend to fight them tooth and nail on this issue. Win or lose, it will cost them. They'll have to wheel out their big guns. If they've got Kavin and Lebenthal corroborating Tortelli, we should hear about it then."

Altogether they talked for several hours, and Jonathan met the other lawyers in the firm who would be assisting in his defense. In the intervals, when they were alone, Jonathan felt Leeds looking at him expectantly. He had no idea what Leeds wanted and, in his misery over Lily, shunted the matter aside, until suddenly it came to him that Leeds wanted him to explain about Tortelli. He hadn't asked for an explanation—he wouldn't—but wasn't that a gleam of disappointment Jonathan saw in those magnified eyes?

Perhaps it was the fact that Jonathan had grown up without a father and Christopher Leeds, though only ten or a dozen years his senior, was an inherently avuncular figure, or perhaps it was some quality in the man himself—but Jonathan found himself distressed at the thought of Leeds's disapproval. He wanted to explain, but how could he explain to Leeds what he could not explain to himself? The Tortelli fiasco was something he had buried long ago, had nearly forgotten until that bastard Barnaby came along and dug up the corpse. What had happened was not Jonathan's fault, but his innocence could be demonstrated only in a context outsiders might regard as corrupt.

He needed for Leeds to understand that there was politics, and there was realpolitik, and each had its own ethic. In the realm of realpolitik, Jonathan played by the Queensberry rules. He might, to use the vulgar phrase, pay off a fellow politician, but never a judge. The minority companies he took under his wing were the real thing, not shells set up to sop up the gravy. He never knowingly dealt with the Mafia or anyone connected to drugs.

Jonathan Fleishman was, in short, a man of moderation, a reasonable man. It was Tortelli who had stepped way out of line.

But when he thought of explaining all this to Christopher Leeds, Jonathan for the first time came close to regretting his choice of attorney. Perhaps he would have been better off with someone of his own persuasion, a political lawyer who knew the way the system worked without needing everything spelled out, who would understand that what happened to the printer was his own damn fault.

What, after all, had they asked of Tortelli? Only that he do what people do if they expect to get business from the city. These things were understood, accepted, no cause for resentment among reasonable men. There were tactful means of handling such matters, with discretion and deniability for all sides.

Considering their opportunities, no one could say he and Michael were greedy. They never approached anyone who didn't stand to make big bucks off the city. They were fair and businesslike: no strong- arm stuff, no threats; the stick implied, the carrot tangible. Tortelli would have been a millionaire by now if he'd played along. Why hadn't he? Jonathan told himself Tortelli was just too small-scale greedy to see the big picture, but he suspected that Tortelli's mistake lay in taking the thing personally, failing to realize that this was just the way the system worked. It costs money to make money.

Whose fault was it that the printer deliberately set out to embarrass them? Jonathan's first instinct had been to refuse the meeting Tortelli demanded, but Solly insisted that the man was basically willing to do business, for Chrissake, he was just very paranoid that someone was scamming him. All Tortelli needed, Solly said, was reassurance that his money was going where he wanted it to go. Michael needed an infusion and was willing to play along, conditionally. "Just this once," he said, "then Solly takes over."

Jonathan should have stuck to his instincts; he knew that now. But the problem with Tortelli happened to arise at a sensitive moment. One week earlier, Jonathan had paid a fortune for Gracie's sweet-sixteen party at the club—a surprise party, because if she'd known about it, his perverse daughter would have stayed away. (As it was, she walked around all night scowling at the guests.) Next month Paul's tuition was due, and the *Water Lily* needed an overhaul. So he had let himself be persuaded. After all, it wasn't the first time they'd asked for a donation, and nothing had ever gone wrong before. The suppliers might not have been delighted, but they were men of the world who knew without having to be told which side their bread was buttered on. Tortelli, too, would fall into line.

The printer chose the venue, some off-the-map bar and grill in south Eastborough. He was waiting when Jonathan and Michael arrived. They shook hands, sat down, ordered a beer each. But before the beer was served, Tortelli got up and with many winks and nods went into the men's room. Jonathan and Michael exchanged a look: what's with this jerk? They shrugged, and followed him in.

Tortelli locked the door. He reached under his shirt, pulled out a fat manila envelope stained with sweat, and thrust it into Jonathan's hand. (No class, Michael said later; none at all, Jonathan agreed.) Jonathan bobbled the envelope to Michael, who shoved it into his briefcase.

"Open it," Tortelli said. "Count it."

They told him it wasn't necessary, but Tortelli stood between them and the door and kept insisting. Finally, to shut him up, Michael opened the envelope and counted out eighty hundred-dollar bills.

It seemed to take forever. All the while, Tortelli stared at Jonathan, who glowered back. "Now split it," the printer said when Michael finished counting.

"The hell with this." Jonathan shouldered Tortelli aside. In the warped mirror that hung on the back of the door he glimpsed a familiar but distorted face; a moment later he recognized it as his own. He started, as one does when an acquaintance from one sphere turns up unexpectedly in another. Then he averted his gaze and hurried out.

In his piece-of-shit article, Barnaby had attributed Tortelli's loss of his premises to his subsequent refusal to pay kickbacks. In fact (and Jonathan longed to explain this to Leeds, but how could he?), Tortelli had lost what he lost right there in that stinking john, among the urinals, when he humiliated Jonathan and showed him his face in a distorted mirror.

Tortelli knew it too. That, and not his outraged ethnic pride, was why he had quit paying.

None of this, however, was explainable to Christopher Leeds, who in any case turned out to be less concerned about the state of

Jonathan's soul than the state of his pocketbook. Leeds asked, as Jonathan prepared to take his leave, how he proposed to pay for his defense if the prosecution won its motion to freeze his assets.

Jonathan flushed, embarrassed not to have brought the matter up himself. He would pay up front, he said, before the motion could be heard. Had Christopher prepared an estimate?

Leeds named a figure. Jonathan turned gray. "You think I've got money like that lying around the house?"

With great reluctance, Leeds spoke tentatively of liquidating assets, mentioned the *Water Lily,* and suggested that Jonathan consult with his accountant.

"Just so I know," Jonathan, "what if I can't come up with all this cash on three days' notice? Are you going to dump me?"

The lawyer wiped his glasses. His watery eyes, de-magnified, looked hurt. "I am not going to 'dump' you, Jonathan. You can be sure of that, just as I am sure that you don't expect me to take this case pro bono."

Jonathan, who'd harbored hopes if not expectations, said, "Of course not."

The problem occupied him on the long drive home to Highview. Selling the *Water Lily* was out of the question, even if he could on such short notice. She was his pride and joy, the tangible symbol of his ascension. It would have to be stocks and bonds, but if he sold those, what would they live on? Already he'd lost the income from his and Michael's informal arrangements, and he didn't know how much longer he could resist the mounting pressure to step down as party leader.

It was rush hour and the parkway was jammed. Jonathan arrived home with just time enough to change his shirt, pick up Lily, and drive back to the city, to Columbia Presbyterian, in time for their appointment with the neurologist Tamar had recommended.

The appointment had been hard to come by. Jonathan had had to beat a path through three layers of secretaries, wielding Tamar's name like a club, to get through to Dr. Lawrence Barrows. Once he got him on the phone, though, Barrows proved both affable and accommodating. His office schedule was impossibly jammed, the doctor said apologetically, but if they would care to come into the hospital one evening that week, he would be happy to see them after rounds.

Barrows turned out to be a younger man than Jonathan

had imagined, almost too young, in his late thirties. He had a friendly, open face, a lanky body that looked like it would be efficient on a handball court, and shaggy brown hair. Altogether he looked more like an English professor at a small liberal-arts college than a topflight neurosurgeon. "Pleasure to meet you, Mr. Fleishman," he said, shaking hands with such enthusiasm that Jonathan had him pegged as a political supporter, until Barrows' next words dispelled the illusion. "Brilliant doctor, your sister. I had the pleasure of working under her my second year of residency. We've kept up ever since." Then he greeted Lily, gazing with a physician's unself-conscious interest deeply into her eyes. He ushered them into seats, settled himself behind his desk, and pulled a pad of paper toward him.

Jonathan said, "Good of you to make time for us—"

Barrows cut him off. "Anything for Tamar. Flattered she recommended me." He turned to Lily with an air of instantly forgetting Jonathan. "Tell me everything. From the beginning, including all the little things that don't tie in and don't seem important, but are odd. How do you feel?"

"Different," Lily said.

Barrows' face changed: he withdrew behind his eyes. Jonathan distinctly saw it happen.

"In what way?" the doctor asked.

"It's not just the headaches, or hearing my mother's voice. It's not the dreams either, though they're bad enough. It's just a feeling, an awareness, I don't know how to explain it, that something is wrong. Something's changed, but I can't say what."

To Jonathan it sounded like mumbo-jumbo, but the doctor nodded gravely. Barrows had about him an air of unlimited time, an affect Jonathan understood well, having seen it among certain high-ranking politicians. Their offices were hard to get into, but once inside, you felt no pressure to hurry. The layers of secretaries and aides acted as a kind of insulation that allowed their principals to inhabit a bubble of hastelessness, a temporal pocket.

Barrows asked many questions. How did the headaches and auditory occurrences—Jonathan noticed he didn't call them hallucinations—begin? Was there ever a warning, a physical marker or premonition? When Lily heard her mother's voice, was she hearing something she remembered, or remembering something she'd heard? Did she ever smell or taste or see anything unusual? Had she noticed any change in her vision? He scribbled notes without taking his eyes off her face.

Jonathan followed the progress of these questions and felt a chill that started in the pit of his stomach and radiated outward. He saw where Barrows was leading, and though he recognized the magical nature of the notion, nevertheless he could not help feeling the man was playing with fire, as if questions like his had the power to chisel an amorphous mass of symptoms into a coherent, devastating form.

Then the doctor turned his eyes on Jonathan, who felt the force of the man's concentration. "Have you noticed any change in your wife over the past few months?"

"No," he said. "Yes. I don't know. Lily, please don't misunderstand, but would you mind . . ?"

Lily went to sit the waiting room, shutting the door behind her.

Jonathan placed both hands on the doctor's desk and leaned forward. "I know what you're driving at, and I don't like it."

"I don't suppose you would," Barrows said. "I'm not crazy about it myself. *Have* you noticed any change?"

Jonathan swiveled his chair toward the window. They were in the heart of Spanish Harlem, and the street below was lively, lined with open-air markets and crowded with shoppers, strollers, stoop-sitters calling out to one another.

He looked at Barrows. "We've been married almost twenty-five years. You get to know a person, how they'll react in a given situation. Lately I never know how Lily's going to react, or what she'll say. It's like sometimes she's very much there, and sometimes she's nowhere to be found."

The doctor nodded.

"The little conventions of a marriage, the things you say and don't say—somehow they've lost their hold. When she's not totally out of it, she's more... forthright. Uncomfortably so. As if she doesn't have time to waste on nonsense."

Barrows, his face a blank, scribbled a note.

Jonathan scowled. "Let's have it, then. What are we dealing with?"

The doctor kept writing. "Too early to tell."

"You have to take into account the stress of our situation, all the publicity, the filth that's been written. It's hard on her." He felt as if he were plea-bargaining.

Barrows put down his pen and looked straight at Jonathan. "It's not stress. Stress might have been the trigger, but it's not the cause."

"Those questions you asked—you're thinking some kind of tumor, aren't you?"

"With any sudden onset of seizure activity, we consider that possibility. But there could be other causes, or it may be something else entirely. We won't know until we've done a CAT scan, which I will have my secretary schedule in the morning, and an MRI. I also want her to have a complete physical. There's someone here I'd like you to use. We'll make the appointment for you."

Jonathan clenched his fists. "The hell my wife has been through these past few months is enough to make anyone sick, without conjuring up a goddamn brain tumor."

"I'm not in the conjuring business," Barrows said gently. "And we're still a long way from a diagnosis. I'm just telling you that with your wife's constellation of symptoms, stress alone is unlikely to be the underlying cause."

"You're not saying what is, though." Jonathan walked to the window and gazed out. It was full dark now; his own reflection stared back at him. "Look, if we're going to work together, I need more from you than final conclusions. You're going to have to think out loud, take me with you every step of the way. I want you to talk to me as you would to Tamar. Can you do that, Dr. Barrows?"

Barrows met his eyes in the window. "I can if you can, Mr. Fleishman. The truth is, I don't know what's wrong with your wife; but you're right in suspecting there's a possibility of tumor. Mrs. Fleishman stated that she feels 'different,' that something indefinable is wrong. This vague feeling of something wrong, which the patient can't pin down or even express clearly, is almost a signature of certain types of brain tumor. When I hear something like that, I take it very, very seriously."

Jonathan, having demanded this disclosure, at once rejected it. "I want a second opinion."

"You haven't had a first one yet. So far, all of this goes under the heading of borrowing trouble. Let's first do the tests, then see where we stand."

As they walked toward the door, Jonathan brought up the matter of payment. Barrows waved him off.

"Whatever your insurance pays is fine. You'll get no bill from me. We look after our own."

Jonathan said, "Better watch out, Doc. An attitude like that could land you in prison."

22

EVERY MORNING, GRACIE WAS AWAKENED at five o'clock by a knock on her door. She dressed and washed, and by five-thirty she was in the kibbutz dining room, eating bread and jam and drinking the thick, bitter coffee the Israelis called *botz,* mud. At five-forty-five, Ezra, the driver, came with the flatbed truck to take the volunteers and their Israeli overseers to the orchard.

She had arrived during late-summer harvest and was assigned to the orange orchards. It was expected that she would work—everybody did—but it was her own choice to live among the volunteers. Tamar and Yaacov both invited her to stay with them, but Gracie had not left one family to seek out another.

"Those rooms aren't very comfortable," Tamar had said doubtfully when" Gracie announced her decision. "They're not air- conditioned; they're the settlers' first homes, from the earliest days of the kibbutz."

"I don't care," the girl said, though she nearly recanted when she saw what was to be her room: a shack with three narrow iron beds, straw mattresses, a standing wardrobe, a couple of rickety chairs, and stacked orange crates for shelves. The floors were bare concrete, the walls as thin as rice paper. The room was uninsulated, hot as an oven in the daytime. In a room such as this her grandparents had lived when they first came to Israel. No wonder Clara ran away, Grace thought with dawning empathy. The charm of austerity, she was learning, lay in its being chosen, not coerced.

Like all the volunteers, Gracie worked from six a.m. till four p.m., a net of seven and a half hours. Three people worked each row of trees, each with a ladder and a burlap bag that slung around the shoulders. They picked from the bottom, working upward. The oranges had to be clipped near the branch, with the stem intact; without the stem, the fruit would rot before reaching market. When her burlap bag was full, or as heavy as she could bear, Gracie would climb down the ladder and pour the oranges into a large bin.

At seven-thirty the truck came to take them to breakfast; by eight-thirty they were back in the trees. Around ten o'clock there was a short break; the workers rested in the shade of a tree, ate oranges, and sipped water. The break for lunch, the main meal of the day, was from twelve-thirty till two; then they worked till four. Friday afternoons and Saturdays were free. Sunday was the start of the new work week.

The weather never varied. Harsh sunlight, unmediated by even the hope of rain, lay upon the earth like a heavy, relentless lover. Hawks and vultures circled in the sky. Once, before she learned the right way to walk, Gracie kicked over a rock and a yellow scorpion ran over her sandal. Luckily it didn't sting her. Yellow scorpions were more poisonous than black ones, she'd been told. Their sting would make you sick for a week, but snakes were worse. There was no antidote to the venom of the black viper.

For the first three days of work, Gracie's head, back, arms, and legs ached constantly. By the fourth day, her body had calibrated the necessary adjustments; by the fifth, the pain was gone. She learned by imitation to cope with the heat the way Israelis did, moving with long fluid strides and no extraneous motion.

Talking burned up precious energy, she told herself, but in fact she enjoyed her cocoon of silence. There was a rhythm to the work, and if you found it, the work went easier. Picking oranges provided a fine sense of closure. When she started, the tree was full of oranges; when she finished, it was bare. No ambiguity, no room for misinterpretation.

To amuse themselves, the pickers competed, team against team. Gracie progressed from a liability to an asset within two weeks. As she grew stronger, she discovered that more was expected of her. She began to measure herself against the kibbutzniks instead of the other volunteers.

Some of the volunteers were cordial, others, the veterans, aloof. Gracie made no friends. Occasionally she was invited to join a group going to swim in Nachal David, the wadi-oasis of pools and waterfalls that adjoined the kibbutz, and she went. But when she wasn't swimming, she kept her nose buried in a book.

A steady stream of men, kibbutzniks and volunteers, came onto her. Their methods were distinct. The American and European men tried to befriend her, disguising their sexual interest. The Israelis were clear and hard-edged, their advances direct and physical; they were more aggressive than the Americans but less likely to take offense when turned down. On the whole, she preferred the Israeli approach, which seemed to spring naturally from a desert environment in which life was reduced to essentials: food, water, shelter, and sex.

But she was never tempted. It wasn't the men, several of whom in her previous life she would have found acceptable; it was her. Grace had renounced men and fancied herself a sexless creature now, a kind of secular nun.

Being thus outside the fray, she was free to observe, and her observations were sharpened by loneliness. She saw clearly how the gulf between the kibbutzniks and the volunteers was bridged, and the hierarchy defined, by sex. The more attractive volunteers had affairs with Israelis, while the less attractive settled for their peers.

The kibbutzniks and volunteers sat at separate tables in the dining room; there was no rule of segregation—it was just the way things were done. Even the girls who were sleeping with kibbutzniks didn't sit with them. Each volunteer was formally "adopted" by a kibbutz family, which meant that once a week, on Saturday afternoons, the volunteers put on clean clothes and crossed over to the kibbutzniks' neighborhood to spend some time with their respective families. But as each of these families had "absorbed" countless transient volunteers over the years, the relationships remained carefully superficial.

Here Gracie's situation differed somewhat from the others'. Hers was not an assigned adoptive family, but her own flesh and blood, her grandfather and aunt. To her embarrassment, Yaacov distinguished her from the other volunteers. He brought her extra food from the kitchen and liniment for her aching muscles. Like Clara, he complained she was too thin, and if she skipped a meal he would lumber down to the volunteers' houses, which they called the slave quarters, to find out why.

He was a tall man with a limp, who should have used a cane

but wouldn't. Volunteers who worked in the kitchen feared his tongue; but they liked him anyway because he never locked the larder, even though he knew they raided it. Once, rumor had it, a member had had the temerity to criticize him in a kibbutz meeting for letting the volunteers steal food. "Idiot!" he'd thundered. "What do you think they do with the food, sell it to the Arabs? These youngsters work for nothing, and you would begrudge them even a full belly!"

Gracie visited his two-room house and was shocked by its bareness: no pictures on the wall, no carpets, no ornaments of any kind except two framed photographs on top of the dresser. One was of Tamar and a man with a shrewd, kind face—her husband. Between them, and towering above them both, stood a teenage Micha. The other photo was a portrait of her family, taken at a wedding: a handsome group, she thought with an odd sense of detachment.

It was hard to imagine Clara married to Yaacov. Both were so strong, yet so different, so set in their disparate ways. Though he rarely mentioned her, she felt Yaacov's attention sharpen when Clara's name came up; but whether this represented animosity or some strange remnant of love, she could not have said. Of his son, Yaacov was inordinately proud, and he had the habit of effacing their long estrangement, as if the bond that he imagined actually linked them both. Grace did not disillusion him, did not tell him that Jonathan rarely mentioned his name, and then only in the context of his absence.

If her grandfather showed an unexpected and somewhat alarming tendency to engulf, Tamar was quite different. She was, of course, much busier than Yaacov—head of the oncology department at Arad Hospital and this year also acting chief of staff, replacing the regular chief, who was away on sabbatical. Yet it was to Tamar's house, not Yaacov's, that Gracie gravitated every Saturday afternoon; it was to Tamar's intensely focused gaze, which brought to bear all the concentrated intelligence that in another sphere sufficed to run a hospital, that she was drawn. Her aunt was always welcoming, even when fatigue lay like dust in the lines of her face; yet she was restrained in a manner that, even to one who barely knew her, seemed uncharacteristic. Tamar never spoke of Gracie's family, and if Yaacov did, she changed the subject.

Gracie spent hours in the orchard wondering about Tamar's

reticence. Sometimes she thought it stemmed from disgust; she had not forgotten her aunt's ill-concealed dismay at the way they lived, the time she visited them in New York. Other times she attributed her attitude to forbearance and respect for Gracie's privacy.

She had no way of knowing the true cause of Tamar's silence, and Tamar couldn't enlighten her, for she'd been strictly forbidden to tell about Lily's illness, the tests she was undergoing, the speculations she herself refused to countenance. That was Lily's decision, and these days, Jonathan would oppose her in nothing. Tamar had argued; she warned them, "Gracie won't thank you for keeping her in the dark." In the end, though, she had to accept Lily's injunction.

Since she couldn't speak honestly, Tamar preferred not to speak at all. For the most part, they talked instead about the desert, its ecology and archaeology. Gracie's gratifying interest owed more, at least initially, to the teacher than to the subject. Tamar's intuitions of the past were as real to her as the imaginings of a child; and when she brought out her treasured collection of artifacts to show Gracie, her face shone with a shy, childlike enthusiasm. She handled them with love; to her they were tactile evidence of continuity, of a time frame so vast it dwarfed the daily tribulations of her life.

They took long walks together. "In this place," Tamar told Gracie as they wandered among the waterfalls and pools of Nachal David, "there has always been water, as far back as recorded history goes. Therefore, there have always been men. David hid from Saul in the caves of Ein Gedi, and even then those caves were ancient. When you walk through this wadi, you walk in his footsteps."

This was seductive stuff, but Grace was determined never to be seduced again. She had been sent here as punishment, and she would do her time and do it well, as a matter of self-respect; but she would not demean herself by loving her prison or embracing her guards.

And yet... Tamar's wonderment was hard to resist. There was in her a connectedness to place that Gracie, who had grown up in a world of interchangeable suburbs, had never encountered. And once her eyes were opened by Tamar, the land worked its greater magic on her, answering a need she had not known she possessed and could not even name. One night after supper, she walked down to the Dead Sea and lay on the pebbled beach, head pillowed on a boulder. The sky, stretched between mountain and sea, blazed with dense clusters of stars. When Gracie closed her eyes, the starlight burned through her lids. She floated on the salt-laden breeze.

Sometimes Tamar and Gracie hiked through the more formidable wadi of Nachal Arugot or along the barren salt-licked shore of the Dead Sea. This was not the intimidating, grandiose splendor of the Alps or the Rockies, both of which Grace had toured with her family, but beauty in a more intimate mode; not a landscape, but a land, full of nooks and crannies that invited exploration.

Tamar was a serious walker, no Sunday mall-stroller. She didn't talk while she walked, and Grace emulated her. But when they stopped to eat or swim in one of the hidden pools among the rocks, their conversation would resume from wherever they had left it, an hour or a week ago. They talked of many things, but never about Gracie's family, and never about Micha, who had not been seen in Ein Gedi in the three weeks since he deposited Gracie on his mother's doorstep.

Then, late one afternoon, as Grace sat beside the deserted kibbutz swimming pool, soaking her feet in the cold water and reading a tattered copy of *Mansfield Park,* a shadow fell upon her; and she looked up with a start to find her cousin towering over her. No doubt, she thought, he was used to sneaking up on people.

She'd forgotten how good-looking he was. The female volunteers rated Micha a major catch, a great big slippery trout whose allure was enhanced by legend: he was said to have been often hooked, never landed. Grace regarded him with no welcoming eye.

He hunkered down beside her. "Still here?"

"Looks like it."

"How's the head?"

She tapped it. "Solid as a rock, thanks."

"I hear they put you in the orchards."

"Yep."

"They say you're not a bad worker."

"I'm bucking for parole."

He laughed. When she turned back to her book, Micha looked her over carefully, in the direct manner of Mediterranean men. His eyes lingered thoughtfully on her body, slender but full-breasted, in a simple yellow tank suit. Her skin had tanned to a deep almond color, much darker than when he'd seen her last. Long hair as black as his curled damply around her shoulders. He wondered if any of his brethren had had her yet. If not, it wouldn't be for want of trying.

It shouldn't have bothered him. He'd dipped into the volunteer pot often enough himself. The kibbutz women disapproved, though they weren't above the odd raid themselves. It wasn't nice, and you wouldn't put it into a recruitment brochure, but everyone knew the volunteers served a dual function in the kibbutz ecology: as a source of cheap labor and as the sexual equivalent of a stocked pond, constantly renewed by the annual tide. As far as Micha was concerned, as long as you kept it honest, there was no harm done. All the same, he didn't like the idea of his cousin being treated like a piece of prime meat.

She looked up from her book and caught him staring. "What?"

"Come for a walk."

That was how most of the kibbutzniks prefaced their moves. "You're not planning to jump me, are you? We are cousins."

Micha laughed. It was a nice laugh, warm and deep and masculine, and despite her intentions, Grace found herself liking him a little. He was different out of uniform. Then he said, "Don't flatter yourself," and she went back to hating him.

He pointed up the mountain at whose foot the kibbutz nestled. "Have you been up there yet? Ma'ayan David is there, the Spring of David. It's the source of the Nachal David water."

Gracie had heard about the spring from other volunteers, and had proposed a hike to Tamar; but her aunt had said no. "Too hot, too steep—go with someone younger." No doubt she'd sent Micha down for that purpose. Gracie squinted up at the stark white cliffs, then at her cousin, weighing the advantage of a guide against the disadvantage of its being him.

"What about dinner?" she asked.

"I'll bring sandwiches."

She walked back to her room while he went to the kitchen. When they met a few minutes later, Grace had on blue work shorts and blouse and the hat Micha had bought for her in Jerusalem.

The trail rose steeply up the mountain behind the kibbutz, not long, but steep and rocky. Midway up the slope Gracie was panting, but her legs were steady, strengthened by weeks of working in the orchard. Several times she dislodged rocks, which crashed down the slope. She felt clumsy beside surefooted Micha, who moved with a grace akin to that of the ibex she'd glimpsed from afar. His sandaled feet seemed to mold themselves to the ground; he was at home in this place in a manner Grace had never known.

Just over the summit was a beautiful green glen, its centerpiece a sparkling pool surrounded by boulders and reeds, shaded by prickly acacia trees. Gracie headed for the pool like a sleepwalker. Micha waited, watching as she pulled off her blouse to reveal the yellow swimsuit underneath. Then he said, "Wait—there's a better place farther on."

They followed a trickle of water, a blue vein cut in the soft pale bone of the sandstone mountain. Except where the water flowed, the terrain was barren and stark, strewn with rock formations eroded into strange shapes by time and flood. They passed a cave, curtained by a waterfall and carpeted by moss. Great boulders balanced precariously at the edges of cliffs. Once Micha stopped and pointed wordlessly across a gulf: it took several moments for her eyes to discern three buff-colored ibex poised motionlessly against the rocks, not twenty meters away. Here and there were obstacles to be climbed over or sidled past. When he helped her, Micha made a point of touching her no more than was necessary.

They came upon a ledge with a sheer ten-foot drop. Micha leapt down and caught Grace as she lowered herself by her hands. She found herself in a small rock grotto surrounded on three sides by white stone walls; at their feet was a deep, still, sunken pool of indigo water (the precise color of Micha's eyes), sparkling like an opal in a setting of bone.

"Are we really allowed to be here?" Gracie whispered.

Micha smiled. "Why not?" He took off his shirt and sandals and dived in. Gracie stripped down to her suit and followed.

The water was ice cold, a shock to the system. When she rose, gasping, to the surface, Micha splashed water in her face with the heel of his hand. She splashed him back, and for several minutes they played and yelled like the children they had never been together.

Later they lay side by side, a few feet apart on the hard rock floor of the grotto, warming themselves like seals in the waning rays of the sun. Micha was thinking about Marta, the first woman he had ever had. He had been sixteen and it had happened right here on this spot. She was a volunteer from Austria, three years older than he, but it was he who'd taken the initiative—he'd kissed her, pulled off her bathing suit, and made love to her right where Gracie lay now.

Since then there had been many. The little grotto had a well-deserved reputation on the kibbutz. Its elemental beauty and isolation, and the delightful mix of frigid mountain water and brilliant sun, evoked a natural eroticism. It was almost impossible to bring a girl up here and not make love to her. Unless, of course, she was your cousin.

Grace stretched and yawned like a cat, unselfconscious in his presence, unaware that he was not in hers. Without planning to, Micha reached out and cupped her head.

She drew back

Micha forced a smile. "Wound's all healed."

"It wasn't much to begin with."

"Have your feelings about the Palestinians changed since you were beaned by one?"

Gracie narrowed her eyes and sat up, hugging her knees. "I keep seeing that boy's face, just before he threw the rock. He looked straight at me."

"He aimed straight too, the little bastard."

"I keep wondering why."

"Feels different, doesn't it, when the rocks are meant for you?"

"It feels different," she said slowly, "but I don't see that it *makes* any difference. Why did you search that woman's home?"

Micha turned his face up to the sky. Overhead, a hawk circled watchfully.

"She was kind to us," Gracie said.

"Yes."

"Then why humiliate her? Just because she's an Arab? Or is that just standard procedure for Israeli soldiers?—someone invites you into her home and you automatically search it."

"Did she seem humiliated?" Micha asked, with an irritating air of patience.

"No."

"That's because she knows the game as well as I do. You're the outsider."

"Tell me what I'm missing."

"She was too decent a woman to leave a young girl bleeding on her doorstep. That doesn't tell you a thing about her politics, or more to the point, her husband's and her sons'. For all we know, the boy who stoned you was one of hers."

Gracie regarded him somberly. "It must be hard to live with so much suspicion and distrust."

"It is what it is," he said.

23

AFTER DINNER ON FRIDAY NIGHT, two kibbutz women, Rachel and Havatzellet, drew Tamar aside. "How is Gracie doing?" Rachel asked, with a frown of concern. "Is she really happy here, or do you think she'd be better off elsewhere?

Tamar, having lived most of her life on the kibbutz, knew these questions were not questions at all, but rather an ominous signal that, with that amorphous unanimity that is the kibbutz's most quelling mechanism, Grace had been judged and found wanting. Tamar loved her kibbutz, but she suffered no illusions as to its nature. Like many an institution founded on the highest ideals, its judgments on individual matters tended toward the narrow and mean-spirited. In the name of equality, the gifted were sometimes penalized and expressions of individuality were perceived as threats to the integrity of the commune. Every kibbutz had its ghosts, the lingering spirits of members who didn't fit in, children who were forced out. She was damned if Gracie would be one of them.

"Why do you ask?" she said. "Is something wrong with her work?"

"No, she's a good worker."

"Well, then?"

"She seems so unhappy," Rachel said.

"She seems to *enjoy* her unhappiness," Havatzellet added.

"If she's unhappy, maybe she has cause to be. Leave her alone."

"But she never joins in any of the activities," Havatzellet said. "When she's not working, she's either in her room or wandering alone."

"We wonder if she's really comfortable here," Rachel said.

Tamar fixed the two of them with a scalpel-edged look. "Listen to me, and pass it on. Gracie is my flesh and blood. She stays as long as she chooses to stay. I absolutely will not have her ostracized."

The delegates took a step backward. "As if we would," Havatzellet said in a wounded voice.

"You heard me. Let Gracie be."

They seemed suitably cowed. Still, Tamar knew that feelings must have been running high for them to approach her at all. In any society of equals, some are more equal than others. Tamar, Yaacov, and Micha were a formidable triumvirate, not lightly to be crossed. If Gracie had been anyone but who she was, she would have been simply and efficiently expelled from the kibbutz, and the communal memory would have closed over her like the sea over a sunken ship. Her position was a protected one; nonetheless, Tamar worried. She had not forgotten what Micha told her, that Gracie had been forced to come to Israel.

The next morning, she invited the girl on a hike through Nachal Arugot.

They set out directly after breakfast. Arugot was a deep gorge bounded on the north by a sheer cliff that was the southern edge of the kibbutz, on the south by a slightly gentler slope, with ridges just wide enough for a hiking path. It was a steeper and longer trail than the one through Nachal David, with less protection from the sun. Tamar was pleased to find that Grace kept up without difficulty, or at least without complaint. Moreover, she moved intelligently, which to Tamar meant silently and efficiently.

After about an hour and a half, they came upon a rocky plateau. The main trail traversed the plateau, but another, barely discernible footpath led steeply downward at a right angle to the main trail. "Just down there, in the wadi, there's a hidden waterfall and a deep pool," Tamar said. "Quite a pretty place, but it's a steep climb down and then back up. Do you want to go down?"

"Yes, please," Gracie replied.

The path was not only steep but also covered with a layer of slippery pebbles. Gracie's legs soon ached with the effort of keeping her balance and controlling the speed of her descent. But the way was not long; within fifteen minutes the two had reached the floor of the wadi, where a frigid stream ran among the boulders. They waded upstream. The gorge diminished to a narrow, winding passage, opening up in a deep blue pool that bubbled and hissed with the turbulence of the fifty-foot cataract crashing into its far side. Iridescent dragonflies darted over the water, and some came to investigate the intruders, hovering fearlessly about their heads.

They stood on the lip of the pool and Grace looked about in wonder. "This is Eden."

Tamar laughed. "Don't eat any apples." She left her sneakers and backpack on the pool's rocky margin and dived in wearing her shorts and blouse. Gracie jumped in after her. The shock of icy water on her burning body made her gasp. She turned to find Tamar waving at her from underneath the waterfall, where she dog-paddled against the current. Gracie swam to her side. Water streamed over her head and shoulders, reviving her weary, aching muscles. Water in the desert, the essence and origin of baptism. You don't have to be a Christian, Gracie thought, to feel born anew.

Later they sat on the rocky ledge peeling oranges and waiting for the sun to dry their clothes. Tamar said, "This is such a magical place. I often wish I could bring patients here."

"Why don't you?"

"Too strenuous for most of them."

The sun was high overhead, framed by the canyon walls. Gracie scratched her back lazily against a rock. "I wish I could stay here forever."

"Here in Ein Gedi, or here in this spot?"

"Here in this spot."

"And the kibbutz? Are you happy there?"

"I'm okay." Gracie looked at Tamar and narrowed her eyes. "Why? Have they said something to you?"

"You know kibbutzniks. Well, maybe you don't. We have a hard time keeping our noses out of other people's business."

"What do they say about me?"

"That you seem sad."

When Gracie's eyebrows came together in a frown, Tamar could see Jonathan in her face. "How I feel is nobody's business," the girl said. "I carry my weight. Or did they criticize my work, too?"

"They say you're a very good worker." Tamar peeled another orange and handed half to Gracie.

"Am I supposed to pretend?" Gracie said. "Put on a happy face, sing songs around the campfire?"

It would help if she did, Tamar thought. The kibbutz didn't care how she felt, only how she acted. But this girl was a wounded animal; she needed solitude, a safe place to lie up while she healed. There was little enough Tamar could do for Grace, but at least she could provide privacy, protection, and time. "You are welcome here for as long as you want. But you don't have to stay if you don't like it."

"Why would you say that?"

"Micha told me you didn't want to visit. He said your parents made you come."

"That was chatty of him. I've never heard him string more than five words together."

Tamar smiled but was not distracted. "Is it true?"

"Yes. But now that I'm here, I figure I might as well stay for a while."

Tamar nodded. After a while she said, "Why did they send you?"

"I was in the way."

"They couldn't have said that."

Gracie looked at the older woman pityingly. "Of course they didn't say it. They never *say* anything."

"Why were you in the way?"

"Because I have a big mouth."

"You?" Tamar said, laughing. "You hardly talk."

"I've learned to control it."

With mixed success. Tamar smiled as she thought of her son, who came out of every encounter with Grace like a dog with a noseful of porcupine quills. "But what did your parents say?"

"They said it was to protect me. But that wasn't the real reason."

"What was?"

"A failure of imagination on my part. I couldn't see my father the way he wanted to be seen."

"What do you mean?"

Grace didn't answer.

Tamar felt a sinking sensation. There was only one interpretation of her silence. "You think he's guilty."

Gracie scowled at the ground, looking as if she wanted to cry but had forgotten how. When Tamar reached out to her, she flinched. Pain and anger: Tamar knew them well, met with them every working day. Some patients had the pain without the anger. Years of observation had taught her that "easy" patients, who followed doctors' orders unquestioningly and made few demands on nurses, usually adopted a similarly passive approach to their diseases. On the other end of the spectrum were the ones the nurses called patients from hell, habitual scrappers whose aggression, properly focused, was a valuable weapon. These were the patients who would grab a disease by the collar and go eyeball to eyeball.

Gracie was a fighter, a fighter and a survivor. Tamar's greater fear was for Jonathan. She had believed in her brother's innocence, not because he was incapable of venality, but because he was too smart to endanger himself. But Grace believed he was guilty; and Grace was an observant child.

For some reason, she felt sorrier for Jonathan now than she had when she'd thought him innocent.

"Have you thought how strange it is," she asked Grace, breaking a long silence, "that I ended up living with Yaacov, and Jonathan with Clara?"

"Why strange?"

"Because I am really more like my mother, while your father is like Yaacov."

"How do you figure that?"

"Clara and I are peasants. Our attachment is to place, not ideologies. Yaacov and Jonathan are a whole other breed. They're idealists."

"But you're a doctor. You *are* an idealist."

"I'm a worker," Tamar said firmly. She held up hands as hard and muscled as any laborer's. Grace thought of her mother's hands, slender, blue-veined, delicate. Her aunt's hands evoked the potato pickers in Van Gogh's paintings. Tamar was solid flesh, deeply rooted.

"But you and Yaacov both chose to stay here."

"We did, but for different reasons. Yaacov fell in love with Zionism, but I fell in love with the land."

"And which am I?" Gracie asked after a pause. "Peasant or idealist?"

"What do you think?"

A thing without roots, Grace thought. "I don't know."

"Then you must find out."

"Why?"

"A person needs to know where she belongs."

"Another Delphic utterance. Care to translate?"

Tamar smiled. "I'm saying that nothing matters more than knowing who you are and where you belong."

Grace's thoughts turned to an incident of the day before. She had been standing with Yaacov outside the dining hall, watching Micha play soccer with a bunch of kibbutz men, when the old man squeezed her arm. He said, "I look at those boys, and I know it was all worthwhile, just to produce such fine healthy animals."

Would he have said the same, she'd wondered, watching Paul play tennis? Paul played well, but Gracie didn't think so. Yaacov's approval had had to do with the dual nature of those young men cavorting on the lawn. Each had another life, a secret life into which he would disappear for a month or two each year, returning home in a dusty green uniform, leaner and harder than before. These men handled rifles and Uzis with the same seasoned ability as they did soccer balls and tractors.

Grace had felt hurt, obscurely criticized. She felt the same way now with Tamar. "You think my father lacks roots?"

"I think," Tamar said slowly, "that of the two of us, I was the lucky one."

Micha lingered like a cold that won't go away. Though he claimed to be on leave, week followed week and he showed no sign of returning to duty. No one who knew why was telling, but Tamar looked grim, and Yaacov slammed about the kitchen with his jaw clenched. Rumors flew like bats at dusk. Some people whispered that he had been booted out of the army for some obscure offense, others that he had taken leave or quit altogether. Volunteers came to Gracie for inside information. She would have enjoyed keeping his secret but was denied the opportunity; no one had confided in her, and she was too proud to pry into matters that were none of her concern.

When Micha had first come home, he'd said he was going to the Sinai for a week or two to get away, touching off a quiet but intense competition among the female volunteers. None secured the desired invitation, but it hardly mattered, since after announcing his plan, Micha kept delaying his departure. Instead he settled in as a tractor driver; and after that, Grace seemed to run into him everywhere she went: in the dining room, in the kibbutz clubhouse, at Tamar's on Saturdays. In public he rarely sought her out, but she often felt his eyes on her; and if any of the kibbutz men talked to her, Micha was sure to notice and afterward warn her off. "Coby's unreliable," he'd say. "Yair's married."

If he were anyone else, she'd have assumed he was interested in her himself, but if there was one thing Gracie was certain of, it was that Micha was not attracted to her. His own behavior made it clear. He was more like a sheepdog than an aspiring lover: vigilant and protective when wolves were about, uninterested when the flock was safe.

Then, one day, the explanation came to her. Micha was following orders, and those orders could only have come from Tamar. Silly woman. Couldn't she see that if there was one thing Gracie Fleishman could do, it was take care of herself?

Gracie wasn't the only one to notice Micha's odd behavior. He endured some ribbing, especially from his friend, Coby. "What's your problem, man?" Coby demanded one night when they met in the tractor shed. "You want her yourself, is that it?"

"Get fucked," Micha told him equably.

"I'm trying, but you keep getting in the way."

Micha popped him lightly on the chin, a love tap. Coby tapped back. They teetered on the edge of blows until Coby backed off. "Fuck it, man," he said. "You want her, take your best shot."

"It's nothing like that," Micha said.

"Yeah, keep telling yourself that."

Why shouldn't he, when it was by far the simplest and most useful explanation? Micha, no simpleton, nevertheless preferred uncomplicated solutions when they were on offer. He was not a deep thinker. His intelligence was considerable, but by nature and training it was geared toward action, not analysis. Tactics, not strategy, were his forte; in that respect he was the perfect army man. Lately, though, Micha had run up against matters that absolutely required thought, and not merely thought, but the most painful reexamination of long-held tenets. Decisions had to be made. With his future hanging in the balance, Gracie was a distraction he didn't need, but one whose removal from the scene he had sometime since ceased to desire.

One night after dinner, he followed her down to the Dead

Sea. He didn't purposely sneak up on her; it was just the way he walked.

Gracie started. "Jesus Christ. You should wear a bell."

He sat beside her on the rocky shore, close to the sea. The air was as salty as tears. She said, "Why are you dogging me?"

"Who says I'm dogging you? Can't a man get some fresh air?"

"I don't need a baby-sitter."

"You sure about that?"

She scowled. "Tell Tamar I can look after myself."

"What's Tamar got to do with it?"

"I know she put you up to it. Piss-poor choice, if you ask me. It's obvious we don't get along. You made it clear from the start that you didn't want me here."

"You made it clear you didn't want to be here."

"Don't you get it, cuz? School's out. You can go."

"What if I don't want to go? Besides, you're wrong about Tamar. She hasn't got a devious bone in her body."

"Then why are you hanging around?"

Micha sighed. "Damned if I know."

A star fell into the Dead Sea. They watched it sizzle.

24

JONATHAN READ THE VERDICT in Dr. Barrows' face. His smile of greeting seemed painted on, like a clown's; his eyes were remote, armored.

He clipped an X ray onto a lighted screen and picked up a pointer that lay atop the screen.

Jonathan saw a convoluted white mass: his wife's brain. He averted his eyes.

"Here is the problem," Barrows said without preamble. "This dark mass here is a lesion. Its location, on the surface of the superior temporal gyrus, accounts for all your wife's symptoms."

"A lesion... ?"

"A tumor."

"Not acceptable," Jonathan said. "I don't buy that."

He could hear God taunting him, thumbing his nose: Lily has a brain tumor, nya nya nya nya nya. Dr. Barrows' face appeared in his narrowed line of vision, peering into his face with a comical expression of concern, like someone seen through a fish-eye lens. His mouth moved soundlessly; Jonathan could hear nothing over the roar of God's derisive laughter. He stood, frozen with fear, like a rabbit caught in rushing headlights.

A strong hand pressed him downward into a chair. Barrows disappeared, then reappeared. A glass was held to Jonathan's lips. He drank. The brandy warmed his soul. God's laughter faded to a murmur.

"Are you with me, Mr. Fleishman?"

Jonathan spread his arms, as if to say: Where could I go?

Barrows pulled up the other visitor's chair and sat knee to

knee with Jonathan, who took this as a positive act of charity. In another era, this man would have doctored lepers.

"I know it sounds dreadful. I know it's frightening. But I assure you that there is hope. This is not an automatic death sentence by any means. We don't know, you see, what kind of tumor it is."

"Does it matter?"

"It matters a great deal. Some tumors are relatively benign—they're contained, they progress slowly. Some can be completely excised. Others can't."

Hope seized Jonathan in its cruel claw. "Can hers be?"

"I don't know. It's impossible to say without a specimen of the tumor."

"You want to do a biopsy."

"That's one possibility. We could do a needle biopsy, remove some tissue."

"One possibility?"

"The other is a procedure called debulking, and in your wife's case, that's the course I would recommend. Debulking simply means going in and taking out as much of the tumor as we can. Killing two birds with one stone."

An image flashed before him: he saw Lily lying on a table and this man, hidden behind a mask, opening her skull. Who were the two birds? Jonathan put his hands to his temples and pressed hard. The hospital's air conditioning was inadequate, yet he shivered.

The doctor's voice was calming, almost matter-of-fact. "We know the tumor's there, Mr. Fleishman. Whatever kind it is, it's got to come out."

Jonathan found his voice, or someone's. "I want another opinion."

"I understand. But time is of the essence. This thing isn't going to stand still while we discuss it. Your wife needs treatment now."

"Dr. Barrows, I don't care if my sister thinks you walk on water. I am not letting you or anyone else cut up my wife's brain without a second opinion, and a third if I'm not satisfied."

"Then do it fast. If you want, I'll have my office set up the appointment."

"What the hell am I supposed to tell Lily?"

"Ah." Barrows sat back with a sigh. "What do you think? You know her best."

"I don't think she wants to know."

"Why not leave it up to her at this stage? I won't lie to her, but I'm certainly willing to let her ask the questions before I answer them."

Lily asked no questions.

Told she could not drive, she did not inquire why. She agreed to see another doctor without expressing any interest in Barrows' findings. If anything, her mood was lighter now, as if by telling all to the doctor, she had literally unburdened herself. Serenely, if a bit absentmindedly, Lily went about her ordinary business, maneuvering around the reporters who clustered at the gate, gardening, shopping, visiting with those few of their friends who still called. Either Jonathan or Paul was always around to drive her wherever she wished to go.

Clara and Paul knew. Clara had read his face the moment he came from the hospital, followed him into his study, and demanded to know. He told her what the doctor had said. She listened with her hands over her mouth. When she took them down to embrace him, a wordless cry escaped.

He planned to keep it from the children until no doubt remained; but Paul walked into the study that evening and caught Jonathan weeping at his desk. In a moment of weakness, desperate for comfort, Jonathan broke the news.

Paul called him a liar; then he, too, burst into tears. Moved to a tenderness he had not felt since the boy outgrew him, Jonathan came around and knelt beside Paul's chair to embrace him.

His son pushed him away. "Don't. You're the kiss of death. This is all your fault."

"My fault," echoed Jonathan, amazed, not at this idea, upon which he had already seized, but that the boy had had the wits to conceive it.

"She was fine until all your shit started coming down. God damn you," Paul sobbed, "she was the only one in this family who cared about me."

"Is, not was. And she isn't. The only one."

But Paul had already run out, slamming the paneled oak door behind him.

Later the boy came back and apologized. The shock, Paul said, had rattled him; he hadn't meant the things he'd said. But Jonathan knew they were true. It *was* his fault, though he knew better than to say so. People only say such things to be reassured that they're wrong: *No, of course it's not your fault—you did everything you possibly could.* Whereas Jonathan knew damn well that somehow or other, Lily's illness *was* his fault. He was certain that this catastrophe could not have happened if he had cleaved to his wife as he had vowed to do. His failure to notice that she was ill was but an extension of earlier failures, not of love, but of attention.

For many years Jonathan had clung to the belief that everything he did, he did for his family. In the days that followed Barrows' diagnosis, he realized that he'd never asked Lily what she wanted, but rather had assumed he knew. Mistakenly, it appeared; for Jonathan could see her cancer in no other way than as a reproach to him, Lily's way of saying: "No, dear, this isn't it. This isn't what I wanted at all."

The great crisis that had so recently preoccupied him was as nothing. Whatever the outcome of his impending trial, his career was ruined. In a strange way, his awful guilt over Lily helped temper the agony of what he still regarded as wrongful accusation. There was solace in the discovery that he was not, after all, entirely innocent. And yet his true culpability would never be laid at his door, for who, besides Jonathan and Lily, knew how he had failed her, and who would believe him if he confessed? On the contrary: when Lily's condition became known, even his enemies would pity him.

He went through the formality of scheduling another examination for Lily, by a neurologist whose name he attained from their own internist. Not because he doubted Barrows' diagnosis—he knew damn well God wasn't playing potsy with him—but to provide God with every possible opportunity of changing his mind. After all, God had stayed Abraham's hand as he lifted it, on Jehovah's own orders, to smite his beloved son, Isaac. A miracle, Abraham would later proclaim piously, but don't you think he waited, arm poised, for just such an intervention? One does not sacrifice the innocent to punish the guilty: this is such a basic moral law, men expect even God to understand it.

To sweeten the deal, Jonathan offered incentives. For the first time since his daughter's bat mitzvah, Jonathan went to synagogue and prayed. Lord, take the cancer away from Lily and give it to me, he bargained, and I'll praise you on my knees every day of my life and die with a prayer of thanksgiving on my lips. Only let Lily be well, and the jury can find me guilty and sentence me to life; strike me dead if I murmur a word of complaint. Relieve me of this guilt, O Lord, for I cannot bear it. Have mercy, Lord.

The day's reading was from the Book of Job: *For the arrows of the Almighty are within me, the poison whereof drinketh up my spirit: the terrors of God do set themselves in array against me... The things that my soul refused to touch are as my sorrowful meat.*

Jonathan's eyes filled with tears of recognition. He felt a terrible bond to Job, as if he, too, were sitting on the floor in ashes and sackcloth. *If I justify myself, mine own mouth shall condemn me: if I say, I am perfect, it shall also prove me perverse. Though I were perfect, yet would I not know my soul: I would despise my life.... He destroyeth the perfect and the wicked. If the scourge slay suddenly, he will laugh at the trial of the innocent.*

The prayer service continued, but the rhythm of statement and response faded as Jonathan read on, transfixed. Coming upon this particular reading at this time was like hearing his name spoken in an empty room or picking up a bottle at the seashore and finding a message addressed to him. His heart swelled with anger at Job's false comforters. Hypocrites. *Forgers of lies, physicians of no value.... Miserable comforters are ye all.*

He felt he was reading a parable of his life. The only difference was that Jonathan, unlike Job, could not flaunt his unblemished righteousness in God's face. Once, he would have dared; lately, however, he had come to understand that his was not an absolute but a relative virtue—relative to his times, to his peers, to what he could have done, had he chosen to be greedy. His affliction, on the other hand, was not relative but absolute, so disproportionate to his sins and so cruelly misdirected as to stand with the trials of Job.

When God spoke to Job from within a whirlwind—*Gird up now thy loins like a man: for I will demand of thee, and answer thou me. Where wast thou when I laid the foundations of the earth? Declare, if thou hast understanding."* The lawyer in Jonathan cried out an objection. "Irrelevant, your Honor!"

Hath the rain a father? or who hath begotten the drops of dew? Out of whose womb came the ice? and the hoary frost of heaven, who hath gendered it? Canst thou bind the unicorn with his band in the furrow? Or will he harrow the valleys after thee? "Your Honor, I object! Dewdrops and unicorns, hoarfrost and rain—Your Honor, kindly instruct the witness to confine himself to answering the question."

Hast thou an arm like God? or canst thou thunder with a voice like him? "Your Honor, please; is this a court of law or a wrestling match? This is God's justification? I'm stronger, tougher, older than you, so I'm right? This is playground justice, your Honor, this is bullying on a cosmic scale."

But whom was Jonathan addressing, and whom was he kidding? There was no higher authority, no court of appeal. When he looked around him, he saw nothing but an old man leading a pack of other old men in meaningless prayer.

After the service, Jonathan stayed behind. Following an impulse of which he was ashamed, yet which he could not resist, he confronted the elderly rabbi, a pink-cheeked little man with a Yiddish accent. "What crap, what absolute bull," he said furiously. "This book of Job subverts the whole goddamn religion."

"Come into my office," the rabbi said.

"What's the point?" But he followed the old man down the hall into his comfortable, book-lined study.

The rabbi sat behind his desk and peered over his bifocals at Jonathan. "I know you."

"Probably. But I'm not here to discuss my situation."

"I see. You're here to talk about the book of Job."

"I can't understand how they let that story in. Here's a man who's been unjustly punished, and he damn well knows he doesn't deserve it. He asks why, as he has every right to do. He speaks so eloquently that God himself is moved to respond. Great. But what does God have to say for himself? Crap is what he has to say. Bullshit. Cosmic bluster. God beats his chest like Tarzan and comes off looking like a total shmuck—am I right or am I wrong, Rabbi?"

"Mr. Fleishman," the rabbi said, "we Jews take the world as we find it. The questions Job poses grow out of the world; we do not invent them. The good suffer, the innocent die horribly, and sinners prosper. Natural and unnatural disasters descend upon us. We see this. We try to understand. But we cannot wring answers from God's throat; and such answers as He volunteers are likely to seem paradoxical. 'For he is not a man, as I am, that I should answer him, and we should come together in judgment.' If a five-year-old child asked you, 'Daddy, why do people fight wars?' what can you say that is both true and comprehensible to him? The book of Job teaches us that the answer to the problem of innocent suffering lies outside the scope of human comprehension."

"In other words, God cops out. 'The devil made me do it,' He says."

"No. It's the author of Job who blames Satan, and that passage about God's wager with Satan is not something we Jews feel compelled to take literally. God himself says something quite different. He tells Job, 'You cannot judge me because you are incapable of understanding me.'"

"You're telling me God works in mysterious ways. That's not an answer; it's a tautology. Where's the comfort in that?"

The rabbi spread his hands. "Only the poor comfort of faith— the belief, the hope that somewhere out there, there are answers; that there exists a perspective from which all this suffering makes sense; that redemption is possible."

"That's *your* reading, from this cozy study, from this comfortable niche you've carved for yourself, interpreting the uninterpretable word of God."

If the rabbi was offended, he showed no sign of it. "What's your reading, Mr. Fleishman?"

"If I were God's lawyer, I'd advise my client not to testify. His best defense is to keep quiet and play dead. Otherwise, your almighty God hasn't got a prayer."

Reckless talk, but what precisely did he have left to lose? The age of miracles was past. "Curse God and die," Job's wife had advised him, but since then God had refined his punishments; now it was: Curse God and live.

The judge in Jonathan's case had handed down her decision, granting the prosecution's motion to freeze the Fleishmans' assets. And the day after his visit to the synagogue, Jonathan learned that with regard to the other matter, God, like the judge, had turned thumbs down. The second neurologist's diagnosis was identical to Barrows', and he too urged immediate surgery.

25

THE KID SWAGGERED UP to the table in Maxie's where Barnaby sat alone swilling boilermakers. Three empty shot glasses and three empty steins were lined up in front of him. Barnaby knew the face—he worked for some downtown Trotskyite rag, circulation twenty-seven. "What do you want, kid?"

"I heard what you did to that Fleishman bitch, bro."

"*Bro?* Where'd you get that, *Miami Vice?* Goddamn pasty-faced suburban maggot."

"Easy, my man—I am here to shake your hand."

"Say what?"

"You heard me," the kid said. "Hey, my philosophy? I say fuck 'em all; and if you can't fuck them, fuck their wives, fuck their daughters, fuck their fuckin' dogs, man."

"Fuck you, asshole," Barnaby growled.

The kid faded. Real reporters came and went; none approached him. Barnaby kept on drinking. For a man who had recently scored the scoop of a lifetime, his dance card was surprisingly blank.

His body was in Maxie's but his head was still in Hasselforth's office. Thinking what he should have said, replaying what Roger had said. Hasselforth was in his sanctimonious mode, puffing away like Fred MacMurray in a cloud of smoke. "You compromised yourself and you compromised us. There's no way you can be objective anymore. I'm taking the Fleishman story away."

"You can't," Barnaby had said reasonably. "It's mine. I broke it miles ahead of the competition."

"And how did you get there?"

Barnaby ignored this remark. "Since when is objectivity a virtue around here, anyway?"

They went a few more rounds, till Hasselforth pulled rank. "I'm the editor, I call the shots. Like it or lump it, you're off the story."

The hell with them. The hell with all of them. Barnaby signaled for another drink. He still didn't get it. What was the fucking big deal? It wasn't as if he'd broken any of the real rules. Yes, he'd used the girl, but that was what reporters did. They were all parasites, but by God they were useful parasites. As to the sex: if you silenced every reporter who ever balled a source, newspapers would be nothing but blank space and ads. So what if she was a few years younger than he? She was old enough. When Woody Allen nailed Mariel Hemingway in *Manhattan,* the crowds roared. But him, he walked into his own newsroom and everybody looked at him like he was Freddy Kruger. Journalistic ethics, his ass. As far as Barnaby was concerned, it all boiled down to sexual and professional jealousy.

Take a vacation, Hasselforth had said. Damn straight he'd take a vacation, and spend it doing what he did best. He'd put together a story that would make Hasselforth sit up and beg. And if he didn't, there were plenty of other fish in the sea. Barnaby knew his industry. If the product was good enough, they'd be lining up at his door, all sins forgiven and forgotten.

The next day, he phoned Jane Buscaglio. Her secretary said she was tied up. "So untie her," he joked. The secretary didn't laugh and Buscaglio didn't return his call.

He didn't need her—no single source was crucial—but it irked him. He checked her schedule. That afternoon, he went downtown to the federal courthouse and waited outside a courtroom till she emerged.

"Hello, Jane," he said.

She looked at him as she would have at a steaming pile of horse manure and stepped around him, taking care not to soil her shoes.

He trotted beside her down the long corridor. "What's going on, Buscaglio? All of a sudden I'm a leper?"

"Get away from me."

"Not till you tell me why."

She stopped on the courthouse steps. Quitting time; a stream of gray suits poured out of the building, parting around them, then smoothly rejoining. "You lied to me," Buscaglio said.

"What about?"

"Grace Fleishman—ring a bell?"

"Who told you?"

"Who didn't? It's all over town."

"You don't believe that story. The girl's a fucking basket case. What's her word next to mine?"

"Gold," Buscaglio said.

"Even if it were true, which it isn't, the girl is free, white, and over eighteen."

"Just barely."

"Come on, Jane, this is bullshit. You need me. I'm a better investigator than anyone on your staff."

"If anyone on my staff had pulled that kind of shit, he'd be out on his ass. Rayburn called me in."

"Yeah?"

"He'd heard too. Said he knew I used you sometimes, and told me to cut it out. Called you a few choice names. Bottom line, you're off the mailing list."

"There's gratitude for you," Barnaby growled. "If it wasn't for me, he wouldn't have Kavin or Fleishman. That's what he's really pissed about. Lucas is of two minds about this prosecution, or hadn't you noticed?"

"Fuck you, Barnaby We're done. If I were you, I'd get myself another beat—better yet, another line of work." She marched off, heels clicking on the stone steps.

Harsh words, but Barnaby knew she didn't mean them. Buscaglio knew as well as he did that no scandal lasts forever. Especially ones that never made the papers to begin with.

For days after the incident at Maxie's, Barnaby had lain low in an agony of waiting. Every time the phone rang, his stomach turned over as if it were wired to the bell; but no reporter called to ask for his comment. When the story didn't appear in the next day's press, he figured they were fleshing it out, looking for confirmation of Gracie's accusations. A week, two weeks went by; nothing happened. Gracie Fleishman disappeared from view. The rumor was she'd been sent away. Barnaby figured he was home-free. His colleagues were standing up for him, after all.

Roger read it differently.

"They're protecting the girl, not you," he said. "And themselves. You make us all look bad."

That was the attitude: Barnaby had fucked up. It was enough to make a strong man weep. Barnaby was sustained by whiskey and the knowledge that *this too shall pass*. New scandals crowded out the old. A year from now, no one would remember. A year, hell; two months at the outside, and they'd be lining up for his autograph again. In the meantime, he kept working.

Buscaglio kept her word and refused his calls. No one else in Rayburn's office would give him the time of day. This was unfortunate, because Fleishman's indictment had totally changed the story, taken it off the street and into the attorneys' conference rooms. The question was no longer what Jonathan did but how he did it and with whom. If Fleishman was retailing favors and contracts, he had to be purchasing them somewhere. Whose strings did he pull, and with what currency did he pay? Above all: was Fleishman talking?

Working from his apartment, Barnaby went back to his original sources on the Fleishman story. Most wouldn't take his calls; those who did gave him nothing he didn't already have.

He tried another approach. From the private treasure chest where he kept all his confidential material, safe from the prying eyes of his colleagues, he drew a list of names, office addresses, and phone numbers: fifty-four city employees who had gotten their jobs through Jonathan Fleishman's recommendation. The list had cost him two pairs of front-row seats to a Giants game, but it was cheap at the price.

Barnaby lay on his bed with his reporter's notebook propped against a knee and the list by his side, and one by one he phoned the names on the list.

It took the best part of four days, with multiple calls to most, to work his way through. Most hung up when he gave his name; others had their secretaries screen him out. Barnaby didn't take it personally; some resentment was inevitable, but by the law of averages, he expected that some of Fleishman's people would be looking around about now, getting ready to jump ship, maybe score a few brownie points with the press. Yet the few who agreed to talk with Barnaby did so only to harangue him. Words like "persecution," "vendetta," "distortion," and "fabrication" were carelessly tossed about. And for all this abuse, he ended up with nothing more than he'd had when he started: a list of names.

It pissed him off, this unseemly loyalty to a villain; it tested his patience. By all the laws of politics as he knew them, and he knew them from the ground up, Fleishman's former proteges ought by now to be turning on their wounded mentor in a kind of feeding frenzy. Instead they were rallying round, supporting him like a goddamn pack of dolphins, while Barnaby's colleagues did a piranha number on him. What the hell did Fleishman have that Barnaby lacked?

What really hurt, what kept him up drinking and smoking weed late into the night, was the way the lines were getting blurred. By all rational standards he was the good guy, Fleishman the bad. Fleishman had betrayed the public trust, and Barnaby had exposed him: you would think people would be grateful. You would think that at the very least, they would turn against Fleishman.

Oh, the high-ranking pols kept a wary distance—they were scared to death. But the people whom Fleishman had robbed and whom Barnaby defended, whose side did they take?

One night Barnaby turned on his TV and gnashed his teeth in rage as he watched a delegation from three south Eastborough housing projects present Fleishman with a check for $12,485 for his defense fund. The money had been raised entirely in the projects, through hundreds of contributions of five and ten dollars each. All three networks covered the event. The Hispanic woman who led the delegation recited a little set speech whose gist was: You've been on our side all these years, Jonathan; now we're proud to be on yours.

She hugged him. The cameras pulled in close, and Fleishman wiped a photogenic tear from his eye. "This means more to me than I can say."

Barnaby hurled an ashtray at the wall, banged his head against the back of his chair. The injustice of the thing drove him mad. Letters to the *Probe* were running three to one in favor of Fleishman, ten to one from his borough. Some were damned offensive attacks on Barnaby's motives, competence, and parentage. "Who are you?" one woman wrote to him. "When you do for the people a tenth of what Mr. Fleishman did, then you can talk."

Idiots. They treated Fleishman like Robin Hood, when all the while he was picking their pockets. The businessmen Fleishman hit up didn't foot the bill; they passed it along, in increased prices, lower wages.

But people see what they wanted to see, which as far as Barnaby was concerned was damn near nothing. He was the fool, painting pictures for the blind. The people were ungrateful; almost, they deserved what they got.

Although, officially, Barnaby was on vacation, the biorhythm of his life was set to the *Probe's* weekly cycle. Tuesday was the deadline for that week's edition; by Monday evening, when he had nothing new to report, his blood pressure began to rise. Again and again Barnaby went back to the list of Fleishman's political debtors. Slowly an idea began to emerge, like a chick pecking its way out of a shell. Barnaby, like most writers, thought better with a pen in his hand. He took a yellow legal pad and turned it sideways. On the bottom he drew a small circle around the initials J.F. He divided the page into vertical columns and headed each with the name of a municipal agency. Then he took the list of names and began slotting them in. When he'd finished, he had a kind of flow chart, a diagram of one man's political reach.

From a chaotic-looking desk drawer Barnaby pulled out another list, compiled during the early days of his investigation. Beside the typed names of the six companies that paid Fleishman or Kavin in one capacity or another, he had penciled in a list of favors, services, exemptions, and contracts facilitated by Fleishman (presumably it was Fleishman, not Kavin, who had far less power citywide than his friend). Barnaby laid one list next to the other, and his eyes went back and forth. After a while, without noticing, he began to hum a Beatles tune.

Tuesday morning, Barnaby entered Hasselforth's office and tossed a thin stack of papers onto his desk.

"What's this?"

"Read it."

Roger read one line. He looked up. "Do you have a memory problem, Barnaby?"

"Yeah—too many of 'em."

"Not one week ago, in this very room, I took you off Fleishman."

"Just read the damn piece."

"Sit down," the editor said testily. "You're looming again. I hate it when you loom." He skimmed the pages rapidly, a cigarette dangling from his lower lip. Hasselforth watched too many old newspaper movies. Once, for a gag, Barnaby had given him an old-fashioned eyeshade. Roger wore it till it fell apart.

He read the piece a second time, more slowly. Barnaby lolled in his seat, batting away smoke. When Roger finished, he fastened his eyes to Barnaby's face but said nothing.

"Well?" Barnaby said.

"You expect me to print this?"

"Up to you, Rog, old boy. If you don't, there's plenty that will."

"No, they won't," Hasselforth said. "This is garbage."

Something lurched inside of Barnaby, but he kept it off his face. "Harsh words," he said very gently.

"All this putrid moralizing, Jesus. Did you ever stop to think how it would read, coming from you?"

Barnaby yawned delicately.

"The other papers would come after us with machetes, and who could blame them? It really is the most awful crap, Barnaby. That trite old corruption-equals-cancer bit, for example."

"I thought it was a damned good analogy," protested the writer, stung more by this attack on his literary taste than the slur on his morals. "Corruption really does spread exactly like cancer, once it metastasizes."

"Apparently it does; everybody says so."

Barnaby winced.

"And all the hyperbole about Fleishman himself." He turned to a page at random and read; "'Fleishman played Lancelot to his own King Arthur, Iago to his own Othello: a great man brought down by his own evil impulses.'"

"That's a great line!"

"Aw, please. You wanna preach, go preach in the subways. I got news for you, my friend. Jonathan Fleishman is just another politician on the take, one of a million. Your problem is you got snookered; and that hurts your pride."

"I never denied it." Barnaby crossed his arms over his chest and studied the ceiling. "Fine," he said in the tone of one making a great concession. "Cut that part."

"Sure, cut that, and what have you got left? A bunch of names, Fleishman appointees. So the system runs on patronage: welcome to America."

"You're missing the point. I've broken down the services Fleishman provided by the agencies he needed to manipulate. He's got people in every one."

"So what? At this stage of his career I'd be surprised if Fleishman didn't have people in every city agency. Ditto for the Democratic leaders of the other boroughs."

Like a teacher instructing an incorrigibly stupid child, Barnaby said, "Every one of those people owes Fleishman their job. Do you really think they'd refuse him anything?"

"Just because he recommended them doesn't necessarily mean they're corrupt. You've got to *show* they bilked the system for him, not just imply it. Jesus, Barnaby, I feel like I'm talking to a tyro here. What's happened to you?"

Barnaby scowled. "This from the King of Guilt-by-Association."

"I'm worried about you, man. This piece doesn't even sound like you. Another reporter turned this in, you'd burn his buns."

"I don't have to take this shit." Barnaby lunged for the pages.

Hasselforth slapped a hand on top. His face assumed a crafty look. "I'm not saying it's totally worthless. I can't run it, but it's suggestive, okay? It opens up lines of inquiry. Leave it with me; we'll work on it."

Barnaby snatched the pages from under Roger's hand, folded and stashed them in his pocket.

The editor sighed. "Did you even try for confirmation?"

"Of course. I called everyone on that list."

"So? What'd you find out?"

"I found out that Fleishman's people are a hell of a lot more loyal to him than mine are to me."

"Tell you something about loyalty, Barnaby. It's like social security. What you pay in is what you get out."

"You're saying I wasn't loyal to the *Probe?*"

"The *Probe* was your power base, you said it yourself a million times. You were out to make a name for yourself."

"I never heard you complain."

"I didn't. It worked for us too. But not anymore. Not like this."

"Tell me how I wasn't loyal. Tell me one single thing I did that wasn't good for this rag."

"Just one?" Roger blew smoke at the ceiling. "How many women on this paper have you screwed?"

"Jesus fucking Christ."

"Fifteen? Twenty? Half the female work force? Look at the grin on your face. You're proud of it."

"You're jealous."

"No, just sick of you treating every new female employee like fresh meat in a lion's cage. Leaving aside what this says about your emotional maturity, it's bad for morale."

"Whose, yours?"

A geyser of smoke spewed from Hasselforth's mouth. "Go home, Barnaby."

"Kiss my ass."

"Do you have an appointment, sir?" The receptionist looked doubtfully at Barnaby's jeans and black T-shirt. He'd thought of going home to change but had discarded the notion. He was Barnaby, not some kid out of school applying for a job in the mailroom.

"Just tell Rossiter I'm here," he said.

Rossiter himself came out to greet him. They shook hands, and the *Times* editor led him to his office. A secretary served coffee while Barnaby gazed around appreciatively. Leather chairs, mahogany bookshelves, perfect order, and a secretary who did coffee; why had he wasted so much time?

"What can I do for you, Barnaby?" Rossiter asked when they were alone.

"The question is what I can do for you." Barnaby tossed his story onto Rossiter's teak desk.

"What's this?"

"My dowry."

Rossiter's eyebrows took flight. "Hasselforth fired you!"

"Hell, no. He tried to take me off the Fleishman story."

"I see."

"It was my story. So I walked."

"Quite," Rossiter said dryly. "But are you sure this is the best time to make a move?"

"Better late than never. Do I really have to sell myself to you? You know my work. You know your people have been eating my dust for years."

"That's true. And two months ago I'd have said absolutely, Barnaby—come on board, write your own ticket."

"I'm the same man I was two months ago."

"Probably. But we didn't know you then."

A hard knot formed in Barnaby's gut. He stared at Rossiter.

"It's an ugly story we've been hearing, Barnaby."

"What story's that?"

"That you had an affair with the Fleishman girl at the same

time you were investigating her father; that you kept her in the dark and used information she gave you."

"That's a total distortion."

"According to my sources, you publicly admitted the affair."

"I see I've been condemned without a hearing."

"It's a shame. Everyone knows you're one hell of a reporter. But you're tainted goods now."

Barnaby smacked his own forehead. "Look me in the eye and tell me your dick had never led you anywhere you shouldn't have gone. The point is, that thing with Grace Fleishman—at worst it's a personal failing. It's not as if I plagiarized or fabricated. What matters is the work, not the man."

Rossiter listened with his lower lip thrust forward, nodding as if he agreed; but he said, "Not gonna fly here, my friend. You can peddle that line elsewhere."

When he looked at it objectively, Barnaby could see it was Gracie's fault. She had trashed his reputation with her outrageous scene, ruining his chances with the *Times*. But somehow he could not bring himself to hate her. The girl was obviously in love with him. What else could have compelled her to make such a spectacle of herself? Fleishman's Victorian power trip was further confirmation, if any were needed. Sending her away was a transparent attempt to sever her, once and for all, from Barnaby.

He exonerated Gracie on the grounds of female weakness, himself on the grounds of duty. That left Jonathan to bear the blame, and rightly so, for it was his corruption that had brought them all to their present pass. Fleishman was like a dragon who, with his dying breath, singed the hero who slew him. But the dragon's ward was the hero's rightful prize, and Barnaby, despite all that had happened, meant to claim his due.

He did have one regret about Gracie. For all the trouble their affair had cost him, he ought to have gotten more out of it. The one time they'd made love, he had been too frantic to savor her properly. All that remained were incomplete impressions: the scent of green apples, a flash of brown thighs, an air of culpable innocence. Poor Barnaby: his bewitchment was of the senses, the hardest to dispel.

26

THE WEATHER WAS CHANGING. After months of unrelenting heat, a subtle transition had begun. The daytime winds blew as hot and dry as the land they swept, but late at night another breeze arose, moist and chill. The land licked its pale, dry lips, remembering rain. Too early yet, the kibbutzniks told each other, but nightly the clouds piled up and no stars were observed.

Summer's crop of volunteers dispersed, university students returned to the cities, and last June's graduating class, Grace's contemporaries, entered the army. The kibbutz settled in on itself. Overhead, flocks of pelicans and cranes flew south, headed for the Arabian peninsula and Africa.

One Saturday afternoon, the wind blew in birds of a different feather. Three men in khaki fatigues, without insignia, strode into the dining hall, looked about, and approached the table where Micha sat with five other kibbutzniks.

The oldest, a man of about fifty with a scarred face, planted himself in front of Micha. The others flanked him. "I want to talk to you," the scarred man commanded.

Micha lounged in his seat, legs outstretched. "Pull up a chair."

"Outside."

One of the soldiers put a hand under Micha's arm, as if to lift him. Micha didn't budge, but the kibbutzniks at his table surged to their feet. The dining room fell silent. There was a moment in which it seemed that anything might happen; then the soldier released Micha's arm.

"No problem," Micha said, and he went outside with the men—soldiers, unmistakably, though they wore no uniforms.

From the dining-hall window the kibbutzniks and volunteers, Gracie among them, watched as they stood outside, arguing. Or rather, the older man argued, waving his arms and stabbing a finger at Micha's impassive face. When the older man finished, Micha spoke a few words, sketched a salute, and walked away.

Later that afternoon, Gracie entered Tamar's small house, which smelled pungently of baking bread. The kibbutz's bread was excellent, delivered fresh each morning from a Jerusalem bakery, but on Saturdays Tamar liked to bake her own. Micha was visiting his mother, sitting beside her on the living-room sofa. They had been talking, but fell silent when Gracie appeared in the doorway.

She stopped on the threshold. "I'm interrupting."

"Come in," Tamar said with a welcoming smile, though she was clearly distracted. Micha scowled at the tiled floor. Gracie knew they'd been talking about what had happened at lunch. Discretion struggled against curiosity, an unequal battle: she sat herself down cross-legged in Tamar's armchair and waited.

"Tell her," Tamar said. "She'd better hear it from us and not…"

Micha stared past Gracie. "A prisoner died in army custody. He'd been severely beaten. The man happened to have dual citizenship. His family went to the American consulate and the foreign press, and the government was pressured into setting up a commission to investigate. I've been called to testify."

A prisoner died; he'd been beaten—the passive verb form, redolent of guilt. Once again, Grace discovered that the world was made of Tinkertoys. One touch and it collapsed. "Who beat him?" she said. "You?"

"No!"

"Then why are you being called to testify?"

"I witnessed it."

Tears came to her eyes. "You watched and did nothing?"

Micha sighed. "When I saw what was happening, I stopped it. But it was too late. The man died the next day."

Gracie drew a long, shuddering breath. "This prisoner was an Arab?"

Micha's face curdled with disgust. "You think they would do

that to a Jew? They didn't even use their fists. When I came in, he was lying on the floor and they were using him like a trampoline."

"Micha," Tamar said warningly.

"Tell her, you said. Our Gracie likes to have all the facts."

"And those soldiers today... " Gracie said.

"Came to remind me where my true loyalty lies."

"But you know what you have to do."

"No doubt it's clear to you," he said bitterly.

"Isn't it to you?"

He leaned back in his chair and stared at her. "We have a name for people like you: *yefei nefesh*, beautiful souls. People who always know the right thing to do."

"That's certainly not me."

"People like you have no idea what it's like on the ground. Every day I send my soldiers into danger. I've had men kidnapped and tortured, knifed in the souk, shot from behind. I've seen them broken by what *they're* forced to do. One kid, nineteen years old, He'd shot at the legs of a man holding a firebomb and killed a five- year-old girl. He tried to hang himself. And by the way, the prisoner who died wasn't just some random Arab. He was a leader of the Intifada."

"You're saying you won't testify?"

"I have to," he said miserably. "It's the end of my career. But there's no choice."

"Why? Because they subpoenaed you?"

"Because he was my prisoner. My responsibility."

"I'm sorry," she said. "For what it's worth, " I admire your courage."

"Did I ask for your admiration? You know nothing."

The telephone rang. Tamar went into her bedroom to answer it. She was gone a long time. Gracie smelled the bread burning and went to rescue it. As she returned to the living room, Tamar emerged from the bedroom, pale and thin-lipped.

"Leave us," she told her son. "I need to talk to Gracie."

That night, after everything was packed and readied for her flight the next day and Gracie lay sleepless on her iron cot in the airless room, an urgent desire came upon her to go into the desert. Her thoughts turned with longing to the hidden waterfall of Nachal Arugot, where Tamar had taken her. It seemed to her that if she could only visit that sublime place one more time before she left, if she could once see the sun rise in Eden, that would sustain her through all that lay ahead. It was three A. M. If she left now, she would be back by breakfast, long before anyone missed her.

She dressed in blue work shorts and a sweatshirt against the night chill, and set out down the long road to the Dead Sea. The full moon conspired, hiding behind a cloud as she traversed the exposed section of the winding drive. Though two guards patrolled the kibbutz at night, neither saw her go.

The moon emerged as she reached the entrance to Nachal Arugot, bathing the trail in an eerie glow. Bats swooped silently through the wadi, from whose depth she heard a wailing cry. The coolness of the moist night air made climbing easier, but the moonlight ebbed and flowed; parts of the path were overhung by rock, in deep shadow. Everything looked different by moonlight. Keeping to the trail required so much concentration that, for the first time since Tamar had broken the news about her mother, Grace was able for minutes at a time to forget it.

The gorge at night was dark and primordial. Under the flattening sun it had seemed lifeless, except for the green swath cut by the stream in its depth. But at night the wilderness teemed with invisible life that buzzed and rustled, clicked and swooped all around her. Disoriented, Grace passed the unmarked trail down the gorge to the hidden waterfall and continued for half an hour more before growing convinced of her mistake. Retracing her steps took a long time. By the time she found the turnoff, she was impatient and exasperated with herself. Halfway down the steep slope, she skidded, lost her footing, and began to tumble. Her fingers dug at the ground but found no purchase. Her bare legs scraped and bumped along the rocky ground. As she fell, she gathered speed and momentum. At the bottom of the slope, Grace shot over the lip and plunged twelve feet to the floor of the gorge.

She landed in water, feet first. Her left foot sank into soft silt, but her right collided with a boulder. Then both legs gave way, and she pitched forward into the shallow stream.

For some time she lay as she had fallen. Quick moving in in its channel of stone and sun-baked mud, the frigid spring water sluiced over her bruised body and washed away the blood.

At length, Grace stirred, sat up, took stock. She had multiple aches and scrapes, and a deep, ugly-looking bruise where her canteen had dug into her side, but the pain in her right ankle eclipsed all the rest. It hurt so badly she was afraid to look at it, but she forced herself. Nothing protruded, but the ankle was blue and distended, already swollen to the width of her calf. She wiggled her toes experimentally. Fiery arrows shot up her leg, but the toes obeyed. Using both hands, she lowered her leg from the boulder into the rushing stream.

She nearly fainted from the pain, but as it subsided, the cold water numbed the ankle wonderfully. Feeling better, Gracie cupped her hands and splashed water onto her face. A patch of forehead burned. When she touched it, her hand came away grotty with blood and bits of rock.

A fine sight she would look, thought Gracie, hobbling off the plane at Kennedy all bandaged and bruised. Clara would have a fit, seeing her worst fears realized. With that thought, Grace glanced down at her watch to find it clinging uselessly to her wrist by a shred of a leather band, the dial smashed to bits. Abruptly she awoke to her plight. There was no way she could climb out of here alone on one good leg; it was challenging with two. And no one knew where she was. Like some fool of a tourist, she had broken the cardinal rule by wandering off into the wilderness without leaving word. She knew exactly what the kibbutzniks would say when they realized she was gone: that she'd slunk away without a word of farewell, like Paul had. They wouldn't even look for her.

But no, she thought; her clothes, her wallet and passport were in her cabin. And her canteen was not. Micha and Tamar would figure it out, and they would search for her. Eventually help would come; but when?

Her flight was to leave at two p.m. She had planned to leave Ein Gedi by ten. Unless some early-morning hiker happened by, which was extremely unlikely, there was no way she'd be found, much less extricated, by then.

When she thought of her poor mother waiting at home, Gracie wept. It was the first time Lily had ever needed anything from her, and she was letting her down. What would they tell her? What would they tell Jonathan? Gracie, who had never prayed in her life, prayed now that Tamar would have the wits to lie, to conceal her absence until she was found. Tamar could do it. She'd had no problem lying to Gracie all these weeks. Gracie had a dreamlike recollection of Tamar standing like a piling in stormy seas while she, Gracie, sick to death of adult lies and deception spewed outrage. She'd considered Tamar her friend, and Tamar had betrayed her.

Even when all else was revealed, she'd gone on pretending there was hope. Many tumors were operable, she'd said. Some cancers could be cured. But from the instant she heard the words "tumor" and "brain," Gracie knew she was going to lose her mother—lose her, worse yet, before she ever found her.

Above all, she felt cheated. There was supposed to have been a time when she and her mother would come together in understanding and love. That time might have come when Gracie had a child of her own and thus learned a mother's secrets, or perhaps sooner; now it would never come at all. She understood that every time she had said or thought or written in her diary the words "My mother and I don't get along," the essential context had been that once they had done so and someday they would again. That context had suddenly, shockingly, ceased to exist.

Whoever said "Ignorance is bliss" had lied. Ignorance is pain deferred, payable later with interest.

A sudden flash of lightning cleaved the sky. Thunder cracked, resounding through the gorge. Gracie raised her head in amazement, wiping the tears from her eyes. After she'd told her about Lily, Tamar had said, "The sky won't fall if you shed a tear or two, Gracie." See how wrong she was. Another streak of lightning lit the world. The air had turned chill, and the wind carried a strange, electric scent.

Shivering, she pulled herself out of the stream and reclined on a narrow stone bank with just her right foot in the water. Her sweatshirt was soaked. She took it off, wrung it out, and put it back on. Now there was neither moon nor stars; mist drifted through the gorge.

Hours passed. Gracie dozed fitfully. In a dream, she heard her father call her name, but she couldn't see him. She wandered alone in a desolate plain without boundary or feature, crying like a child who's lost its way. Marooned, bereft, she had nothing left except a sense that something remained, something abided. Grace squatted down, clasping her knees; a stone arch grew up around her, like the gateway to a Roman citadel, and a white bird came from nowhere and perched upon her head.

She awoke to darkness and pain. But she knew where she was; she no longer felt lost. Dawn was approaching. Ten yards upstream, a female ibex stood on the rocky verge of the stream, head raised and nostrils flared. Gracie stared at the ibex and it stared back. A wordless acknowledgment passed between them. Then the ibex lowered her head and drank.

27

ON SUNDAY, AT SEVEN A.M. ON THE morning of the day Gracie was coming home, Tamar phoned.

"The flu," she shouted over a static-filled line. "We waited till the last minute, hoping she could fly, but she's not up to it."

"Let me talk to her," Jonathan said. "Put her on."

"She can't talk. She's lost her voice on top of everything else. We'll call tomorrow."

He believed her; it was just the way their luck was running these days. Listening to his end of the conversation, Lily began to weep. He put his arms around her and tried to comfort her. Just another day or two, he said; Gracie would surely be home before the operation. Lily covered her face, but tears seeped through her transparent fingers. She cried a lot these days. When they'd closed up the East Hampton house she'd cried as if... well, as if.

Two hours later, as Jonathan was finishing a solitary breakfast at the kitchen table, the telephone rang again. He picked it up.

"Mr. Fleishman, it's Elsie, from the answering service? There's a Mr. Elliot from the New York *Times* on the line, sir."

"You have standing orders about calls from the press."

"I know, sir, but I thought you might want to take this one. He says it's about your daughter."

Briefly Jonathan closed his eyes. It had come at last. He was surprised that it had taken so long, surprised too that it was the *Times,* this kind of scandal being more the province of the tabloids.

"Put him through."

"Mr. Fleishman? Dave Elliot, *Times*. Thanks for taking my call."

"What's this about my daughter?"

"Is Grace in Israel, Mr. Fleishman?"

"No comment."

"Sir, our Israeli correspondent picked up a local report of a girl gone missing in the Judean desert. The girl's said to be an American named Fleishman, first initial G. We know you've got family in Israel, and no one's seen Grace for a while. We wondered if it could possibly be your daughter."

Jonathan leaned against the refrigerator and stared out the window. Though last year's ivy had taken hold and spread over the terra-cotta garden walls, its roots were engulfed by weeds. Lily hadn't the strength to tend the garden these days, but Jonathan didn't have the heart to hire a gardener. He lit a cigarette with shaking hands.

"No," he said. "It's not my daughter."

"Where is Grace, Mr. Fleishman?"

Jonathan hung up. Moving slowly through the house, as if its corridors were full of a viscous fluid, he drifted upstairs to check on his wife. After a restless night she was sleeping at last. Clara sat beside her in an armchair; she gave him a reassuring nod. He walked down the hall to Paul's room and peeked in. His son was lying on his back on a mat, lifting a barbell.

"Be careful with that," Jonathan said.

"It's only forty pounds."

"Just be careful."

He continued down the hall to his study. As the oak door closed behind him, he sank to the floor, where he sat for some time, hugging his knees to his chest. The room looked different from this angle. The floor-to-ceiling bookcases seemed to lean inward, looming over him; the desk looked unscalable. The clock on the wall read nine-fifteen, which made it four-fifteen p.m. in Israel, where Sunday was an ordinary workday. If all was well, Tamar would be at work in the hospital. He got up, crossed the room to his desk, and punched in her home number. She answered on the first ring.

He said, "What the hell is going on there?"

"Jonathan... ?"

"Have you lost my daughter?"

Silence stretched over seven thousand miles.

Tamar said, "I was trying to save you a few hours' anxiety. We'll find her, I promise you."

Jonathan laid the receiver on the desk and wrapped his arms

tightly across his stomach, gasping for breath. Dark spots danced before his eyes; for the first and only time in his life, he thought he was going to faint. Gradually the darkness subsided and his breath returned to him. He picked up the phone. Tamar was calling his name.

"What happened?" he said.

"Are you all right, Jonathan?"

"Just tell me what happened."

"Yesterday, after you called, I told her about Lily. She was upset, and very angry with me for not telling her before. Eventually she calmed down. We booked her flight; then she said she wanted to be alone and went back to her room. This morning she didn't show up for breakfast. We checked her room. Everything's there except her work clothes and canteen. It looks as if she went out for an early-morning walk."

"How long has she been gone?"

"We can't be sure when she left. Probably ten, twelve hours."

"What are you doing?"

"We have search teams out looking. Gracie's a sensible girl. She'll stay put. We'll find her, Jonathan. It's not the first time someone's wandered off and gotten lost. They always turn up."

Sooner or later, he thought. Dead or alive. "Who's looking for her?"

"Veteran search teams, people who know the area well: kibbutzniks, field-school guides, Bedouin. We'll find her, Jonathan, I promise you. In a few hours this agony will be over."

"Helicopters? Dogs?"

"Not yet."

He drew a pad toward him, uncapped a pen. "What about the army?"

"They only come in after twenty-four hours. We expect to have her back long before then."

They spoke a short while longer. Then Jonathan hung up and made a list. His hand shook but his head was clear. He knew what he wanted and how to get it, and he reached for his Rolodex with the air of a knight unsheathing his sword. In less than two hours Jonathan got through to two senators, a member of Knesset, a deputy minister at State and his counterpart at Defense, a contact in the CIA, the Israeli ambassador in Washington, and the American ambassador in Tel Aviv. "My daughter is lost in the wilderness," he told them, and to a man they assumed he was speaking metaphorically. Apprised of the truth, they were shocked, sympathetic—and vulnerable.

From the Israelis Jonathan demanded that the army immediately join the search for Gracie; he demanded helicopters, dogs, and the involvement of Israel's security services. From the Americans he required massive pressure on the Israeli authorities. Everything he asked for was promised to him. When he had crossed the last name off his list, Jonathan phoned Christopher Leeds at home.

"Christopher," he said, "I've got to go to Israel."

"Me, too, some day. Good morning, Jonathan."

"I've got to go today."

"What are you talking about?"

"Gracie was staying on my sister's kibbutz. She's lost. They think she wandered off into the desert."

In the silence that greeted these words, Jonathan imagined Christopher crossing himself, a gesture he'd never seen the lawyer make.

"How long has she been missing?" Christopher asked.

"Fourteen hours, maybe more."

"My God."

"I need my passport." At his arraignment, Jonathan had been ordered to surrender his passport to the U.S. attorney's office.

"They'll never go along with it."

"They must. I want to see Lucas today, this morning."

"Jonathan, they'll suspect you of faking this thing to get out of the country and into Israel. Israel, as you know, is exceedingly reluctant to extradite Jews."

"Lucas won't believe that."

"Lucas is not your friend."

"He was. He's known Gracie since she was born."

"Which means he's got to bend over backward to avoid any sign of favoritism. At best he'll leave it to Buscaglio, and there's no hope there."

Jonathan's voice was steely. "I'll handle Lucas. Just get me in to see him."

"I'm sorry," Lucas Rayburn said. If eyes are the windows to the soul, his were barred, shuttered, and protected by steel grates. "Your attorney must have warned you. It can't be done."

"Lucas, we're talking about Gracie."

"If she is missing, the authorities will find her."

"There's no 'if.' She *is* missing."

They glared at one another from opposite sides of the conference table. Christopher Leeds sat beside Jonathan, Jane Buscaglio beside Lucas. Neither had yet spoken a word.

Lucas said, "Maybe it's just Gracie's way of saying she's not ready to come home."

"She's needed and she knows it. She wouldn't have missed her flight for anything."

"Let Lily go over, then. She's under no restraint."

"Lily can't travel."

"Why not?"

"You don't want to know."

Lucas rolled his eyes. "No, let's hear this."

"Lily's sick."

Still skeptical. "Sorry to hear it. What's wrong with her?"

"Brain cancer." No one spoke. Jonathan took a card from his jacket pocket and slid it across to Lucas. "Her doctor's name and home number. Call him. He'll confirm what I've told you."

"Jesus fucking Christ."

"In three days they operate. So you see, Gracie would have been very anxious to make that flight."

"I can't believe this."

But Lucas did, and they all saw it. Jane Buscaglio caught her boss's eye and gestured toward the door. They stepped outside and walked down the deserted corridor. Buscaglio had been reached at her gym and wore training shorts and sneakers. She barely reached Lucas' shoulder, but she walked like she had no idea they weren't equals. "Tell me you're not buying this bullshit," she said.

"You think that's what it is?"

"Please. His daughter, his wife—what is this guy, a modern-day Job?"

"I can't see him making this up. I know Fleishman. The man lives and dies by his family, especially that daughter of his."

"Then how come his lawyer never heard it before?" Buscaglio said triumphantly. "I saw Leeds's face when Fleishman pulled that final rabbit out of his hat. He was flabbergasted."

"Is it true?" Christopher Leeds was asking at that moment. "Is it possible?"

"It's true."

"Why in God's name didn't you tell me? I could have gotten a postponement. I could have used this in the hearing on freezing your assets. I can still—"

"No, you can't. We're not using Lily's illness as capital. I'm not dragging her into this, and I'm not hiding behind her skirts."

"Jonathan, you're upset, and God knows you have cause. You're carrying enough of a load. Let me do my job."

"I'm not stopping you—but you're not using Lily."

Jane Buscaglio hung up the phone in her office and shrugged. "He confirmed it, the cancer, the surgery."

Lucas rubbed his eyes. "Did he say what her prognosis is?"

"I didn't ask. You realize that when the press gets hold of this, Fleishman's going to drown in sympathy. Not to mention what happens if the daughter really does turn up missing. We'll need a change of venue to Alaska just to get an impartial jury."

"That's your concern? You think Lily got brain cancer just to fuck with us?"

"Easy, Lucas."

"I've known Lily Fleishman half my life. She's a fine woman."

"She can afford to be, on what he rakes in."

"She was the same when they had nothing. Given the situation, what's your call on the passport?"

She stared. "Frankly, it scares the shit out of me that you're even asking that question."

"He's not going to walk out on Lily now."

"For all we know, she put him up to it. For the children's sake, naturally.'"

"You're a hard woman, Jane."

She drew herself up to her full height. "Hey. I'm sorry she's sick, but basically I don't have a whole lot of sympathy for the lady, okay? Because as far as I'm concerned, either she knew what he was up to or she deliberately closed her eyes. Either way, she had no problem spending the loot. And, just 'cause someone obviously has to say it, we'd be crazy to let Fleishman go abroad."

"He's not going to run. He won't desert Lily."

"You're the boss," Buscaglio said. "But if he jumps....Think about it, Lucas. Do you really want to put your career in that man's hands?"

* * *

They returned to the conference room. Lucas went around the table and sat down beside Jonathan. "I know you don't want my sympathy, but that's all I can offer."

"What's it going to take," Jonathan said, "to get that passport?" Christopher gave him a sharp look, which Jonathan ignored.

"No deals," Buscaglio interjected. "What good is a deal once you're over there?"

Jonathan ignored her, directing his words to Lucas. "You want me to plead guilty? I'll do it unconditionally. I'll sign a confession here and now."

"The hell you will." Christopher jumped up and tugged Jonathan's arm. "Come on, we're leaving."

"Listen to your lawyer," Lucas said. "Go home."

Jonathan turned to Buscaglio. "A full and complete confession. An admission of all my sins, in return for permission to go find my daughter and bring her home."

"Worthless," Leeds said quickly. "I'd have it thrown out in a minute,"

"Would you name your accomplices?" Buscaglio asked.

"I said *my* sins," Jonathan said. "No names, but I'll plead guilty to every count of every charge."

"No, you won't." Christopher looked past him at Lucas. "If you have any decency, Rayburn, you'll put a stop to this now."

"Forget it, Jonathan," Lucas said. "The passport's not on offer, and anyway, you know as well as we do that a confession under these circumstances would be worthless. But you know,"—he leaned in toward Jonathan, holding his eyes—"I've got this crazy feeling that maybe you really *want* to confess. I'm wondering if somewhere inside you, the principled man I once knew is buried alive, fighting to get out."

"Shame on you," Christopher cried. "You're telling a depressed, traumatized man to go ahead and jump."

"No, sir, I'm telling him it's okay to do the right thing. I'm saying it's the only way to salvage anything from a career that was once exemplary. You're advising him to squander his last shred of dignity on a desperate effort to deny the truth, and I hate that. I don't blame you; I know your job is to get him off, not to save his soul. But he still has choices. And you know that, Jonathan. Somewhere inside, you know that."

28

"HALF THE GODDAMN MORNING WASTED waiting for you prima donnas to get your tutus on," Micha said disgustedly, "then a fucking drop of rain falls and you're afraid to go out."

"A drop of rain?" the other said. Sheets of gray rain curtained the window of the dining hall, whose atmosphere was dense with smoke and steaming bodies.

Micha was getting a civilian's brush-off from an old comrade, currently the commander of the army's search team. Lieutenant Mordecai Rachamim, called Motke, came from a small development town in the Negev. His parents were Tunisian immigrants, and Motke had been a fanatic Likud supporter since he was big enough to sling a tomato. Micha was a third-generation Labor man. They had nothing but the army in common, and outside, their paths would never have crossed; the friendship dated back to the first push northward through Lebanon, where the two young officers argued politics by night and fought grueling house-by-house battles by day.

Micha said, "If you'd gotten the fucking dogs here on time, we'd have had her by now."

"Too late now, that's for sure. Which reminds me: Yossi, cancel the dogs," Motke said into his radio.

"I just want to know one thing. Is this personal? Are you sitting on your ass because this girl's my cousin?"

"Fuck you, Kimchi. It's not her fault she's related to you. She'll find shelter, and we'll find her as soon as the weather breaks, *if* she's out there."

"What if she's hurt? What if she can't reach shelter? It's been nearly 36 hours. She could die of exposure."

Motke lit a new cigarette from the butt of the old. "Those trails could wash out any minute. The wadis are flooding already. Plus, for all we know she's drinking coffee in a Tel Aviv café."

"With no money and no clothes."

"Maybe she met someone. She's an American, right? Look, I don't give a shit how much heat I get from headquarters. It's my call, and I'm not risking my men's lives for nothing. It's a question"—he blew smoke in Micha's face—"of loyalty toward our men."

"So that's what it comes down to."

"You got it."

"How much loyalty, Motke? Enough to close your eyes to murder?"

"It wasn't murder."

"Why not? Because he was an Arab?"

"Goddamn kibbutzniks. Who set you to be a light to the nations?"

"It's as much my army as yours."

"Not for long," Motke said.

"Well?" Tamar said as Micha entered her house on a gust of wind and rain.

"Nothing. They're waiting for the rain to end."

"Bastards," Yaacov said, pacing back and forth on his gimpy leg.

"Same with Udi," Tamar said. Udi Heskel was chief ranger on the Ein Gedi nature reserve and head of the regional search team. "They've pulled everyone back for fear of floods."

"I don't understand how you could let her go off like that," Yaacov said. "Such terrible news, and then you just let her go."

Micha sprang to his mother's defense. "No one could have anticipated this. Gracie should have known better."

Tamar passed a hand over her eyes. Yaacov was right, she thought. She never should have left the girl alone.

"And then to run and tell Jonathan before we even get her back. What will they think of us?"

"I didn't tell him," Tamar said wearily. "He found out somehow."

"Clara will never forgive me."

"Dad, the woman hasn't spoken to you in twenty years. How're you going to know the difference?"

"I'll know."

"I'm off, then," said Micha.

Tamar looked from him to the window, blasted by rain. "I'll go with you."

"You'd only slow me down. And I need someone to man the radio in case I get lucky."

"Yaacov can do that."

"You're not coming," Micha said flatly.

They locked eyes. Finally Tamar nodded. "Take my medical kit. Where will you go?"

"Nachal Arugot," he said. He'd been over it again and again in his head. Nachal David was the most accessible of her haunts, the hills above the kibbutz the most dangerous; but both areas had been thoroughly searched the day before, without result. That left Nachal Arugot, where Grace had hiked with Tamar.

Yaacov said, "Udi's already been there."

"Only along the upper trail. Udi doesn't really believe she's out there. He thinks she's holed up somewhere, giggling at all the fuss."

"I took her down to the hidden waterfall. She loved it." Tamar's voice was full of dread. No one needed to say what they all knew. When the first rain fell as early and hard as this unseasonal deluge, flash floods were sure to follow. Six years ago, two young boys hiking through Nachal Arugot had been caught by a flash flood. They'd drowned in the wadi.

Micha slipped Tamar's medical kit into his knapsack and shouldered the pack. He nodded good-bye.

"Be careful," Tamar said.

"I'm always careful."

"That's not what I meant."

He paused at the door, looking back.

"Be careful with Gracie," she said. "How is it with you and your cousin?"

Her son stared at her. "Really, Ema? Is this the time?"

"Precisely the time. If you find her, she'll be a very grateful girl."

"As well she should be."

"Don't hurt this child, Micha."

"Whatever Gracie is, she's not a child. And if you're going to worry about someone, worry about me."

* * *

The Greek philosopher Zeno said that one can never step in the same river twice, for the river flows and changes constantly, sweeping all with it. Toss a stone into moving water and both the stone and its impression vanish instantly; excavate a river and all you'll find is silt and more silt. Not so the desert, whose nature is to desiccate and thus preserve. Excavate a desert and layer upon layer of human and natural history is revealed, indelibly inscribed in rock; press your ear to the ground and hear, beneath the thrumming of everything that moves, the faint temporal echoes of those who came before.

When these two elemental forces meet, rushing water and impermeable rock, the potential for destruction transcends the present. Not only all that is, but all that was is swept away; time itself is stripped to the bone. Thus it was that when God chose to undo the world, his instrument was flood.

This was the sight that greeted Micha when he left his jeep at the beginning of Nachal Arugot and embarked on the path that snaked along its northern wall: a stream that should have been a mere trickle, swollen into a raging river, flooding the wadi floor and surging toward the Dead Sea. Micha, who knew the wadi intimately in all its moods and seasons, had never seen it so distempered.

On ordinary days it was possible to stand at one end of Nachal Arugot and holler, and the sound would echo and reecho down kilometers of canyon, loosening rocks and sending the skittish ibex flying. Micha cupped his hands to his mouth and bellowed Gracie's name, but could not even hear himself over the pounding of the rain and the roar of the stream below. Beneath the hood of his slicker he wore an army cap with a visor, but the wind spiraled through the gorge, blinding him with rain. His anger at Motke abruptly disintegrated. If Micha had commanded the search team, he, too, would have sent his men home to wait out the storm.

He took the walkie-talkie from his backpack. "Ema, can you hear me?"

There was a loud crackle of static, then Tamar's voice: "... are you?"

"I'm just entering the wadi now. It's badly flooded. Let them know—they're going to have to close the road."

The radio crackled but he couldn't make out the words.

"There's zero visibility and the noise is tremendous. I'll try the path first, then cut down lower."

"Be careful." Her voice was suddenly clear.

Micha hunched his shoulders and set off. He hated worrying Tamar, who had the harder part of waiting, but it couldn't be helped. They had to know where to look in case of accident.

As he walked, he searched the ground. It told him nothing, all sign of human passage washed away. Frequently he stopped, looked about, and called Gracie's name. No answer came. Micha passed groups of ibex huddled motionlessly beneath stone overhangs. They lowered their heads at him but did not flee. Twice the trail was blocked by rockslides; he had to pick his way around the obstructions.

At length he came to a small plateau where the path forked. To his right the trail rose into the mist; to his left it descended a steep slope toward the hidden waterfall. Before heading down, Micha tried the radio, but raised nothing but static.

Halfway down the slope he came across the first sign of Gracie's passage, a sodden swath of blue material, snagged on a rock. A little farther on he found a torn sandal, which he recognized as hers.

He picked it up. "Gracie!" he cried. The wind took his voice and flung it back at him. Micha scrambled down, crouching back on his heels in a controlled slide that took him to the very lip of the land, below which was a sheer drop of four meters to the bottom of the gorge. The wadi was particularly narrow at this point, its spring-fed waters usually contained in small pools and rivulets, closely bounded by stone walls. He stood upon the verge and gazed down in awe at a rapid, cascading stream, some two meters deep.

"Gracie!" he cried. Throwing off the hood of his slicker, he listened but heard only the rain clattering around him and the stream sucking and spitting great spumes of protest as it crashed into boulders. Then, from within the storm's great bluster, came a faint, irregular, unnatural sound, a metallic clink. Micha sidled along the edge, following the sound to its source: a canteen caught by its strap between two massive boulders. The rushing water battered the canteen repeatedly against the rock. It looked dented but new, as well it might; he'd bought it only weeks ago.

Micha stepped back, away from the verge. He hunkered down

and clapped his hands over his eyes. From the darkness, a vision arose, of Grace tumbling down the slope, grasping desperately at rocks and ground and thorny bushes, then sailing over the edge and into the rocky ravine.

The fall alone wouldn't have killed her, but it might have immobilized her, pinning her down helplessly as the waters rose and rose.

He crawled back to the verge and peered over. "Gracie!" he shouted. The wind laughed back at him. "Gracie!" he cried, but his voice sank like a stone in water. Yet a third time he called her name, so hopeless of response that, when it came, he doubted his ears. It wasn't until the second answering cry that he jumped up and looked around.

He saw no one. A voice had spoken, but no one was near. A shiver of primordial awe ran through him: *Who calls my name in the wilderness?* But as he turned back to the gorge, a hail of pebbles rained down from above. He spun around in time to see first an arm, then a disheveled head emerge from a crevice in the hillside, twenty meters above him. The arm waved vigorously, and Gracie cried out to him.

Later, when he thought of this time, he could never remember crossing the distance that separated them. He remembered hearing her voice, seeing her; then they were huddled inside her tiny cave and she had thrown her arms around his neck and he was hugging her.

Gracie recovered first and pulled away. "Sorry I pounced."

"Pounce away."

She laughed. "I never thought I'd be so glad to see you."

"Likewise." Micha took a thermal blanket from his knapsack and wrapped it around her shoulders. She was shivering and her skin was hot to the touch; but her eyes were focused and clear. "Are you hurt?"

"My ankle."

Her right ankle was tightly bound in a wet bandage that turned out, as he unwound it, to be a bra. For the life of him he couldn't help replaying their embrace, reassessing what he'd felt under her damp shirt. Unwrapped, the ankle was puffy and blue, but didn't seem to be broken. Assuming a dispassion he didn't in the least feel, he told her to lie down, then checked her over. The sole of her left foot was mottled with small bruises and cuts, probably from clambering barefoot on the rocks; the right was unscathed, indicating that she'd put no weight on it. There were dark bruises along her left side; when he probed them, she winced. Micha added a possible broken rib to his inventory of injuries. When he was finished, he wrapped her in the blanket.

"How the hell did you get out?" he said.

"Climbed out."

"On one leg? Bravo, Gracie."

She shrugged. "The water was rising. I had no choice."

"Why didn't you answer sooner? Didn't you hear me calling?"

"I'd fallen asleep. When I heard you call, I thought I was dreaming."

"When I saw your canteen, I thought..." He didn't say what he thought.

"The strap got caught and wouldn't come loose, and finally I thought I'd better leave it and get higher. All the animals were gone by then."

"The animals?" he said, wondering if he'd overlooked a head injury.

"They came to drink in the morning, the ibex and those furry little mammals. I was glad to see them; till then I'd had only mosquitoes for company. Then the rain started, and they ran away up the hillside. After a while, something amazing happened. Snakes and crabs crawled out of the water and from under rocks, and they started slithering up the slopes. It was raining hard by then, and I got the feeling they knew something I didn't. So I decided to climb out."

"You decided to climb out," he echoed.

She gave him a silencing look.

Micha poured hot coffee with milk into the cap of his thermos and supported Grace with a strong arm as she drank. He gave her some biscuits and dates; she wolfed them down and asked for more. Afterward she leaned against him comfortably, not saying anything. He put his arm around her. Micha could have stayed in that cave forever, but he knew the heat radiating from her body wasn't passion, but fever.

"I have to leave you for a little while."

Gracie sat up in alarm. "Why?"

"I've got to get far enough out to radio for help. Then I'll come back. It won't take long."

"I can walk out, if you help."

"And do more damage to that ankle? No—we'll lay on some transport for you."

Gracie knew people were waiting, worrying about her, so she said, "Go ahead." But as Micha crawled toward the cave's opening, she panicked. "Wait, please. Don't leave me alone yet."

He looked out at the slashing rain. There would be no rescue till the weather cleared. He came back and sat close beside her.

"It's funny," she said. "Somehow I knew it would be you who came for me."

He turned to her with burning eyes. "And did you know why?"

"Fear of Tamar?"

He laughed. And then somehow it happened that he was kissing her. He kept waiting for her to push him away, but she didn't. After a moment of what felt like astonishment, her lips parted under his and she kissed him back hard. She tasted of dates and honey. The kiss felt like hello and goodbye all at the same time.

Micha wrapped his arms around her, and her body melted into his. The blanket fell off her shoulders. She was shivering, though her skin was hot to the touch. *Be careful,* he heard his mother say, but he didn't need her to tell him. He let go of Gracie and backed away as far as he could in the tiny crevice.

"Regrets already?" Gracie asked; then, when he didn't answer: "Don't worry, I get it. You rescued me, and now here we are, just the two of us, marooned in a cave like the last two people on earth. It's situational."

"You think?"

"What else could it be?"

"Could be love," he said. "Crazy, stupid love."

A moment passed while they looked into each other's eyes. Neither one was laughing now. A blush spread over Gracie's pale face.

"I guess we'll never know," she said. "I'm needed at home."

"For now," Micha said.

29

IT'S JUST LIKE FALLING ASLEEP," the anesthesiologist said. "You'll feel no pain. When you wake up, it will all be over."

"To sleep, perchance to dream, ah, there's the rub," Lily said almost gaily, the sedative having had that effect.

"Do you have any questions?"

"Where's my daughter?"

"On her way," Jonathan said, taking her hand. The doctor nodded to him and slipped out of the room.

"I won't go till I've seen Gracie."

"Paul called. The plane landed, he's got her, and they're on their way."

"She'll be here, *tochter*. Don't worry about Gracie," Clara said. She sat on the far side of the bed, half-hidden behind an enormous spray of late-blooming salt-spray roses. Jonathan, unable to sleep the night before, had driven all the way out to East Hampton and back to bring Lily roses from her own garden. Their sweet, wandering scent filled the room, displacing the antiseptic odor.

The door opened and Gracie rushed in, casting aside a crutch as she knelt at the bedside. She burst into tears of relief. "I was so afraid I'd miss you."

Lily laid her hand on Gracie's dark head. "Thank you," she said fervently to Paul, as if he had personally plucked Grace from the wilderness.

He shut the door. "No big deal."

Lily said, "Are you all right, darling? Your poor ankle."

"I'm fine, forget about me. I'm so sorry for the worry, the trouble I caused."

"Your father had the worry. They didn't tell me till you were found."

Gracie looked up. "Dad...."

Jonathan reached down and helped her to her feet. He put his arms around her and she laid her head against his chest. She was thinner, her body harder than the last time he'd embraced her. Paul, seeing the tears in his father's eyes, turned away in disgust. Gracie, his Teflon sister: was there nothing she could do to lose their love?

"What a naughty girl," Clara said, " worrying us all to death." Jonathan growled and she subsided. "Thanks God, is all I got to say."

A short while later, an orderly came with a gurney to take Lily to surgery. Paul kissed her and moved away to the window. Gracie said, "I love you, Mommy."

"I know, darling. I love you, too."

Jonathan walked beside the gurney, holding Lily's hand. They rode up in the elevator and passed through a labyrinth of corridors until they came to a pair of green swinging doors. "This is where we leave you," the orderly said, stepping away.

Jonathan bent and kissed her on the lips. He couldn't speak.

"Don't worry, love," Lily said.

The orderly swung her around and backed through the green doors. Dr. Barrows was waiting on the other side. He leaned over the gurney, pulled down his mask, smiled. "Hello, Lily. How're you feeling?"

"Scared."

"Don't be. With Tamar breathing down my neck I wouldn't dare be less than perfect."

Lily felt woozy, uninhibited. "Don't take out my mother," she pleaded.

"You're in the best hands," said a nurse with kind eyes.

They wheeled her into the operating room and asked her to slide onto the table. Lily looked up at the lights, then around. The room was full of people. In the corner stood a table full of terrible-looking instruments. Her heart began to pound. A masked man loomed from behind. She didn't recognize the upside-down face until it spoke. "Did your daughter make it back in time?"

"Yes, she did."

"Good. What's your favorite flavor, Lily?"

"Strawberry."

"Strawberry it is." He placed a mask over her face.

It was nothing like falling asleep. There was no transition. She was; then she was not.

Gracie's return from the wilderness was a sign to Jonathan that all was not lost. His pending trial had faded to insignificance. His priorities were finally clear. They could confiscate his property, they could incarcerate his body; but there were things, infinitely more precious, they could never touch.

In the surgical waiting room, Jonathan sat on a sofa between his children, holding their hands and watching the clock. Clara, exhausted, fell asleep in an armchair. She slept, snoring lightly, for three hours. Then Dr. Barrows came, still in his greens.

He didn't smile. "She's out of surgery and resting comfortably."

Jonathan was already on his feet. "Can we see her?"

"Not yet, no. She's still in recovery. Let's go to my office and chat."

The invitation was meant for Jonathan alone, but Gracie jumped up. "I'm coming, too." She intercepted a warning look from the doctor to her father. "Please, Dad. No more secrets."

Jonathan said, "No more secrets. Paul, do you want to come?"

"I'll stay with Grandma."

Barrows led them down the hall to a small office. Gracie leaned her cane against his desk and sat beside her father.

"We got the preliminary path report," Barrows said. "It's not good news."

Jonathan had prepared for this in his imagination. It was important to bear up, to be calm, rational, in control, a pillar of strength to his family. He had practiced saying the word "malignant" as if it were an ordinary word, like "lamp" or "mayonnaise." He opened his mouth. An awful sound came out, a kind of bleat.

"Do you want me to go on?" Barrows asked.

Jonathan nodded.

"It's a type of tumor called glioblastoma multiformi. We were able to debulk the primary lesion, but the tumor has spread. It's probably metastasized to other organs, but that's not going to matter. It's the damage to the brain that's critical."

Gracie closed her eyes. For a moment she was back in the wadi with the water rising around her.

"What can you do?" Jonathan asked.

"We've bought some time with this procedure. Radiation therapy could buy some more."

"How much time?" He felt outside the scene, above it, watching like a spectator at a play.

"With radiation, a couple of months. Maybe less. A lot depends on her willingness to fight." And to endure, Barrows thought but did not say. There was only so much people could absorb at one time. In this case, the ultimate prognosis was grim enough without bringing in the stages of the disease.

"If we'd caught it sooner... " Jonathan began.

Barrows interrupted. "Wouldn't have mattered. This kind of tumor, by the time it's symptomatic, it's already spread."

"What now?"

"First, she'll need to recover from surgery. Then we'll see where we stand. There are several options."

Grace emerged from her stupor to turn a dangerous look on Barrows. "Options?" she echoed. "You sound like a goddamn stockbroker."

"It's not his fault," her father said. "He's trying to help."

"Why operate on her if it's hopeless? Why put her though all this, if he can't save her?"

"We couldn't know until we tried," Barrows said gently. "And today's surgery has prolonged her life."

She looked him up and down. "Tamar said you were a great doctor, but I think you're a fraud."

"Gracie," Jonathan said, "that's unjust and uncalled for. You're not helping."

"How can I help? Tell me what to do and I'll do it, whatever it is."

"Just be with her," the doctor said.

Barnaby nursed his fourth whiskey and flipped channels with the remote. Lily Fleishman's surprise surgery led the eleven-o'clock news on all three networks, each of which ran identical footage of the family leaving the hospital, followed by old clips of Lily looking vibrant and lovely. "Tragedy strikes the Fleishman household." "Hospital sources described Mrs. Fleishman's condition as 'guarded' after surgery to remove a cancerous tumor." "The family remained secluded in their Highview home tonight following..."

Sympathy dripped from their tongues. The anchors shook their heads, looked grave, and sighed.

"Goddamn pack dogs." Barnaby felt sick. Those shots of Fleishman leaving the hospital with his arms around his children (yes, Gracie was back, but he wasn't going to think about that now) were utterly beyond the pale. Had the man no shame? Did he need to grovel for pity, degrading not only himself but also all those who once believed in him? It was pathetic, and so was the manner in which the media pandered to this blatant bid for sympathy, instead of examining, analyzing it. There was, despite Roger's denigration, a natural and enlightening analogy to be made between cancer and corruption. But did they make it?

He switched off the television, picked up the phone, and punched out Hasselforth's home number.

"Did you believe that shit?" he said.

Roger sighed. "What shit?"

"Lily Fleishman's alleged cancer."

"Alleged? You think they made it up? They cut her brain open, asshole."

"There's a great story here, and you're missing it as usual. Corruption as political cancer; the conflation of the public and private realms."

"What are you, married to that metaphor? You ought to get off the sauce and start thinking again."

"Fuck you too." Barnaby hung up. He tried to roll a joint, but his hands were shaking. He lay back, and thought of Gracie as she'd appeared on his television screen. She looked like she'd been beaten up. There was a bandage on her forehead and a cast on her foot. None of the networks so much as mentioned her injuries, which had to be Fleishman pulling strings as usual. What the hell had he done to her?

Gracie had stared into the camera almost as if she were searching for someone. Barnaby had no doubt it was him. He thought about calling her, just to make things right. He knew exactly what he'd say. "We fucked each other over; now we're even. No hard feelings, kid."

He ought to rescue her, take her away from Jonathan. The idea excited him, though he knew it was premature. In the meantime, no point wasting a perfectly good hard-on. Too smashed to get up for his phone book, Barnaby dialed the one number he knew by heart.

On the fourth ring, a slurred voice answered.

"Hey, Ronnie," he said.

"Who the fuck is this?"

"Your lover, babe."

"It's two fucking o'clock. What do you want?"

"I want you, babe. I'm willing to forgive and forget if you are. Why don't you hop in a cab and come over?"

Silence. Then: "Are you out of your mind?"

"I miss you, Ronnie."

"Try jerking off." She hung up.

30

L EAVES CLUNG TO THE WINDOW SCREEN like drowning passengers to a ship's debris; then the wind's tide swept them away. The framed sky was patchy gray and white, the ivy brown against the terra-cotta walls. Lily scorned the waste of precious time that was television, and spent her rare hours alone gazing out into her garden, watching the season change.

She lay under three blankets, for the room was chilly. Once, her friend Margo had come to visit. As she bent to kiss Lily, her face crinkled with repugnance, an expression gone in a moment but not before Lily registered it. Cancer had an odor all its own, a sickly- sweet stench like rotting flesh that exuded from the mouth and pores; and though she herself, immersed in the disease, could not sense it, others could. From then on Lily had insisted that the bedroom window remain open. Even so, her son rarely entered the room, and didn't stay long when he did.

She had come home over Dr. Barrows' objections. He'd pressed her to stay for radiation. "Will it save my life?" she'd asked him flat out. He seemed surprised by the question, but Lily waited him out, her ostrich days over.

"It's not a cure," he said. "It will prolong your life."

"Prolong my death, you mean. No, thank you."

The doctor appealed to Jonathan, but her husband would not oppose her wishes; if Lily wanted to come home, he said, then home was where she belonged. The couple had, in these last days, reverted to the posture of their first. They were partners again, back to back against the world, as if all the years of growing apart had never been. Jonathan turned to Lily for counsel and comfort, she to him for strength and reassurance.

"I'm a coward," she told Jonathan matter-of-factly. "I'm not afraid of dying, but I'm scared to death of pain. I want you to promise me... "

He promised.

Their rediscovered intimacy was an anodyne to the second passing of her mother, excised by Dr. Barrows' scalpel. No more sweet lullabies to smooth the passage into sleep, no more the sense of someone close behind her. Was Greta's voice really no more than a side effect of Lily's disease, an effluence of cancer? Lily could not think it. Perhaps it was the imminence of the end, or an inability to conceive of her own nonbeing, but Lily had come to imagine death as a barrier to perception, not being. She believed the cancer had not generated the voice, but rather blocked the censor that kept it from being heard. Thus, unseen, unheard, her mother yet lived on within her, as Lily would in some sense live on in her children.

But these were thoughts for the empty hours when she gazed out at her garden, idle speculation, for soon enough the issue would be proved, and if she was wrong she would never know it. Far more absorbing, far more pressing, were the problems of the living, and herein lay the bitterest pain of all, that Lily was not to know how their lives turned out. There was no greater sorrow than the loss of a child; and whether it was the child or the mother who died, the severance was the same.

Thus Lily mourned for and was comforted by her children, especially Gracie; for contrary to all reasonable expectation, it was her difficult and distant daughter who cleaved to her, her loving son who stayed away. When he did visit, Paul acted as if he were angry with her. Though he spoke all the right words of encouragement and sympathy, his eyes accused her of desertion. But Lily's relationship with Gracie was utterly changed, for the awful constraint of time had eradicated all others, and together with sorrow came moments of lightheartedness, laughter, and love.

Not only in relation to Lily was Gracie changed. The whole family marked it and wondered. Clara walked into her own room one night, after Lily had fallen asleep, to find her granddaughter sitting on the floor with tears on her cheeks. A photo album lay open on her lap. "My rough, tough Gracie, crying over pictures?" the old woman said in amazement.

Gracie scrubbed at her face with a sleeve. "I didn't know you saved all these old photos."

Clara sank heavily into her upholstered rocking chair and laid her knitting bag beside her. "So who told you to go snooping in my room? You want I should go snooping in yours?"

This, in Clara, was a mere hiccup of ill humor, a conversational tic that Gracie ignored. She said, "Yaacov was a smashing man, wasn't he?"

"Jacob," Clara corrected. She looked down at their wedding photo and snorted. "A million years ago I wasn't so bad myself."

"You were beautiful. He's still a good-looking man, you know."

"And I'm an old bag. Life's unfair."

This seemed too self-evident to invite comment. Gracie turned to a photo of Clara and Jacob holding a newborn baby girl. All three stared solemnly into the camera, he in black, Clara stout in white with a high ruffled collar, the infant in a stiff white bonnet.

"How come neither of you ever married again?"

Her grandmother laughed deep in her throat. "Once is enough."

"That's the same thing he said."

"Shows what a fool he is," said Clara, not without a note of self-satisfaction.

"If he's a fool, what are you?"

"It's different for women. Women marry for *kinder*. I already had my children."

"They marry for husbands too."

Clara sniffed. "Men *are* children."

"My father's not."

"No. But look what it took for him to grow up. What is it all of a sudden with the questions? Eighteen years you didn't care, suddenly you got to know everything?"

"It interests me, that's all. I've been thinking about families and what makes them stick together or fall apart, and I thought about you and Yaacov, how you're not together but not really apart either, since you never got divorced."

"It's not so easy, divorce."

Gracie said, "I just wish they were here, that's all. I wish our family was together."

The old woman rocked and sighed, and after a while she said quietly, as if speaking to herself, "So do I, *maideleh*. So do I."

That Gracie had changed was as apparent to her family as its cause was obscure. Something had happened in Israel, that was certain. Was it Tamar's effect they were seeing? Israel's? Was it Gracie's ordeal in the desert, or some unknown factor, a secret lover, perhaps? When Lily asked, Gracie just smiled.

"Will you go back to Israel?" she asked.

Gracie looked amused. "Someday, maybe. I was asked."

"By whom?"

"Tamar, for one."

"What is she like," Lily asked, gently mocking, "this paragon aunt?"

"Tamar? Solid. I have an image of her as a kind of ancient Indian fertility figure, short and squat, with a center of gravity right around the pelvis. Don't know why, since she's neither squat nor particularly fertile."

"Was she good to you?"

"She didn't mother me, if that's what you mean. She liked me."

"She always did. And Micha," Lily said slyly, for little had been said of Micha, "did he like you too?"

Gracie laughed. "Strangely enough, he did."

"Nothing strange about it, my darling."

"I wasn't very nice to him."

"Just as well. If you're too nice to men, they get ideas above their station."

They laughed, two women together, allies at last. Then Grace asked: "Were you too nice to Dad?"

The smile faded from Lily's face. Gracie was still Gracie after all, with the same instinct for the jugular.

"Maybe. Things might have turned out better if I'd been more forceful. You, my darling, on the other hand, are much too hard on him."

A ghost of her old truculence crossed Gracie's face. "We're doing better. Mostly I stay out of his way."

"That's not doing better. You misjudge him, Gracie. If only you would trust what you know, instead of what you hear. You know him better than any of *them*."

"Do I? I'm not sure."

"Whatever they say he did, whatever mistakes he made, your father is a thoroughly decent man. And you know that, Gracie." Lily took her daughter's hand and squeezed it hard. "You know it."

* * *

Jonathan's trial had progressed to the stage of pretrial hearings, which required his presence in court. He did not so much participate as audit, politely attendant but disengaged. All decisions he left to Christopher Leeds, except one. Leeds argued strenuously for a postponement on the grounds of Lily's ill health; Jonathan refused.

"What's the point?" he whispered as they stood in the corridor awaiting the start of a hearing. "She's not getting any better."

"The point is, you're useless to me in this state. Your body's here, but your mind's a million miles away. The prosecution won't object. Ms. Buscaglio as much as told me, 'Ask and ye shall receive.' Why not, for heaven's sake?"

"Because I want it resolved. I want an end to it, and so does Lily."

"I'll go to the judge," Leeds threatened. "I'll get a ruling that you're temporarily incapable of assisting in your own defense."

"You do and I'll fire your ass."

"Which would just prove my point. What would firing me accomplish? You've got no money. Who's going to defend you, some pimply-faced P.D. fresh out of law school? You want to spend the rest of your life in prison?"

"Of course not!"

"Sometimes I wonder if that's not just what you crave, a nice safe cell where nothing more can happen to you."

"Stick to the law, Christopher. You'd make a lousy shrink." The case was called, and they went inside.

Afterward, Christopher Leeds drove up to Highview to call on Lily. She received him in her bedroom and heard him out, and he thought from the way she nodded as he spoke that he had won her over. But when he finished, Lily said, "I won't let my husband go through this ordeal alone."

"But he is alone. You can't come to court, and your children, quite properly, won't leave you."

"But I'm here when he comes home. We talk. Later," Lily said gently, "he won't have even that."

Frail and gaunt, her golden hair replaced by a wig, she was so shockingly unlike the lovely woman of just a few months ago that it nearly broke his calcified lawyer's heart. For Jonathan's sake, Leeds tried once more. "Don't you see, Lily, he's so distracted and distressed over you, he can't think straight."

She put her hand on his, and hers was as dry as parchment. "But he *is* thinking straight, Christopher. We both are. Straighter than we have in years."

"Maybe he's right," Jonathan said later, watching from the bedroom window as the lawyer, his head sunk between his shoulder blades, walked slowly to his car. "What's going to happen will happen. Why waste precious time in court that could be spent together?"

"Doing what? Reminiscing about our salad days? No, Jonathan. For as long as I have left, I want to be part of your life, your real life."

Though many things were said between them that once would not have been, some things remained unspeakable. The worst was Jonathan's growing fear that the trial would last longer than she would. From week to week he watched her grow weaker, until she could no longer get out of bed unassisted. Pain etched fine lines on her flawless face. It came and went, assaulting in modulated waves like labor contractions, rising to a similar intensity. In these peaks of pain, Lily abandoned herself as women do in childbirth; she lost all inhibitions, howled and screamed and soiled the bedclothes with vomit and urine, as if she were struggling to give birth to death.

Jonathan began to feel he could bear her death better than her pain. He begged her to take more morphine, but she resisted; the drug made her groggy and increased her nausea. Dr. Barrows told him that marijuana could relieve the nausea, so Jonathan went out one night and bought a couple of lids. He rolled a dozen joints and put them in a box on her night table. Sometimes he smoked with her and they got stoned together, just like old times. But when the pain was at its worst, she banished him from the room and would have no one but Clara or the nurse he had engaged for her. Closed doors could not block out the sound of her retching. Gracie wept in sympathy, and Paul stalked the house with a Walkman glued to his ears. Jonathan thought of his promise. How much more could she endure? How much more could they?

The hearings concluded, and jury selection was set to begin in ten days. Christopher Leeds came to the house to see Jonathan, bearing a bouquet of asters and mums and a jar of his wife's strawberry preserves for Lily. They sat in Jonathan's study and Leeds said, "There have been some developments. Our discussions with the Eastborough Democratic party have reached the point where they're willing to accept a voluntary suspension, with pay and benefits, pending the conclusion of your trial." He paused for comment. Jonathan stared blankly, rubbing his brandy snifter along his lower lip. "It means, among other things, that your health insurance continues," Leeds said. "I don't have to tell you how important that is."

Jonathan stirred. "Is that why? Did you bring her into it?"

"I didn't have to. They know."

"So they did it for Lily."

"No doubt her condition affected them."

"Tell them to go to hell. We don't need their charity. Tell them it's too little, too late."

"I already accepted."

"You had no right."

"Shut up, Jonathan," Leeds said equably. "You're in no position to take that attitude. Besides, they're entitled to care about Lily. You have to allow other people their decent impulses."

This drew a tight smile out of Jonathan, and a tacit concession. "What's the other development?"

"Ms. Buscaglio called again."

"What's the offer?" he asked, without much interest.

"Reduced charges and a recommendation for leniency in sentencing."

"In return for... ?"

"Basically for what you offered that day in Rayburn's office. A full admission of guilt."

He was quiet for a while. "What do they mean by leniency?"

"We didn't get into that. I wanted to find out first if you're interested." Leeds's eyes, magnified behind monkish glasses, gave out nothing.

"What's your advice, counselor?"

Leeds laced his fingers and gazed into them. A snifter of brandy sat untouched on the table beside his club chair. Jonathan's study was redolent with an almost sybaritic atmosphere of leather and smoke, old books, cognac, and Persian carpets. Fleishman was a man, thought Christopher Leeds, who liked his comforts, who, more than most, defined himself by what he had. Though it was not his habit to indulge in negative thinking, he couldn't help wondering how such a man would fare in a prison cell.

He said, "It's a chance to avoid the possibility of a substantial prison term. We both know what that means, given the circumstances. But you would have to plead guilty. I cannot tell you to do that."

It was a measure of how profoundly Jonathan's life had changed that this prospect, which months ago had so appalled and disgusted him, should now hold a powerful attraction. He thought for a long time.

"If I agreed, would they allow me to postpone prison till Lily... till Lily's situation is resolved?"

Leeds said gently, "I think that's obtainable."

"What are my chances if we go to trial?"

"Hard to say. It depends on three witnesses and an X factor."

"The witnesses being Michael, Solly, and Tortelli."

"Correct. Of course, Messrs. Kavin and Lebenthal are guilty by their own admission of the very crimes of which they accuse you, and that will help us. But if the jury sees Tortelli's testimony as corroborating theirs, it will go hard on us."

"And the X factor is the jury?"

"No, Jonathan. It's you."

"What's that mean?"

Leeds walked over to the desk and stood with his back to it, facing Jonathan, hands linked behind him in a courtroom pose. "When I took this case, you were full of the fighting spirit, chomping at the bit. Now we're down to the wire, and suddenly you're pulling up.

"Lord knows I'm not blaming you, Jonathan. In all the years I've been practicing, I never saw such an avalanche of troubles fall on one man. You told Lucas Rayburn that he couldn't hurt you anymore, and right now you're so numb you probably believe that. But I am here to tell you, my friend, that one day the anesthesia will wear off, and you are going to wake up and find yourself someplace you never wanted to be. And you're going to say, 'How the hell did I get here?'"

Jonathan lit a cigarette. "You're telling me to take the deal."

"No, I'm not. If you want to fight, we'll give them one hell of a fight; but I can't win without you, my friend. You want to cut a deal, that's okay too—but you've got to go all the way."

"All the way? What haven't you told me?"

Leeds returned to his seat and said with a slight shrug, "You'd have to cooperate. Name names and testify."

"That wasn't the deal I offered! I made it clear—no names, no testifying against others."

"That's the only way they'll do it."

Jonathan laughed mirthlessly. "I should have known there'd be a catch 22. No way, Christopher. Tell them no."

"Maybe you should talk to Lily first."

"I know what she'll say."

"Are you sure?" Leeds said sternly. "She has her children to consider. You do, too."

"My daughter once said something to me I'll never forget. She said that whenever I do something for my family's sake, it's the wrong thing."

Christopher Leeds cocked his head. "Harsh words from a daughter."

"Harsh?" Jonathan considered. "I don't know. Accurate."

Nonetheless, he was tempted, and not by the vague offer of leniency. Lucas had been right: something in him longed for confession. For the first time in his life, Jonathan regretted not being Catholic. With Jews, he thought, you go to them with a tale of guilt, and they'll talk and tell stories about their Uncle Nate who had the same problem once, and their Tante Faigele, and then they'll throw in some dybbuks and golems and the angel of death for good measure; so by the time you leave, your head is spinning, plus you've still got the same problem you came in with. Catholicism seemed to him a much more efficient religion. Confession, penance, and absolution all under one roof, like a car wash.

In bed that night, he told Lily about Buscaglio's offer and asked her, "What should I do?"

Lily said, "You know what to do."

"I wish to God I did. If it was just a matter of pleading guilty, I could live with it. At least it would spare us all the expense and agony of a trial."

"Do you know things that would be useful to them?"

"I know things that would make their hair curl. I know how the system works. I know all the players."

"Can you see yourself standing in court testifying against them?"

"No."

She smiled. "There you are, then."

"Christopher said consider the children."

Lily raised herself painfully onto one elbow. "Look at me."

He gazed up at her face, which had not lost its beauty in his eyes.

"Don't think about the children. The children will survive. And for God's sake, don't do what you think is best for me. Just do the right thing, Jonathan."

"And all will turn out for the best in this best of all possible worlds? Ah, Lily, have you gone soft on me?"

"Best isn't an option. This is strictly a salvage operation. It would comfort me," she said, "to know you'll be okay."

Between love and regret, his heart was rent. "What am I going to do... "he began, and could not finish.

Lily put her thin arms around his neck, her mouth to his ear. "You'll do fine, love. I know you."

The autumn wind knocked hard against the windowpanes, fluttering the curtains. The temperature had dropped and snow was in the air. They fell asleep in each other's arms, like young lovers. Jonathan dreamed it was summer and he was drifting in a gondola down a canal in a city of white stone. In the dream, Lily was with him: one of her hands held his, the other trailed through the water. But when he awoke, Lily had gone.

31

THE FUNERAL WAS PRIVATE, BUT MANY came who were not invited. Jonathan posted himself just inside the parlor door, greeting visitors, shaking hands. He and Lily had stood in so many reception lines in their lives that, even as he accepted condolences for her loss, he kept imagining her by his side. Each time he turned to her and saw Gracie standing in her place, he felt a shock of reawakening that mimicked the first shock.

It all still seemed so tentative. Yesterday morning when he had awakened, the sense of her absence was so palpable that even as he gazed at her, lying beside him with her eyes wide open and free of pain, it seemed to him that she had just risen and gone into the next room.

Voices came at him; faces blurred. Now and then one stood out. Lily's friend Margo, smart in black, makeup streaked with tears. His loyal secretary Maggie, weeping. "They say God works in mysterious ways, but this is incomprehensible." That funny little man who'd come to the house several times to visit when she was sick, Lily's hairdresser, pressed his hand and said, "I loved her, Mr. Fleishman." All the while Christopher Leeds hovered nearby, a *goyishe* guardian angel. Old allies from various tenant associations came, the staff of the Democratic headquarters, political associates who hadn't spoken to him in months. Our prayers are with you, they told him. When he looked around the room, part of him took pleasure in the diversity of people who had gathered to see her off. Blacks, Hispanics, Asians, and whites, working people, socialites, and politicians: their only common denominator was Lily.

The mayor's entrance was heralded by a commotion at the door. Trailed by his entourage, he strode up to Jonathan, clasped his hand. "Jonathan, my deepest condolences. Lily was a mensch, as good on the inside as she was lovely on the outside."

"Thank you for coming," Jonathan said with all his heart, for it seemed to him that whatever harm his colleagues had done him mattered far less than their goodness in coming now.

The mayor shook his head. "How many times have I sat at her table?"

Certain truancies were also felt. Jonathan understood full well why Michael and Lucas couldn't and shouldn't have attended; yet their absence caused phantom pain, like the missing limb of an amputee.

A small elderly man hurried in, wiping rain from his glasses with a large white handkerchief. With a jolt, Jonathan recognized the rabbi who'd presided over the reading of Job. "What are you doing here?" he said, not rudely, but with surprise.

The rabbi stood close to him. "Ever since our talk, I've felt guilty. When I heard about your wife, she should rest in peace, I knew I had to come."

"Why should you feel guilty? You didn't do anything."

"That's why. You came to me at a time of terrible trouble, in agony of the soul, and me, what did I do? Like a dumbkopf, like Job's *ferkakte* comforters, instead of consoling, I lectured. You asked a question and I pretended to have an answer, when the truth is, I have none. Forgive me, Mr. Fleishman," the old man said, "for I, too, am bewildered by God's ways."

The mourners were ushered into the chapel. When all were seated, the doors opened again for the family. Jonathan led Gracie in on his arm; Paul followed with Clara. Like a wedding procession, Jonathan thought, except that his bride lay in the coffin beneath the ark. Gracie sat on one side of him, Paul on the other, with Clara beside Paul. His son and mother sobbed throughout the service, but Gracie sat dry-eyed. She had not wept since Jonathan broke the news, and her face was like a gathering storm, ponderous and dark with unshed tears.

He heard nothing of the eulogy. Instead the little rabbi's words played through his head, over and over, until they shed their mantle of customary meaning and were revealed in their nakedness. I too am bewildered. Bewildered: lost in a wilderness, as Gracie had been, as he was now, stranded without moral compass in a world governed only by the inscrutable laws of nature.

When the Lord smote Job, he left him his wife. Jonathan's wife had been taken. Jonathan no longer asked, "Why me?" Instead he asked, "Why not me?" For him, at this stage of his career, dying would have made perfect sense; for Lily it made none. Her death was not only unjust but also offensively arbitrary, as if whatever god was hurling thunderbolts at Jonathan had struck Lily by mistake.

Now and then portions of the service reached his ears. He tried not to listen. If they spoke of God's mercy, he would have to rise and bear witness: "Here before you stands a living example of God's bountiful mercy."

Nevertheless, when the rabbi recited the Kaddish, Jonathan stood and repeated after him the Hebrew prayer for the dead; and though he could not have said what they meant, the ancient words comforted him the way a man, wandering alone in a desert, is heartened by signs of other men's passage.

A cold, steady rain accompanied them to the cemetery. Standing by the open grave, Jonathan felt his composure start to crumble. He lowered his umbrella and let the rain sluice down on him. The chill discomfort alleviated a little the pressure within.

"Ashes to ashes, dust to dust." Lily lay in her grave. When the rabbi motioned him forward to throw soil on the coffin, Jonathan turned and walked away.

He was ashamed. He was not so lost to the world but that he wanted to behave with dignity; yet how could he do it to her? Only yesterday she had died, and already they were burying her. It seemed hasty to him. What if Lily relented, what if she decided to come back?

Gracie came after him, took his arm, and led him back to the graveside. She pressed a fistful of wet earth into his hand and said softly, so only he could hear, "It's over, Daddy. Say good-bye."

After the burial, everyone hurried to get out of the rain. Jonathan noticed a man standing some distance away, his head averted, as if he were visiting another grave. A rain hat concealed his face, but Jonathan would have known that rangy, overlong body anywhere. He said he wanted time alone. When his family had gone, he walked over to the man and said, "Lucas."

Lucas Rayburn lifted his head. "Didn't mean to intrude. Just wanted to pay my respects."

"You could have come through the front door."

"I didn't think you'd appreciate that."

"You didn't think it would be politic."

"It wasn't *politic* to come at all," Lucas said with a shrug. "I shouldn't even be talking to you."

Jonathan nodded. Rain dripped down his face into his coat collar. Presently he said, "Michael didn't."

"Would you have wanted him to?" When Jonathan did not reply, Lucas continued: "I'm sorry about Lily. I know she must have hated my guts at the end. But I never stopped caring for her."

"I know."

"I always said marrying Lily was the smartest move you ever made, my friend."

The words slipped out—my friend. Jonathan heard them but knew they meant nothing.

"Twenty-five years with a woman like her," Lucas said, "even ending the way it did, I figure you're still ahead of the game."

"I guess," said Jonathan. He stood like a lost soul, hands in his pockets, shoulders hunched.

Lucas looked at him with pity. "You'd better get back. They'll be waiting on you."

Jonathan nodded but lingered. "Decent of you to come," he said gruffly.

"Will you give me your hand?" Lucas asked, extending his.

"Let me wipe it first. It smells of mortality."

Lucas grimaced, reached out, and pulled Jonathan to him. He spoke in Jonathan's ear. "I don't want to see you rot in jail. Take the deal, old friend."

The many rituals attached to death had seemed from the outside sterile and insignificant to Jonathan; but now he found them comforting. Expressions of an interior bereftness, they served to align the outer world with the inner.

The lapel of his jacket was torn, signifying mourning. Jonathan and Paul let their beards grow. Mirrors were covered, and the family sat on benches or stools instead of chairs. Just as narcotics after surgery knock out the body while it recovers from the insult, shiva acts upon the traumatized mind. Who can think with a houseful of visitors yammering away? People have needs they carry with them, as the more self-sufficient snail transports its house. They must be fed, listened to, comforted. His mother was beside herself with grief. She tried to hide it from the children, but when she was with Jonathan, she couldn't stop crying. "Why Lily?" she asked a thousand times. "Why Lily?"

For Jonathan, the hardest part of each day came after the visitors departed and what remained of the family was left to its own devices. Then Lily was always almost there, just missing. At supper their conversations were spaced for her; the resultant silences were like an empty chair. The house felt much too large, but if he sought refuge in Lily's neglected garden he was sure to sense her lingering presence, just out of sight. She was in his mother's sighs, his children's forlorn looks.

He was conscious of his children's misery but sensed that it excluded him. Grace continued to behave with ominous propriety. At the house as at the funeral, she greeted their visitors with calm dignity, courteous even to those former friends who had put aside expediency just long enough to call. With Jonathan she was solicitous, but quiet and thoughtful. She did not speak of her mother.

Tamar phoned frequently. In the absence of the hospital's medical director, she could not leave the country; she apologized to Jonathan for missing the funeral with such heartfelt regret that he grew aware for the first time of his own callous behavior when her husband died. Several times, she had long talks with Gracie, who closed herself in her room and emerged afterward with reddened eyes. But Jonathan never saw her cry.

Paul avoided his father, spending most of his time alone in his room. Thus Jonathan saw that his children, too, were slipping away.

At night the house was silent but for the hum of its systems. Jonathan wandered like an unquiet ghost from his bedroom to his study to the library. His ears rang with Lily's stubborn, baffling silence; was she angry with him?

The library was cold. He built a fire. Without thinking what he was doing, he brought out their wedding album, sat on the rug before the fire, and opened to a picture of his bride. Lily stood beneath a flower-draped chupah in the garden of the Cloisters, wearing a white off-the-shoulder peasant dress. A garland of lilies crowned her hair, which flowed like a golden waterfall about her bare shoulders. She was barely older than their daughter.

On the facing page was a shot of himself flanked by Michael and Lucas. At first he laughed aloud at his youthful self, all hair and beard and dark, hungry eyes. What a contrast to the lovely Lily. He'd wondered then, and still did, why she'd chosen him to love. But when his eyes fell upon his two best friends, dressed for the occasion in rented tuxedo jackets and jeans, mugging for the camera, his laughter gave way to a tidal desolation.

He shut the album and, staring at the fire, fell into a kind of waking dream in which a myriad of flickering images from the past appeared and disappeared. These did not reach back to his earliest years, for Jonathan had been one of those impatient souls who spent their childhood preparing to leave it behind, but rather began with his emergence into manhood, the dawning politicization that was inextricable from his friendship with Michael and Lucas. In the wash of memory, their lives were a medieval tapestry and Lily a golden thread woven through the cloth. She was his lover but their collective lady, their anima, their revolutionary muse. All for one and one for all; they played at war amidst the ivied towers of the university, and their victories, which had seemed so permanent but proved so ephemeral, they laid at Lily's sandaled feet.

Time rushed by, stuttering now and then, freezing for an instant, then eliding whole decades. Images: Lily naked in his sleeping bag in the back of Rosinante. Martin Luther King's face close to his; the whisper of his breath, the extraordinary energy of his presence. Paul's birth, and Gracie's: a tiny fist thrust out of the womb. Lily in her first garden, a patch of ground behind their Martindale house, laughing up at him with mud on her cheek. Moving vans; a picture rescued from the garbage. The three Musketeers together again, side by side on a dais—this time, their tuxedos had matching pants. The images turned discordant. Three stooges standing admidst urinals, fumbling an envelope from hand to hand. Lily in her rocking chair, staring up at him. Yellow roses upended in a trashcan. Michael in the locker room, tearing the leech from his chest, crushing it underfoot. Lucas' presence in the graveyard; Michael's absence. How had they come to this? There was no pivotal point, no sudden turn. One thing led to another, and options closed behind. Do the right thing, Lily had said, enigmatic as the sphinx. There had been a time when he knew what the right thing was.

The door opened. Gracie came in and settled cross-legged on the rug. As if they were becalmed in the night, Jonathan looked at his daughter and perceived with muted wonder that she had become a woman, with a woman's listening face. The kind of woman men would tell their secrets to; and she would hear what they said and what they didn't, and weigh these things on her secret scales; and they would never know what she thought unless she chose to tell them. Such a strange, knowing look on a face still soft with childhood filled Jonathan with a sense of mournful wonder. Her precocity was a reproach to him. He had tried to build a wall around his children, but it collapsed about their heads. A smaller wall would have kept them safer.... But what good is wisdom when it always comes too late?

Somewhere, a clock struck three. Jonathan said, as if continuing a conversation, "I used to think you were making a mountain out of a molehill, but lately I've realized it's the molehills that count. You were right, Gracie. I never should have sold that house."

32

"ARROGANCE," BUSCAGLIO SAID, "Greed and self-deception. It began with arrogance, with a man who held himself above the law because he believed that he alone knew what was right for the people of this city, and he alone could accomplish it, by hook or crook or whatever means it took. Benign extortion, tit for tat: a favorable lease in exchange for a day-care center, a city contract in return for a commitment to minority hiring. It worked. And this powerful man, Jonathan Fleishman, saw that it worked; he saw how much people were willing to pay for the favors he could dispense, until there came a time—I don't pretend to know precisely when, but I suspect it came gradually, little by little—when the nature of his demands changed.

"That's when greed entered the picture. As Jonathan Fleishman ascended the social rungs of the city, he turned his eyes from the disadvantaged and fastened them on the wealthy, the entrepreneurs. He saw how they lived, with their penthouses and second homes, their trips abroad, their yachts and limousines; and he came to covet those things for himself and his family. Ever conscious of his public image, he didn't drop the old, altruistic demands. He merely added new ones: a personal piece of the action, a lucrative consulting contract, a gift of stock.

"Now, there is nothing wrong with desiring wealth. Entrepreneurs are valued in our society, more so than politicians. We all live in a material world. Jonathan Fleishman could have chosen with perfect honor to leave public service for the private sector. Given his energy, intelligence, and talent, we cannot doubt that he would have succeeded. But wealth alone was not enough for this man. Ladies and gentlemen of the jury, Jonathan Fleishman wanted to live like a king, but he also wanted what he'd had before—the admiration of the masses, the esteem of the press, the aura of Robin Hood."

"I mentioned a third element, and that is self-deception. For self-deception there must have been: how else can a man lead two lives, unless he finds a barrier to protect his right hand from knowledge of his left?

"Now, to those of us who work in the criminal system, self-deception is nothing new. Because of it, true remorse is a rare commodity in these halls. Not a criminal comes through this system but believes that he had good and sufficient cause for whatever he did. Thieves, rapists, murderers, even child molesters find ways to justify their crimes.

"Here, however, we have a defendant who is exceptionally intelligent, professionally persuasive, charming; a man, moreover, who has known tragedy in his personal life. Therefore I feel a need, ladies and gentlemen, to warn you most strongly not to buy into this man's self-deception. Do not let him confuse, deceive, or distract you; for, I assure you, he and his lawyers will spare no effort to do just that. Nor must you allow pity to cloud your clear judgment. The question is not whether or not the defendant has suffered. Suffering is not expiation, nor does it bring absolution.

"His attorney will try to persuade you that Mr. Fleishman's pattern of private arrangements with companies that depended on his goodwill in their dealings with the city was perfectly innocent. Failing that, the defense will undoubtedly contend that his extortion was simply business as usual, the way things are *really* done: as if the laws that apply to the rest of us don't apply to the upper echelons of the business and political worlds.

"You will reject this unjust view. And as the trial unfolds and you learn the extent of this man's corruption—not only the extent, but the state-of-the-art sophistication of it, the labyrinthine deceptions he employed to escape detection—you will also deduce the existence of a guilty mind. So much, you will say, for business as usual.

"The defense will bring a string of witnesses to attest to all the good Jonathan Fleishman accomplished for this city. I tell you now: we have no quarrel with these witnesses. The state does not claim that Fleishman was always a thief and a rogue; we say he became one. And we say further that not the least of his sins is the theft of his own valuable services, the good he did and the good he could have done for this city.

"But for that theft, Jonathan Fleishman must answer to a higher court. In this one, we will concern ourselves with his violation of those mundane laws that govern the lives of lesser mortals such as ourselves. We will prove to you that Jonathan Fleishman committed the grave crimes of extortion, solicitation of bribes, influence peddling, and conspiracy. Most of the criminal defendants we see in this court commit their crimes out of desperation; Jonathan Fleishman has not even that excuse. Before this trial is over, you will know that his motive was the lowest, the most contemptible of all: greed.

"Greed, arrogance, and self-deception reduced this man who had everything to the level of a common thief; and as such, ladies and gentlemen, he must be judged and punished."

With one last sweeping look at the jurors, Jane Buscaglio returned to her seat. Christopher Leeds arose. His gray suit was slightly rumpled, his demeanor modest as he stood blinking through his glasses at the jury. Myopically he examined every face as if for the first time, though in fact he had come to know each one intimately through hours of *voir dire*. He saw a middle-class housewife. A bus driver. A waitress. A professor of economics. A supermarket manager. A retired dry cleaner. A part-time computer operator. A school custodian. A beautician. A retired special-ed teacher. A bank teller. An office-supply salesman. A motley crew: five whites, three Hispanics, four blacks; six men and six women. Leeds was well-pleased, Buscaglio less so. Christopher Leeds smiled at the jurors and turned toward the prosecutor.

"Very good, Ms. Buscaglio," he said with the pleased wonderment of a teacher whose student has far exceeded his expectations. "Bravo—that was very fine indeed. Most persuasive," he said, turning once again to the jury. "Indeed, if I were sitting in your place and heard such an opening, why, I'd vote to convict on the spot.

"Dramatic construction," he counted on his fingers. "Vivid language. Fascinating characterizations. Ms. Buscaglio's little narrative contained all the elements of good fiction. One suspects that my colleague has missed her true calling; though I wonder about the part about the right hand doing this and the left hand doing that, and the right not knowing what the left is doing because there's some barrier in between... " He glanced down at his own hands in perplexity. "This I found a bit confusing. One wonders, you see, how the poor man fed himself, or dressed in the morning." Some jury members laughed. Others smiled.

"As fiction, there is much to admire in Ms. Buscaglio's presentation. But in the guise of nonfiction," Leeds said with quick- gathering anger, "it was unforgivable. She knows, you see, just as I know, that the pathetic, contemptible man she describes is not Jonathan Fleishman, is not like Jonathan Fleishman, indeed has nothing to do with Jonathan Fleishman!

"And, by God," Leeds said quietly, "I ought to know. In the past few months, I have watched this man undergo the trials of Job—"

"Objection!" shouted Buscaglio, who'd been sitting on the edge of her chair, waiting.

"To what?" the judge said, irritated at the interruption.

"May I approach the bench?"

"Mr. Leeds, will you join us?"

Both attorneys stood before her.

"He's about to bring up the wife," Buscaglio said. "This is exactly why we moved for a change of venue. Mr. Leeds is obviously trying to sway this jury."

"It was never our intention to mention my client's tragic loss, your Honor. But once Ms. Buscaglio brought it up, we have no choice but to air it."

"I brought it up?"

Leeds looked only at the judge. "She said that Mr. Fleishman recently suffered a personal tragedy."

Judge Malina peered over the top of her glasses at Buscaglio. "So you did, Counselor."

Buscaglio flushed. "I only said that to forearm them against just the sort of—"

Leeds said, "Irrelevant, Your Honor. She raised this issue, and unless I clarify it, the jury will be left with lingering doubts: What was this tragedy, and was it somehow my client's fault?"

"You're picking at straws," said the prosecutor, who could see in the judge's face which way the wind blew.

"If you hadn't referred to Mr. Fleishman's loss, Ms. Buscaglio, I might have ruled it prejudicial. But since you did, the question is moot. Objection overruled."

Buscaglio scowled all the way back to her table. Leeds, turning back toward the jury, was arrested by Jonathan's voice calling his name. He returned to the table and they put their heads together. At last Christopher Leeds shrugged and walked back to the jury with a pained look.

"My client instructs me that his tragic personal bereavement is not the business of this court. He tells me that he seeks, not sympathy, but justice. I can only respect his wishes."

Jane Buscaglio smiled, but her triumph was short-lived. The jury was gazing at Fleishman with the very emotion he had eschewed. They knew, of course they knew. Even if they had somehow avoided learning the news from television or newspaper headlines, the presence of the two Fleishman children dressed in black was eloquent testimony. Fleishman ended up not only with the benefit of their knowing but also with the credit for not having told them; and Buscaglio seethed, convinced they'd set her up.

Christopher Leeds leaned on the jury box and spoke quietly. "Ms. Buscaglio has told you a fairy tale, a muddled and malicious fairy tale. Now I will tell you the truth. This man"—he pointed to Jonathan—"has dedicated his entire life to serving the underprivileged in our society. After graduating at the top of his class in Columbia Law School, he received offers from leading private law firms, offers that would certainly have led to a lucrative career. He turned them all down to follow his conscience down south, where he became one of the original Freedom Riders, a young disciple of Martin Luther King Jr. Unlike many of us, however, who were inspired by great causes in our youth, only to turn our mature energies toward our own betterment, Jonathan Fleishman never strayed from the path he had chosen.

"Ms. Buscaglio portrayed a greedy, venal man. Reluctantly, but wisely, she acknowledges Mr. Fleishman's tremendous contributions to this city. Wisely, I say, because she could hardly hope to deny them. Instead, she has the audacity to claim they are irrelevant. A lifetime of selfless, principled service: irrelevant. A man's character: irrelevant.

"Well," Leeds said magnanimously, "she has to claim that, doesn't she? And I think we must also forgive her for that rather bizarre left-hand, right-hand theory, because without it she cannot possibly bridge the unfathomable contradiction between Jonathan Fleishman's lifetime of altruistic service and the crimes she claims he committed. During his life, Jonathan Fleishman had untold opportunities to go into business for himself, to get rich legally and honorably. He turned them all down. He had different priorities. Is this the behavior of a greedy man? The moment you look carefully at this man's character, the prosecution's case goes out the window."

Leeds removed his glasses and wiped them with a crumpled white handkerchief. "The truth is, this case is not about money. They pretend that it is; but it's not. It's about power. Because power, unlike money, is something that did interest Jonathan Fleishman. Power interested him exceedingly, for power is the primary tool of his trade, without which a politician is totally ineffectual.

"Jonathan Fleishman learned some things from his years as a freedom fighter, from his lifetime of advocacy for migrant workers, battered women, abused children, the homeless. He learned that no one ever gives up power willingly. He learned that power is a finite quantity and there's never quite enough to go round. He learned, in short, that to give power to the people it is necessary to take it from someone else; and this is a lesson that served his constituency well, though it cost him dearly. For in doing this, ladies and gentlemen, Jonathan Fleishman made enemies. Powerful enemies, including some disguised as friends.

"You will meet some of these so-called friends," Leeds said, his lip curling with disgust, "as the prosecution attempts to make its case. I trust you will know how to judge them. And now, before the trial begins, allow me to leave you with one thought. If there ever was a man more sinned against than sinning, that man is Jonathan Fleishman."

Coverage by the press was largely sympathetic. This was partially a matter of sportsmanship: going after Fleishman now presented all the sporting thrill of kicking a wounded bird. The man was grounded. He was out of the game. In addition, Lily's sudden death had shaken even seasoned reporters, who through months of intense observation had achieved a kind of one-sided intimacy with the family. Jonathan and Lily were perceived as an exceptionally close couple; since her death, Fleishman had looked like hell. There was nervousness among the reporters, a fear unspoken but shared, that Fleishman would kill himself and that they would be blamed for hounding the man to death.

The exception, naturally, was Barnaby.

He was back at work on the *Probe*, but Hasselforth had not

only kept Barnaby off the Fleishman case, he'd rubbed salt in the wound by assigning the trial to Ronnie Neidelman.

Barnaby stayed cool, kept busy, and acted like it didn't bother him. The list of Fleishman's contacts in city agencies had proved to be a gold mine, and he was riding the crest of two new scandals like a circus performer astride two horses. Once again, his rivals on the papers that had stupidly failed to hire him were eating their hearts out.

Doors that had been closed were reopening. Buscaglio still wasn't taking his calls, but others in her office were. In return for a few helpful hints on other matters, Barnaby managed to keep a finger in the Fleishman pie. Hasselforth could take him off the story, but he couldn't prevent Barnaby from writing whatever he pleased in his column. Nor could he stop Barnaby writing a book about the Fleishman scandal, a possibility to which he was giving serious consideration.

Several years ago, a couple of *Voice* reporters had made a bundle on a book Barnaby could have written, an expose of the last municipal-corruption scandal. It wasn't the money alone that attracted Barnaby, though God knew he wouldn't turn up his nose at a hundred grand or so. It was also the forum—a second shot at setting the record straight.

During the first session of Fleishman's trial, Barnaby sat far to the back of the crowded courtroom, well out of Gracie's sight but not Ronnie Neidelman's. Ronnie spotted him and glared; he blew her a kiss. When court recessed at four o'clock, following Christopher Leeds's opening statement, Barnaby raced back to the *Probe* to write his column.

"One day after Lily Fleishman's funeral, Assistant U.S. Attorney Jane Buscaglio went to court and appealed in an *in camera* session for a change of venue. Fleishman lawyer Christopher Leeds objected; his client had a right to be judged by his peers, the people with whom he had worked and lived, blah-blah-blah.

"Judge Malina ruled for the defense.

"Buscaglio, whose aggressive prosecution of this case has so far been exemplary, then pressed for a postponement. She argued that in the atmosphere of bathos created by the death of Fleishman's wife, it would be impossible to impanel an unbiased jury.

"Again Leeds objected. His client's sole desire, he said, after the tragedy of his wife's sudden demise, was to get on with his

life and let his children get on with theirs. Prolonging their ordeal
would be cruelty. In full confidence of his acquittal, Jonathan
Fleishman demanded his right to a speedy trial.

"Judge Malina's ruling was a slap to the prosecution's face.
It was the first time, said the tart-tongued judge, that she had
ever entertained an appeal for postponement on the grounds of
ambience. The trial would proceed as scheduled.

"And so the trial begins, and Jonathan Fleishman drags into
court his grieving children and his old mother, draped from head
to toe in black; and he has the gall to pretend, in a staged scene
with his lawyer, that he's looking not for sympathy, oh no, but for
justice. The hypocrisy thickens."

He was printing out the copy when the door opened and
Ronnie Neidelman barged in. Barnaby stood to block her view
of the printer.

"What do you mean," she said, "by horning in on my story?"

He hooted. "Your story?"

"I'm covering this trial, not you."

"And I'm sure you're doing a fine job of it. Now, run along,
little darling." Barnaby swung her toward the door and gave her
ass a pat.

Ronnie wheeled around and mashed his instep with her heel.
"Oops."

"Goddammit, bitch, that hurt!"

The printer clattered to a halt. Ronnie's eyes narrowed. "Let's
see your story."

"I'll show you mine if you show me yours." She left the office
without a word and returned with a typescript. They swapped
and sat down to read.

"Pathetic," Barnaby sneered.

"You took the words out of my mouth."

"Do yourself a favor—don't submit this drivel."

"Roger's already approved it," she said, gloating. "I can't wait
to hear what he thinks of yours."

"What's happened to you, Ronnie? You used to be a reporter;
now you're writing for *Seventeen* again."

Ronnie blushed. She'd done a stint on *Seventeen* in her early
days and didn't like to be reminded of it. "I call it like I see it. I'm
not saying Fleishman should walk. I'm saying the U.S. attorney is
taking the easy way out by scapegoating Fleishman."

"You can't scapegoat a guilty man."

She rolled her eyes. "Fleishman couldn't have delivered without help from friends higher up. Why aren't they on trial with him?"

"That's got nothing to do with Fleishman's guilt. You publish this—" he waved her copy—"you're aiding and abetting the enemy."

"You're obsessed with him."

"I'm not obsessed with him. He just happens to be the devil incarnate." Barnaby laughed.

Ronnie didn't. "That's what I mean. You've lost touch with reality. Can't you see that after what happened, you're the last person to accuse Fleishman of hypocrisy? Christ, talk about people in glass houses."

"Fuck that shit. I'm sick of hearing about that."

"Then you picked the wrong girl to screw."

"Oh, shut up, Ronnie, you moron. You know as well as I do, we do what we gotta do. You want to tell me that if that girl had talked to you, you wouldn't have used it?"

"I wouldn't have slept with her to get it."

He guffawed. "You've never slept with a source?"

"She's a baby."

"She's no baby."

"It was a repulsive thing to do."

"I'm not running for sainthood. My personal life has nothing to do with my work."

Ronnie looked at him thoughtfully. "You know, I bet that's what Fleishman tells himself."

"Don't compare me to that prick!" Barnaby exploded. "Ask yourself this, Lois Lane. Who's really abusing Gracie? Who dragged her into court, who put her on display days after her mother croaked?"

"Have you considered the possibility that she wants to be with her father?"

"Right. I've seen her little Stepford-wife routine. Holding his arm, smiling bravely for the cameras. God knows what goes on in the house."

She threw up her hands. "You're nuts, you know that? You're really nuts."

As the door slammed behind her, Barnaby shouted, "Someone ought to pull her off that sinking ship. Someone ought to save Grace."

33

ON THE DAY MICHAEL KAVIN TESTIFIED, Jonathan rejoiced in his wife's death.

Sitting in court, listening to the testimony, which Michael delivered in a stilted, rehearsed monotone without ever looking in Jonathan's direction, he could not take his eyes off Michael. It was like looking into a mirror, the face was that familiar; and though he'd known all along that Michael was going to testify, the actual hearing and seeing of it shook him to the core, as if the words issuing from that too-familiar face pierced straight to the very marrow of Jonathan's bones, without mediation of ear or mind.

He didn't lie, Michael. He said nothing to which Jonathan could unequivocally reply: "No. This didn't happen. You made this up." What he did was more insidious: he showed things in the wrong light, or at least (for lately Jonathan had grown wary of words like "right" and "wrong") in a light other than the one in which they had tacitly agreed always to regard them. In the fluorescent glare of the courtroom, understandings became conspiracy, friendly accommodations revealed themselves as extortion, and the fine line that Jonathan had always trod, with Michael in his footsteps, between what was acceptable and what beyond the pale was utterly obscured. "Michael's going to turn on you," Lily had said, but not even she could have envisioned the sheer awfulness of Michael's betrayal, which used, not lies, but discolored truth as its weapon.

The witness before Michael had been Arthur Speigel. Arthur blinked his rabbity eyes and answered questions in a defensive yet sanctimonious whine, imperfectly secure in his blanket of immunity. Jonathan listened with impassive disdain. No Speigel, no matter how ignoble and ungrateful, could touch him.

Michael's treachery did touch him, though, in a place he had ceased to feel, ceased almost to believe in. The pain was exquisite yet not without a certain clarifying value. For the first time since his trial had begun, Jonathan felt oriented. Michael's betrayal had supplied a point of reference, a base line against which he could measure himself.

Afterward, in a small office in the courthouse, he said to Christopher Leeds, "Thank God Lily isn't here. I wish to God I'd died before I saw this day."

They were waiting for the press to give up on them before venturing outside. At the moment, though, Jonathan would rather have faced an avalanche of reporters than his children and mother, who waited in another room.

Leeds said, "I expected worse. This wasn't so bad. And tomorrow"—he all but rubbed his hands—"we get him on cross."

An image flashed before Jonathan's eyes of Michael, plump and pinkly naked, crucified on a cross. He shook his head to clear it. "What are you going to do to him?"

"As he did to you, so shall we do to him."

"How?"

Leeds clasped his hands behind his back and paced up and down. "So often," he said sadly, "when a man has most cause for gratitude, he feels resentment. Such a man is Michael Kavin, whose secret envy of his friend and benefactor led him at last to a terrible betrayal. Michael Kavin turned on his mentor and sought to destroy him, concocting a scheme to elevate himself while simultaneously diminishing Jonathan Fleishman. He inveigled my client into a series of increasingly compromising situations, culminating with the absurd farce of the Tortelli episode, the stoogelike, fumbled bathroom handoff he so graphically described in his testimony."

Jonathan heard him out. Then he applauded. "Excellent, Christopher. Very plausible, psychologically speaking. But it won't fly."

"Why not?"

"No one who knows us is ever going to believe that Michael inveigled me into anything."

"The jury doesn't know either of you."

"If anyone could pull it off, you could," Jonathan said. Leeds bowed his head. "But I don't want you to."

"Actually," the lawyer said, "that's my call."

They eyed each other like boxers before the bell.

Jonathan said, "I will not lower myself to do to Michael what he's doing to me."

"We talked about this."

"I don't recall. It doesn't matter anyway. I'm finally finding my feet, Christopher. I'm coming back to myself."

"I'm happy for you."

"I've discovered that there are limits to what I will do."

"That's a dangerous attitude for a man in your situation. You ought to know by now it's a dog-eat-dog world."

"We still have choices."

"Not many." Leeds cast him a worried look. "Not anymore. This case requires aggressive handling. We can't just respond to their version of events. We've got to put forth our own scenario."

"That Michael 'inveigled' me into everything? I never told you that."

"But that is what I think happened," Leeds said blandly.

"No, you don't. Christopher, don't think I'm not grateful. Your support means a great deal to me. It's just, there's more at stake than you realize."

"Your future is at stake. That's all that concerns me."

"My future, yes. Mine. Whatever happens, I need to be able to live with myself."

"My friend, if you hobble my defense, you will be living with yourself for a long, long time."

"Possibly. That's outside my control."

Leeds's plump face puckered with distress. "You're not seeing things objectively."

"No, I see them subjectively."

"Lily's passing has affected you."

"Yes. She told me to do the right thing. I'm feeling my way toward it."

"With all due respect," Leeds snapped, "Lily's not running this defense. I am. And I cannot defend you with my hands tied behind my back. Michael Kavin is the prosecution's star witness. I have to discredit him, or the game is lost."

"Ah, but there's always another game for you."

Christopher Leeds drew back, blinking rapidly behind his glasses.

"I'm not complaining," Jonathan said. "That's how it's supposed to be. But I'm the one who has to live with the consequences, so I'm the one who has to decide."

"Decide what? What have you got in mind? Tell me now, Jonathan. I don't like surprises in court."

"I'm thinking of changing my plea." He astonished himself with these words, which seemed to have sprung full-blown out of nowhere. They filled him with a sense of elation, even giddiness.

Christopher Leeds gazed up at the ceiling and pressed his plump palms together. "Lord, give me patience."

"Listen to me. If I've got to go, I want to go with a bang, not a whimper. I won't be dragged down like a stag by a pack of dogs. I'd rather hurl myself off a cliff."

"And land in jail, you silly man. You mustn't despair, Jonathan. That's what they want you to do. That's why they used Kavin so early in the trial."

"It's not despair. Oh," he said, "it's hard in there. It's foul, listening to that miserable woman talk of things she's incapable of understanding. I feel, God help me, like Gulliver among the Lilliputians, tied down, totally immobilized, tormented by hordes of tiny creatures. But that's not it, Christopher. That's not the reason."

"What is the reason? No—don't answer. It doesn't matter. It's too late to plead guilty. You've got to stay the course."

"I'm entitled to change my plea."

"You had the opportunity to plead guilty to reduced charges. You turned it down."

"And I'd turn it down today, on their terms," Jonathan said indignantly. "I'm not interested in passing the buck. The buck stops here." He thumped his chest.

Christopher Leeds sighed. "My friend, do you know what happens to people who are too good to live?"

"You think I'm off the wall?"

Leeds put a hand on his shoulder. "I think you're exhausted. I think you've had an emotionally draining day. I think you need to go home and put your feet up and have a drink. Have two. Tomorrow everything will look different."

He led Jonathan into the room where Paul, Gracie, and Clara waited. Clara jumped up as the door opened. Her face was ravaged. "How many times has that boy eaten in my kitchen?" she demanded.

"Mama..." Jonathan held out his arms.

She hugged him. "Such a good friend, like my own child I treated him—look how he stabs us in the back. God curse him forever, the *gonif*, the liar."

"Let's go home," Jonathan said. Over her head he looked at Gracie, whose face was pale and grim, and at Paul, who would not meet his eyes.

Christopher Leeds led them to a back door that opened into an alley. The car was waiting on the corner to their left, he told them. He took Jonathan's arm and opened the door.

A shrill whistle sounded from their right as they emerged into the fading light. "Come, let's hurry," Leeds said, breaking into an ungainly trot. They reached the limousine only steps ahead of a dozen pursuing reporters and cameramen, all shouting Jonathan's name. The driver, a young clerk in Leeds's office, jumped out and opened the back door. Jonathan stood back to let his mother and daughter enter first, but Christopher Leeds shoved his head down and bundled him into the car, sliding in beside him. Clara followed, and Paul went around the car to the front passenger seat.

Above the baying of the reporters: "Fleishman! Fleishman!" one voice stood out: "Gracie!" it shouted.

Gracie looked back. Barnaby emerged from the crowd. She didn't recognize him at first. Not because he'd changed, but because he hadn't. By her internal reckoning, years had passed since their affair; decades. She'd aged. What a shock to see him looking younger than she felt, hale and hearty. How strange to look upon that frank and open face, that shaggy beard, tousled hair, the puppy-dog friendliness of his brown eyes.

"Gracie," he said warmly, as if all that had happened hadn't.

Jonathan bent down to see what was delaying his children. "Son of a bitch," he cried. "I don't believe—" He lunged for the car door handle.

Leeds stopped him. "Let her handle this. She's capable."

Paul vaulted over the hood of the car, landing beside Grace. "Leave my sister alone, you prick. She doesn't want to talk to you."

Barnaby ignored him. " Gracie, darlin', we need to talk. Let's go somewhere."

She said nothing, but looked at him with such disdain he took a step backward. Poor girl, he thought. They've really got to her.

The reporters had forgotten Jonathan. Their attention and cameras were focused on Grace and Barnaby. He ignored them and spoke to her alone. "Gracie, you have a choice. You don't have to play Daddy's good little girl. You don't have to stay with him."

Paul shook his head in wonder. "You really believe she'd go anywhere with you?"

"Let's get some coffee. Then, if you still want to go home, I'll take you." Barnaby held out his hand.

Gracie slapped his face, hard. Flashbulbs and strobes flared all around. "Once again for the cameras!" someone yelled.

Hurt and astonishment suffused Barnaby's face. He put a hand to his cheek and backed away. A woman surged into his place and thrust a microphone toward Gracie. "Why'd you do it, Miss Fleishman? Why'd you slap him?"

"It's what you do to mosquitoes," Gracie said with a shrug.

Jonathan followed his lawyer's advice: he went home, closed himself in his study, put his feet up, had a drink. Had two. Waited for rational self-interest to reassert itself. At eleven o'clock he watched *Eyewitness News*. Gracie had upstaged him: all the clips were of her slapping Barnaby. When he heard what she had called him, Jonathan burst into cleansing laughter.

"You didn't know who you were messing with," he said to the screen. "You didn't know my Gracie."

Suddenly he felt hungry. He switched off the set and went down to the kitchen, where he made bacon, toast, and scrambled eggs. Lily, who'd watched his cholesterol count like a hawk, had rarely allowed bacon into the house; but since Jonathan had begun doing the shopping, he'd made it a staple. What the hell did he care about cholesterol?

When he finished, he washed the frying pan and put the dishes into the dishwasher. Upstairs, he made the rounds that, since Lily's illness, had become habitual, almost compulsive. No sound came from Paul's room, though light shone through the keyhole. From Gracie's room came a light, rhythmic thumping.

He knocked and entered. She was kneeling, fully dressed, on the mattress that was her bed, pounding a pillow with her fist. Wispy feathers floated through the air; some had settled in

her hair and one stuck to the corner of her mouth, giving her a
feral look. Grace looked up at him and suddenly he saw himself
reflected in her face: she had his eyes, his bone structure, his
intensity.

"What's the matter, Gracie?"

"I hate him," she said.

"The mosquito? He's not worth hating."

Gracie stared blankly. "Not that pest. Michael Kavin. I hate
him. He's the lowest slime that ever crawled on earth. He has no
right to exist, no place in this world. I despise him, I loathe detest
shit piss spit on him."

Jonathan shut the door. "I pity him."

"Pity? After what he did to you?"

"What he did to me is nothing compared to what he's done to
himself."

"Which is what? He made a deal, he'll walk away with a slap
on the wrist, that bastard. Oh, God." She hugged the battered
pillow to her stomach. "I feel like I'm exploding."

"There's nothing left to hate. My old friend Michael is no more.
He destroyed himself today."

"I wish he had. I wish he'd shot himself. A dead man couldn't
do what he's done to you."

"He didn't," Jonathan said. "I did it to myself."

34

JONATHAN SAID, "I NEED YOU TO BE ALL right with this."

"I'm not 'all right with this.' I'll never be 'all right with this.' You want to put a noose around your neck, that's your business. But you're asking me to knock the chair out from under your feet, and that's very much my business, and I'm damned if I'll do it."

They sat alone in the back of Christopher Leeds's car, traveling to the courthouse. The lawyer's cheeks were a fiery red, stained by anger or distress or both.

Jonathan said gravely, "I am absolutely convinced this is the right thing for me."

"It's madness, man! You think you're going to stand up in court and say, 'Mea culpa,' and the judge will say what a good boy you are and send you home? You'll go to jail, Jonathan. You could rot in prison for twenty years. Is that what you want?"

"Of course not, but I'm prepared to accept the sentence of the court. Don't desert me, Christopher."

"You're deserting yourself, fool," he groaned.

"On the contrary: I'm finding myself."

Leeds ran his hands over his bald pate. "You feel a need to confess, you want to cleanse your soul, talk to God, not the court."

Jonathan said coldly, "I have nothing to say to God."

"Think how your enemies will gloat. The prosecution will say they had us beat so badly we just lay down and died."

An acerbic note crept into Jonathan's voice. "I'm fucking up your batting average, is that it?"

"I don't deserve that, Jonathan."

"No, you don't. Sorry."

"We could win, you realize. You could walk out of that court a free man."

"You think I should?"

Leeds smacked himself on the forehead. "Whose side are you on?"

"I'm trying to get back on side."

"It's Lily. I should have anticipated this. You feel life's not worth living anymore."

"I think she would approve. But I'm not doing it because she died. It's an act of hope, not despair."

"It makes no sense," the lawyer said. "What's changed? Why are you doing this?"

"I've changed. Little by little, bit by bit, I became a man I would have despised as a boy. And now that I see it, I want to get back."

"You're asking me to betray you. You want me to play Judas."

"Which would make me what, Jesus Christ?" Jonathan said with a laugh. "Christopher, I chose you for my advocate. If you really are my advocate, you'll help me do the right thing."

Christopher Leeds closed his eyes and remained for some time with his head sunk onto his chest. Presently he said in a resigned voice, "Have you told your family?"

He had, that morning at breakfast. Next to tossing dirt onto Lily's coffin, it was the hardest thing he'd ever done. He'd told them what he had decided and why. When he finished, there was silence.

The children looked in their laps. Clara stared straight ahead. Her lipstick was a brilliant red slash across her ashen face.

"Mama," he said, "are you all right?"

"Sure, sure. You stick a knife in my heart and ask if I'm all right? Don't do this, Jonathan."

"I have to."

Clara pushed back her chair and walked out.

Paul said, "She was right about you, that prosecutor bitch. She said you were full of pride, and she's right. Tart it up however you want, that's what it comes down to."

"How can you say that, Paul? To stand up and publicly admit I did wrong, I betrayed my own principles—is that pride?"

"It's pride dressed up as humility."

Jonathan looked taken aback. "Call it what you like," he said, "it's all I have left."

"If you do this thing, if you shame us this way, so help me God, I'll never speak to you again."

"Son—"

"Don't call me that." Paul stalked out, leaving Gracie alone with her father.

"You don't have to do this," she said. "It's not necessary."

"Yes, sweetheart, it is."

"The last time I talked with her, Mom said I had misjudged you. She said I was always too hard on you. I think she was right."

"I'm not so sure," he said.

"Is the prosecution ready?"

"Yes, your Honor."

"Is the defense ready?"

Christopher Leeds stood. "Your Honor, my client wishes at this time to change his plea—"

"Objection!" Buscaglio screamed.

"How can you object to that?" Leeds said, not looking at her.

Judge Malina rose. "In my chambers, please. You too, Mr. Fleishman."

"Mr. Leeds," the judge said, when the door closed behind them, "is there something I should know? Have you and the prosecution reached an agreement?"

Leeds and Buscaglio answered in unison: "No, your Honor."

"Have you advised your client of the possible—I might even say probable—consequences of pleading guilty?"

"Indeed I have, your Honor."

Malina's hawk eyes fastened on Jonathan. "Do you understand, Mr. Fleishman, that you could be sentenced to twenty years in prison for these offenses?"

"I do, your Honor."

"Do you harbor some hope that because of your record, you will be let off with community service? Because if that is your thinking, Mr. Fleishman, let me advise you that in my opinion, sentencing you to community service would be like throwing Brer Rabbit into the briar patch."

"No, ma'am, I don't."

"Do you imagine that as a reward for pleading guilty, you will be let off lightly?"

"No, your Honor. All I ask, and it is a request, not a condition, is that before you dismiss the jury, you allow me to address the court."

Judge Malina sat back and stared pensively at Jonathan. She was a woman in her sixties, gaunt-faced, with eyes as sharp as her tongue and a reputation for severity in sentencing.

She said, "Are you mad, sir?"

"No, your Honor, not mad. Guilty."

"Guilty of the crimes with which you are charged? Or guilty of surviving your wife?"

Jonathan's face darkened. "Both; but one has nothing to do with the other."

"So you say. I tend to doubt it. I'm not sure I can allow this change of plea. It seems to me you're acting under the stress of your bereavement, against your own self-interest."

"With respect, your Honor, I am the best judge of that."

"What do you say, Mr. Leeds?"

They all looked at Christopher Leeds, Jonathan with some anxiety. The monkish lawyer opened his mouth and closed it without utterance.

"It's a ploy, your Honor," Buscaglio burst out. "It's a preemptive bid for sympathy. The defense knows they've got no case."

The judge gestured impatiently for silence. "What say you, Mr. Leeds?"

He replied, "It's an act of conscience, not despair."

Buscaglio spluttered.

"Ms. Buscaglio," Judge Malina said testily, "what exactly is your problem? If Mr. Fleishman changes his plea, you've won your case."

"But she doesn't get to grandstand," Christopher Leeds said in an unusual display of spite.

"Your Honor, the defense was given a chance to plea-bargain before the trial, and they turned it down flat. I'll be damned if we'll renew the offer."

"Who asked you?" Jonathan growled.

"Do you want some time to consider?" the judge asked.

"No, your Honor."

"Very well, Mr. Fleishman. It's your funeral."

The courtroom was jammed. Reporters jockeyed for position; spectators crowded in behind the last row of seats. Among them, standing head and shoulders above the rest, was U.S. Attorney Lucas Rayburn. In the section reserved for the defendant's family, Gracie sat alone.

The only clear space in the room was the arena circumscribed by the judge's bench, the witness stand, the tables of the prosecution and defense, and the jury box. The tall windows of the courtroom, dingy with the accumulated grit of the city outside, transformed brilliant sunlight into a diffuse gray mist. Jonathan, facing the jury from the center of the court's arena, was illuminated darkly.

He closed his eyes, then opened them. "I came in planning to fight," he said. "I'm no Christian. When someone attacks me, my gut response is not to turn the other cheek, but to strike back. Sitting in that chair, listening to *that woman* savage my reputation and belittle all that I have done and made of my life, I felt rage.

"She called me a hypocrite. She said I was greedy and arrogant and that I abused my position to enrich myself at the expense of the people I pretended to serve. She described a vile remnant of a man, with no shred of decency or honor to his name, and she said I was that man.

"Then it was Mr. Leeds's turn. He described a very different man: an altruist of the highest order, who sacrificed his self-interest for the good of the people, whose only offense was his effectiveness. And that man, too, was said to be me.

"Thus the prosecutor drew one man and Mr. Leeds another; the two were as different as Dr. Jekyll and Mr. Hyde, and yet both described the same man. I don't know how you felt; I was perplexed. I wondered how a single man could be two such different things.

"I used to believe that if a man knew who he was, it didn't matter what others thought of him. The past few months have taught me different. I'm not saying a person can't have hidden qualities. I'm saying perception stems from something real. It's reflection, not invention. Men are not infinitely elastic creatures. There are limits to how far we will stretch. That's why when a man is seen with such radical divergence as that woman and Christopher Leeds saw me, that man can lose his cohesion. He can lose his grasp on who he is."

Jonathan stopped, searched the jurors' eyes for understanding, found only puzzlement. He walked closer and tried again.

"It was Michael Kavin who gave me the answer to the riddle that plagued me. Michael was my oldest and closest friend. You heard him betray me; but did you see, as I who loved him saw, how he betrayed himself in the process? As painful as it was for me, the cost to him was greater.

"And yet, much as I would like to, I cannot say he lied. The things he said happened did happen. At the time, of course, we called them by different names or didn't name them at all. Not because we feared surveillance, but because we convinced ourselves that if things aren't spelled out, if acts aren't named, then somehow they don't really count. There are ways," Jonathan said with a thin smile, "of talking about things without ever saying what they are. We were good at that. You might say I'm a man who thoroughly outsmarted himself."

Now he saw them smile and nod with comprehension. Next would come sympathy. Politician to the core, Jonathan couldn't help working the crowd, even though he wanted nothing from them.

He harshened his voice, pushing them away. "You know what we did. Michael told you. We extorted money. We forced companies to pay us for concessions from the city. And all the time we did it, we never felt it was wrong. It seemed so amicable, you see. Handshakes, drinks, smiles all around. No one ever resisted... until Vito Tortelli.

"I watched and listened as my friend Michael destroyed us both; and suddenly it came to me: I saw that the degenerate ogre described by the prosecutor and the selfless altruist described by Mr. Leeds really were one man, but a man divided in two, a man who was not whole, who had no integrity, who'd convinced himself that he could be one thing in his private and another in his public life." Jonathan looked from face to face. "As if there were a difference. There is no difference. You can't divide yourself into separate selves, you can't live by separate sets of rules. What you are is what you do and how you do it. I knew that once. I managed to forget it. Now I know it again.

"Therefore," he said, turning toward the audience, "I have decided, against the advice of counsel, to lay down my arms. I will not defend actions I now find indefensible. For the sake of the man I used to be, as much as for the sake of the people whose trust I abused, I confess to the charges against me. I blame no one but myself."

Jonathan's gaze came to rest on Gracie, who sat up straight and haughty and so dry-eyed it seemed she would never cry again. He smiled at her, then turned back to the audience, to the avid reporters.

"The prosecutor was right about one thing. It doesn't work without self-deception. You've got to sell yourself a real good line of goods to do what I did. Nor does it happen overnight. It takes years of gentle, steady shifting. You move, and the center moves with you.

"Once in a while, something happens. You see your face in a distorted mirror. Someone close to you says, 'You're not the man you used to be.' But you explain it away. You grow layers of excuses, removable skins.

"Me, I told myself I needed the money in order to deal with the power brokers on their level. I told myself everybody did it. At the deepest level of excuse-making, I told myself I did it for my family. Why should my children pay the price of their father's principles, which anyway were too deeply embedded to be compromised by a little finagling on the side? What right had I *not* to provide them with the best our society has to offer, when I possessed the means to do so?" Again his eyes touched on Grace. "Young people judge everything in black and white. Older people see shades of gray. As we grow older and take on the responsibilities of a family, as we acquire mortgages, debts, possessions that need to be financed and insured and maintained, we grow more tolerant, less critical, of ourselves as well as others.

"I'm not opposed to tolerance," Jonathan said. "It's just a hell of a dangerous commodity. A little goes a long, long way. More than a little, and a man gets lax in his views. He starts tolerating things he's got no business tolerating.

"Not that I knew it at the time. That would have been intolerable. I convinced myself that this was a game in which everybody won, nobody lost.

"It's not true. There may be victimless crimes, but extortion isn't one of them." He placed both hands on the railing that separated him from the rest of the courtroom and leaned forward. "One thing only I'll say in my defense, and then I'll shut up. Regardless of the other stuff going down, *I never stopped doing my job.* I never stopped fighting for my constituency.

"The prosecutor told you it was all a sham. She said I used my office solely to enrich myself. That's a lie. Serving the people of this city was my reason for being, my heart and soul. The other stuff was something I drifted into.

"But I make no excuses. I take responsibility for everything I did, the good and the bad. They don't cancel each other out. That is my only consolation."

He walked back to the defense table and picked up a glass of water. There was a spontaneous eruption of applause that spread through the court— not only spectators, but also jurors and hardened reporters joined in.

Judge Malina pounded her gavel, but it was Jonathan who silenced them. "Why would you applaud?" he said in astonishment. "I'm saying I'm guilty." He walked to the center of the court, where the gray city light shone down on him. "A ruined man stands before you. I have lost everything; soon even my liberty will be gone. I expect to serve many years in prison for the same offenses Michael Kavin will walk away from. But I wouldn't trade places with him for the world, because with this act, I reclaim myself: a battered old self, spotted and bruised, like the last peach in the bin, but my own."

A female juror sniffled. Jonathan returned to the defense table and slumped against it. He looked spent, terminally weary. "I apologize to the people of my borough for betraying their trust, to my family for using them as an excuse for my own failings, and to my noble lawyer, Christopher Leeds. I apologize especially to Vito Tortelli, the only businessman we approached who had the guts to call a spade a spade, and who paid for his courage. Thank you, your Honor, for letting me speak."

He nodded to her and the jury. As he walked around the defense table toward his seat, Gracie stood and stretched her arms out over the railing. Jonathan hugged her and let go.

Lucas Rayburn bulled his way through the crowd. Buscaglio rose to intercept him, but he passed her by and grasped Jonathan's hand. They shook, and Lucas squeezed his shoulder. Then Jonathan sank into his seat.

Christopher Leeds put an arm around him. "You're a dead man," he whispered. "But no one will ever say you didn't go down in style."

EPILOGUE

Eighteen years later

GRACIE TIPS THE BELLBOY, locks the door, and leans against it with a sigh of contentment. She loves hotels, and this Albany Hilton is a good one, better than she could afford if she were paying. There was a time in her life when she lived in a series of hotel rooms much less luxurious than this, a time of healing suspension that left her with a taste for privacy and a recurrent hankering for motion. Though the privacy of hotel rooms is illusory, violated daily by unseen intruders, as illusions go it's a strong one.

She is in this room by choice; she has been asked, indeed strongly pressed, to stay elsewhere. To this invitation she replied, with as much tact as she could muster, that she is too anxious before speaking engagements to be fit for human company. And while it is true that she is nervous, both she and the one who invited her understand that on this particular occasion there are more than the usual grounds.

Gracie orders a salad, an omelet, and a half-bottle of white wine from room service. While waiting, she unpacks. On the night chest goes a framed photograph of her children: David sitting on a tractor, holding baby Talia. A stab of longing, a physical pain, pierces her as she gazes at their faces. A week has passed since she kissed them good-bye, and two more will pass before she holds them again, assuming David lets her, for at the advanced age of eight he is getting too old (so he tells her) for mushy stuff.

Tamar claims he is the image of Jonathan as a child, but Gracie sees the resemblance only in his eyes, which are gray with flecks of green and lit from within by an almost painful curiosity. Much as she loves her firstborn child, she's relieved to be away from him; for Grace is a secretive soul, and David's inquisitiveness knows no bounds.

The day before she left the kibbutz, she walked into her house to find him studying the photo album she keeps hidden in a trunk. "That's private," she said angrily. He didn't even hear. With eyes as round as silver dollars, he stared at the yellowed front page of the New York *Post*. "Fleishman arraigned!" the headline blared, but although he speaks his mother's tongue fluently, David cannot yet read it. He was studying the photograph of her family standing on the steps of the municipal courthouse.

"That's you," he said, jabbing at her image with a grimy finger. His eyes traveled from her face to the face in the picture and back again, suddenly unsure. She knew why. The girl who stands on the edge of the step, her body poised like a pugilist's, wears a fierce and wild look, an expression Grace's children have never seen on her face and please God never will.

"Who's that?" David demanded, pointing to the sober young man who stands close beside her, holding her arm.

"My brother."

He looked up suspiciously. "You have a brother?"

"Yes."

"Did I ever meet him?"

"No," she said, taking the album from him, closing it firmly. "And I'll thank you to stay out of my things."

"Why haven't I?"

"He lives very far away, in America."

"So? We've been to America. Do you write to him? What's his name?"

"Paul."

"Paul Fleishman?"

"Paul Mann."

"Why isn't his name Fleishman, like yours and Grandpa's?"

"He changed it," Grace said.

"Why did he change it?"

She ran her hands through her hair and tugged. Then the door opened and Micha walked in. David launched himself at his father and wrapped his skinny legs around his waist. "Did you know Mommy has a brother?" he said in Hebrew.

Micha's eyes went from his son to the album to Gracie's face.

He said, "Come on, sport, let's shoot a few baskets before dinner."
David whooped and raced outside.

A temporary reprieve, she knows, artificially prolonged by
her flight abroad. The boy has a sponge of a memory and he is
relentless. The questions will come, and what will she tell him?
She has buried her past without requiem; yet what did she gain
by forgetting her mother, forsaking her father, and accepting her
brother's desertion? Her son looks at a photo and asks, "Is that
you?", and she is confounded. Perhaps people aren't meant to rise
like phoenixes from the ashes.

Someone knocks on the door, and she starts, but it's only
room service. The waiter wheels in a table, pours the wine, palms
his tip, and leaves.

The omelet is warm and good, but Gracie eats insensibly, lost
in thought. What will she tell her son? She cannot lie to him.
Though little remains of her childhood, the pain of being lied to
is indelible.

The truth, however, is not hers to give. That night she reread
her old diaries. They told her little, evoked nothing but pity and
impatience toward the child who wrote them. What happened
to her family went beyond personal tragedy; Jonathan's disgrace
was resonant with the falling-away of a generation. None of
this, however, emerged from the journals, in which all is filtered
through the prism of her adolescent angst. And that girl wanted
to be a writer, Grace thinks mockingly, forgetting, for a moment,
that she became one.

Grace writes fiction because fiction has form to it, fiction makes
sense. Her books are political, set for the most part in the Middle
East. Grace has never written about her father's fall from grace,
though her publishers have hinted on more than one occasion that
such a book, even in the form of a *roman a clef,* would be welcome.
The fall of Jonathan Fleishman has not been forgotten.

The idea exerts a powerful fascination, composed equally of
attraction and repulsion. Now and then over the years, she's
played indirectly with the story, tunneling below and above and
around it, like a mole faced with an impassable boulder, but her
explorations went nowhere.

Gracie's not a coward, but she's no fool either. Writing is
a process of naming things that may or may not have existed
before they are named, but do after. (One may ask whether a tree
that falls unheard in the forest makes a sound, but there can be

no such doubt about a tree whose fall is witnessed.) Grace fears the application of that process to her family. As a mother, she recognizes magical thinking when she sees it; and yet she fears that to write their story would be to visit upon it another mode of reality, an even greater immanence. To write it, she would have to conjure up her father, her mother, even Barnaby. Such visitations are easier to invoke than to exorcise.

In any case, she doesn't much care for the story's conclusion, which offends her novelist's sense of justice. If she *were* writing the story, it would end with the judge being so moved by Jonathan's confession that she refused to send him to prison. The family would then draw together in a grand epiphany of reconciliation, the children cleaving to their father, the aged mother forgiving her son; and if Grace could find some way to bring Lily back from the dead, she would do that too. Gracie likes happy endings; she believes they provide more of a sense of closure than sad ones. In real life, too much is left unresolved; not every problem has a solution; and terrible mistakes go unrectified.

In real life, Judge Malina was affected by her father's confession, but not enough to set him free. Nevertheless, she was charitable. Citing his confession, his obvious remorse, she sentenced him to three years on each count, to be served concurrently. In addition, the judge recommended early parole. Jonathan ended up serving less time than Michael Kavin, whose deal with the U.S. attorney netted him a two-and-a-half-year jail term.

Clara was devastated by Jonathan's confession to crimes that, in her view, he never committed, and that even if he had, were not crimes at all. He was still her son and she loved him; she visited him in prison and befriended his guards, whom she bribed with home-baked babka and apple strudel; but honest, from-the-heart forgiveness was beyond her power to bestow. After Jonathan's release from prison, Clara moved to Florida. They wrote, visited, but never again lived together.

An odd consequence of their breach (one that Gracie as writer would have scorned to use) was to throw Clara back on the other branch of her family. After Jonathan's sentencing, she wrote to Yaacov, breaking a silence that had lasted decades. Her letter was reproachful: she blamed Jonathan's confession on Yaacov's quixotic long-distance influence.

He replied: "Where did he get the idea that money is so important you should do anything to get it? Not from me," an outrageous allegation Clara could not allow to pass unanswered. Thus, after a hiatus of nearly forty years, they were quarreling again, a kind of geriatric War of the Roses that gave them both a little something extra to live for.

They all survived, each in his or her own way. Life does go on. When her first existence ended, Gracie fashioned a second; and if traces of the old remain, they are not, for the most part, the kind that require noticing. They are small things, like the care Gracie takes to keep her house bare, her dislike of burdensome acquisitions. She is one of the few for whom it truly is more blessed to give than to receive—not on moral or religious grounds, but rather because giving brings relief from ownership, whereas receiving is fraught with anxiety.

She visited her father in prison only once, early in his term. For thirty minutes they sat on hard benches and talked awkwardly. Gracie told him he looked well, surprised to find it true. Jonathan had regained some of the weight he'd lost during Lily's illness; he seemed fit and relaxed, the tension around his eyes and mouth gone. But the sight of him in prison clothes upset her deeply. The ill- fitting coveralls diminished him, made him seem what he had never been to her, a man like any other. Gracie found it hard to look him in the face. When their time was over, he kissed her good-bye and asked her not to come back, but to get on with her life.

Grace could have argued. She could simply have disobeyed. Instead, she agreed and went abroad.

She wanted to be a good daughter, to support her father in his hour of need; but we cannot always be what we want to be. Her family had exploded. Grace had no more control over her life than a piece of shrapnel.

She flew to London and set out from there, tramping through England and much of Europe, working when she needed money, carrying her possessions on her back. Once she began moving, she couldn't stop. From Europe she went to Africa, and from there she slowly made her way up the Sinai coast, through Egypt and into Israel, where she came to a sudden and profound halt. For the first full year of her stay in Ein Gedi, Gracie never ventured out of the region, much less the country, but rather burrowed her way deeper and deeper in. Tamar said it was all the same, the burrowing and the running; but the observation implied no criticism. She was deeply pleased that Grace had come back, and with nothing left to stand between them.

Micha was smug, certain she'd returned on his account. Yet it took him well over a year of unreasonably stubborn persistence to consummate the promise of their last meeting; and when Gracie finally did sleep with him, it was only to prove once and for all that he didn't really want *her,* he just wanted to have her.

It didn't work. She'd neglected to take account of her own reaction. Micha proved to be a wonderful lover. He lifted her out of herself, he made her forget her name. There was a whole side to Micha that came out only in bed, and Gracie fell in love with that side.

They stayed together. Eventually she moved into his room. The kibbutz acknowledged them as a couple. But Gracie wanted nothing to do with marriage. She had lived five years on the kibbutz (four of them with him), become a member in her own right, and published her first book before she consented to marry him. And even then, he told their friends, only half-joking, she agreed only to mollify Tamar, and with the understanding that he would remain in the army and she on the kibbutz. It was not the kind of marriage Micha had ever envisioned for himself. But he knew that in her own cautious way, Grace loved him; and he was content.

The waiter knocks, enters, and removes her tray. Somehow the omelet has been eaten, the wine drunk. Gracie lies on the bed and reads over her lecture, entitled "Politics and Fiction." It is the same lecture she's delivered in four cities so far, apparently to her listeners' satisfaction, but now, knowing who will be listening, she reads more critically. It seems to her a paltry thing, bare-boned and passionless, nothing like her real work. Though she enjoys the traveling and, yes, the fuss and attention paid to the Visiting Author, she feels like a fraud. If her work were nonfiction, if it emanated from some area of expertise, that would be different. But novels, if they're any good at all, invariably speak better for themselves than their authors can for them. After attending numerous lectures and readings by well-known writers, Grace had concluded that however brilliant their work, novelists themselves were rather stupid creatures who had much better stay home and write than go abroad and pontificate.

At last she puts the text aside and, turning out the lights, sinks into the darkness as if into a warm bath. In the vestibule of wakefulness and sleep, her children's faces dance before her. She smells the dust on David's hair, baby Talia's sweet, milky breath.

She drifts into a dream. It is children's hour on the kibbutz, the time between the end of work and the start of dinner. Micha is home for the harvest. He enters the house in his blue work clothes, smelling of sweat and oranges, to shower and change and play with the children. These are precious moments and she does not take them for granted, not even in sleep; for Grace is her mother's daughter, and there is that in her that waits and watches and does not presume.

Then Micha and David are gone, and Grace is with her daughter and Lily, who is seeing the child for the first time. Talia has fallen asleep. Her round head, too heavy for the plump little body, lolls against the side of her infant seat. Mouth open, she snores lightly. Grace watches her with a love so exquisite it hurts. Lily gazes adoringly over her shoulder. "All good things come to an end," she says with a sigh.

"Not necessarily," Grace answers quickly, and suddenly the dream ends and she wakes in a strange bed, soaked with sweat. Lily, more substantial in memory than in life, has evoked the fear that in Grace lies close to the surface. Once, when she was very young, she saw a movie about a young servant girl who feared she was turning into a witch. The harder she tried not to, the more witchlike she became. The movie had terrified Grace. Its vision struck the shore of her childhood like a bottled message from the adult world: that which we most dread, it said, we become.

The telephone rings. Eyes shut, Gracie reaches out for it.

"Good morning," a man's voice says.

"Good morning."

"Shall I come get you? We could have breakfast."

"No, thanks. I have to go over my notes."

"All right," he says reluctantly. "But afterward... "

"Yes, yes; as we planned."

She washes, dresses, and puts on her writer's face. At two o'clock that afternoon, she sits on a stage in the auditorium of the State University at Albany, gazing queasily at a sea of young faces. Her hands are shaking, and her body is dank beneath her respectable author disguise. A distinguished-looking gray-haired man stands at the podium. Clumps of words pierce the fog of her panic. "Critically acclaimed... new realism... escape from escapism and brand-name minimalism... political consciousness... " He turns toward her and holds out his hand.

"I'm very proud to present my daughter, Grace Fleishman."

She crosses the stage and stands beside him. "Laying it on a bit thick, Dad," she murmurs. The microphone picks it up, and the audience responds with friendly laughter.

Ordinarily Gracie's stage fright dissipates the moment she begins to speak. Her lecture touches only lightly on her own work, focusing instead on her elders and betters, her favorite writers: Nadine Gordimer, Graham Greene, John le Carré, Walker Percy.... This time, however, her father's unseen presence saps her authority. Grace feels like an imposter.

She picks out a few faces from the crowd and concentrates on those. There's a restless boy in the front row, who crosses and uncrosses his arms and legs every minute, an intense young woman in the third row who takes notes feverishly, a blond girl, glowing with hostility, who stands in the back. A red-and-white keffiyah is wrapped around her neck. That one will be heard from during the Q-and-A.

She recites her lecture by heart, feeling like a zombie, but when she finishes, the applause is sincere. Jonathan comes to stand beside her. He gives her an incandescent look, then turns to the audience and raises his hands for silence. "Ms. Fleishman will take questions now."

Hands shoot up. Gracie points to the back: best to get it over with. The girl in the keffiyah takes a combative stance, legs spread, arms akimbo. "How do you reconcile your ostensible humanism with your choice to live in a racist country?"

Gracie answers: "There are racists in Israel, as there are everywhere. The disease is endemic. No one is immune. I suggest that if you examine the premise of your question, you will see that."

"Do you deny that you're a Zionist?"

"No, why should I deny it? It's perfectly possible to be a Zionist and still favor a separate Palestinian state. Lots of us do."

"What you *do*," the girl says shrilly, "is shore up a fascist, racist regime with your facade of liberalism," and she storms demonstratively out of the room. No one else stirs. Grace points to the boy in the front row, who is waving his arm.

He stands. "All your books are political, and most have to do with corruption of one sort or another. Yet you had a front-row seat at one of the biggest corruption scandals in New York's history, and you've never written about it. Why?"

As if the audience were a single beast, its eyes shift to Jonathan, sitting in the shadows in the back of the stage. Only Grace does not look. She folds her hands on the podium and says shortly, "I prefer to write fiction."

"Why? Why trivialize important political issues by novelizing them?"

"Good fiction doesn't trivialize, and it has one advantage at least over nonfiction: it never pretends to be the one-and-only right way of seeing things. I think it was Einstein who said, 'Imagination is greater than knowledge.' I believe that. It's at the heart of what I do. And you know, we all do what we can."

Slowly, staring at her, the young man sits. The questions that follow are ones she's answered many times before. Where do you get your ideas? Are your books autobiographical? Do you know when you start a book where you're heading, or do you just go with the flow? She answers graciously, without thought.

Afterward there is a wine-and-cheese reception: faculty members and a few handpicked students. Then her father takes her home.

Jonathan lives in a little country house in northern Columbia County, a forty-minute drive from the university where he teaches three days a week. It's a simple two-story farmhouse, with wide-board oak floors and fireplaces in the living room and the library. The house is set on twelve open and wooded acres; behind it stands a small apple orchard. "Macouns," Jonathan tells her. "Their season's short, they're hard to grow, and the apples don't store well. But they're the best damn apples I've ever tasted."

Grace has never seen this house. The last time she visited, Jonathan lived in a rented apartment in Albany. The land and the house, which he owns, speak of a life regenerated, if solitary. "It's lovely," she says; he answers a bit defensively, "I like the quiet. In prison it never was. You develop a lust for peace."

In the living room he kneels to light the fire, then holds his hands out toward the flames. They are liver-spotted and translucent, an old man's hands grafted onto a younger man's body. The rest of him looks vital, strong. The years of suffering have carved deep lines from his nose to the corners of his mouth, and his hair is completely gray. But his back is straight, his eyes are clear and full of light.

The telephone rings and Jonathan goes into the kitchen to answer it. Gracie pokes around the room. The furniture is a pleasing hodgepodge: woven Navajo rugs and Shaker cabinets, a padded deacon's bench that does duty as a sofa, a heavy oak rocker, and two wing chairs set before the fireplace. None of it comes from their old houses. In a box of kindling and old newspapers, she spies a desiccated copy of the *Probe*. She carries it to the rocking chair and flips through. Barnaby's name is nowhere to be found.

Her father's voice drifts in from the kitchen. "Of course they say that, what would you expect them to say?... It doesn't work that way. The whole point of bureaucracy is obfuscation and delay.... Sure, if that's what it takes...If you get a good show of students, you can count on most of the tenured faculty. The untenured obviously have more to lose.... That's not nearly enough.... Yeah, but if you want to get their attention, you need numbers...."

When he returns, Grace tosses the paper aside hastily.

Jonathan laughs. "Afraid I'll slap your hand? He doesn't work for them anymore."

With elaborate disinterest she replies, "Who does he write for?"

"No one, as far as I know. While I was still in prison, he left the *Probe*. There was some talk about a book, but it never materialized. For a while he did a radio talk show, but that fizzled out, and I guess at some point he gave up and left town. That name you pinned on him stuck, you know. Mosquito Man, they called him. It didn't help his career."

Gracie nods toward the kitchen. "I thought you swore off politics."

"I did. It's just a student thing. The university has endowment money in nasty places and the kids are agitating for divestiture. Well," he says with a lopsided smile, "they asked for help, I didn't thrust it upon them."

"You can take the man out of politics, but you can't take the politics out of the man."

"Look who's talking." He sits beside her on the deacon's bench. "I meant what I said today about your work."

"I had a good teacher."

Jonathan laughs. "In the 'Do as I say, not as I do' mode."

"I don't *do* anything. I just write." Lately, Grace has felt a growing dissatisfaction with the safe and sheltered life she's fashioned for herself. Her father's apprentice, she was intended for a larger life than the one she has chosen to live. Her books are her emissaries; they march out into the world like obedient toy soldiers, but it's no longer enough. Month by month her country grows more polarized. The second-class status of Israel's Arabs compares itself to that of southern blacks before the age of civil rights; and Grace is one of those who has always said enviously, "If only I'd lived in that era... " Like a war horse, she quivers at the call to arms.

He regards her closely. "Just? You must know your books are more effective than another body on a picket line."

"Maybe." She changes the subject. "Do you hear from Paul?"

His face freezes. "Not much. Do you?"

"Christmas cards. With pictures of Theresa and the children gathered around the tree, and a cheery little mimeographed note." Her brother lives in the Midwest, an executive for Philip Morris.

"I get those too. Fine-looking children." There's a silence, uncomfortable on her part, forlorn on his. Jonathan has never met these grandchildren, never spoken to them. He doesn't know their birthdays. He used to send Christmas presents but they came back unopened. Paul's phone number is unlisted and he doesn't answer letters.

"Jerk," she mutters; but she's thinking that Jonathan has met her own son only once, Talia never. If she's the white sheep, it's only by comparison.

Jonathan shrugs. "He means well."

"No, he doesn't. He's rubbing salt in the wound is all."

"We don't know that."

"I know. Though I expect that if my books ever make me really famous, he'll decide I'm worth knowing again."

Gracie spends the night beneath her father's roof. She tosses and turns but cannot fall asleep. When she was small and sleep wouldn't come, she would creep into her parents' bed and take comfort from their slumbering warmth. They were her rigid poles, the moorings against whose fixity she could rail and buck, secure in their fastness. When they broke, she was cast adrift. Was it fair that now, in the safe port of her marriage, in the harbor of her own motherhood, she should feel such unanswerable longing?

Toward morning she falls into an uneasy sleep. She dreams of her daughter, who has recently discovered her hands, but cannot yet control them. Talia lies in her crib, eyeing the mobile strung across it. Her little mouth puckers with desire, her tongue protrudes, her whole body begins to quiver and shake. She kicks her feet and arches her back, and suddenly her two arms fly out and brush the mobile, which rattles and chimes. Seeing what she herself has done, the infant laughs aloud.

Waking, Gracie knows at once that she was dreaming of herself. At eighteen she had the same passionate, haphazard coordination, not physically but morally. She saw no difference, then, between a person and his deeds, recognized no degrees of guilt. Good and evil were absolute, and to the perception of evil she reacted with blind and spastic indignation.

Given time, she would have gained coordination. Given time, she would have seen for herself what her mother tried to show her, that Jonathan's failures were of judgment, never love. But they were given no time.

Gracie loves her father. She never stopped, even when she betrayed him. The ocean she keeps between them is the measure of her love, and of her fear.

When she thinks of family, she thinks of Micha, Tamar, and the children, not her parents. And yet she is aware that the family we are born into is the template for the one we create. This theory fills her with dread, for if it is true, then she is bound to lose the ones she loves. Grace believes in free choice and binding love, but she has seen how one erodes the other.

Jonathan wakes her, knocking on her door. "We have so little time," he says by way of apology, and leaves a cup of steaming coffee by her bed.

The house is full of winter light, so quiet that with her eyes shut she can imagine herself back in the desert. Barefoot, Gracie carries her cup to the window. Outside, the ground is covered with a thick white quilt. The trees in the orchard are silver filigree. The road cannot be seen. She wonders how she will get to the airport, and decides, with an odd satisfaction, that she probably won't. The smell of bacon drifts in under her door. She dresses quickly and goes downstairs.

The kitchen is pungent with burning wood, and the table is set for two, with a covered dish of scrambled eggs, a plate of bacon, sliced tomatoes, thick-sliced sourdough rye bread, and creamery butter. Grace sits down and says, "Tell me you don't eat like this every day."

Jonathan looks over from the counter, where he is pouring fresh coffee into mugs. "You don't like it?"

"It's a great treat, but have you checked your cholesterol lately?"

A slow smile spreads over his face, deepening the lines around his eyes.

She says, "What?"

"For a moment, you sounded just like your mother."

"You're avoiding the question."

He sets the mugs on the table and sits beside her. "I'm in perfect health."

"You look it, actually."

"So do you. Israel agrees with you."

"Yes."

"And you're happy," Jonathan says; it is neither a question nor an answer, but something in between. "It's still your choice to live there."

"Come see for yourself," Grace says, looking at him.

The room is so quiet she can hear the snow fall.

Her father says, "I've never been asked."

"You have, lots of times. Tamar's asked you, Yaacov's asked you... "

"You haven't."

"No," she says. "But I'm asking you now."

Jonathan gets up from the table and feeds the wood-burning stove. When he returns, his face is flushed.

"Feeling sorry for the lonely old man?"

"Not at all."

"I've got a life, you know. I have friends. I have work. I have my books and my own writing."

"That's nice. All you need is a dog and you're set for life."

She catches him with a mouthful of coffee. When he laughs, the coffee spurts out over the table. "God, Gracie, I've missed you."

"I've missed you too, Daddy. I love you." As she speaks these words, Grace is seized with dread. It comes to her that no sooner did she say them to her mother than Lily slipped through her arms and died.

But her father shows no signs of succumbing. He doesn't melt away, clutch his head, or crumple to the floor. He just takes a slice of bread and butters it thoughtfully.

"How about April?" he says.

About the Author

Barbara Rogan has spent virtually all of her career in the publishing industry: as an editor, a literary agent, a writer, and a teacher. She graduated from St. John's College with a liberal arts degree and started working as a copyeditor with a major New York publishing house. Shortly thereafter, she moved to Israel, where she became the English-language editor of a Tel Aviv publishing house, and a while later she launched the Barbara Rogan Literary Agency to represent American and European publishers and agents for the sale of Hebrew rights. Among the thousands of writers she represented were Nadine Gordimer, Isaac Bashevis Singer, Abba Eban, Irwin Shaw, John le Carré, and her childhood favorite, Madeleine L'Engle.

At the age of twenty-six, she was appointed to the board of directors of the Jerusalem Book Fair, the youngest director ever to serve on the board. During this period, her first novel, *Changing States*, was published simultaneously in England, the United States, and Israel. For some time, she continued to write and run the agency, but eventually followed her passion to become a full-time writer. Since then, she has produced seven more novels, including *Hindsight*, *Suspicion*, and *Rowing in Eden*. Her fiction has been translated widely and graciously reviewed. About *Suspicion*, the *Washington Post* wrote, "If you can put this book down before you've finished it, it's possible that your heart may have stopped beating."

"What *Bonfire of the Vanities* tried to be," *Library Journal* wrote of *Saving Grace*. *Café Nevo* was called "unforgettable" by the *San Francisco Chronicle* and "an inspired, passionate work of fiction, a near-magical novel" by *Kirkus Reviews*. Rogan also coauthored two nonfiction books and contributed essays to several published anthologies. To read more about Rogan's work, visit her website, www.barbararogan.com.

Rogan taught fiction writing at Hofstra University and SUNY Farmingdale for several years before trading her brick-and-mortar classroom for a virtual one. Her online courses and editing services are described on her teaching website, www. nextlevelworkshop.com. As a professional whose experience spans all aspects of publishing, Rogan is a frequent presenter at writers' conferences, seminars, and retreats.

OPEN ROAD

INTEGRATED MEDIA

Open Road Integrated Media is a digital publisher and multimedia content company. Open Road creates connections between authors and their audiences by marketing its ebooks through a new proprietary online platform, which uses premium video content and social media.

CPSIA information can be obtained at www.ICGtesting.com
Printed in the USA
LVOW11s2126110215

426711LV00001B/49/P